The Fontana Resurrection

BY DAVID EDEY

Copyright © 2014 by David Edey

First Edition – July 2014

ISBN

978-1-4602-0192-3 (Hardcover)

978-1-4602-0190-9 (Paperback)

978-1-4602-0191-6 (eBook)

All rights reserved under International and Pan-American Copyright Conventions.

No part of this publication may be reproduced in any form, or by any means, electronic or mechanical, including photocopying, recording, or any information browsing, storage, or retrieval system, without permission in writing from the publisher, except by a reviewer, who may quote brief passages in a review.

This book is a work of fiction. Names, characters, places and incidents are products of the author's imagination or are used fictitiously. Any resemblance to actual events or persons, living or dead, is entirely coincidental.

Produced by:

FriesenPress

Suite 300 – 852 Fort Street

Victoria, BC, Canada V8W 1H8

www.friesenpress.com

Distributed to the trade by The Ingram Book Company

For Linda... family matriarch, whose wisdom is emulated by elephants.

CHAPTER 1

Doubts

Scene 1
The Morning News...

> *"Death was a friend, and sleep was Death's brother."*
> *~John Steinbeck, The Grapes of Wrath*

July 27, 2010, 5:32 a.m.

It had been another night, a night of dreams. Dreams no one really could have, though he had lived them profoundly as if they'd been real experiences; set in eras he had never known nor studied; in locales he had never visited; about things, try as he might, he hadn't been able to fathom—events he had tried unsuccessfully to chronicle for Chelsea, hoping she would help interpret facets of them for him. But these effusions had dissipated into thin air in their attempts to traverse the short distance across the breakfast table between them.

"Everyone dreams," she had offered, or variations of that, always listening politely, mostly enduring patiently, not caring to go there.

Nights had never been his friend—nights like the one he had just come through. But when the night was gone, completely gone, he said to himself in the absence of anyone to say it to, the smell of freshly brewing coffee would be there, dripping into a pot that had come to equate the sound of hope for a new day—new things to look forward to, new things to do. Hopefully, old friends to see, perhaps new friends to be made, out there, beyond the window. Hope. And charity. Are these the characteristics of age, he wondered? Perhaps not age regretted, rather of age savoured. Of maturity denied too long in a headlong rush to become somebody, to acquire more than others, to cry out with huge uncertainty within one's head, "Hey world, look at me! I'm something! Somebody? Or maybe not. Please don't tell me I'm not. I don't think I could handle that."

Maybe if I just shouted it a little louder—within the universe that swirls inside my mind, that is. Not out loud. It's not *said* out loud. It's part of the male solitude that comes of being suspended within humanity's guileful togetherness, like a tea bag hanging by a string beyond its depth in uncomfortably hot water. It takes us, he thought, each of us, a very long time to get used to being steeped.

He shuffled through disheveled sheets of torn-off-the-pad foolscap—some crumpled, a few dog-eared, most pencil-smudged—laying on the kitchen table, looking for his last draft of a memory he had put together during the night's sleepless hours, wanting to take a fresh look, perhaps revise it. Again. With his right brain smoking on the words, he read it to himself—*a last time*—he promised the left side of his head:

STATIONS

> *I'm from the west; maybe that's why it's so pleasant to reflect on it. Manitoba, actually. A two-elevator town near the Saskatchewan border; elevators long gone. They even tore down the CPR station. Pity. One doesn't see them anymore, except in wrinkled watercolour paintings done by nostalgic, displaced prairie weeds like myself, or imprinted on coffee mugs once offered as promos to sell Shell gasoline. A few of them are still in my cupboard.*

They never break; the dishwasher won't chip them. Their handles are a bit worn, like the fingers of a favourite old leather glove, but the image is still there: brown, fading lines; a small-town train station, tracks coming and going; somewhere inside a telegraph clicking to the attentive ear of a long dead station agent, his green visor pulled well down over a balding forehead, pencil poised over a dog-eared pad, furrowed brow, concentrating on a rattling stream of dots and dashes. A different era, before bits and bytes; an era of singing-wire clicks, of locomotives that could flatten a penny placed on a polished track. A time for an attentive boy to lie in wait for a train, just a fishing pole's length from where it must hurtle past, flattening his body over scattered rain-washed stones sloping gently down and away from roadbed ties, his head turned to one side but with the penny still in view, the smell of summer creosote hanging heavily in the noon air; and, beneath him, crushed, sun-stunted wisps of clover, fragile and unlikely to survive his uneasy, excited presence.... The lad all the while keeping a close eye on his coin lest it be cast out of sight by the massive four-in-a-row drive wheels: wheels bearing tons of blackened iron and steel along at speed, the earth beginning to tremble beneath him as the single lamp, centered perfectly in the circle of the locomotive's boiler, floating now above shimmering heat that makes its connection to an advancing cow-catcher, and its dependency on parallel rails for its westward guidance, indistinct.

Nearby, a gopher, not trusting the boy but unafraid of the train, becomes a sudden flicker of light, folding itself deftly into its burrow—a best-kept secret—tenaciously excavated over time through the roadbed's compacted clay, with a lightless shaft opening narrowly, surreptitiously into the shadow of withered, khaki fox-grass.

Time. A time it was, indeed. Time etched deeply into memory, triggered by a coffee-cup's image, overlaid by imagined clicking wheels, a clicking telegraph.

And there, beside the cup, a flattened penny, caressed softly between thumb and forefinger of an aging hand; memories of youth fading but nurtured in the uncertainty of a quiet smile, dimming like the dish-washed outline of a bygone station, still there, faintly, on the curve of a coffee cup; and still there, too, on the sound of a phantom whistle, floating back through the wispy smoke of decades gone…in misty eyes and coffee growing cold.

He supposed that all could bring a smile to anyone sitting alone in the dawn, listening to the quiet hissing and dripping of a coffee pot, waiting for a first warming cup, hearing the ticking of the kitchen clock. A clock from the Orient, Macau actually, older than the fingers that now twist the key that winds it, the clock that will announce another dawn long after those fingers—shaking now to await their first caffeinated relaxation—grow still…with someone else to do the winding.

July 27, 2010, 5:10 a.m.

The evil men do, he thought to himself with characteristic cynicism, could be mitigated if nudged toward the lighter end of the gray scale by political foresight. However, he considered, *political foresight* was just another oxymoron.

Reluctantly giving politicians their due, he had to admit that nobody could now or ever could see the future. In life, he had long ago concluded that bad beginnings could be avoided if lessons from the past had been well enough learned. But, after beginnings were initiated, endings were inevitable, and they weren't always pretty.

"Just as well we can't see them coming—can't *truly* see them coming—given that our tomorrows are beyond us," he muttered into an emptiness that seemed apparent but was in truth populated with dust motes jittering in the space above the kitchen sink. They glimmered there in a shaft of the dawn's first light, passing through the kitchen window and dancing weightlessly, like autumn's first fruit flies to some unseen choreographer's direction, eventually to coalesce with flakes of ageing skin and fallen hairs into dust bunnies that would drift into shadowy corners and behind the kitchen appliances. That, he knew, would annoy his wife. This was, after all, a dusty house, no matter how hard she tried to keep it otherwise.

His mind grew more clement in the solitude he had claimed for himself in the morning's stillness. He was getting old. He had made peace with this inexorability. *Old* hadn't been an easy journey. Life's meaning, to the extent that there might ever have been one, for him had managed to get twisted around a tree limb like some parasitic vine, pursuing him apace as he had tried to climb his way through two careers—both of which he would too late realize were never things of value. The first had been, in the way he saw it now, an unintentional step on his part toward crimes against humanity. The second had ended much like the Hindenburg dirigible, but without the flames.

The darkness of mornings often left him wondering about the lie that sunrise too often attempted to have him believe. On a clear day, why does it hold such promise, he asked himself, returning to the moment. Why is hope so fragile, so brutally extinguished, so often? Of course there was no answer; he knew there never could be. Not for him.

He smiled his mother's smile at the dance that made the air above the sink seem a miniature lighted stage. Her smile was one of the few things he hadn't admired about her—a reflex response to any juxtaposition of uncertainty and fear, a redoubt to hide within when truths and confidences were being ripped apart by a brutally unpredictable husband. Often her smiles preceded a beating of the bruised- and blackened-face sort, which gave neither of them pleasure, but which, once initiated, he had pursued as if caught up in a moment of insanity. Hers was a trait, a head-hanging passivity, which he, her only son Stanley, had inherited—something he wished he had not.

The phone jangled with all the unpleasantness of its ill-chosen ring tone, as if maliciously practicing a couple of musical bars he had never cared for—as if, he thought, just to annoy him.

He glanced at it, at the clock, then away. It was 5:10 a.m. He stirred his coffee inattentively and again squinted against the morning sun as it edged over his neighbour's roof. Today's was a clear sky; the forecast was without threat of rain, for a change. The weather people had foreseen that. Or had they, he wondered, dubiously? Had they indeed found *foresight?* He smiled at the thought, this time an honest smile.

He had immersed himself in these little rituals, more or less every morning, assessing the weather and guessing the whereabouts of the fellow next door. The window above the sink was well positioned to offer him a clear view and was enticing because it always, in daytime, glowed invitingly, like the allure of a left-on computer screen, begging any passerby to check for new e-mails or a bit of inconsequential trivia on Facebook. At least that's what he told himself. In fact, whatever the guy next door might be doing was none of his business. Perhaps, though, making the attempt, daily, surreptitiously, was the shard of a habit left over from his first career.

They had their differences, he and the fellow next door. Friendship probably was off the table, forever. Early on, there had been a problem with encroachment from his side of their property line. The man was a motor-relic collector, mostly cars and superannuated World War II desert-war Land Rovers, some motorcycles, a three-wheeled Triumph. He had built a barn to contain many of them, contrary to his property's covenants, and he often had assorted machines, nosing over ground that wasn't part of his fiefdom. At one point he had collaborated with a couple of other pretenders—possibly South Africans—who had brought in a beaten-up military light-armoured vehicle. They had worked on it together, rebuilding the engine and restoring the body to near-battlefield authenticity. Perhaps as a retaliatory gesture against earlier issues regarding the barn and the ever-changing eclectic disorder of the neighbour's dandelion patch, the wannabe soldiers had taken to parking their war wagon with its gun pointed at the kitchen window from which he was now peering. A subsequent hedge planting, which—by tree and shrub and supporting lattice-screen framework—had grown into a tall living fence and now softened much of the view.

The Fontana Resurrection

The annoying sound in his head, he knew, was the phone ringing again. He ignored it. In defiance of its having broken his reverie, he continued rotating his spoon around the white dab of foam forming in the centre of his cup. Odd, he deduced, looking at his watch—it was a bit early for anyone to be calling. Not that many people *did* call, except to solicit funds for one or another purportedly good cause, or to try to flog something. Of late he had found a perverse pleasure in taking these calls, especially if he could fit the handset back into its cradle somewhere in an offender's midsentence.

A decent majority of neural dendrites, however, knew that whatever was going on beyond the hedge wasn't any of his concern, although it persistently tweaked a mischievous curiosity. What would the man be up to today? Probably nothing, at least nothing useful to the aesthetics of projects undertaken but never completed. His ageing yellow Triumph was still idle in its familiar place, up on blocks, headlights swivelled up like afterthoughts bolted onto its front fenders, no doubt left popped out due to some electrical fault. The man's toy—this one, anyway—looked to him like a jaundiced frog awaiting an incautiously buzzing fly to let itself get snapped up as catch of the day.

There was that interruptive noise, again: the bloody phone! He looked in the direction of the toaster and adjusted his glasses to improve his chances of grabbing the talk-into part on a first pass, rather than knocking it over, as he often did, suppressing a small annoyance that the thing always seemed half hidden. It would be nice if this call were from one of his insomniac buddies, he thought, maybe looking to go somewhere in the village for breakfast. He pressed the talk button just before the call defaulted to the answering machine.

"Hello?" he offered, groping for an elusive pseudo-cheeriness.

Then he slowed the process of stirring his coffee, the swirl of foam melting into the brown opacity of his cup. The caller began, not really in a businesslike tone, saying that he was the RCMP detachment commander in Sherbrooke, Nova Scotia.

"Mister Watson?" he asked, with a sensitivity uncharacteristic of most policemen he had known.

"Yes, I'm Stanley Watson…"

"Hi. I'm Corporal Jason Elujah," the man on the phone said. "I wouldn't be calling you directly, but folks at our headquarters tell me that you were a serving member of the Force some years ago. Is that true?"

"Yes," Stanley paused. "Back in the day. Is there a problem? I've been a long time gone."

"There might be," he continued, now in a manner more suited to an undertaker consoling a recently bereaved client. "May I speak to you openly, as one police officer to another?"

"I think so," Stanley said. "Why not? What's happening?" He took a sip of the coffee, not knowing what to expect. He realized that he was a bit more apprehensive than might have been the case thirty years ago, had he then received such a call.

"Is your wife there with you?"

"No. She's sleeping. But she'll soon be up. She has an early tee-off with some of her golfing buddies. They'll probably end up having lunch together, but she ought to be home by midafternoon. Can I ask her to give you a call?"

"Umm…no, not yet," the officer said. "I was just concerned that she might be inclined to pick up another phone." There was a pause. "Is her mother by chance Marion M. Barber?" He drew the name out a bit apprehensively.

Stanley wondered why the "M". "Yes," he said. "Is Mae in some sort of difficulty?"

"If we have the right person, yes." Corporal Elujah paused. "She's dead." He pressed forward quickly. "We've been chasing the identity of a Jane Doe here for a couple of weeks, with the help of our forensics people. They're still working on it. Our person washed ashore at Port Hilford Beach, about fifteen minutes' drive from Sherbrooke Village, in Guysborough County. She'd be in her early eighties. No jewellery. Wrapped in a wool blanket, strapped in with a couple of belts. Looks like there may have been one or more other bindings. The belts weren't of the same type; both had been pre-used, maybe first-owner discarded, according to Forensics.

"The blanket doesn't have any label or identification, although there may be some hope for it. The wrapping had started its journey with a satin binding. In a short section where the stitching had given way it had apparently snagged a severed, possibly overlooked medical bracelet. The bracelet had been clipped from her wrist with something other than scissors, maybe wire cutters or some other nonmedical tool. We've been focusing on the bracelet itself. The salt water had washed out all but traces of the name on the paper sleeve we found inside it, but our science guys were able to make out traces of some of the letters that had been there. It's allowed them, we think, to connect our Jane to an Ottawa City Police missing-persons report. But the identity is tentative. The Ottawa folks were okay with me contacting you directly, given our headquarters' request—at my suggestion—to do that, based on your previous service."

Stanley let something like a snuffed-match puff of smoke drift around inside his head for several seconds before responding. "Christ, you're kidding," he managed, softly, the words coming out as little more than a whisper.

His coffee had gone from warm to tepid. He tried it again, tasted its age, and spilled it into the sink.

"Unfortunately not," the corporal added. "We'd like to ask you to try to identify and, if possible, speak to her dentist. Our Miss Doe at one time had a partial upper plate. It wasn't with her when she drifted onto the beach. Forensics would like to get any available data related to it. Do you think that you or your wife could do that for us?"

Stanley struggled with the emotional complexities that he knew would propel themselves upward through the crust of Chelsea's sometimes volcanic nature. He hedged from offering an immediate commitment. "This'll be a sword in her side," he suggested, wanting to say yes but knowing he'd be tightening his own nuts in a vice. "She's been worried about her mom for at least two months. Maybe we'd better hold off involving her until we're a bit further along with confirmation."

There was a pause at the other end, before the corporal asked, "Might you possibly be able to do it without her?"

He allowed himself another moment to consider the discomfort likely to worm its way into that unwanted little mission. It had been a long time, a very long time, since he had done anything like this. "Maybe," he said. "Let me mull it over for just a bit. I'm gonna pour myself a fresh cup of coffee, okay?"

Using the moment, he groped for remnants of any professional objectivity that age might not yet have robbed from him. "Listen," he tried, this time a bit more brightly, as though he might be able to slither toward the end of this part of their discussion more easily. "I could grab a flight out there; I think I could visually ID her."

"I doubt that," the corporal said, dropping his earlier attempt at congeniality. "She's been in the water a while; mostly on the bottom. There are indications she may have been weighted."

"Weighted?" Jesus Christ, he thought, this just keeps getting better, doesn't it? "With what?"

"We can't be sure," the corporal said. "Compression marks in sections of the blanket suggest that she may have been packaged along with some fishermen's weights. They could have fallen away, or perhaps she drifted or was dragged away from them when the crabs and other bottom-feeders began working on her. She isn't quite skeletal; remnants of the blanket, wherever it was belted tightly enough to her, protected some of her flesh and organs. She still has her left eye and ear, and quite a bit of her scalp and some hair remains. But her lips and nose are gone, as is the soft flesh around her remaining eye. Where the blanket had loosened, her face looks to have been eaten away vertically along an irregular line, separating relatively well-preserved flesh from the whiteness of her skull, as you might see on a mouse left for a few weeks on an anthill.

"That's more or less what our medical examiner and the pathologist have been left with. The assistance of specialists in forensic dentistry, if needed, is available to them and through them to us, and our RCMP Forensic Laboratory in Halifax will do what it can. But, overall, there's not much to go on. And that's why we need your help. Until we can confirm who she is, or was, we'll have a hard time tracing her back to wherever she came from and whomever killed her."

Stanley's age-misted mind tried sluggishly to process all the implications of what he was hearing, and then it bid him to ask, "*What* might have killed her, do you think?"

This time the corporal was a bit slower to respond. "We don't know," he said. "Our forensics and the medical people haven't been able to find a cause of death. That shouldn't be considered unusual, given what they've had to work with.

"Might your wife have kept something of her mother's that could help our folks with a DNA link? A toothbrush would be ideal, or a hairbrush maybe, or a piece of clothing—perhaps a coat or sweater that might have one or more hairs caught on it. Could you have a look? If yes, I'll get one of the Ottawa City Police techs to come by and collect it. But just *find* it, okay. Don't touch or disturb anything that might help us in our investigation; the OCP folks will want to do that.

"My number here is 902-522-2200. Ask for me, personally. That way we can keep any of my team members from calling back and unintentionally upsetting your wife."

Stanley still wasn't sure he wanted to, but he knew he needed to help if he could. Rust had long since corroded much of whatever he had once known about legal niceties, such as the rules for continuity of possession of evidence.

"Yes," he found himself mumbling, "I'll get on it; I'll call you back soon."

Without really being conscious of what he was doing—his mind still awash with the description of Corporal Elujah's Jane Doe—he watched his coffee dregs dry into a stain on the bottom of the sink and then poured water for a fresh pot.

Could it really be Mae, he wondered? If so, how in the hell did she ever end up in the ocean off the southeast coast of Nova Scotia? Who might have put her there? And why? When should he try to edge Chelsea into this uncertainty? Definitely not now, he judged, not until the police had a confirmed identification. Whenever he could—presumably whenever she was out playing golf or bridge with her friends—he would have to sift through Mae's records and the basement closet. The good news was that Chelsea had meticulously kept her mom's records; she had power of attorney for the past three years and she organized everything in folders in logical order. It was Chelsea's way. They would be easy to go through. Just not right now.

He stirred a small pour of cream into his new coffee, walked the short length of the kitchen to the patio door, opened it, and stepped out onto the deck. Setting his cup on the shore-side railing, resting both hands on the now sun-warmed cedar beside his cup, eyes closed, he tested his weight against it.

Moments like this, bringing with them unanswerable questions about what might be, often dredged up reflections of what *had* been: thoughts of the people in his life and his interaction with them. His memories were of little comfort, yet he had always had a hard time re-interring them until they had their way, like serpents writhing around Medusa's head, waiting for Perseus to sever it at the neck. Eyes closed, he surrendered himself to the inevitability of a rerun.

Scene 2
Stan's Life, on Reflection...

> *"The average man, who does not know what to do with his life, wants another one which will last forever."*
> –Anatole France (1844 - 1924)

July 27, 2010, 5:57 a.m.
How was he going to tell Chelsea? His mind filled with her in a kaleidoscopic rush, images like shattered bits of mirror reflecting in their turn her face, her dreams, her likes and dislikes, and scenes of their life together.

He cherished two photos of her above all others—no, three, actually—and he had been able always to bring them into his mind's eye, at will. Two had been taken in Fort Macleod, Alberta, in the autumn of 1959. She had been eighteen then and in the full bloom of a physical perfection that nature had graced her with, a beauty that occurs in women perhaps one time in a thousand.

It amazed him, always, that she had accepted him into her life.

Overall, thanks to her magnanimity, their partnership had been a happy one, but he knew that he hadn't really deserved her. Her willingness to remain with him often had seemed a miracle, something he guarded now at the core of his being—one that she might easily be forgiven not to have allowed him to keep. But somehow she had; she had reassured him that she had stayed because she wanted to. Later, in moments of his often-troubling depression, which of late had been rather too frequent, it had become the thing that lengthened the distance between where he stood and where a rope lay coiled, waiting. Indeed, his life had stretched out in two directions: life before her and life since having met her.

She initially had been a case of mistaken identity. He met her at a YMCA dance in Ottawa toward the end of his RCMP training. He went to the dance with one of his buddies on a Friday night with no great expectations. He had seen her across the floor and could hardly believe it: a girl from his hometown with whom he had been infatuated since the age of six. And there she was! Or so he had thought.

It had been an unrequited nonstarter, one which he nurtured for years.

He had despaired that, beyond the pleasantness of a returned "Hello," and the courtesies that were expected as part of day-to-day life in a small Manitoba village, she would have nothing to do with him. She had been his first-ever rejection. On Christmas Day of his sixth year he had given her a packaged toy tea set, wrapped in white tissue with a red bow and ribbon. Her older brother had answered his knock at the door, looked at him and then at the package, and grinned. Turning away from the still half-opened door, he had called to his sister, Celeste. She had come to see who it was and, hiding her embarrassment as best she could, she accepted the gift and closed the door, leaving him standing in the cold. He didn't, of course, initially *know* it was a rejection. In fact at that age he didn't know what rejection *was*. The only other girl in his life had been his mother, and she had always loved him, even when she was angry with him.

A bit later, when slowly it had begun to dawn on him that Celeste didn't really like him, he couldn't quite grasp the concept: What was there not to like? Not just about him, about anybody? He couldn't think of anyone whom he didn't really like, and didn't know why the *like* feeling wouldn't automatically be reciprocated. He knew that love was different, special, that there was a variance in its intensity. But he couldn't get his mind around why everybody wouldn't simply like everybody else. It was perhaps his first lesson in what he would later discover to be one of humanity's many insoluble quandaries.

Celeste and he had been classmates from the first grade through the end of high school. Periodically he tried to date her, and she always politely refused. In his senior year he'd been voted the school's student-body president. In that same election she was elected student-body secretary. With a rush of hope he'd realized they would need to work closely together throughout that year; maybe he'd have another chance. But no, she'd remained steadfast, though polite, in her refusals. She didn't date often, but she wouldn't date him. She didn't actually tell him that of course, he'd just been left watching her back as she'd walked away or had hung up the phone.

After high school, he had gone to a community college in Winnipeg, and from there he had joined the RCMP. They had sent him to Ottawa for training. Boot camp was a grind, but he had done well.

* * * * * * * * *

Toward the end of boot camp came a life-changing dance, and Chelsea. In looks she and Celeste could have been twins. But Chelsea never rejected him, not then, not ever—at least not *totally* rejected him.

On April 3, 1959, Chelsea tentatively accepted the engagement ring he had gone out on a limb—a bit too far on a limb perhaps—to finance for her. Really, he had *no* money, but the owner of the small jewellery store, recognizing the close-cropped haircut and rigid bearing of an N-Division recruit, had accepted the risk. It was a small risk he knew;

the Mounties would chase the guy down and wring the debt out of him were he to default.

On April 9, he had shipped out for southern Alberta, ending up in a three-person detachment a half-hour's drive from Lethbridge. Chelsea had remained in Ottawa to complete her year at teachers' college. She had persuaded her parents to take her West for a visit during the college's summer break. At the end of that trip, she informed them she wasn't going back. This had been his first introduction to her tenacity: She found a job and a place to stay, and they entered into the beginning of a life together.

After Taber, the RCMP moved him to Fort MacLeod where he had lived for a time with another Mountie in a replica of the town's original fort. Chelsea had followed, found a new job, and shared a residence with two other girls.

Then came Claresholm, a smaller town, but essentially an echo of the Fort MacLeod experience, other than that there was no fort to live in.

From there they had spent a summer following the ponies in Alberta and Saskatchewan as part of a pari-mutuel racing supervisory team. Oversight of these racetracks was an annual collaboration between the RCMP and Canada's Department of Agriculture. The Fed's interest was twofold: keep the racetracks' betting honest and the horses free of steroids, and more importantly, collect the half-percent of the daily take due and send it to Ottawa.

At the end of that summer they had gone back to Ottawa to get married. Shortly after they had come home to Claresholm, Stanley learned that he had been transferred into the Security Service—an RCMP behind-the-scenes outfit, about which he knew almost nothing, except that such an organization had existed and protected its shadowy presence within the force's midst with pussyfooting zeal.

They moved to Lethbridge where he turned in his uniform for a plain-clothes allowance. Chelsea began again to look for a job. She found one in the RCMP's Lethbridge subdivision headquarters, and for a time they had been able to work relatively close together.

Two years into their marriage, Chelsea, by her own design, had become pregnant. They were transferred to Ottawa, where he found himself wedged into a ubiquitously meaningless niche within the Security Service's headquarters at 1200 Alta Vista. There he became a "reader", the Service's aphorism for any entry-level intelligence analyst.

They had supposed he was methodical and analytical, and they were right, of course. But it had metastasized to become, later in life, more a liability than an asset. He had been able to, from the get-go, as had hundreds of others in that place just like him, find and flag the few kernels of relevance from sheaves of coloured-cardboard covered paper brought to his and others' desks in a seemingly endless parade of clerk-propelled shopping baskets. He soon realized that he was merely a pawn; forces greater than he or his peers could at that time have hoped to understand were watching him.

He had no previous idea of the vastness of Canada's secret cadre of peekaboo players, nor of the extent to which their interoperability and cooperation with the West's intelligence framework stretched. His peers and he did what they were told—*believed* what they were told to believe. In hindsight, how incredibly naive he had been. And he wondered, now, why he hadn't asked out early, to return to the uniformed side of the force. But it had never occurred to him *then* to bow out of what had come to be called, within intelligence circles, the Great Game. It had been, at times, actually quite fun, but in ways that brought humanity no great good.

By 1967, the organization had decided it wanted him in Europe: specifically, Vienna. He, Chelsea, and their two kids had shipped out, first class, from Montréal on Cunard's *Carmania*. They docked at Le Havre, France, and, after a stopover in Paris, caught the Orient Express to Vienna.

His job in Vienna was a bit different from anything he had experienced at home. Austrian culture shock had taken them both a while to overcome. His job had gone well enough, initially, but it had left Chelsea isolated, trying to cope with two young kids, one less than six weeks old when they had arrived, mired in a quasi-hostile society still licking its wounds from defeat in World War II.

He was the third man within a three-person operation, working out of the Canadian Embassy's *Auswanderung Abteilung* in the city's Inner Ring. It was a dual-purpose function: to filter out undesirables from the immigration stream and to maintain liaison with accredited intelligence and police agencies in the host country, including those of its resident allies. He had managed to fit himself in fairly comfortably, but at a cost to his relationship with Chelsea. He had tried too hard to perform well at work, thus having left her to her own struggles in a house she didn't like and in an environment that remained entirely alien to her.

She had grown ill-disposed toward their landlord, a senior bureaucrat in the Austrian government who had lost an arm in a war that was, quite understandably, too recently behind him. He had an Austro-Germanic proclivity for expecting that women would deem themselves subordinate to their men and would do as they were told and accept whatever they were apportioned. That didn't work for Chelsea, although the landlord had to learn that lesson the hard way. They had needed to move, for her sake, and they did—to Bad Vöslau, approximately thirty kilometers south of the city.

Their new home was magnificent by any standard. It was a walled villa, stuccoed in Schönbrunn-Palace Maria-Theresa yellow, and came with a housekeeper who did all the things that housekeepers do, four days a week. The house had a wide central hallway with a red-carpeted, two-tiered set of steps leading through double French doors to a living room large enough to obscure its concert grand piano, ensconced in a corner. From there, looking straight ahead, the great room led through twin pillars that introduced a large, glassed-in winter garden, lush with exotic plants, and an ornate iron settee and chairs nestled comfortably into its greenery. Double doors beyond that led out to a garden dominated by a billowing chestnut tree, encircled at its base by a bench. The garden had apricot trees from which they could pick fresh fruit. A man hired by the landlord attended to the garden, so Stanley didn't have to cut the grass and Chelsea didn't have to tend the flowerbeds.

Summer passed. The senior assistant liaison officer was posted to Trinidad. Vienna station's second man then had been moved to Athens. For a time, it had left Stanley alone as the only operative who knew and could deal effectively with local contacts. Word came from Cologne that a new person, senior to Stanley, would be arriving from Milan to take charge.

The Milan person had introduced himself. He was a bad choice. It became apparent from the outset that there was something very wrong with him, a mental tic that Stanley hadn't been quite able to name. But, seldom are people allowed the luxury of picking their supervisors; it was then and still is that way. He had realized that he was the one who would have to adjust. He tried. He really did.

The 1968 Czechoslovakian October crisis came along. Alexander Dubcek had overstepped the bounds of conformity that Moscow had set out for him and his government. In his speech to the Communist Party of Czechoslovakia Plenary Session, held between May 29 and June 1, about *The Prague Spring*, he had said, among other things, that his aims with reform policies were to transform rather than to destroy the system. Part of his address read:

> The Party should not slow down the democratization process.
>
> If we want to arrive at a truthful picture we cannot see only extremes and speak in absolute terms....
>
> The fundamental nature of the current situation is determined by the positive social process begun in January.
>
> The contradictions and conflicts that are quite natural in the current process and that are at times brought to a critical head perhaps even too dramatically, are neither the product nor the consequence of the policy on which we embarked in January. They are, rather, the fruit of a long social crisis that has been maturing over the years, a crisis in which a host of unsatisfied needs and unsolved problems had accumulated without redress from the previous regime. What is more, the previous regime by its actions

even deepened these problems, even though many people had drawn attention to this fact.... In January we cleared the road to their solution. This naturally does not take place without conflicts and a certain degree of spontaneity. So, the fundamental source of the current difficulties lies in the burden of social conflicts, mistakes, and deformations that reached a critical state, especially over the past few years when personal power was so concentrated....

But since then the situation has changed: Anti-communist tendencies have grown stronger and certain elements are attempting to engage in more intensive forms of activity. The large majority of the party has come to realize this danger, which is today the main threat to the further progress of the democratization process. Increasing sections of the progressive public are beginning to be aware of it as well.

We maintain that the fundamental path to follow is one that will have the full backing and recognition, above all, of the working masses, the working class, and cooperative farmers. The Party leadership knows only too well that if anti-communist, right-wing forces emerge, the foundations of socialism cannot be safeguarded without the working class. That is what will guide the policy of the party....

"There are also now fears of the conservative forces in the party and of a return to the situation before January 1968. This danger stems from remnants of stereotyped thinking of the past and from the inertia of bureaucratic methods and activities.

Although the proponents of these views pay lip service to the new policy, they have not yet overcome old thinking, and instead assess social developments by fanning nervousness and mistrust in the policy of the Party leadership and by readily giving the worst possible labels to each deviation from inertia or to even a slightly different socialist initiative. Some of these people are even pursuing deliberate actions against the policy of the Party....

It goes without saying that such views and attitudes undermine the Party's capacity to act and could discredit the party in the eyes of the broad mass of the people, who are rightly coupling their hope in a new policy of the Party with efforts to overcome old sectarian and dogmatic working methods....

Both extremes have the same objective impact in the final analysis and obstruct progressive development, which is and must be our main goal. We must and will not stop half way....

It would be naive to expect extremist tendencies not to exert pressure that might lead to attacks against the socialist system itself in our country.... That is why the exceptional measure we are proposing—to prepare the congress during the three summer months—is a fundamental issue for the development of the entire internal political situation.

The Kremlin's take on this essentially was that Dubcek was a threat, an obdurate ant seeming to beg to be stepped on. Moscow threatened military intervention unless he backed away from his confusing attempts at promoting democracy.

He didn't. Russian tanks rolled in; his defiance too soon was to be crushed. The BBC on August 21 reported it this way:

1968: Russia brings winter to *Prague Spring*

Dozens of people have been killed in a massive military clampdown in Czechoslovakia by five Warsaw Pact countries.

Several members of the liberal Czechoslovak leadership have been arrested, including Prime Minister Alexander Dubcek.

The Soviet news agency, Tass, claims "assistance" was requested by members of the Czechoslovak Government and Communist Party leaders to fight "counter-revolutionary forces".

But in a secret radio address, Czechoslovak President Ludvik Svoboda condemned the occupation by Warsaw Pact allies as illegal and committed without the government's consent.

US President Lyndon Johnson said the invasion was a clear violation of the United Nations Charter and that the excuses offered by the Soviet Union were "patently contrived".

It is a sad commentary on the communist mind that a sign of liberty in Czechoslovakia is deemed a fundamental threat to the security of the Soviet system," he said.

The Czechoslovak authorities have ordered their vastly outnumbered army not to fight and are appealing to the public for restraint.

Czechoslovakia's abortive path to freedom began when Mr. Dubcek, a Slovak, became Communist Party leader in January.

A programme of wide-ranging democratic reforms had been gathering pace in the face of Soviet disapproval and the rebirth of social and political freedom became known as the *Prague Spring*.

Resistance

In the capital of Prague today, crowds of people gathered in the streets chanting support for Mr. Dubcek and imploring the foreign troops to go home.

Much of the resistance was centred around the Prague radio station. As the day progressed, Czechoslovak youths threw homemade missiles and even tried to take on Russian tanks.

Reports say some tanks and ammunition trucks were destroyed, but Soviet troops responded with machine-gun and artillery fire and at least four people were shot dead.

In the Wenceslas and Old Town Squares, hundreds of youths made barricades out of overturned lorries to try and halt the advance.

Soviet and eastern bloc commanders have now imposed an overnight curfew and are threatening to shoot on sight anyone caught breaking it.

All rail, road and airline routes out of Czechoslovakia have been closed as troops continue to enter the country—now estimated to number nearly 175,000 men.

The Czechoslovakian intelligentsia, first to recognize that they were the most threatened and perhaps best positioned to make a hasty exit, did so. Vienna was their nearest and best hope of throwing themselves into the benevolent arms of an empathetic Western group of nations. Out they poured, overwhelming the resources of several Western embassies. Mainly, those that had fled to Austria were temporarily accommodated within the Drieskirken refugee camp.

Canada was approached and agreed to take a fair share of asylum seekers. Bureaucratic processes were sharply truncated, and people were squeezed through the hasty acceptance requirements and then onto tag-team Air Canada DC-8s, assigned to accommodate virtually all applicants fleeing a country at odds with Cold War communism.

Attempting to screen *undesirables* from the stream of humanity coming through the Canadian Embassy became notional at best. Each day the Immigration Department's reception area was filled well beyond capacity. People packed the hallways and spilled into the stairwells. Assistant Liaison Officer Wagner, marginally stable when things earlier had been quiet, withdrew to a stationery stockroom, finding there a place to cower within a tightly shelved solace he so desperately needed. Stanley, with Wagner now an ancient-mariner's albatross hanging around his neck, was left at the helm.

He called the service's European headquarters in Cologne to give them a situation report. He would soon need help.

Help came. The liaison officer in charge of operations throughout Europe flew in to personally assess the circumstances. He had arranged for the immediate withdrawal of Wagner, who went back to Cologne just long enough to allow Ottawa time to facilitate his admission to a Canadian mental institution. Then the Cologne office put together a trans-European team to come to Vienna. Bernard Castleman came from Stuttgart. Richard Angleton was dropped in from Cologne, as was the personal secretary to Europe's liaison officer, who would handle the post's administration. All others would deal with applicant interviews through interpreters, and Stanley, being the only man left on post who knew the local contacts, would handle interagency liaison and provide the glue to hold things together.

It was an interesting time. Much earlier, in southern Alberta, Stanley had worked with Angleton, so they knew each other well and put their heads together to help a number of high-risk people safely out of the country.

Everyone on the ad-hoc Vienna team was keenly aware that the Czechoslovakian Intelligence Service, being primarily under the direction of the Russian KGB, had injected operatives into the émigré stream, apparently in an attempt to learn who was headed where in their newly adopted country. There was no way to be sure that some of the Czech agents, possibly tasked with resettling in Canada as sleepers, hadn't already passed through the net.

Workdays for Stanley, including the daily commute from home, routinely stretched into twelve hours, plus. He saw very little of Chelsea and the kids during those many weeks, and the stress on her trying to cope with a Westerner's loneliness in an all-Austrian village—struggling with a language she was still learning and essentially friendless within a culture nurturing residual antipathy toward anyone who had come from a wartime-enemy country—became too much for her. She packed up the kids and went home, intent on an extended stay with her parents.

It got worse. Shortly after they had come to Vienna—with Stanley having left Chelsea alone to sort out her new life in a strange culture and in a strange neighbourhood—she had wanted to arrange for help with the kids. Assisted by the embassy's local staff, they had advertised in a couple of the Viennese newspapers for an English-speaking *au pair*. They found one: Anastasia Buranekova, a Czech girl who had been living in Austria and whose English seemed adequate. She was pleasant enough, but was playfully immature and soon became, to Chelsea, more a liability than help around the house or a caregiver to their children. Later, when Chelsea gave her notice, she had announced that she would like to immigrate to Canada.

Stanley realized that Anastasia's desire presented a dilemma. If she were going to be filtered through the embassy's immigration process, he wanted to make sure that she not discover his role within it. He had taken the precaution of screening her through the usual allied agencies, but didn't want to interview her, for what he'd presumed were obvious reasons. Thus, when all agency checks came back negative, he had passed her through the security stage of the acceptance process.

Big mistake.

At more or less the peak of the Czech crisis, he had a second visit from the officer in charge of European operations. Their meeting was blunt, one-sidedly confrontational. The officer handed him a sheet of paper with Stanley's signature on it, which he had instantly recognized as Anastasia's immigration security clearance document. The first question out of the officer's mouth was "What information have you been passing to this woman and for how long have you been doing it?"

That melted way any possibility of casualness from where Stanley sat, although in a bizarre way it had let him relax into an in-the-chair conclusion that his career was over. What was left to lose? He also recognized an interviewing technique that was common within the Service: never ask a question to which you haven't already researched the answer. So, Stanley knew, from the very end of his inquisitor's first statement, he must not lie. Not that he had wanted to nor that he had any reason to.

Stanley gave the officer his Anastasia Buranekova story, keeping to the bare-bones. The officer wanted to know whether or not he had been sleeping with her, an implication that Stanley had expected and had been able to truthfully deny. The officer then showed him a photograph, ostensibly of Anastasia. It was indeed a picture of a beautiful woman, but it wasn't Buranekova. Stanley told him that; however, the officer stated in a flat, determined voice that a reliable source had given him the photo and remained adamant that it was authentic. It couldn't be, Stanley insisted, and added that he didn't know who the pictured woman was.

Apparently the Brits had tagged the woman in the photo as a Czech intelligence-service operative. Not a good thing, to be sure.

The interview dragged on and hours passed; the tone perceptibly softened. Was this guy beginning to believe him, Stanley wondered? He became confident enough to try for a chess player's stalemate—a standoff of sorts, where neither would be left feeling the loser—in the event that the game might not end here. He intently watched the other man ease into his longer, I'm-really-your-friend strategy, two protagonists attempting to determine what the other's next move might be and trying to mentally counter any loss before it could be declared: queen takes knight...whatever. In a further effort to dilute his inquisitor's judgment of him, Stanley suggested that the officer have a conversation with his wife. She was, he devised, in a better position to offer an assessment of Anastasia, knowing that Chelsea's would be a more acrid version. But the officer declined. The afternoon lengthened. The session gradually played itself out, ending in what seemed to Stanley like a non-acrimonious cessation. They didn't shake hands of course, but Stanley silently congratulated himself on not having had to lay down his king. There would be no checkmate—at least not in this round.

But the shadow of that day lingered, and in its shade Stanley's career languished for months and years to follow. The intensity of the Czechoslovakian crisis churned on toward the 1968 Christmas holidays, becoming for him mentally exhausting and physically a wipeout. Not surprisingly, he supposed, he had received notice from Cologne that he would be posted to that city, to become part of the European regional headquarters group, a place where the Service could keep a closer eye on him.

During the course of his having worked through the preliminary logistics of that move, the embassy received notice from the Austrian government that he was to be declared *persona non grata*, apparently for activities that were outside his mandate and in violation of Austria's criminal law. Meanwhile, the officer in charge in Cologne—his former inquisitor—had been replaced by a new fellow, who had opted, happily for Stanley, to challenge the Austrian declaration and was successful in getting it annulled.

Stanley tidied up his impending relocation to Cologne as the Czech crisis tailed off into a gradually diminishing urgency. His replacement in Vienna—an upwardly mobile striver from Stuttgart—took over his chair in the *Abteilung*. Life went on. Dubcek, in Prague, was replaced, at least for the time being. The Soviet Union had prevailed. Later though, a BBC assessment put it in context:

> Following the invasion, Mr. Dubcek and others were
> banned from office and replaced with a famously

repressive communist regime. All the reforms were annulled or abandoned.

The invasion drew condemnation from across the globe. Significantly many western communist parties and communist Yugoslavia and Rumania dissociated themselves from the USSR's actions.

As with Hungary in 1956, the West took no action. The Soviet defense minister is said to have recommended invading even if it meant a third world war. Moreover, the US was in the middle of a presidential election campaign and entrenched in Vietnam.

The Communists were finally ousted on 24 November 1989, and Mr. Dubcek made a triumphant return to Prague.

He became chairman of the new post-Communist administration in what became known as the *Velvet Revolution.*

Once more Stanley had become a desk-bound intelligence analyst, of sorts. But, happily, things were more laissez-faire than they had been in the Ottawa headquarters. Life in Cologne eased itself more into a foreign holiday than a work assignment, and after he had settled in, Chelsea and the children returned. From the outset, Chelsea liked her new house. It was less ostentatious than the villa in Bad Vöslau, but homey, with a more Canadian feel to it. He got on well with the new officer in charge, and during the next year they became friends, good friends.

In 1969, with the end of his tour looming, Stanley learned he was to be returned to Security Service headquarters in Ottawa.

Once there he found himself in a three-person unit responsible for drafting procedural guidelines and regulations for the Service's overseas operations. He wasn't promulgating them, of course, just drafting them. He had been assigned to a more senior overseas veteran whom he soon came to like. He also got on well with the third man in the unit, and work had taken on a more meaningful importance than he had anticipated. The atmosphere within their shared office space became relaxed and quietly congenial.

Months passed, uneventfully. Stanley's world and the world outside his purview continued to turn. In spite of a generally shared McCarthyist expectation, no holocaust had transpired.

In the summer of 1971 a call came for him, mandating an interview with the Service's headquarters personnel officer. Could this be, he worried, the fall of his carefully structured defense around the Vienna incident? But no, it turned out to be good news: he had scored well in a military-supervised language aptitude test. The test had been an all-day grind, with each participant having been consigned to a semi-isolated booth, alternating between headset-and-microphone exchanges and pencil-and-paper exercises, all with the intent of determining each candidate's speed of recognition and assimilation of spoken and written words, numbers, and phrases borrowed from the Kurdish language.

No crumbling Austrian wall. No shadow of his former inquisitor. At least not yet.

The Service had decided that it wanted him to relocate to Monterey, California, to enroll in a meat-grinder American military language institute. He was to undertake—between 1971 and 1972—Asian Studies, majoring in Cantonese. His career was about to change focus, toward the Far East.

The college enforced an American military approach. The army felt that relaxation was not a comfortable cohabiter with academia. Teachers had a mandate: to force-feed students in much the same way the Chinese traditionally had fed Peking ducks—lots and often. The rules were made clear within the first week: Every Friday the department's professor would test students. Fall below a 70 percent average and under-the-line students would be on their way home.

The coursework had been gruelling—the hardest work he had ever done. Rote memorization was key. The material was cumulative, exponentially so. He knew that his mind would need to become a flexible vessel and that that accommodation would have to happen quickly.

A torrent of new words—written (or, more correctly, stroked) and spoken—tumbled over the class daily.

Because self-confidence had never been one of his strengths, fear of failure came to haunt his every breath. Homework initially took anywhere from five to seven hours of post-class evening time. He spent weekends in isolation, staring at Chinese-character flashcards, trying as he might to burn them into some recess of his still-rebellious mind.

"Nothing is more perishable," his professor was fond of saying, "than the memory of a Chinese character." Then he would occasionally add, "You're lucky. In my time, we Chinese kids used water to bush our characters onto a hot brick, outside, in the sun. When the image evaporated, we would be required to do it over again. And again. Until we knew it." All teachers, including the professor, were from the Chinese mainland; all were, within their own disciplines, recognized experts. They had a mandate: be intense and unforgiving. A war was on, this time in Vietnam, and China was backing the North.

Days passed, then weeks. He hadn't yet flunked out. He had top-of-the-mountain moments, just as he also encountered no-light-at-the-end-of-the-tunnel days. For the latter he had an ally; the Service had been astute enough to send a Toronto-based member to attend the same course. When either of them noticed the other beginning to slide, the one on firm ground would throw out a lifeline. It had worked. In fact, varyingly, it had saved them both.

The sheep's bladder that his brain had become expanded, asymmetrically and sometimes stretched at the seams, but with an ever-increasing capacity and sufficient stability to not let him fall behind. The days became easier; weeks seemed shorter. He could finish his homework in about three after-supper hours.

The school—or the army—had invented a failsafe method to keep its students attentive, euphemistically named "the daily dialogue". In fact, it was a monologue and was the class's first activity each morning. It took the form of a daily two-page handout, printed back-to-back. Each was a short story, interwoven with Chinese characters and idiomatic expressions, the latter recently having been daytime taught. The noncharacterized text was in Romanized Chinese with added *tone-marks*. Cantonese has nine tones, of which each word-syllable owns a different meaning according to the pitch at which it needs to be *sung*. Students had to memorize daily handouts verbatim and then sequentially recite them the next morning, each standing beside his desk. And there, in front of him—wristwatch ceremoniously removed, its metal wristband folded inward upon itself and set on the classroom's lectern, glasses adjusted and pen poised over a grading sheet—the professor would raise a scrutinizing eye and softly call out, in Cantonese of course, the name of the first student to recite. He would time each recitation, listening for pauses that might be a telltale sign of flawed memorization, always with an ear attuned to tonal correctness.

It was terrifying. The daily grading, along with results from paper exercises and tests, went toward each student's weekly average, hopefully—for the student—to hover somewhere above the 70 percent self-destruct line.

Weeks ground into months. The months became a calendar year, leading into another. Final exams were written and spoken and were finally behind them. The professor's charges' heads had been filled, and it was time to send them home. He passed with a grade average of 93 percent. His best subject had been Chinese calligraphy—the art of Chinese-character painting and writing. As a child he had been artsy and won prizes at a local fair for his pencil drawings. Thus, after having locked the image of the characters into his mind, he had little difficulty replicating them on paper. In that subject he achieved 99 percent. The professor had been unwilling to show him his error. One of the teachers later explained that it was not the Chinese way to recognize a perfect paper.

Stanley's sense of self-esteem—previously having hovered between low and nonexistent—had received a welcomed boost. For the first time in his life he realized he had a talent: *languages*. Not a particularly useful talent, but better than none.

He was called back to an unexpected and painful obscurity within the Service's headquarters' Chinese counterintelligence and counterespionage operations, once more to become just a pawn. He shared an office with his new supervisor, a likable guy with a recalcitrant disrespect for the Service and what it had apparently been striving to achieve. The man's denigration of the work they were doing and the people they were doing it to, and for, was disconcerting. For much of the time, his boss just read the daily newspaper. When new intelligence material came in for analysis, he would comically chip away at Stanley's endeavours to deal with it. It had quickly become a depressing environment.

He had to live within that work encapsulation for almost two years. But it wasn't totally uneventful. In coffee-time chats with colleagues one of them had mentioned, perhaps inadvertently, the code name of a file—a dossier that had long intrigued him—about his Vienna misadventure.

Aided by a schmoozing acquaintance with the two women guardians of the Top-Secret registry, he had managed to sign out the file and openly carry it to his office. He had the proper clearance level, although the women had rightfully queried him, regarding the Service's need-to-know rule, which was a second level of protection for secrets that were particularly access-limited. He had explained that *of course* he had a need-to-know; he had been involved with the situation that the file dealt with during his time in Vienna. They had bought the explanation, having known he had once been posted there. Although this posit was technically true, the ruse had been a disingenuous circumvention, and would later be questioned—rightfully so—by Internal Security.

So there it had been, the whole story, temporarily his to digest. The Service had taken a hard look at him and the Vienna incident's uncertainty. It had turned out his then-inquisitor and superior hadn't believed him. The officer had suspected him of having been "compromised," which was Service double-speak for concluding that Mr. Watson had left himself open to blackmail, or perhaps even had been co-opted by Czech or Russian Intelligence. In short, Watson might now be a spy—a traitor. They had tracked and were continuing to follow Anastasia Buranekova's activities. They had interviewed her at length about any affiliation she had with Czech Intelligence and had delved more deeply into her relationship with him. She denied that she had ever been anyone's "agent" and declared that she hadn't been screwing her former employer, Mr. Watson. Of course that's what the Service would have expected her to say, true or not. So the shadow of doubt still hung there, smoke from a smudge hindering his career options and advancement. The investigation was ongoing. He couldn't do much but wait and watch.

Time passed. Curiosity prevailed. He had wondered how the investigation might be proceeding. Again he drew the code-named file and checked for any conclusions the Service might have reached. But conclusions in any spy case, barring a confession, are usually tenuous; reaching an absolute yes or no is often difficult. So, the case had been left hanging. And there, in the top-secret registry awaiting discovery were Stanley's two signatures, showing received and returned dates for the file.

Internal Security's role was to be ever watchful for moles in the organization, and it was a tough thing for them to undertake successfully. Hard evidence was difficult to develop, even in cases involving the Opposition's defectors; believing intelligence gleaned from defectors was always a Damocles' sword. They may have been plants tasked with offering disinformation.

But the internal people had to remain vigilant, always. Their first visit to Stanley had been unannounced and totally unexpected. He knew the guy whose chore it was to tease the truth out of him; in fact, he knew him well.

It opened with a disingenuous grin and a "Good-to-see-you-again!" proclamation, effused self-assuredly as the fellow invited himself into Stan's office and unbuckled his apparently tired knees to let a heavy-but-not-fat torso fall, as if he had been at home, into the only visitor's chair that fronted the tiny monk cell's—which it had once been—typically small civil-service desk, simultaneously scratching a match and holding it to a wonderful smelling cigar. There had been a few minutes of diversion as Stanley went next door to try to borrow an ashtray. In the moment, Stanley had been happy that he had never smoked.

Although tense from Stanley's perspective, the interview was relatively congenial, following unwritten rules that advantaged him because he knew only too well what the questions were going to be and which of his answers would be further pursued for verification and/or contradiction.

Even before the end of the cigar-smoker's smilingly proffered "Hi," Stanley knew that his friend-for-the-day would have just come away from an intense reexamination of the file—code-named *Burnt Bridge*—almost certainly done in collaboration with colleagues. He'd have absorbed all nuances of the investigation to date.

So, once again Stanley cautioned himself, "Don't let yourself get caught in a lie."

The investigator didn't take any notes; he would have jotted them down later if the conversation hadn't been more than likely tape-recorded. Stanley would of course look for the installed device later, but he knew the organization would be one step ahead of him in retrieving it. Or his Smiley would have been wearing a wire.

The Security Service had adopted more the MI-5 style of internal interrogation than the CIA ever would have countenanced, the latter's inquisitors being notoriously harsh. The Canadian approach was to keep all tangential chats off the direct line of questioning quite chummy. But, throughout, it was always a cat-and-mouse game, and top-of-mind caution was warranted.

The day had ended tiredly for them both. His interrogator left, Stanley supposed, having gleaned nothing new to document whatever his professional judgment might have deduced. But Stanley had a thread of truth going for himself: *he knew* that he wasn't a spy.

Months passed; his chum dropped in, back for another chat. Again it became a protracted game of truth or consequences. Again, he stuck with the truth, keeping his responses pointed, succinctly aimed at the heart of each question and avoiding its wavering, suction-cupped tentacles. But there had been few new things for his hidden-hand's go-between to bring up; the session's apparent intent having been to find out if he had *ever* done anything for which he might be, or to become, susceptible to blackmail.

"Would you submit to a polygraph?" his smiling friend asked.

"Yes, of course," Stanley replied.

But no polygraph had ensued. Perhaps they were actually trying to *clear* him, he had thought. He had been no angel, but he would never have sold out his country or his colleagues, not for anything he'd done or would do.

But, he had known—stuck in his little green-walled cell that had once been a monk's bedroom, watching the one maple tree that had been his saving-grace view from a miserably small window turn green in springtime and orange in October—that he was going nowhere, career-wise. He still had the same disenchanted supervisor next door, chortling over what had been deemed a subordinate's misplaced diligence, offering up new cynicisms and doubts of purpose daily.

It began to rub off on him, and he was ready to get out from under, to move on.

With a hint dropped here and a favour called there, he had planted the necessary seeds in the hope of harvesting another foreign assignment. The Service was hesitant, still a bit nervous about his loyalty and about the suitability of his wife to endure another offshore posting. But he had prevailed, conjuring up and persisting with the necessary assurances.

In 1974, the Service finally sent him and his family to Hong Kong.

They took residence in a high-rise tower halfway up the mountain from a then-teeming Victoria Harbour. The building had the look and feel that it might have been shaken off its hillside stilts by little more than a magnitude 6.0 earthquake. Once again, Chelsea had been dropped into an alien environment. Once again, the assignment was a culture shock from which she would never adjust during their time on the island. But she had coped—bravely and largely alone, except for the company of their two young children—for their first two years. It was to have been a three-year posting.

Happily, the business community and the then-largely British governing class were accommodating; all the principal players spoke English, second language of commerce and first language of officialdom.

He had been in his element, given his modest Cantonese comfort level, steeped earlier in the dark tea of Asian culture and history: his differentiation from most *Kwai Lo's*, south-China's favourite ethnic slur for Caucasians.

The liaison officer overseeing operations for Asia-Pacific, based in Hong Kong, was replaced shortly after Stanley's arrival. The new man, eventually to become an RCMP assistant commissioner, exemplified gentlemanly behaviour to an anachronistic extreme, exuding that behaviour in day-to-day dealings with peer-level, other-nations' counterparts, and his own bevy of subordinates. He carried with him an air of superficiality that made him somewhat unpopular back home. But, in him, Stanley found an almost instant kinship, which, later, he had never been able to completely explain to his colleagues. Cornelius Sutherland and his wife Katrina were to become lifelong friends. The gap in rank and social status between this new officer and him should've been insurmountable, but somehow it wasn't. Cornelius was of Scottish nobility. Until relatively recently rural Scotland was dominated by a narrow clique of aristocrats and landowners; some of whom with titles, deeds and rights stretching back centuries. Often living in castles and mansion houses, these men owned vast tracts of land, counted in the hundreds of thousands of acres; dominated the local political environment and controlled the bulk of the wealth. Virtually everyone else either worked directly on their estates or paid rent to farm them. Cornelius, it turned out, was a direct descendant of the Sutherlands of Dunrobin Castle, seat of the Countess Sutherland. But Cornelius had made nothing of that, ever. He didn't like anyone abbreviating his name, though; found it an unacceptable effrontery. Although an impeccable dresser, he had daily hung up his jacket, literally rolled up his sleeves, and got on with the mission he had been sent to command.

On the other hand, Stan's immediate supervisor—midway between himself and Cornelius—had been an insufferable dolt. Cornelius was able to stomach this man's buffoonery for a time, but found he would need to bypass him if he was to get all necessary things done. Cornelius thus had come to rely on Stanley as a subordinate, and Stan had done everything in his power not to disappoint. They worked together, laughed together, played together, drank together. When Cornelius had to undertake one or another delicate mission in a country where his presence required treading softly, he had sometimes taken Stan with him.

Burma had been such a venture. They had slipped into Rangoon for a briefing by Cornelius's Australian military counterpart, an army colonel. With all the necessary security precautions in place, the Aussie officer had given them a wanted-back-home, unvarnished update on the state of Burma's military vis-à-vis the country's rebellious factions. Then they had beaten a path back to Hong Kong, all of which had entailed overnighting for a couple of days in the capital's infamous Strand Hotel.

The Strand by then had been reduced to a relic of its former British glory era. In the dining room, a waiter, attempting to maintain the essence of the country's historical formalities, had presented them with the day's menu. No, he had indicated apologetically, their first choice would not be available that evening. Nor, it turned out, would their second choice. By the time they had worked their way through most of the items listed, they had to ask what *might* be available. Immensely relieved, the waiter had offered up whatever had been in the pot that day. They would be able to skip the menu next time, and did.

After one of their dinners, having sat otherwise alone in the hotel's lounge, they had begun to place bets on whose gecko would first cross an agreed-to crack in the ceiling. Cornelius's smallish lizard did the politically correct thing and crossed the line first. Stanley made good on the bet: a small-denomination *kyat* note, long since demonetized in its particular iteration by the Burmese government.

The good part—and what had forever cemented their friendship—was the consumption of a bottle of Canadian whisky that Cornelius had stashed in his luggage, downed all in a one-night go. They had retired to Cornelius's room, where he had a story to tell about a dominating father who had become a senior officer in the RCMP. Before that, Cornelius's grandfather had been a sergeant major in the Force—maybe not a good thing for Cornelius. Between father and grandfather they had managed to press a malleable child into their own, soldierly mold—there to keep him until Cornelius, in his turn, became a senior officer.

But in some circles Cornelius's father had been disliked. Personality traits that others found disagreeable had been imprinted on Cornelius, who had spent a long time trying to shake them. And he had wanted to talk about it with someone he knew and could trust. To Stanley's mind, the man had been completely successful in reshaping himself. Others disagreed, although there may have been a level of professional jealousy at the root of that disagreement.

Stanley, when it came his turn to share stories, divulged that he had been no stranger to harm imposed by an unyielding father. His own dad, Everett—a World War II veteran wounded in France, short on tolerance, long on abuse—had attempted to turn him into a little soldier. But Stanley was too soft a soul to be molded into anything approaching a trained warrior. Yes, he had liked the uniforms his mom had made for him as a child, and he had embraced the parade-square discipline that came with having been enrolled in Virden's army cadet corps. But, *shoot* someone? He thought not. The disparate parenting model that he had experienced—loving gentleness on the part of his mother and judgmental rigidity from his father—had left him with a crippling indecisiveness and accounted, he thought, for his lack of self-esteem.

So, he and Cornelius had found, in a shabby hotel room in the capital of Burma, something in common, something that would become an inseparable bond.

Stanley's Hong Kong tour of duty had thus turned out to be a good one, mainly. Cornelius had trusted him alone with ventures into several Asian uncertainties. Thailand was his first such sink-or-swim trial. He had to feel his way at every step. But that responsibility soon had become comfortable turf for him; he could move about there without feeling at risk. He got along well with his counterparts in the Royal Thai Police, the government organization charged with performing police functions throughout the country. The unitary agency's power and influence in Thai national life had at times rivalled that of the army. The department played an important role in the government's efforts to suppress the remnants of the Thai insurgency. Their Special Branch, a label customarily used to identify units responsible for matters of national security in British and Commonwealth police forces, was tasked with acquiring and developing intelligence, usually of a political nature, and conducting investigations to protect the State from perceived threats of subversion, particularly terrorism and other extremist activity. The headquarters in Bangkok administered all the components of the police system. Bangkok usually was his first in-country destination. As his relationship with Thai colleagues strengthened, they had enjoyed some interesting adventures, including an audience with an Ayutthaya—the country's ancient capital—monk whose fortune-telling gifts were regarded by many local officers as having been a gift of their deity.

Meanwhile, farther east, the quagmire that the Vietnam Conflict had become was always a back-of-mind concern. By April 1975, all of America's input had disintegrated. By April 23, 100,000 North Vietnamese soldiers had advanced on Saigon, which by then had been overflowing with refugees. US President Gerald Ford declared, on that day, that the conflict was "a war that is finished as far as America is concerned." But, it wasn't quite. By April 27, Saigon was encircled. Approximately 30,000 South Vietnamese soldiers were inside the city, leaderless, with the North Vietnam Army firing rockets into downtown civilian areas. The city erupted into chaos; looting became widespread. Two days later President Ford ordered *Operation Frequent Wind*—a helicopter evacuation initiated with a radio broadcast of the song *White Christmas* as its prearranged code signal—that triggered the extraction of 7,000 Americans and South Vietnamese from the city. None of which was easy. At Tan Son Nhut Air Base, frantic civilians began swarming the helicopters. The evacuation was shifted to the walled-in American embassy, still secured by US Marines. Thousands of civilians attempted to get into the compound. In support, three US aircraft carriers stood by off the coast to handle incoming choppers. Those in excess had to be pushed overboard, empty, to make room for more arrivals.

The country was literally falling apart. As Saigon came under full siege by the North Vietnamese, few resources remained to care for children found abandoned, some of whom had been fathered by American soldiers. Those children's mothers feared what would happen to them if the North Vietnamese found them out. Others were orphans who lost their parents and families to the war. Some were simply abandoned due to poverty or disability.

The South Vietnamese ambassador to the United Nations and many humanitarian groups were by then pleading to the American government for assistance in rescuing the little people. On April 3, weeks before the collapse, President Ford announced *Operation Babylift*. On that day, private and military transport planes began to fly out Vietnam orphans with Canada's participation.

One of the first official flights of *Operation Babylift* ended in tragedy. A C-5A Galaxy flew the initial mission. The C-5 departed Saigon's Tan Son Nhat Airport shortly after 4 p.m. on April 4. What seemed to be an explosion as the lower rear fuselage was torn apart happened just twelve minutes after takeoff. The locks of the rear-loading ramp had failed, causing the door to open and separate. A rapid decompression occurred. Control and trim cables to the rudder and elevators were severed, leaving only one aileron and the wing spoilers operating. Two of the four hydraulic systems were out. The crew wrestled with the controls, managing to guide the plane with changes in power settings and by using the one working aileron and wing spoilers. They descended to an altitude of 4,000 feet on a heading of 310 degrees in preparation for landing on Tan Son Nhat's runway 25L. About halfway through a turn to final approach, the rate of descent increased rapidly. Seeing that they couldn't make the runway, full power was applied to bring the nose up. The C-5 touched down in a rice paddy. Skidding for a quarter of a mile, the aircraft again became airborne for a half mile before hitting a dike and breaking into four parts, some of which caught fire. According to Defense Intelligence Agency figures, of the 305 aboard, 138 people were killed in the crash, including 78 children and 35 Defense Attaché Office Saigon personnel.

The last flight out of Vietnam for *Operation Babylift* was on April 26, 1975. Overall, approximately 2,700 children were flown to the United States and about 1,300 more were flown to Canada, Australia, and Europe.

But many less-fortunate people were abandoned and in need of humanitarian consideration. As a result, the United States launched

Operation New Life, with Guam becoming a focal point for the processing of about 110,000 Southeast Asian refugees. Some 40 percent of them transiting Guam were from Vietnam's ethnic Chinese population; other groups disproportionately represented were the South Vietnamese military and civil service, many of whom would have faced imprisonment and re-education camps had they remained. Individuals made suspect to the victors by virtue of their international education also departed; by one count, Vietnam lost two-thirds of its physicians in less than a month.

During the second phase of the operation, 1,546 politically sensitive refugees were kept under guard in a separate part of the American camp. All were former Viet Cong caught in the mass migration and later returned at their own request, quietly offloaded from a ship onto life rafts by US Navy personnel a short distance off the coast and instructed to paddle back to Vietnam. They did so, having stripped off US-issued clothing and jettisoned US-provided relief supplies.

The Canadian government concurrently established a presence on Guam, announcing that Canada too would accept refugees. At that time English-speaking immigrants to Canada were upsetting a political balance between Québec and Canada's English-speaking provinces, and—perhaps because Vietnam's colonial language had been French—the Canadian government sought, found, and accepted French-speaking, professionally educated people from within that stream.

The time was busy for everyone involved, either directly or peripherally, including staffers and wives of the Canadian Commission in Hong Kong, Stanley and Chelsea among them.

Apart from the Vietnam experience, Hong Kong itself had had its moments. The Chinese had initiated a honeypot attempt at recruiting Stan, which, oddly for a professional, had caught him unawares. He had actually felt rather flattered. Perhaps they had a source at the Monterey language school or maybe they had discerned something of interest in what he had been doing in a general sense. He believed they couldn't have sifted him out as a person of interest from the relative anonymity of his home Service's Alta Vista headquarters. There he had been nothing but a cork bobbing in a sea of minions all doing essentially the same thing—low-level people, just cogs on a wheel within a very large, very ponderous, very malignant machine.

In hindsight, the attempt had been amusing. He had enrolled at Hong Kong's *Alliance Francaise* to study French, knowing that he would be able to continue the program back home. By the third or fourth week into this initiative, a new student joined the class. She was a tall, lithesome Han girl, selected, he had presumed, by the Chinese Intelligence Service for her remarkable beauty. She was gracious and unnervingly attentive, her raven hair swaying in its midnight cascade onto white shoulders, reflecting diamond highlights like sheets of water tumbling over pristine falls in the fullness of an August moon. Her English would have been the envy of Britain's Royal Palace.

She had made the most of her classmates' several offers of assistance to catch her up with lessons missed.

His first off-key note tumbled reluctantly into consciousness when she—rather too soon, he thought—became more interested in him than in others at the school. A testosterone-driven part of him had wanted to believe she was really who she had contended to be: the bored wife of a Singapore lawyer. Quiet a successful one apparently. The CIS would have no doubt planted such a person to cover the eventuality that he might make inquiries.

Money apparently being no object, she had spent part of her time in Hong Kong, finding the colony's lifestyle more upbeat. Either way, she was undeniably an Asian sophisticate—temptingly amorous. She drove, as he might have expected, a current model BMW, and she had offered to take him home after classes. He had accepted a couple of times. But he knew doing so was trouble. *Trouble*. However, that was his mind talking; the other part of his anatomy was struggling to take over the lead.

As he had hoped wouldn't happen, she became interested in what he did for a living. Unhappy with his vague responses, she had digressed into various monologues about Hong Kong politics and had obliquely edged her way into asking where he stood vis-à-vis an upcoming Colony election. When he had persisted with unenthusiastic responses, along the line that Hong Kong's testy coexistence with the Mainland was really none of his business nor of any real interest to him, she had become upset. "How could anyone live here and not care?" she had asked, adding that it was any responsible resident's obligation to be opinionated.

Good point. And an interesting one: he was officially a resident, but he hadn't mentioned that.

He persisted with a dullard's responses…and she dropped it, moving toward where the game—obvious by then—was headed. Would he care to have a fling with her? She had a nice place, she had said, and would enjoy his attentions, although "they ought to drop in somewhere for a Coke first, just to get better acquainted."

In the end, they hadn't gone for the Coke nor did he accompany her to wherever her handlers no doubt had wanted her to lead him. Instead he remained obtuse, feigning disinterest. He told her he must concentrate his energies on the *Alliance* studies. Meanwhile, his wannabe cave dweller was screaming at the still-functioning fragment of his brain that he was lying. But that fragment could visualize the cameras and audiotape reels recording every stroke and murmur. He recognized the pit he would be tumbling into, from which there would be no escape.

Might she just have been a plant, he wondered, to test his resolve—to assess his strength of character, merely to have some other-side voyeur add a line or a paragraph to a CIS dossier? That wouldn't be out of character for any intelligence organization; they all played by more or less the same rules, or lack of them. The more they knew about an enemy the better placed they would be to later counter him, if needed.

She had returned to *Alliance* classes three or four more times, then quietly dropped the course and disappeared, presumably into the anonymity of Hong Kong's 24/7 anthill of humanity. Or perhaps she had been recalled to the Mainland. He never found out and never inquired; it was too risky. But he had told Chelsea and had weathered her righteous tears. For weeks after he felt wretched, recognizing in the mirror the asshole that he had been every time he shaved, and borne, head bowed, the coldness of her silence.

He hadn't told the Organization, however, which he had an obligation to do. He had already been through enough grief with Internal

Security; no point offering a few fresh coals for them to stoke. Had they known, they would probably have put out his fire, career-wise, prematurely.

Two years came and went, which weren't an easy time for Chelsea. Wedging their two kids into Hong Kong's British colonial school system had been difficult. The teachers were underwhelmed by their children's prior academic exposure. Their acceptance had been conditional upon passing entrance tests and, in Cameron's case, some pre-enrollment tutoring. Back home he had been post-kindergarten in a French immersion program, having lived in a non-Francophone household. He had struggled desperately with that. Thus, when facing his starchy British evaluators, he hadn't known the first thing about Roman Numerals, among various other British scholastic anachronisms. Eventually, the school's staff had placed him in a special-education group, leaving him to surmise he was an academic cripple.

Both kids had nonetheless coped. They enjoyed the relative safety, which, as Caucasians, the colony had afforded them. Cameron only once suffered a beating, on the premises of their apartment tower. Accosted by two Chinese youths who had scrambled over the surrounding page-wire fence, they put the boots to him. Tearfully he had described the encounter to a distraught Chelsea, a red shoe-print visible on the side of his face, as were bruises to his body.

Dorian had managed to break an arm while attempting to jump from a low-level ledge on the apartment tower to an adjacent building. He didn't quite make it.

The stifling humidity of summer and the ants-on-a-chocolate-bar crowding of the Colony's beaches and its streets hadn't helped. It had gnawed away at Chelsea's resolve. With a year still to go in their posting, she had declared enough.

He had made his case to his superiors as best he could. Then they had come home, but the Organization understandably wasn't amused.

Back in Ottawa he was placed in charge of the region's field Vietnamese Operations Desk and later the China Desk, working out of an inconspicuous downtown brick building. He got on well enough with the people on this team, two of whom were Chinese, but had difficulty relating to what he sensed was an ethical weakening among more senior intelligence operatives and their headquarters controllers. Morally, things that the organization had been doing were out of sync with his values. He had come to feel out of place.

A continent away, others in the Great Game had come to feel similarly. He recently read *Spy Catcher*, the autobiography of Peter Wright, former assistant director of MI5. It was a compilation of things that Stanley had never realized were happening. Two of Peter's reflections would stick with him forever, and they were hauntingly familiar:

"Shortly afterward Sokolov Grant and his wife left the area. Our inquiries had probably leaked to the village, and he presumably wanted to make a new start. But for all its apparent meaninglessness the Sokolov Grant story has always had symbolic importance to me: an ordinary man suddenly falling under suspicion, and just as abruptly cleared again, his life utterly changed because of something a man he has never met says in a darkened room on the other side of the world."

And:

"The MI5 technique is an imperfect system. But like trial by jury, it is the best yet devised. It has the virtue of enabling a man, if he has nothing to hide, and has the resilience to bear the strain, to clear himself. But its disadvantage is that hidden blemishes on an innocent man's record can often come to the surface during intensive investigation and render continued service impossible. It is a little like medieval justice: sometimes innocence can be proved only at the cost of a career."

Of passing interest to him was Peter's response to a CIA representative when asked by him for help regarding how the Company might better assassinate Third World leaders. Peter's reply was, "The French! Have you tried them? It's more their type of thing, you know.... We're out of that game. We're the junior partner in the alliance, remember? It's your responsibility now."

For him, forcing himself to continue playing his role in the shadowy scheme of things was beginning to corrode his relationship with the world around him, threatening to destroy his soul. The McDonald Commission by then had come and gone. Many of the unlawful activities the Security Service had stooped to could be read in the daily newspapers.

He finally realized that this wasn't his world. He needed out. At the beginning of 1979 he resigned.

He had spent days crafting a résumé, which, with masked disingenuity, was sufficiently convincing to get him a management position in the private sector. And for the next twenty-one years he had worked within Bell-Northern Research and Nortel, returning for a year at one point for a stint in Hong Kong and China.

Eventually he became Nortel's international director of security policy, a position that had taken him to most countries along the Pacific Rim, and to several cities in India where the corporation was represented.

On the opposite hemisphere he often flew to London to help Nortel's security director for England, the EU, and Africa to map out a program consistent with the corporation's intellectual-property protection requirements, which he had earlier written. Twice his offshore excursions took him to destinations which, when dots were connected, tracked circumnavigations of the globe.

He spent other significant slices of time closer to home—in Nashville and Atlanta, and eventually, after a headquarters stint in Mississauga—before returning to Ottawa. There, they bought a house that Chelsea knew she could make over to reflect her own persona, and they settled in. It would be their last corporate shuffle.

Toward the end of 1999, on his sixtieth birthday, he left the corporation, just in time. Soon after, the high-tech bubble had burst; investors' confidence in Nortel had stepped off a cliff. Share value fell from a high of $124.50 to junk paper at near terminal velocity. The company staggered, tumbled, and then went bankrupt.

Two-thirds of his life had come and gone. In many ways it had seemed unfulfilling. His years, he felt, had been misspent. Two things, more than others, bothered him: He had always wanted to write, and hadn't; and he had never wanted to hurt anyone, and had. Life in the intelligence game, he had always known, seldom faded away from any scene without abandoning its victims. That was why he had left.

Memories of it—secrets he had to suppress—remained locked in his psyche. It had been like a mouse trapped under a bell jar, feeling ever more drowsy, never quite aware of the consequence of giving in to sleep.

He came to believe his only hope for redemption lay in reinventing himself. He had set out to do that: to become another person, a *different* person, knowing all the while that time was not on his side. The apocalypse's fourth horsemen soon would be overtaking him; he felt he had already ridden with the other three.

Yes, the fourth horseman—the one astride the pale horse—was *Death*. He knew the others on a first-name basis: *Conquest*, riding the white horse; *War*, on the fiery red horse; and *Famine*, on the black. Perhaps he would ride throughout eternity, not with them but in their shadow, a greeter of humanity's unknowable outcome. In life, he felt like he had ridden always in shadows. If there were to be an afterlife, perhaps this would be his role. Only his children would be able to gauge his in-life humanity, if indeed he had ever had any.

A reflected flash of sunlight off a boat's turning wave in the river brought him back to the moment. He paused, recovered his bearings, and pushed back from the deck's railing. He found his coffee cup, turned it upside down to spill cold dregs onto the lawn a dozen or so feet below, and made his way back into the kitchen.

That morning, 6:23 a.m.

She startled him, not by her actions but by an absence of them, standing in the hallway entrance to the kitchen, waiflike, silent, not wanting to intrude, as had ever been her way.

"Angeline, how nice to see you!" he offered, refocusing as rapidly as his mind would let him. "It's early. How did you get here?"

"My mom dropped me off. She's supply teaching today. I persuaded her that you wouldn't mind driving me to school."

"Of course not," he tried, still adjusting, "but it's early yet. Would you like to practice the piano for a while, or maybe start a game of chess? We wouldn't have time to finish, but I could make you a cup of tea; we could at least open."

"Yes, perhaps chess, if that's okay. Is Grandma here? I wouldn't want to wake her."

"She's asleep; it'll be fine, I'll close her bedroom door. We've time enough for a few moves anyway," he tried, fabricating enthusiasm, but preoccupied by Elujah's phone call. "White or black?"

"Black," she teased, tossing her photographer's-model long brown hair back over a shoulder, "I wouldn't want you to claim an advantage were I to beat you."

They settled in at the game table, its polished-cast pieces and inch-thick glass board mutely calling out for combatants to sit. He treasured it, a gift from his youngest son—a design prototype, unique in the world.

Hurrying, perhaps unwisely to get the game going, he opened: pawn c2 to c3.

She countered: queen's knight to c6.

Good, he thought, sliding his white queen to b3.

She paused momentarily, lifting the felt base of her king's knight over an affronting pawn to h6. She had studied her opponent's early-checkmate attempts before: as in, catch the king while the king is still boxed in.

He paused, lips pursed, working his tongue over teeth not yet introduced to today's brushing. Then he moved the pawn at e2 to e3.

Without even hesitating she picked up her knight at c6, waved it above the board in front of him, smiled contentedly, and with a flourish placed it on e5. "Grandpa, you *are* a creature of habit, do you know that? You'll never beat me in the short game; has experience taught you so little? Freeing up the queen? So early? That's so transparent. Or are you just anxious to get me off to school?"

He tried to care, to be a true part-of-the-moment grandfather, to win her over, not just to beat her at chess. But he was still at the beach, picturing Marion washed ashore, wet, soggy, decomposed, and crow-pecked; probably having scared the shit out of the youngster who had found her.

Angeline seemed—to him anyway—still to be in the game, elegantly relaxed, now the dominant presence in the room.

She sensed it. Good opportunity, she thought. Changing the paradigm casually, she managed to catch him askance.

"Could I see your crossbow?" she asked, as if enquiring about a new wall hanging or an ornament with no purpose other than needing to be dusted.

"What crossbow?" he countered, lamely, feeling himself deflating suddenly, uncontrollably, like a sheep freshly stuck with a shepherd's trocar. It was the best he could manage. She started demurely enough, perhaps purposefully, he thought. He wondered why she had even gone there, suspecting she would follow on with her often-enveloping, ganglial questions. Would she maybe reveal a motive that hadn't yet jack-in-the-boxed out at him? He tried to heel bite a flock of woolly thoughts, but apparently the bearers wanted not to be gathered. Still, within his ebbing cognition, a mother-in-law's image, dead on the beach, prevailed.

Angeline waited, still smiling; tall of body, nestled confidently into tapestried upholstery of her chess-table chair, hands clasped palms up in her lap, just as he had watched her settle herself whenever entering into light conversation with guests at a party. But this wasn't an artifice; her dreamlike motions were real. Her presence was actual; she was as a hologram one could reach out and touch.

"The one Jeremy told me about," she breathed, airily, "the one you used when he went out with you on your togetherness predawn hunt. He first spotted a turkey coming out onto the field that you were both watching. But you couldn't try for it because it was a hen. Then he was first again, this time to spot a wolf come out onto the field."

He retreated; "Humph," was all he could make his throat do. "Well, he *did* have the field glasses, and he was positioned higher within our deadfall than I was. I had placed him there."

"Well anyway," she smiled, winningly, *"that* crossbow."

"Why would you like to see it?" he asked, his mind still struggling to change provinces, trying to get a grip on what this new thing was all about.

"Because I want you to teach me how to use it." She dropped the smile and then continued, "I want to learn how do something other than just ride horses."

"Well, you seem to do chess quite well. You beat me, as I recall, last time we played, albeit with your feigned naiveté about being just a beginner," he muttered, hoping she would drop the hunting offshoot.

"Okay, so I do *two* things, besides go to school."

"What about your artwork? You're away ahead of your years in that!"

"Thank you. But that's what I'll be studying at my next school. I want to try something completely different."

"Crossbow?" he averted, "You'd have difficulty even cocking it. You're still a tender young girl." He hadn't meant it condescendingly, worried that it might have come across that way.

"Grandpa, stop trying to dissuade me. And please don't call my age *tender*. I've never been a tender age."

"That's not what your mom thinks. I got a strip torn off me when I tried suggesting something as innocuous as your needing to eat more vegetables. She would take a teacher's strap to me if she ever knew I was conspiring to coach you on how to shoot a crossbow. The *vegetable* lesson wasn't something I'll need to learn twice."

"They don't use leather straps any more, Grandpa." She had a way of projecting her disappointment that was somewhere between grace and resignation. "Okay then. What other archery gear do you have?"

"What makes you think I have any?"

"Jeremy said."

"Well, maybe he shouldn't talk so much about that kind of stuff."

"You have a compound bow with two sets of limbs, one set rated at 50-pounds pull and the other at 60-pounds. Why both?"

"It seems Jeremy has been quite chatty."

"Grandpa, you're playing this game like you play chess—evasively. Come on, I'll soon have to leave for school. What else are you trying to keep from me?"

"What else do you think I have?

"You have a beautifully crafted traditional recurve bow, a Damon-Howatt Hunter, and its worth quite a bit. It has a 45-pound pull, hidden away with a dozen handmade cedar arrows, all with feather fletchings. Their maker still keeps in touch with you; he's an old-school archer from Montana. But your bow's too strong for you. That's why you bought and had installed the 50-pound limbs for your compound. Anything else about your little secrets you'd like me to out?"

"Jeremy didn't know some of that stuff."

"Doesn't matter. Maybe Uncle Cameron knew. Maybe he told me. Maybe I've been hacking your e-mails. That's how the Montana guy communicates with you, isn't it? Well, isn't it? I get Justin's help with the Internet stuff. He can crack into almost anything. He's a hell of a lot smarter than his teachers give him credit for. And much smarter than his older brother thinks he is."

Jesus, Stanley thought, pushing back in his chair, who *is* this girl?

"Grandpa? Are you going to teach me? I'll learn one way or the other. I have to. One day you'll understand that."

"Angeline, I can't. I've told you the reason why."

"Then let me see your hunting gear. We don't have to shoot it. You won't even have to string your bow. And, you know, you really should have a technician release the tension on your compound. And you should have removed the battery from your crossbow's red-dot sight; it might already have leaked and corroded."

"How can you possibly know that?"

She smiled his mother's smile and then said, "Assistant Liaison Officer Watson, you don't need to know. But you *do* remember the need-to-know rule, don't you? You should. You violated it, twice. Big mistake." Then, bringing the tone down a notch, she added, "You've never quite recovered from that, have you?"

"For Christ's sake, child, you're beginning to scare me! Who *are* you anyway?"

"Grandpa, I'm your granddaughter. That's all you need to know. Remember the rule. Don't break it; third time unlucky. Now, come show me your archery stuff."

And so he had, obediently, watching her closely all the while, trying to puzzle his way through what was really going on.

He watched her select the recurve and studied her holding it at arm's length, pulling an imaginary drawstring to her cheek, releasing it correctly, following some ethereal arrow's path. To where, he wondered, watching her put the bow back down.

"Now we'd better be off to school," she said. "There's some dreary stuff waiting for me there, which I'll have to again put up with."

And they had left, together, in silence.

During the drive to school, she had offered: "You have some very disconcerting dreams, don't you?" it being more a statement than a question. "You should pay attention to them."

He turned into the school, stopped to let her out, and watched a newly arrived yellow bus disgorge its cacophony of sugar-hyped someone's-little-darlings as they played and pushed their way through education's yawning front doors, Angeline among them. She quickly fitted in, dancing their same tune.

He wondered about what she had said. "Dreams? Which ones?"

The car took him home without conscious effort on his part. Sorting through everything that had happened that morning would take some time, like sifting weevils from a sack of flour. He had watched Chelsea do that, in Hong Kong. He remembered that they had eaten the flour. But he had had less time for the Colony's cockroaches. They'd made an annoying clicking sound whenever they had ventured across the apartment's tile floors. And Victoria Island had been host to carpets of them. Billions, literally.

Scene 3
Angeline's Interest in Archery...

July 28, 2010, 5:27 p.m.

The boys were with their father Cameron, a natural-born archer who had mastered his hobby to a level where the target point of a second fired arrow frequently struck the string notch of the one loosed just before, thus splitting the first arrow's shaft. These always became moments of amusement, the split arrows becoming curled and twisted aluminum trophies, albeit expensive ones. They were in their archers' alley, a lane perhaps ten feet wide and forty feet long, untrammeled underbrush competing with young maples and ironwood to encroach upon their shooters' pathway from both sides. At its far end was a weather-sheltered target system of Cameron's own design. Heavy bolts had been tightened down against horizontal steel plates, drilled to accommodate full-height vertical threaded rods; the plates serving to sandwich dozens of identically sized thicknesses of "black joe" to form a rectangular six-foot-high butt capable of stopping even a bolt shot from a 150-pound-rated crossbow. Cameron's compound-bow, at full draw, developed half that energy, Jeremy's only a quarter.

Cousin Angeline had come upon them quietly, although not by accident. Imperceptibly she had remained with them, watching, learning, and drifting in and out of their periphery at will, effortlessly, as was her way. It was a hallmark state of being that allowed her to find a comfort zone in the presence of more assertive people. This gift of gentleness, the ethereal charm, was something she hadn't yet fully realized was part of the woman she would soon enough become, a trait that would serve her well. Or maybe she *did* know.

Jeremy was three years older than his brother Justin and was the dominant of the two boys. Justin had learned to recognize and counter most of Jeremy's self-interest gambits, having realized early on that he would need to establish a survivalist's toehold within the family if he were to have any hope of retaining a unique identity. He had developed behaviours that had allowed an often-peaceful coexistence. But, notwithstanding his innate ability to recognize a proposal being warped into a scam whenever spoils were to be divided, Jeremy usually could manipulate his way into leaving the scene with the lion's share.

When Angeline came upon them, Cameron was giving Jeremy instruction on correct stance and how to breathe leading up to the release of each arrow. Both father and son were using handheld mechanical triggers, allowing them to achieve better accuracy.

Jeremy learned quickly and shot well. He wanted to become as good as his father.

The Fontana Resurrection

Justin only watched. He wasn't sure he wanted to make archery his thing; he was more interested in music, quietly longing for a guitar.

Angeline was attentive. She hadn't wanted to let it show, however, not yet, anyway. She would wait until sometime Jeremy was practicing alone. She had known for some time that he liked her, perhaps more than in a platonic way, and was quite sure she could persuade him to teach her the rudiments. One problem she now realized was that Jeremy shot left-handed; she would have to adapt herself to his bow.

When Jeremy eventually set down the bow to return to the house for "a glass of water," as he had politely put it, she knew he was going to relieve himself. She went over to his bow, picked it up, and tried pulling back the bowstring to get a feeling for the weight of it. She was thus encouraged, so she shifted her focus to how a shooter might align the arrow's string notch with the bow's optical sight. It wasn't initially obvious to her. She could see something like a small washer bound into the centre of the twisted lines that together made up the bowstring. She didn't try to look through the sight though, that could come later, another day. She made a mental note of the machine's—for it looked like a machine to her—make and model. Cameron was still shooting. Justin was watching his dad, not her.

Jeremy returned. Side by side, father and son continued, competing, trying different targets. They tied small underinflated balloons to map pins pressed into the target butt. They were able to pop them almost simultaneously, left then right, father and son releasing together. Looking for something smaller, they thumbtacked dandelion blossoms to the butt. Again, their synchronized shots; one hit, one miss. And so it went on.

An hour passed; energies began to wane. All archers have a finite number of pulls before they lose the steadiness needed to ensure best scores.

Father and son looked at each other, grinned, agreed to an unspoken "enough," and walked to the target to withdraw their last arrow groupings. Content within each other's company, they shuffled back to the house, Jeremy to disappear into the concrete hideaway next to the furnace that had been converted into a bedroom for him, to fire up a video game before delving into his homework.

Cameron, having gone upstairs, craved a beer and maybe a bite to eat. He poked through kitchen cupboards, looking for a bag of potato chips or anything that might take the edge off, at least from now until whenever dinner might materialize. Between work and play, he had begun to feel like it had been a long enough day. But he knew he would need to drive Angeline home, and did.

He had noticed she had seemed preoccupied throughout their hour or so at the archery range. Maybe it was just her usual inscrutability. She was, after all, his brother's daughter, that same sense of purpose and achievability. Her demeanour had a pleasantness all of its own, but he had never been quite able to fathom whatever she might be processing beneath that mysterious countenance.

July 28, 2010, 6:48 p.m.

With supper finished, Angeline eased her way upstairs to her room and uncased her laptop. She clicked on Google and entered "Browning youth bow". The browser took only a moment to flash up Browning Arms Corporation's global website.

She clicked on the *archery section*.

A great site, she thought: colourful and easy to find her way within. And she liked the amber logo: the profile of a 5-point buck, head turned to look behind it.

In the site's sidebar menu, she found and clicked on *Youth Bow*. There, shown in side view and vertically, dressed in breakup camouflage, was a skeletonised machine exactly like the one she had held an hour ago. The site described it axel to axel as: Length: 31"; Bow weight: 3.4 lbs.; Speed: 273 fps at 28 inches; Let-off: 70% actual and 65% effective.

"Let-off," she said. She had learned what that meant: that she would have to come up with 70% of the bow's draw weight before its cams would roll over to let her draw the arrow full length.

She thought she could handle that, were its draw length adjusted to 25 inches. She knew that Jeremy would do that for her. Her effective draw weight thus would become about 26 pounds.

She would practice lifting that amount of heavy metal in her basement, first with her left hand and arm, then with her right, until she was completely comfortable with at least twenty-five repetitions. That should give her the sustainability she would need to shoot well.

She put her laptop away, changed into a T-shirt, and headed for the basement. Her dad's weights were there; she would put them back when finished. He was pretty fussy about that sort of thing.

July 30, 2010, 4:18 p.m.

On Friday she phoned Jeremy and asked what he was doing the next day. Characteristically, he hedged before answering, "Why?"

She could picture the expression on his face and imagined that he would be weighing the possibilities, should she choose to come over.

"I'd like you to teach me to shoot," she said.

"Shoot what?"

"Don't play thick with me Jeremy. I want you to teach me how to use your bow."

Jeremy looked briefly around him to see whether his parents or his brother might be listening. They weren't, apparently, and he responded, "What's your interest?"

"I just want to try it. Maybe it's something I could take up."

"So, that might take some time. What's in it for me?"

She could smell where this was going and thought it best to dampen his libido now rather than later. "What did you have in mind?" she asked, adding an edge to her voice.

"Well, you'd have to be nice to me."

"Nice?"

"You know. You could consider it my tutoring fee," he said with his usual sly little smile.

"Jesus, Jeremy! I'm asking you to teach me how to shoot a bow, not to buy me a diamond tiara."

"Is that what it would take?" he asked, with a slight droop forward.

"You wish!"

"Am I speaking to the Angeline, my *cousin?*" he asked. "This doesn't sound at all like you. You're usually so withdrawn, so introverted, no one can coax more than a 'hello' out of you. Even then they're not certain whether it's a greeting or a good-bye."

"And that's all you'll *ever* coax out of me, Jeremy!"

"What's different here?" he asked, trying to reassert his dominance over his younger cousin. "This doesn't seem like the real you."

"It *is* the real me, Jeremy. Get used to it."

"The 'real you'? The 'real you' is seldom more than a perplexing three-dimensional shadow. What's changed?"

"Nothing's changed. If it would help, you could consider me two people bound up in the same skin. The one you usually find yourself looking at is the one I save for my parents and people who expect me to be polite. But, inside myself, I'm the person you're speaking to now. My parents have always treated me as though I never found my way out of diapers. But I have. I also realized early on that it might be advantageous—less punitive, if you like—to present the other face to the world. So, that's the Angeline the world sees. I'm not a pushover when it comes to what I will and won't do. In short, I'll pay you, but not in the way you'd probably prefer."

"How much would that be?"

"How much do you want?"

"Ten dollars an hour."

"That much?"

"Who else are you going to get to teach you?"

"You'll do, but I get to use your bow," she added.

"What will *I* use?"

"Your dad's."

Jeremy took a moment to think about that, the same brown glint returning to his eyes as to be found there whenever he weighed right-and-wrong options. "I don't think he would let me," he tried, evasively.

"You've used it before, when he *didn't* know."

"How are you aware of that?"

"Never mind, I know. Have we got a deal?"

"I guess. What time Saturday?"

"Two o'clock. Can that work for you?"

"Uh-huh. How will you get here?"

"My bike."

"Your mom won't let you do that. You *know* that."

"She won't know. My parents will be away for most of Saturday afternoon, and anyway, I'll be home by four o'clock. I'll be dutifully doing my homework by then."

"If you say so," Jeremy offered with a slight conspiratorial smile, still hopeful. "See you then."

July 31, 2010, 1:52 p.m.

Angeline leaned her bike against a stable wall at Jeremy's dad's place. Built more than one hundred fifty years earlier to shelter carriage horses, it had been the primary adjunct to an Ottawa-to-Kingston route's stagecoach inn—the adjacent house having been that inn. Since having acquired the property, her uncle had converted the outbuilding into a machine shop.

She looked around for Jeremy and came up empty. He didn't appear to be at the range and hadn't been in the barn when she had checked.

Then, having taken a garden path that looped through the bush at the back of his parents' home, Jeremy appeared, head slightly bowed, carrying both his own and his father's archery gear. With a brief and slightly cool greeting he handed over his bow, his arrow quiver, a mechanical bowstring release, and a strap-on guard she would need for her forearm. He walked the length of the archery butt to pin up a fresh target, then came back part way and gestured for her to move up to the fifteen-yard mark.

They began. She was attentive and followed his every suggestion with an almost military intensity, nodding whenever she got the point he was attempting to make. She followed his example when he demonstrated the correct posture and arm movements she would need to master. With each new thing, he only needed to show her once.

He thought that she seemed really determined to do this thing, but he didn't know why. Did she want to become a bow hunter, he wondered, or keep it just to target shooting? She had never said. But he thought it best to leave that alone, at least for now.

She assumed her stance for the next shot.

"Elbow up, a bit higher," he said. "That's it, hold it there. You'll have a few seconds to keep the bow at full draw, and then your arms will begin to shake. In that short time, you'll need to get a sight picture that you're happy with and squeeze the trigger, gently. Remember don't jerk it. If you were shooting a rifle, you'd pull your shot off to one side. Same thing with a bow."

Yes, she has it, he said to himself. She's going to be a natural, almost like my dad. She won't need much instruction, just practice. After today we'll be able to shoot together. That'll be fun.

He decided to risk exploring her determination. Trying to put together in his mind a quick complement he might pay her without having it come across like a masked harassment, he offered, "You're so different now from your 'other self'. Where *are* you when you're that other kid?" He felt she had let him get away with using the word *kid,* given that he was now sixteen and she only twelve. In truth, they both looked considerably older than their years. Jeremy had incessantly grown like a beanstalk to six feet five inches, and he wore size 13 boots. Angeline was already taller than her mother and grandmother, and had the slender form of a fashion model. Both had inherited their parents' good looks.

Angeline paused before answering. She released the tension on her bow without letting it lose the arrow and tilted it at a 45-degree angle toward the ground. She knew that she couldn't make him understand, but thought it safe to test uncertainties that might end up scaring him. Might not the two of them have inherited similar genetic hand-me-downs that seemed to her a puzzling family characteristic—if one could call what was happening to her *characteristic*. Without moving her feet from their correct shooting position, she sufficiently twisted her body to enable her to look him full in the face before asking her next question.

"Jeremy, are you spiritual?"

The Fontana Resurrection

Where the hell is *that* coming from? Jeremy asked himself. "Spiritual?" he said aloud. "What do you mean by *spiritual?*" It was his best attempt at a quick response—a dodge, really—given that he didn't want to appear startled.

"Are you at all religious?" Angeline asked, her body still partially twisted toward him.

"Well, I go to a Catholic school, and they teach a lot of it there. All our students are expected to be religious, and, in the case of that school, to believe in Catholicism."

"Do you?"

"No, not really."

"So you fake it, then?"

"Yes, mostly."

"Do you believe in the supernatural?"

"Supernatural what?"

"Life after death?"

"What form do you imagine that might take?"

"Well, I don't know, perhaps the form of spirits; that one's soul, at the time of death, might move on to some other space."

"To heaven? Do *you* believe in heaven? I've always had trouble with that. No, I'm not there, personally."

"Okay, maybe not to heaven. But do you think we might exist in some ethereal sense, later?"

"Probably not. I think that when we die, individually our light goes out, like a snuffed candle. And that's it; we come and we go. I've never met a spirit, and I don't believe they exist. Do *you* know any?" he teased, trying on a sideways glance and smile.

Disciplining her body to correctly address the target, Angeline raised her bow and drew it to full length. "Just thought I'd ask," she replied, squeezing the mechanical trigger very gently as he had instructed. No point pursuing this any further, she decided.

* * * * * * * * *

Beyond that day they shot together whenever an opportunity presented itself, becoming more at ease with each other as time went along. It became quite competitive. Jeremy had an edge over her, perhaps because he had spent more time doing it and was taller and stronger. He was also using a superior bow: his father's. It had a better optical sight, which gathered more light and had a longer draw length. It was like shooting a rifle that had a longer barrel: the greater distance between front and rear sights meant the shooter was bound to have a greater likelihood of accuracy. Still, at fifteen yards, she consistently placed her arrows in the centre ring of all presented targets.

"Jeremy, I want to keep the bow," she had ventured, now feeling she was ready and that she no longer needed him. But, their somewhat soporific teacher-student time together having lulled her, she had dropped her guard regarding his suppressed hopes and was about to regret it.

Jeremy's mind, working like the arms of an octopus wrapping in an ever-tightening grip around an unwary prey, relaxed for a moment to savour what he thought was about to be a good catch. "Really," he smiled.

"Yes."

"Why?"

"I would just like to have it. How much do you want for it?"

"Why do you presume it's for sale?"

"Because you've outgrown it. At your height it's like a toy to you."

"Still, the bow has a draw weight almost heavy enough to qualify it as a lawful hunting weapon. You could shoot deer with it if you wanted, although not *quite* legally."

"I don't want to," she responded.

"Turkeys, then?"

"Not that either."

"Then what?"

"It's not so much that I want to shoot *anything*. I'd just like to have it."

"You *have* it this way, and so far it hasn't cost you anything."

"It has cost me ten dollars an hour, and that's been hurtful, given that my allowance barely covers it."

"Well, you do have options—you always have had," he said, letting a lascivious smile deliberately show.

"Jesus, Jeremy. I'm twelve; you're sixteen. Do you know what the law would do with you if this conversation could be overheard by anyone in authority?"

Jeremy's smile and the lips that had shaped it drooped and turned pale. "Whatever happened to this girl's age of innocence?" he muttered, head down, mouthing the words too softly for her to hear, "Can't a guy try without getting all chewed up?" Feigning gullibility, in a scrambling attempt to extricate himself from an awkward situation, he took a deep breath, looked up, then tried, "No, what?"

"Take a shot at Googling this: 'Enticing a minor to engage in underage sex'. The criminal code is online now and has some really interesting stuff in it. You might want to noodle around in some of the related offenses. Perhaps you want to consider trading off your university years for a stretch in prison."

Jeremy felt like he had taken a *tae kwon do* kick to the chest. He paused for quite some time while he considered a plausible exit strategy. This girl was a hell of a lot smarter than he had ever taken her for, he realized, albeit too late.

"So, is the bow mine?" Angeline asked.

"Yes, it's yours."

"Still friends?"

"Yes, still friends," he said, accepting a limp handshake while trying to hide his embarrassment. "The quiver and arrows, too. And the trigger. Where do you propose to keep them? "

"I can't keep all that at home; my parents wouldn't have it. Can we hide it here, somewhere?"

"How about in Grandpa's bee shed? We could slide it behind a stack of old storm windows there that share space with his beekeeping equipment. That way you can still use it whenever you come here, whether or not I can join you."

And like the conspirators that they had thus become, now sharing a secret and a new respect for the limits to which each of them could be pressed, Jeremy slid Angeline's archery gear behind the stack of windows to share the cobwebs and the mouse nest that he there disturbed.

Grandpa never locked the bee shed. In fact, the door didn't even have a latch.

Scene 4
Stanley Returns the Call to Cpl. Elujah...

July 29, 2010, 9:37 a.m.

Chelsea had scheduled an early morning tee time with a couple of her golfing buddies. Stan knew she would be out on the course for at least two more hours, and maybe longer if she extended her outing to include a couple of SallyAnne walk-throughs. Frugality was her constant companion, wherever she went.

He cleaned off the breakfast dishes, arranged them in the dishwasher, poured himself another coffee, creamed it, and stirred while looking through his kitchen window. The window had become a habit, morosely now, having become one of his haunted thinking places.

He squinted, eyes almost shut, as he often did when focusing on options, even if he only had a couple of them. Where to find traces of Marion's DNA? Better, he thought, to first try looking in the bedroom where she usually stayed when visiting them. Later, if necessary, he could start digging for her dental records. He recalled that Mae had asked Chelsea if it would be okay for her to keep a few items of clothing in their visitors' bedroom's walk-in closet. Chelsea had agreed of course. Later, after Mae's last visit, Stanley had noted, sniffing around as he sometimes did, a blue satin bag containing some of her hair rollers. It was in the vanity cabinet of their guest room's en-suite bathroom. Beside the bag was a small wicker basket that contained bobby pins and other grooming bits and whatnot.

He agreed that he would give them a look. Infrequently confident of outcomes, he made his way to the lower walkout level and into the gloom of the larger of their two guest bedrooms. Whenever Marion stayed with them it was hers. The room was tidy, as usual; Chelsea had always kept it that way.

He gave himself a moment to adjust to the room's paucity of sunlight—the vertical blinds were drawn closed as usual when the room wasn't in use—then he flicked on the closet light. Against this small room's east wall and beneath a high shelf burdened with half-forgotten things that should have been foisted off to folks at the SallyAnne hung some of their off-season clothing. He quickly passed over what he could see was his own stuff and glanced along the row, looking for any item that might not belong to Chelsea. He noticed a jacket—Marion's, for sure—but he knew that Chelsea had worn it several times. He would come back to it if needed. Further along, he saw a mauve dress that he knew wasn't Chelsea's. Yes, he thought, that might do, if he got lucky. Carefully he parted the items on either side of the dress, squinting to get a closer look at its neckline. But the light from the ceiling fixture, a compact-fluorescent bulb, couldn't dispel enough shadow. Having retreated to find a flashlight, he swept its oval patch of yellow—still not as bright as he would have liked—over the shoulders and sleeves of the dress, looking for any hair. He worked his way down to the hem. Nothing. He lifted the dress off the rod by its hangar and slowly, carefully turned it around. Still nothing. He looked farther along the row. Drawing a blank, he returned to the mauve dress. Yes, he thought, he would better have another look at it, in a few minutes.

He stepped away, trying to force his mind to think like a forensic specialist's. He was on shaky ground here; he had only ever had three years of uniformed police experience, and that was a long time ago. Although he had attended and protected lots of scenes where there were dead people, he had never been obligated to attend an autopsy nor had he ever volunteered. Answering forensics' scene-related questions about folks of all ages then on slabs in mortuaries? No problem, but admittedly it didn't take a forensics expert to *protect* a scene. Okay, he told himself, just use common sense, move slowly and be patient. Don't blow this.

Looking along stacks of linen that lay on the shelves on an adjacent wall, he hoped to find a black sheet or at least one that was somewhere close to a moonless prairie midnight. Picking the best near miss, still an unhappy compromise, he removed it from the closet and shook it out over a quilt that Chelsea had crafted for Marion's bed. He knew a hair falling directly onto that quilt would be damned difficult to find and impossible to identify positively as having come from Mae.

He turned on all the room's lights and went back into the closet for the mauve dress. Inverting it carefully as it lay on the dark blue sheet, he slowly moved his way over it, hesitantly—again with the flashlight—inch by inch. Yes! There, he saw, elated, just under the neckline, a *hair*, and close by, another.

Leaving his search for a couple of minutes, he went upstairs to Chelsea's side of their bathroom to look for a pair of tweezers. Finding a glass containing an assortment of small feminine-looking instruments—most of which needed updating, he thought—he selected what he had come for. Wanting an envelope, he went to find one in their office's stationary cabinet, that room being a tight, multiuse space that included a closeted washing machine and a laundry sink. Envelope in hand, he went back downstairs to the dress.

Focusing on the flashlight's sweeping circle, he came upon and tweezered away both hairs from the dress and, unable to suppress a small self-congratulatory smile, inserted them into the envelope's yawed opening. Setting his little find aside, he went into the adjacent bathroom to relocate Mae's hair rollers and bobby pins.

The blue satin bag was a soft canoe-shaped contrivance, zipped along its top. Beside it rested her little wicker basket, with lid, which contained her bobby pins and a collection of pink and white plastic hairpins. Selecting one of its plastic pins, he stirred around the basket's tangled contents. Almost immediately he was rewarded with the presence of *another* hair.

He thought he should stop. He dropped the pink pin back into the basket and eased the lid on.

Next, he unzipped the hair-roller bag. It was filled to capacity with things unfamiliar to him—feminine things—things he had never before paid much attention to. He had always regarded women's dressing-room paraphernalia as bizarre nonessentials, to be avoided. The rollers were made up of coil springs covered with light green plastic mesh, tucked in at each end and held in place by what looked like bristles of an oversized pipe cleaner. Many of the rollers had been speared through with plastic hairpins identical to ones in the wicker basket. He gently probed the contents to see what else might be in the bag. At its centre was a crumpled shower cap.

Throughout his search he realized he was professionally out of touch with what he was attempting to do. Out of a concern for losing something potentially of forensics value, he stopped and zipped the bag closed. He believed with reasonable certainty that no one but Marion would ever have used the bag's contents. He should set it aside for a police examination. His best next move would be to consult with Corporal Elujah.

The bag and wicker basket went back into the drawer where they belonged. The dress, still inverted, awkwardly accepted its wire hanger and was carried at arm's length into the closet. He evenly folded the indigo sheet and reinserted it into the stack from which it had been taken.

July 29, 2010, 3:26 p.m.

Still, no Chelsea. Good, he thought.

His appointment with Mae's dentist an hour earlier had been successful. Dr. Beckwith had understood and had agreed to cooperate right from the moment Stan had made his over-the-phone request, using his then-best police-like overtures. On arrival, he had been handed an unmarked envelope containing Mae's dental history, including copies of her charts and X-rays.

Back in his office, he leafed through the contents. Unable to interpret intelligently much of what he was shuffling though, he carefully reinserted everything, deciding to leave it to the experts.

Then he looked for and found the phone number for Jason Elujah.

Someone at the other end picked up on the third ring. No voice. There was a background riffle of paper being shuffled and a closer, hotter sound, like pursed lips recoiling from the edge of a cup of off-the-burner coffee. Probably Jason's.

"Corporal Elujah?" he asked, uncertainly.

"Yes?" The office noises, whatever they were, went away.

"Jason, it's Stan Watson. I wasn't sure if it was you."

"Oh, Stan…yes. Good to hear from you. Sorry, took me a moment, my mind was somewhere else; we've been busy. What's up?"

"I'm calling about Marion Barber."

There was a poignant silence, then a slurping sound at the other end.

"The Jane Doe you found on the beach?" he prodded, gently. "I think I have something."

"Okay. Good. What might that be?"

"Dental records."

"Great," the corporal responded. "Anything else?"

"Well, I went through all my wife's *retrievals*—personal stuff, cosmetic kind of things, collected from her mom's home, at Mae's request, during her stay here. I found some hairs tangled in a brush. Judging by the colour and length, the hairs must've been Mae's."

"Really? That's encouraging. What's the probability, if you were to make an educated guess?"

"It's gotta be hers, beyond just a guess."

There was the sound again of coffee being drawn over the rim of a cup.

"Hmm," Jason offered, "That does give us options. Very helpful, actually. I had best check with Forensics. Don't mess with anything you've found, okay? Later there could be claims of evidence contamination or continuity-of-possession issues. If so, neither of us would like that. Too embarrassing. Lawyers, you know? I should be able to get one of the Ottawa City guys to drop by. Maybe they'll send along a forensics backup. In the meantime, don't touch any of her stuff. It can keep. Okay?"

There was another hanging moment, then "Have you told your wife yet?" he asked, seemingly as an afterthought.

"No, but I will, soon."

"All right. I'll call back when I have something more for you. If she answers the phone, I'll ask for you, without saying who I am."

"Thanks, Jason. I'm not really looking forward to my chat with her."

"Be gentle; don't get too graphic."
"I'll put it softly. No details."

Scene 5
Chelsea's Stories...

"At times, I am the bearer of 'bad news',
much as I'd prefer not to be. I'd rather be honest."
~Author unknown

July 30, 2010, 9:18 a.m.
He tried to break it to her delicately. He had had to do this sort of thing during the earlier part of his first career, whenever next of kin might have had to be advised of a loved one's sudden death. It'd never been easy.

At home, whenever they'd discussed something of importance, they had almost always sat at the kitchen table. He asked her to join him there, and she sensed from his hesitant manner that it must be something exigent.

He managed to get through it, but with difficulty bordering on awkwardness, his voice rolling deeply in his throat.

At first she couldn't believe it, although she knew he wouldn't toy with her feelings about something this serious. Her mom had been murdered? She fell silent, and when he finished, he let the quiet of the kitchen hang between them. Then, pushing away from the table, she asked him to leave her. "I need to be alone for a while," she said. He got up, hugged her for a moment, then put on a jacket and drove almost vacuously into the village. He parked the car in the Village Mews, locked it, and looked around uncertainly for somewhere to go. This would be a lonely walk.

She had watched his back disappear into the unlit gloom of their garage and saw him close the door quietly behind him.

She didn't really know where to turn next, where to go in this house, or even if she should stay in the house. Trancelike, she found herself feeling her way down the stairway to the home's lower level to turn into the shadows of the hallway leading to her sewing room.

She thought about him—Stanley, her husband, quiet man that he was—before she even began to try to come to grips with what had happened to her mom.

He loved her, she knew, gazing at the portrait he had had done of her a few years earlier. She hadn't looked at it in a long time; usually she walked past it without seeing or even thinking about it, hanging there amongst so many other family faces smiling out toward the corridor's opposite wall, their countenances frozen in time.

She found herself wondering—how often had she wondered that?—what life was about. Was she grieving, she wondered, and if so for whom? Her mother? Or herself?

She knew that her world had been dumped upside down one more time. She cast her eyes down to the frame beneath her portrait to the cursive script that he had added. She read it again, absorbing the reflections he'd put there:

> *How fragile a dream, a thought, a wish; moving, all,*
> *in errant flight toward…somewhere: sometimes beautiful*
> *in sunlight, sometimes uncertain in the mist, sometimes lost*
> *for just a moment, climbing some ethereal, wispy net that stays*
> *a celestial mast; floating upward, again upward on gossamer wings,*
> *ever strong, ever delicate, ever elusive.*
> *Blue wings; unfolding then, apparent now, firming, drying…*
> *from the crayon markings of a child's poem to a beautiful family legend.*
> *Forever blue. The lady in blue. The lady in the portrait.*

Nice of him to have done that, she thought. Insightful. Analytical, she supposed, in a way. But if he believed *she* was hard to figure out, he too had been a lifelong enigma—often up, more often down. At the top of his game he had frequently become giddy, his behaviour almost manic. But when he bottomed out, she had at times been unable to reach far enough into the hole he had dug for himself to assist him. It was scary. He had become inconsolable, distant, as if looking in upon himself from somewhere extrasolar, not rejecting her but not wanting her help either.

Finally she had nudged him into seeking professional help. A couple of failed physician's prescriptions later, then a successful one—in conjunction with time on a psychologist's couch—seemed to have evened him out. Things had gotten better. What for so long should have been obvious to both of them was that he had nurtured deeply embedded guilt related to his first career; he had for decades suppressed a sense of having wronged people when he thought he was helping—at least helping his country. He had been a *patriot* or so he had thought, without having paused long enough to wonder about patriotism's often negative impact on a larger humanity. But, with his bleak fascination for rope now hopefully behind him, he had been fine; he still was, provided he didn't forget to take his magic little white pill every morning.

It had been quite a life—bumpy—like one of NASA's ageing fleet re-entering the atmosphere with bits of its ceramic heat shield flaking off, ever in danger of disintegrating in flames. But their relationship had held together. No one could say it had been boring.

She stood there in the pall of the hallway, with overhead track lights deliberately left off, trying to put the whole experience into some kind of balance. As their life together had progressed through their latter years, its hand-in-hand walk through the seasons had seen love mingled with friendship in a way that left the one sentiment entwined around the other. Mostly, they had shared each other's thoughts, often finished each other's sentences. They laughed together, often. And they had their quiet times, separately, although usually within this same house; there was room here for that. And each had felt a palpable void in the absence of the other whenever they'd travelled separately.

He had wanted to hang her portrait in a more prominent place, but her modesty—his term not hers—had kept him from doing so. Instead, the portrait found its place at the centre of the family's rogues' gallery, sharing wall space with generations of dead ancestors, interspersed with medals and awards. Her kids were there, too. She was proud of them both, at opposite ends of a pendulum swing though they were.

She stepped back, allowing her weight to be absorbed by the wall she knew was behind her, to be comforted by one of the quilts she had hung. She looked again at the face in the portrait, and yes, it was hers, only younger.

But who had she *really* been, she wondered, and what had she done with her life that would be remembered? Anything? Or did that matter? Did *anything* matter? She thought not. Gone, she would be, then soon forgotten.

For a while, she totally surrendered herself to this introspection, stepping through rooms of the well-tended museum of her mind, classically decorated as she had always kept them, with memories of times that once were, but now again set adrift.

She was a quilter now; it was her passion. She had always been a sewer; she had made all manner of clothing for the children, her husband, and herself. She had crafted and sold stuffed toys when they were in fashion, but the quilting thing had pretty well taken over those hours of her life that weren't preempted by caring for the well-being of her extended family. She had a sense of colour that showed in everything she put her hand to. She loved playing bridge, another thing she felt she was moderately good at. She also enjoyed golf, read insatiably, and daily prepared gourmet meals. Or so he constantly told her. Her house, except for her sewing room, was in a constant state of being cleaned or renovated.

That was the *now*. The *before* was something she breezed through quickly, not wanting to dwell on it. Old stuff, she thought, ancient history. What was the point? Her husband had told her, often and lovingly, that she was too inclined to understate her own achievements. He had dragged out their earliest photo albums, pointed out the now-yellowing press clippings and pictures to remind her that when she was seventeen she had won a regional beauty pageant—crowned queen of Gatineau's first winter carnival at a dinner hosting some two hundred people. With his finger running along under the text, he had read, "and instantly became the charm of thousands during week-long carnival events." He always insisted on pressing on, wanting her again to see, as he did, pictures clipped from all the city's newspapers. She dismissed that as a momentary blip, although smiled at the thought that those clippings and other pictures like them seemed to have imprinted themselves indelibly in his mind. He kept bringing them up, wouldn't leave it alone. Well, he could be proud of them if he wanted; she didn't need to be, nor was she.

Her mind drifted back to the big house on the hill overlooking the little hamlet of Ironsides. She had been a farm girl. That was a happy time, although a lonely one. Her parents had coalesced their seed into one later sibling, a brother, separated from her by eight years—almost a second family. Amusements and playthings were inventions she had been left pretty much to discover on her own.

She had raised a pair of ducks—Donald and Daisy, having lifted their names from her fascination with Disney's little friends—which followed her everywhere in and around the farm's outbuildings. She also surveilled the barn's hayloft, ladder at the ready, seeking out niches between the bales where mother cats might have hidden their kittens. Whenever successful, hissing and scratches notwithstanding, she adopted the newborns, named them, and spirited some of them into her second-floor bedroom. Her mom didn't like cats, couldn't tolerate their presence in the house, so Chelsea'd had to be secretive about her surrogate families. She'd had difficulty, though, disciplining them to remain in her doll carriage, particularly when she'd dressed them, under duress, in her dolls' clothes. Once, her mom had found a malingering cat in her bedroom and had dropped it from a window. It'd had a hard landing, but managed to walk away.

Her mom actually hadn't liked the farm, nor did she relish living in a house divided between her and her husband's parents. A door in their living-room wall divided the two households, and Chelsea had enjoyed squeaking through it to visit her grandma. Over the years Grandma had patiently taught her to knit, to sew, and to cook. Best of all, she had taken the time to tell her and read her wonderful stories.

She had always liked horses. At age four, a young colt had grasped her by the chest and thrown her a distance, but she had remained undaunted. By age fifteen her dad had bought her an at-auction RCMP saddle and then a horse of her own—Rogue, she had called it. Together they had ranged the hills and valleys of the farm, enjoying an openness and freedom that that solitude had offered them. The farm was beautiful then: unspoiled grazing land, dotted with old-growth trees and occasional patches of brush. Her father's cattle ranged there each day until milking time. In the summers she would help him take the hay off, and in the winters she had waited expectantly to participate in the Ottawa skiers' seasonal takeover of the farm's highest hills, a place that offered city folks the respite of downhill skiing. One hill, the highest of them, had been fitted with a single rope tow, and she had spent her available time there being tugged up the hill and skiing down. She had loved it. Her dad, Cameron, always with an entrepreneurial eye during years when a dollar was hard to come by, had set up a small hot-dog and hamburger concession at the base of the hill. The concession shack was fitted with a sink and woodstove, and her dad and mom each weekend had pulled, from the farmhouse to the hill, the makings of all offerings they would sell, piled onto an open toboggan and balanced precariously as they moved along a rough, snow-covered cow path.

By the time she had reached her teens she could drive a tractor and handle a baler as well as any farmer she knew. She also believed, then and still, that she could do anything a man could. Why not, she had asked herself then and asked herself now. Her father's imposed hard lessons had instilled in her a fierce sense of independence and a determination early in life not to be outdone by him or by any of his cronies.

She had carried a fire within her that energized her every waking movement, unencumbered by remorse at having occasionally exhaled those same flames in a hiss intended to char narcissistic males who had dared attempt to belittle or subjugate her. One of her father's cohorts had found himself needing to extricate his dishevelled remains from a kitchen corner, humiliated, after having tried to touch her. *She* had put him there, not her dad; she hadn't required anyone's help.

In more gentle moments, her dad's buddies had enjoyed collecting themselves around the farm's kitchen table with him to tease and torment her, often over a poker game. She defended both her seat at the table and her pride, squirreling away her winnings to buy something for herself that the family at that time couldn't afford to give her.

She had been, without doubt, the apple of her father's eye, as strong willed as he was, although without the stubbornness that would eventually carry him, as it had his father before him, back to the bush and into a terminal solitude spent in unremunerative toil, alone with his dog.

She had been outstanding at basketball, travelling as captain of her Hull High School team by bus from one community to another, winning tournaments, and walking off once with the MacLeod Trophy during Québec provincial championships at Lennoxville, there to become the 1957-58 Western Québec League senior girls' champions.

Then she met Stanley, and gradually, over the months that followed, her life began to transition away from everything that had become so familiar to her—her home, her friends, and all things that had been so much a part of her experience until then.

Eventually, the farm's hills were developed into a golf course. The rest of the farm was sacrificed to developers and subsequently became tightly packed residential condominiums.

She seldom went back.

It was all so long ago, she thought. Without consciously realizing she was doing it, she turned and moved pensively along the hallway, one foot in line behind the other, legs sweeping in slow arcs barely above the carpet, fingertips brushing the walls as if sensing her way. She found herself standing in what had by now been designated "Mom's room". It was comfortable, as always. But it was vacant now, hauntingly vacant. Mom was dead; she had been murdered.

Kicking off her shoes, she laid her head on the bed's middle pillow. She stretched out her arms, elegantly, almost religiously, in the form of a cross. And there, in the twilight of the room's tightly drawn shades, she let her mother's memory flood back over her like the waves she had imagined had carried her body ashore in some godforsaken cove at the east end of the world.

Scene 6
Marion's Story...

> *"But she wasn't around, and that's the thing when your parents die, you feel like instead of going in to every fight with backup, you are going into every fight alone."*
> ~Mitch Albom, For One More Day

July 30, 2010, 10:46 a.m.

Chelsea knew, lying there, prostrate-—her mind awash and floating, partially detached like an ethereal wreath around her pillow—that her mom hadn't been an entirely bad person. She didn't deserve to die at the hand of some yet-unknown killer. Yes, she had driven her dad into relative isolation during his advancing years, in part perhaps because she had never been able to handle disorder. And her dad *was* inclined to be disorderly, no doubt about that.

She thought back to how, earlier, her dad and mom had a pretty good life together, all things considered. They had their differences, of course—different values: Mom didn't like cows or the barn and was short on tolerance whenever encountering dad stepping into the farmhouse kitchen without first having shucked off his overalls and shitty boots, but still they had fun when fun was to be had. They had hosted parties in that same kitchen, playing poker, drinking whatever could be afforded, swatting flies occasionally for a dollar a hit, and laughing easily with neighbours and friends. The farm kitchen had been a drop-in place, a place where everybody for miles around could feel comfortable, and did. Dad had made sure of that, passing around chunks of block cheddar at knifepoint to be enjoyed with pleasant conversation, crackers, an olive, or whatever might have been available. Usually a glass of gin or whiskey was to be had. Mom hadn't liked the cheese-at-knifepoint thing, but managed to get over it.

Her dad's incorrigibly gregarious nature, often unwillingly, mollified her mom's diffident formality. Within those discord moratoriums they had found a balance they could find their way along, like tightrope walkers, knowing that a wrong step could be more than painful. When alone, though, her mom was a tidy, fussy person, for whom appearances were of the highest priority—an obsession actually—that may have led to her underlying discontent. Staying current with the fickle drift of fashions, both in dress and home decor, had intensified with the passing years. Her house had been kept spotless, with the help of a cleaning woman they could barely afford.

The house had been beautiful and huge for its time—architecturally pleasing, all red brick, topped with a metal roof. Her great grandmother had built it on a hillcrest along the road that still carries their family name. Later, the house had been divided to accommodate the two Barber families. After the death of the grandparents, her mom and dad had rented out the then-vacant half. And so their lives had progressed, years ticking away inexorably.

Chelsea considered that Mom had gone through her journey too short on self-esteem. She had been born poor into a family of seven siblings in a house in Vankleek Hill and had left when she was fifteen to take a job—having lied about her age—with Bell Canada as a switchboard operator. Later, she had moved up to a similar position on Parliament Hill.

She had met Cameron on a blind date at the age of seventeen and married him when she was twenty-one. Three years later daughter Chelsea came along. Eight years following, an unexpected brother, William, arrived. The children had grown up almost separately, Chelsea having left home when she was eighteen.

Marion's latter years had seemed to pass with a certain dreary sameness. Chelsea realized that with Mom there had always been that underlying unease. For as long as she could remember, Mom had lived in a state of agitation that seemed always to come down to the same few questions: What would the neighbours, or friends, or visitors, or the policeman on the block, or any other person in society think? It had been a negative influence throughout her own youth: the notion that things she had done or said or worn had never been quite right or quite good enough. Mother had imprinted a subliminal anxiety onto daughter, which stayed with her until she had moved away, married, and accompanied her husband to Europe. There, she had been expected to entertain and had gradually overcome her self-doubt and shyness.

Mom and Dad had sold the farm in 1984 and moved to a smaller place in the city, after which Dad had spent most of his time on a second family-owned acreage at the south end of Lake Pemichangan. At that property, he had kept a few cows, enjoyed the friendship of border collies, and found contentment in his relative isolation. But the sand was running through his hourglass, and he had died in 1994. Mom hadn't been very attentive or sensitive to any of that; in fact, she had been downright cold. Marion grew averse to her husband's presence and had arranged through her doctor to keep him away from their home, essentially leaving him confined to a seniors' residence. After that he wasn't a welcome visitor. That had been hard to forgive. She knew, lying there on her mother's away-from-home bed, reliving it, weeping quietly, that she hadn't yet forgiven her. Nor could she.

From that point forward she had noticed her mom's increasing dependence on her for day-to-day guidance, on everything. Eventually, she wanted out of her home and into—of all things—a seniors' residence, although Marion had insisted on something more upscale than her dad had endured.

Chelsea needed to shuffle Mom through a sequence of Ottawa's upper-end facilities until she found one that pleased her. Shortly after, she become ill—liver cancer—and languished in the Grace Hospital until a place could be found for her in a hospice. She liked the hospice, taking possession of her room and expecting—later demanding—to stay until her end of days.

But, Chelsea hypothesized, surfacing from her reverie, that impending death wasn't the outcome, was it? Somehow the woman had rallied. Management at the Lilies of the Field hospice—the institution's viability depending for the most part on philanthropic contributions by the city's one-percenters—had asked her to find another placement. Then, inexplicably, all wheels for the move in motion, she had vanished.

Chelsea of course had known something was seriously out of sync. She had thought at first that mom was delusional, proposing the impossible. Oddly, with these imaginings, Marion's spirits had lifted.

She had said that she was tired of being a bother to the family and was strong enough to take charge of her own life. Part of that would entail a move. Not just a placement to yet another seniors' home, but a move to another country, perhaps somewhere in Europe. She hadn't been sure at first which country. She had claimed to have been collecting information and brochures, and was considering lake-side villages on Austria's Lake Attersee where, she claimed, people like Gustav Mahler, Sigmund Freud, and Gustav Klimt had spent their summers. She had narrowed it down to any one of the apparently pretty communities of Unterach, Sankt Georgen, or Weyregg.

Chelsea had tried to reason that her mom didn't speak German. Didn't matter, Mom said; all the *important* folks there spoke English. Right, Chelsea thought, good luck with that! She hadn't noticed any of the alluded-to brochures. But it seemed a harmless fantasy; why not go along with it? Mom had seemed quite excited about it all. Chelsea believed it was a phase; it would pass. After all, she was terminally ill. She hadn't a hope of managing by herself in *any* European-resettlement arrangement.

But her mom had persisted, and alone—having rejected all help—had settled her affairs in Ottawa and departed for Europe, ostensibly. In her farewell note she had forewarned that she wouldn't be in touch for many months, perhaps as long as a couple of years. She wanted to do this on our own and would be fine. She had mailed identical envelopes to William and to her, each containing a cheque for two hundred thousand dollars. She had added, in her shaking handwriting, that she had more, but she would need it to see her through her remaining years. And there were charities she intended to favour at the end of it all.

That was it. Gone! Chelsea couldn't get her mind around it. Yes, Mom's behaviour had devolved into a pattern of unpredictable decisions and odd requests. Okay, she had acquiesced, if the woman couldn't be talked out of it, then she would just have to work her way through it this time. She admitted to herself now that she'd by then had enough. Mom could do whatever she wanted. Go ahead, lady; let's see how you make out. And she had been glad to have it all behind her.

But, as the weeks stretched to months, she had begun to feel guilt bubbling to the surface, slowly, unobtrusively, like an alligator rising off the mudbank of its swamp, wanting not to disturb prey whose incaution it had noted. Why had she allowed herself to let her mom go? Her mom had only ever been to Europe once before, and then she had her now-dead husband to lead the way.

She had talked it through with Stan, tentatively at first. He, too, thought something was a bit off, although he had never been extraordinarily concerned about his in-laws or they about him. It wasn't that he didn't care; he just hadn't been sufficiently engaged to think about Mae's situation, about it possibly being of interest to the police.

They had started to collect data from travel agencies and the Web about seniors' establishments in the places she had mentioned and phoned all on a list they prepared. Nothing. Doing so entailed re-engaging mollusk-encrusted inefficacy in spoken German, but they had managed. Then they had checked the probable airlines and requested a search of flight manifests for the period she had likely have departed. Again, nothing. She was just *gone*. So they had filed a missing-persons report.

And now she was dead, apparently. So all along it had been some kind of scam. Some asshole must have convinced her to hand over her considerable wealth to one or another *worthy cause* and then killed her for it. Well, she thought, her mom had always had an element of the fear of the Lord in her; was religious to the extent that she believed in heaven and hell, and she could easily have fallen for the predations of a bible-thumping son of a bitch offering heaven on earth, or whatever.

Her earlier weeks of anxious inaction had now turned to anger, and when she got angry, her inclination was to get revenge. She linked some of her antipathy to Stanley, who, even with her frequently voiced concerns about Mom, had drifted along in his self-perpetuating introspective dream state. Okay, she thought, if the police can't find this prick, then she would hunt him down herself, and God help him when she caught up with him. His balls would hang from her fireplace, assuming she could find a taxidermist to mount them.

She rolled off her mother's bed and found her way into the lower-level bar fridge to find a cold bottle of Riesling. She drew out the cork, enjoying the pop it made. Picking the largest glass from the bar's cabinet, she filled it just shy of the brim and took a lengthy sip. Her hand was shaking. She moved along the room's riverside windows and drew the blinds tightly, breaking off a limb of her mom's Christmas cactus in the process. She came back around her Heintzman baby grand and sat to play Scott Joplin's "Solace," the keys sinking into their cushions with greater determination than the composer had intended. Finishing on a softer note, she picked up her glass, turned on her stool, and stared, unfocused, into the gloom she had created for herself. She felt the gathering rage for her mother's killer give way to tears.

Scene 7
Chelsea Visits the Beach...

"Carve your name on hearts, not tombstones.
A legacy is etched into the minds of others and the stories they share about
you."
~Shannon L. Alder

July 31, 2010, 9:02 a.m.
At breakfast she told Stanley she would be going to Sherbrooke as soon as she could make flight arrangements. No, she didn't want him to go with her. She needed to be alone with her thoughts for as long as it might take to get through this—maybe a couple of weeks. She would find a place to stay when she got there.

August 2, 2010, 1:14 p.m.
Her Porter flight touched down in Moncton, New Brunswick. She rented a car and made the three-hour drive to Sherbrooke. Roads were narrow and the asphalt patchy. The asphalt seemed a tiresome stretch of black ribbon twisting through the Spruce-Moose Forest and its looming evergreens, tracts of white spruce and balsam fir, bark covered

with pale lichens, the wood useful for lumber and pulp, soil young and nutrient-poor due to its relative youth and recent glaciations. Small, comfy-looking homes and outbuildings stood, arrayed like hens with broods of chicks. Yellow and black signs told her to watch for deer; she paid them little heed. She knew it was more her petulant mood than the road that was causing her to want to just get through it. From the moment she had boarded the plane in Ottawa, her mind had been awash with thoughts of her mom and who had killed her.

In Sherbrooke, she slowed the car to match the pace of the village traffic, turning at intersections and backtracking to get the lay of the place. She stopped for a bite to eat at a main-street restaurant and inquired there about an inn or motel.

The room that the clerk at the Sherbrooke Village Inn gave her turned out to be more than adequate. Yes, she thought, she would make this her base until she could work through her list. In a fog of preoccupation she unpacked her travel bag and set out her toiletries. Finding her notebook, she paged through to where she had jotted down Corporal Elujah's number. After finding it, she called, not initially sure what to expect.

"RCMP Sherbrooke," the female voice said. Well, Chelsea thought, things had changed, hadn't they?

"Hello," she tried, "Might Corporal Elujah be there, please?"

"May I ask who's calling?" the voice asked, more courteously than anticipated.

"Yes, my name is Chelsea Watson. I believe that Corporal Elujah is investigating my mother's death. Her name was Marion Barber.

"Oh, yes, Mrs. Watson. I'll get the corporal for you."

Chelsea contemplated the pencilled to-do items in her notebook as she waited, flicking pages back and forth, annoyed in her haste by the snagging tip of the pad's spiral-wire binding catching at a corner of each leaf. Another dollar-store bargain, she recalled, miffed now at not having picked a better one. Damn, she thought, it was taking the corporal a bit long, wasn't it?

The Fontana Resurrection

"Hello? Mrs. Watson? This is Jason Elujah." There was a short pause; Chelsea let it hang there. "May I say, first off, that I'm sorry for your loss."

It sounded to her like he actually meant it. She wondered why would he care. He surely must be inured to work like this, making first contact with families of victims.

"So am I, rather. How is your investigation going?" She had always tended to get straight to the point, especially on the phone. People had told her that. She tried now to keep her voice from sounding brittle.

"Well, it has kept us busy, certainly."

She sensed he was treading lightly. Not wanting to upset him, although unable to help herself, she asked, "Any progress?"

"We're doing what we can. It has been a difficult case. Even identifying your mom became a complex process. We weren't left with much to go on."

"Yes, my husband told me something of that, although he wouldn't go into detail."

"It's just as well, Mrs. Watson." Again, his pause. "I'm sorry you've lost her."

He meant it, she was sure now. Forcing herself to relax a bit, she managed an obligatory "Thank you." But, wanting to get on with whatever was to come next, she positioned her first expectation as a gentle request. "My husband said she had been found on a beach. Could you possibly take me there?"

"Yes, certainly; now if you'd like. Where can I find you?"

* * * * * * * * *

He picked her up in one of the detachment's cars. They took Old Hill Road to Highway 211 and turned south. At first she remained edgy. He sensed the depth of her anger toward whoever they were both looking for and allowed for that.

The conversation eased somewhat during their drive. She started to relax. Turning off the highway just past the Sonora Road Bridge onto the parking area at Port Hilford Beach, he noted, gratefully, that no other cars were there. He pulled into a spot that left the police car broadside to anyone passing on the road, hoping that would encourage others to stay away.

They walked together in silence, him leading by half a stride, mincing their way over a rivulet running into the cove from Indian Harbour Lake. She stopped for a moment on the stream's other side to take in the sweep of the bay, wondering at the magnitude of bundled seaweed that had washed up on the sand and admiring the birds that poked and prodded among the richness of the sea's leavings. They were all strange to her. It seemed such a lonely place. Quiet and peaceful like a graveyard. Her mother's graveyard.

From where she stood, looking east along a stand of what she took to be black spruce, she could see a couple of houses beyond a boulder-strewn shore, both on the far side of Port Hilford Road. One, with its outbuildings, may have been a fisherman's home. Distance made detail a bit hard to discern. The place was white with dishevelled and sun-curled shingles. It had been added to at some point. Its doors and trim were red; a second level offered a red deck atop a three-season front-room appendage. All seemed sun-bleached and sand-blown. The outbuildings worked their way toward a tall, sturdy fishing dock. No boat was there and she could see none in the harbour. The ruin of a long boat landing stood at the end of Port Hilford Road, the legacy of a fisherman's workplace and pier. These were the first images of what she believed her eyes were trying to have her mind record.

Jason waited for her quietly, respectfully and patiently. He had other police matters competing for his attention, but sensed this was his first priority.

She turned to him, shading her eyes against the sun. "Where was Mom found?" she asked.

Pointing past her, he singled out a huge boulder, appearing to anchor a transition from sea-washed sand to the beach's tumble of rocks. "It was down there. Would you care to see, exactly?"

"Yes, I think I would. Thanks." They started in silence along the shoreline, picking their way among and over the stones as they drew closer.

Wanting to soften the mood, he offered, "Your husband was a member of the Force, I believe."

"Yes," then added, "but that was a long time ago."

"Did you care for the life?" he tried, posing the question uncertainly.

"*He* did, I think. Well, not toward the end, perhaps. He became disillusioned. Until then he really stayed focused on his career. It became a lonely couple of decades for me. We moved a lot. I'd make a few friends in one place and then we'd be gone to another. I was glad, actually, when it was over. He was raised, you know, in a very small village in Manitoba and was forever grateful that the organization had accepted him. In those days it had been hard to get in; few were accepted. I often thought he had tried too hard along the way to prove his worth. I think he never got beyond that. Now he's something of a recluse, stuck on trying to save the world—from his computer. No one listens, of course."

They stopped. They were at the nearest edge of the boulder he'd pointed out. It hadn't looked that big to her from their earlier distance. The rock remarkably resembled a breadloaf.

"Your mom was here, just along this edge of the monument."

"Monument?"

"This boulder," he said, a bit shyly. "It's quite beautiful in its own right, don't you think? It's Precambrian granite, as you've no doubt noticed. It could be as old as four billion years, rounded along its edges and deposited here by one of Earth's ice ages." He paused and looked at her, hoping for some sign of softening. "During the investigation I've come to regard it, at least within myself, as your mom's headstone."

She was impressed by his empathy and moved. They stood together, regarding each other wordlessly for several moments. It became awkward; she was beginning to like him.

"Who found her?" she asked, almost in a whisper.

"A young girl who actually lives near here. She was playing on the beach with her dog, a big yellow lab. They were walking at the water's edge, and she was throwing a stick into the surf for him to fetch. The last time he came out, she said he ran away from her, wanting to play. Then he stopped and she came upon him nuzzling what she'd dismissed as a bundle of cloth washed in from the ocean—not an unusual thing—until she got closer to it." He paused, looking for her reaction. "She was terrified, as you might suppose."

He stood watching this woman stare into the sand where he had indicated, as if studying where her mom had lain. "Are you sure you want to go on with this?"

"Thank you, Corporal, perhaps not. Not for now. But I appreciate your having taken the time to show me this." She moved her eyes away from where she had understood her mom to have been, partially covered then in wet, salty sand, dead, alone, abandoned, deemed detritus to whoever had left her in the water.

Like an Atlantic roller, her anger rushed in again, unexpectedly, mood-changing. She met the corporal's gaze and, with a sharpened change of tone, tears blurring her vision, she blurted, "She wasn't a bad person, you know; she didn't deserve this. She was never an all-loving, all-embracing person, but this seems to me an unspeakable indignity!"

The corporal wanted to embrace her, comfort her, but the Force's policy discouraged that. The RCMP disapproved of any possibly misinterpreted contact, much in the same way elementary schoolteachers are forbidden from hugging their charges when little ones become distressed or feel unloved. Instead, he offered her his hand, placing the other gently on her shoulder, and, lowering his voice to a nearly inaudible undertone, offered, "I'm sorry, I'm truly sorry."

When he dropped her off at the inn's entrance, she was still quietly sobbing. He suggested that they keep in touch during the days that she expected to remain within his detachment's jurisdiction. He knew that she needed to do other things: reclaim the body, arrange for cremation here or transportation of the remains back to Ottawa, and whatever else. He offered to help in any way he could. She told him she appreciated that, and, thanking him again, pausing to offer a smile as she met his eyes, she elbowed the cruiser door closed, scrabbling in her purse for a room key.

August 5, 2010, 4:42 p.m.

She did what she had to do. It had been difficult, but she got through it. Mae's remains were released to Chelsea's care, and she arranged with the G.W. Griffin Funeral Home to manage the cremation. At her age she had been in a lot of similar farewell accommodations, saying goodbye to friends, friends of friends, and sometimes close relatives. These venues hadn't offered her much comfort, although she had usually surrendered herself to society's apparent need for a sombre departure. People gathered together at such places for a couple of hours, reconnecting with folks perhaps not seen in years.

She thought that this one was quite nice; it had an interesting history, as did so much of Nova Scotia's coastline. The shore and the sea effused endless stories—stories of courage, of ships tall and small, and of strong lads and their fathers who had never come home from the sea. And now, added to these stories, was her mother's story: poor Marion, who had arrived uninvited, unexpected.

She had learned it was at Country Harbour that she would find the G.W. Griffin Funeral Home's parent operation. Folks there had traced its history to the 1920s when Hector MacLellan was Country Harbour's local undertaker. He was often assisted by George Parker (Park) Griffin, born in Goldboro in 1903, married to Lillian MacArthur in 1923 and, eventually, a father of eight. Park was just fifteen years of age when he began working at S.R. Griffin & Sons General Merchants Store, and he would work there in varying capacities until his retirement in 1970. Store wages weren't large during the Depression of the 1930s, and a need for added income to support his family was the main reason he helped MacLellan in funeral service. When MacLellan died in 1936, Park continued to operate the funeral business for the widow Ethel MacLellan.

In 1942, he purchased the MacLellan business and together with his wife, Lillian, continued to render the same service to the area, which extended from New Harbour to Cross Roads Country Harbour. Lillian performed the bookkeeping duties and engraved the breastplates that, in those days, accompanied the casket. Park operated his funeral service from the Goldboro area, where some of his merchandise was delivered by boat. The first funeral coach used by Park was horse drawn. Later, a panel truck was purchased and then a station wagon. Following the death of Lillian in 1968, Park continued until 1975 when he retired and his son Wayne continued to operate the business. George Parker Griffin died December 25, 1994, at the age of ninety-one.

Wayne had then taken over the family business, assisted in the firm by his wife Arnita, who acted as bookkeeper and office manager.

It had been deemed a credit to the community of Country Harbour and surrounding area when, on August 3, 1991, Wayne opened a new funeral home there.

On December 17, 1991, he purchased the funeral home located at 34 Main Street, Sherbrooke, previously owned and operated as the Ecum Secum Funeral Home. How quaint, she mused—she had always imagined "Ecum Secum" as a children's play expression. Wayne had extensively renovated the place to become the G.W. Griffin Funeral Home, St. Mary's Chapel. God would have liked that, she thought. Nice touch.

Tracing the firm's ownership from its brochure, she realized the Griffin's St. Mary's Chapel had yet another historical touch. Wayne Griffin, its owner, had been a serving member of the RCMP for 17 years during her husband's era. She wondered if Stanley might have known him and would ask when she got home. Her notebook's wire coil caught again on the perforation of a clean page as she tried to make a note to remind herself. She angrily pressed her pencil in a sweep the shape of a Nike logo checkmark across it, ripped it away, crumpled it, and started afresh.

The staff members at the chapel were empathetic and respectfully reserved during her visit, listening and nodding throughout her story without interruption. They had heard about her mom's incident well before she had approached them. It had been the talk of the town: a death that shouldn't have occurred but did. Death was, nonetheless, their business; they had expected her.

She thanked them and tried to keep the discussion to the necessities: the business at hand and her mom's preparation for interment.

Selecting an urn, though, had brought back tears and anger, which they quietly accepted. They had seen tears before.

August 9, 2010, 11:07 a.m.
During the affair's denouement, when the unpretentious hammered copper container she had chosen was handed to her to take home, she had to take advantage of a gently proffered box of Kleenex. All part of the service, she concluded, noting that the dark suits in attendance seemed silently in agreement; all, she smiled to herself, part of the masquerade death initiates, every time.

She spent a couple of introspective days thinking about how best to wrap up everything, deciding, bit by bit, not to take her mom back to Ottawa. The anguish of a memorial service was more than she felt she would later be able to endure. Anachronistic rituals like that weren't something she would later want for herself; she had resolved to make her wishes quite clear to the family when she returned home.

She decided that she would say here, near Sherbrooke, her farewell, interring her mom at the base of the breadloaf rock. She wouldn't seek anyone's permission to proceed; she would simply wait until a time when no one else was on the beach and then offer her silent good-bye in the presence of shorebirds, seagulls, and that seemingly omnipresent cormorant, its wings in her imagination again wide spread, presiding at a distance as de facto priest while the sun dried seawater from its tertiary feathers.

She didn't rush through her waking hours, having found rather unexpectedly she quite liked Sherbrooke. She spent an afternoon exploring the town's Heritage Village. Entering it had been like walking down any small town's main street, although with this one she was able to cross an imaginary line into a different age to find a welcomed solitude and, with so few others having chosen the same day to attend, a silence akin to an earlier experience she had as the singular seeker contemplating relics enshrined in the transepts of a cathedral. Everything she found here was vintage, of an era earlier than her own.

The anger she had felt began to evanesce. She wanted now to linger, to find herself, to let her mind recalibrate, to think through her future with Stanley, and to try to imagine the rest of their lives together. What would they do next? What *should* they do? Mortality had become her unwelcomed night visitor, manifesting itself within dreams as an apparition staring out at her in a fragmented reflection of death's certainty from angular shards of a cracked mirror. How could they optimize the months and hopefully years left to them? How might she nudge him away from his depression and get him moving toward something positive, without unintentionally vectoring him aside to wallow in the quagmire of his dark memories? Perhaps answers were nearby—*here*, in this village—or, if not, maybe at the beach.

"Yes, the Port Hilford Beach," she mumbled, her words addressed to no one there, "Mother's beach." She decided that she would turn the breadloaf rock that the corporal had sentimentalized into a monument to her mom's memory.

To that end, she bought a small trowel from the local Home Hardware.

She wanted to know more about the beach and about the rock itself, the flora, and the fauna, and not just that there were "stones" there and "plants" and "birds" and "shells". She had been to the town's library a couple of times to explore possibilities. Following introductions, both ladies in attendance had offered their condolences and, with purpose-of-trip niceties out of the way, had been helpful with her search. One of them, Margaret Henderson, she felt, might become a friend. How pleasant to at least contemplate.

The next morning she settled herself into wave-formed folds of warm sand to spread out all her borrowed reference materials, laying them onto overlapping bath towels that she had liberated from the inn. She found herself alone there, happily so. The sky, Atlantic-overlay blue, free of big-city smog, was individuated by faint cumulus billows, looking very much like a puffed cotton softness that might have been plucked from Egyptian bolls as many as 12,000 years ago. The sun had actually begun to melt away the remaining ice in her soul, and she had stopped thinking, for a time, about the spoiler: what had happened to her mom.

She stepped away from her nested minilibrary, underlain and bounded by snitched inn's linens, and wandered the beach gathering samples—assorted shells, bits of green struggling for existence among the rocks, and a blossom here and there. Her curiosity was wide-ranging, a childish sense of discovery having overtaken her. She brought her gleanings back to the towels, paged through her borrowed literature, and learned that she had been gathering, among her other things, the carapaces of rock crabs, or as one of her books had added as a pedantic touch, *Cancer irroratus*. Who but a paleobotanist, a linguist, or the book's author would have been likely to know *that*, she wondered? Minus the Latin pomposity, she felt everyone from the region would have known all or most of the native species and would have thought her silly. But, as a stranger, *she* didn't know these things and didn't feel at all uncomfortable having to look them up. Anyway, it served to take her mind at least temporarily away from her mom. And her mom would forgive her this, she imagined.

The crab shells particularly fascinated her. She wondered in a macabre way whether some of them had dined on whatever had been left of her mother. In their own deaths, the crabs' exoskeletons had remained yellowish with purple-brown speckles. She counted nine marginal teeth along the edge of each shell, on each side of their eyes, and three more between the eyes. Apparently, in life, they scurried around on their four hind legs looking for things to eat—alive or dead—holding in reserve their front legs, claws really, to grab and tear apart prey.

According to a page she was anchoring against a light breeze, another sample she had found was of a soft-shell clam. But it was rather unremarkable, apart from once having had a long sand snorkel, like a submarine's periscope. These soap-dish items seemed to be everywhere.

More interesting were the northern moon shells with their smooth and whorled carapaces with shades of gray and tan. She found that these aquatic niceties dined on other mollusks by using their file-like tongues, along with acid produced from internal glands, to bore a hole in each victim's shell and then inserting their snout into that drilled perforation to suck up the victim's body. Lovely, she thought—yet another nasty life-form—humanity apparently was in good company.

Next she organized her assortment of circular, puffed-up pincushions, as she likened them to, and found from her echinoderm book that they were green sea urchins. Forget about the Latin, she decided, having struggled and failed with earlier shell pronunciations. In life these creatures apparently had a top covering of protective spines, each movable on a ball-and-socket joint. Long tube feet had stuck out beyond the spines for breathing, sensory reception, seizing food and anchoring the animal to rocks. They would have had strong teeth on their undersides, used to scrape and grind seaweed and other food. But when they had died, their spines had fallen off, leaving the bumpy shells she was now examining. The bumps had been the knobs on which the spines had moved within their joints. Tiny pores visible in the carapace were where the feet had extended when they were alive. Chuckling at her own absence of god-created-the-world belief, she said in a soft voice to no one listening, "Wouldn't the creationists have had fun with this!"

Never having lived near the Atlantic, knowing it only from maps and books, she found herself not at all bored with this exploration. Rather, she became quite fascinated. Cracking open yet another of her tomes, she moved on to sort through seaweed samples, wanting to better understand what comprised the rotting hawser of red, brown, and green organic mix that stretched along the beach for hundreds of yards, taunting her imagination to accept that it looked like a gigantic, bloated python. She paced off, with soggy steps, its width, and visually estimated its depth to get a better sense of its overall mass.

Again she began to feel like a duffer. Who else would do this? How could it matter to anyone locally? Probably *wouldn't* matter to anyone because they would already know all this stuff. Well, it mattered, now, to her, she told herself without apology. This gift of the sea, if anyone else thought of it that way, was approximately two-and-a-half meters wide by a half-meter deep, and it arced across as much as a half of the entire strand area. A gift, she thought, that the sea kept on giving.

Shuffling through her books to get the right one, she found that seaweeds in general didn't have any leaves, flowers, roots, or stems.

Instead, their leaflike fronds which photosynthesize and produce a jellylike coating to prevent water loss in the sun and wind. Their seeds are released as reproductive cells directly into the water. A holdfast foot that looks like a root anchors the plant to sand or rock. The holdfast doesn't absorb nutrients as roots do; no need—the plant is bathed in nutrient-rich water. Nor are stems needed, the plants simply float.

She looked out along the length of this malodorous deposit and realized the incoming tide must bring in tonnes of similar matter, perhaps daily. She thought this sea-emanating salad could make fertilizer if harvested. Perhaps that was happening, or it could become the base for commercially produced biofuels. She had read about energy companies experimenting with using seaweed to yield ethanol, but didn't think the idea had caught on with investors or, more importantly, with governments.

She got up, looked for, and found a length of suitable driftwood and poked around within the mass. She stretched out tendrils of it and pinched her nose as it dried and released a drift of noxious gas. She found within it clumps of Irish moss, finger sponge, dulse, and ladder wrack. She also identified sugar kelp, eelgrass, and beach grass. She felt a bit smarter for her effort, if only she could remember it all to describe to Stan when she got home. She went back to her notebook and scribbled several new entries.

Moving higher onto the beach's reach up toward the road, looking among grassy patches, she found a trailing vine with lavender flowers. Its curly tendrils clung to other plants as it spread along the ground. She identified it as beach pea. And, nearby, blossoms she had mistaken for dandelions turned out to be coltsfoot, the earliest plant to blossom amongst all the region's wildflowers. Apparently it could reach half a meter in height by midsummer. She picked one, roots and all, and placed it into one of her larger books to press and later take home. Its leaves were reminiscent of the skin on frogs she had caught as a child in a creek near home—a virtual camouflage of flat green interspersed with dabs of brown, each dab ringed in a deeper shade, like splats of pigment flicked from an artist's brush.

The birds she had seen on her first day with Corporal Elujah turned out to be semipalmated plovers. She jotted it down on a fresh page. The other gaunt-looking black birds she had wondered about, sitting on rocks offshore, turned out to be double-crested cormorants. They had seemed at first to be ugly harbingers of death, apparitions feigning crucified avifauna, if there could be such a thing. Why, she had wondered, did they stand so erectly there with their wings hanging out like priests offering a benediction? Did they perhaps know her mother? Had they welcomed her ashore?

There was an explanation, of course; she knew there would be. The cormorants weren't pallbearers or death symbols; it was all in her imagination. Turned out that the birds' feathers lacked oil for waterproofing, enabling them to better swim underwater to catch fish. Obviously, she now could see, their plumage got wet when in pursuit of dinner, so they had to perch somewhere with their wings spread to dry. Any rock would do as a perch—no cross was needed, no nails either. No virtual coffin to carry.

But her by-now playful mood had begun to fade. A returning sense of responsibility seeped in to grey it out. The sun had grown hot to her skin; a breeze wafting pungently over the day's deposit of seaweed wasn't helping. She knew, with lessening reluctance, she would need to give it up, at least for today. She hadn't, after all, come to Sherbrooke to play on the beach.

She started gathering together her books, her shells, her collected organic samples, and the inn's towels. Fumbling one of the books in her haste, it'd opened fanlike as it fell, pages splaying against loosely packed sand. She stood, muttering an obscenity as she brushed it off. Her car was hot as she drove back to town. She rolled down the windows, intentionally leaving off the air-conditioner. The wind in her face better suited her darkening mood.

Margaret Henderson, alone when Chelsea arrived at the library, sensed Chelsea's anxiety as she bumbled an explanation about having dropped one of the books, opening it to show minuscule damage, and offering to pay for a replacement. Margaret gave it no more than a passing glance. Attempting imperceptibility, she had appraised Chelsea's fretted expression as she had rambled on with her overwrought apology, tears not more than a gasp away. Here, Margaret felt, was a person in need of someone to be with. Gingerly she invited her for a cup of coffee. She turned a key in the library's front door, and they went together to the nearby Village Coffee Grind, Margaret's arm gently resting around her shoulder until they arrived. Chelsea, embarrassed, held a cupped hand gently to her mouth as the unwanted tears welled up, spilling onto her cheeks.

"It's okay," Margaret offered, gently. "You're a long way from home and probably feel like a stranger. But you needn't go through this odyssey friendless; others and I can be—*want* to be—here for you. Folks in the village know about and feel your loss. We've been shocked by it. Events like your mom's cruel ending don't happen often in our little community. This isn't the big city. Murdering elderly women isn't something we're a party to every day."

"Thank you," Chelsea sobbed, gasping for breath as she tried to speak. "I've spent so much of my life alone; we've moved so often. For a long time my husband seemed insensitive to all that. At times it's left me not knowing which way to turn. Friendships made have faded with distance and time. I've become hardened to it. Or so I had thought. Now I feel like one of those hard-shelled creatures I've gathered on the beach: hard on the outside, vulnerable inside. You know what I mean?"

"Yes, of course I do. This land is no stranger to death. We all feel it when one of ours goes out to sea and doesn't come home. The sea seems always to exact a price for what it's willing to give up. Our men and their boats pay it, often."

"I shouldn't let myself get like this, really; my mom wasn't exactly a sweetheart." Dabbing at her cheeks with a tissue, she added, "It's *how* she died, I think...I think that's what has me so angry."

Margaret nodded and added nothing, except her look of profound, honest sympathy.

Chelsea took a distracted glance at her surroundings. They had brought their coffee onto the patio where it was quieter and more pleasant, even somehow relaxing. She felt she would like to come back here, to spend time getting to know this stranger who had been so willing to talk to her, to *care* about her. "Thank you for this," she said, "Could we do the coffee thing again, maybe soon?"

"Of course." Margaret replied.

"I don't want to keep you. You're probably needed back at the library."

"It's okay," Margaret said. "It hasn't been a busy day. I'll run over there if somebody comes along. In the meantime, why don't you tell me more about yourself?"

Dabbing at her nose and trying to regain her composure, Chelsea thought, yes, she would, but felt a concurrent need to keep it brief—no blubbering.

"There's not much to tell, really. Farmer's daughter. Married a police officer—RCMP—who became…something different than that. Eventually we got old. Nothing outstanding."

"Really?" Margaret queried, offering a smile she hoped would invite this stoic presence to open up more, to trust her.

But Chelsea wasn't ready for that, not yet. She knew she liked this person; it wasn't that that held her back. She could tell that Margaret's sincerity was real. She wondered if all folks who lived near the sea were this friendly. Could that be? Back home, she mused, they wouldn't give a damn. If you were a beggar, most would pass you on the street, and wouldn't drop a loony into your hat. Survival of those who were able, she thought, and leave the rest to wander, hungry, lost to everyone: to their loved ones, to society, to themselves. Who cared? Only other unfortunates who had been there. Humanity was cruel, most times. But not this lady.

The silence amplified between them as if in an anechoic chamber, Margaret holding her smile, waiting. She had dealt with grief before. She had learned that life was something people had to help each other through, and here was a person who needed a sounding board.

Chelsea was able to whisper, "Give me a couple more minutes, okay?"

Margaret nodded, leaving herself open to a response whenever the other was ready. No hurry. She saw a pair of distraught lips drawn tightly together, quivering, as Chelsea tried to regain her composure.

Chelsea took her eyes away from Margaret. Focusing for a first time on the cafe's surroundings, she noticed its name: the Village Coffee Grind. Neat moniker, she thought. Cute place. The sign on the roof showed a coffee grinder—quite appropriate. Smart idea. The building itself was reminiscent of a small bungalow. It had flat-blue board-and-batten siding and was roofed with gray asphalt shingles. The trellis over the patio, filled with hanging baskets of white and blue flowers, was supported with four-by-four uprights that had been left unstained. Their chairs were wicker and comfortable. Empty Adirondacks lounged under a rectangular orange umbrella, backed by a large rock. Another heavyweight stone anchored the left side of the property, kept company by a couple of superannuated lobster traps. She wasn't quite sure what they were; she thought of asking Margaret, but she didn't. Too off topic. Too trivial for the moment. She was beginning to feel better.

Only then did she really notice the property next door: St. Mary's River Lodge. Swiss, apparently. She had missed it when she first came to town, instead staying at the Sherbrooke Village Inn, which of course had worked out quite well. The lodge was prettier, though. It appeared to be one-and-a-half stories, with white siding, red shutters and gray shingles on its upper front, and was painted dark brown below. Its add-on was fronted by an archway that suited its setting, laden with baskets of yellow pansies, the arch itself shingled with graying unfinished boards. It had a European look. If it indeed were Swiss, perhaps she would have been able to practice her German had she stayed there. German, she thought. Germany. Austria. Switzerland. *Schweitzer Deutsch*. It had been a long time since she had used it.

Margaret was waiting, smiling, taking small sips of coffee without taking her eyes off Chelsea.

"You've been very understanding with me, Margaret. Thank you for that." Chelsea paused, wanting to remain in this person's company, to get to know her better. "Could you come to the beach with me?" she tried. "There's a huge boulder there I'd like to show you. Maybe you've already been there and seen it. I'd like to ask your opinion on something."

"A rock? Well, maybe I *have* seen it," Margaret said, "but yes, I would like to see it again. What's special about it?"

"It's apparently where my mom washed up, came to rest beside it. I'd be in better shape, I think, to talk there. The beach has taken on an unexpected significance to me. I want…I want my mom to remain there."

"To *remain* there?"

"Her ashes, yes."

"But can you *do* that?"

"Who else would know but me and you?" A softness had crept into her tone. She was becoming herself again; she knew she was moving away from grief toward a new friendship and felt a burgeoning happiness about that.

"When would you like to go?" Margaret asked.

"When could you get away?"

"Well, today's Tuesday. The library is closed tomorrow. I could meet you here in the morning for coffee. We could go after that.

August 11, 2010, 9:23 a.m.

They sat inside the Coffee Grind for their morning cup, a little easier in each other's company than they had been the day before. Over Margaret's polite objection, Chelsea paid the tab before they set out for the beach.

Margaret could tell that her chimerical friend felt an affinity for the place, like a child anticipating the building of a Sunday sand castle. The sea's horseshoe strand had shortly morphed before them into a garden of Chelsea's plants, home to *her* fauna, all effused as examples of things she had been able to identify from the library books—the wash of seaweed thrown up by the tide, fresh shells that hadn't been there for her before, and blossoms that Margaret could only smile at, eyebrows raised.

Breadloaf Rock was about a hundred yards down the beach. She pointed it out to Margaret, who needed a few minutes to absorb her companion's enthusiasm. A few steps ahead of her, Chelsea whispered in a voice intended to be unheard, "Mom, where are you now…right now?" She paused to listen, but there was only the sigh of water rolling into their end of the bay, its weight felt under foot, she thought, more intensely than the sensation of rolling surf being telegraphed to her mind. Her body, she surmised, was perceiving a compression of wet sand at her feet, sensing it pushing upward, like railroad ties flexing up parallel tracks against the weight of an oncoming locomotive, the train felt before being seen, perhaps as experienced by the horse running toward its rendezvous with destiny in Alex Coleville's famous painting.

All of which brought them to the moment. Chelsea thought the day was perfect—cloudy bright with just enough cover to keep the two of them from having to don sunglasses. Margaret walked slightly behind, wanting her presence to remain unobtrusive, to offer whatever reassurance in silence that it might. They abandoned their shoes at the edge of the freshet running down from the lake, spilling into fingers of a daily varying delta, yielding its form to the sea's unpredictable dictates. The water was cold; pebbles pressed ruddy indentations into the soles of their feet as they minced their way across, arms waving, outstretched as if attempting some form of semaphore not yet memorized. As she looked back, their limp-wristed limbs seemed to Chelsea to resemble the wings of her priestly cormorant, now sitting out there on its outcrop, presiding over the human goings-on, offering its mimicry without caring about their intent. Her mind, given its innate stubbornness, was determined to have its way. She wondered if the beach's Prophet of Darkness had watched her mother drift in. What did it think then, she wondered? Perhaps, to it, death wasn't a new show—not new at all. She knew from Margaret's books that it wasn't a carrion eater. But then her mother wasn't carrion, was she? Not to the bird. Perhaps just to the crabs.

At her rock, she stopped. Margaret came to stand alongside. Chelsea extended her arm, her hand palm down, stroking the granite's smoothness. "What do you think?" she asked. Margaret still hadn't been able to quite get her mind around where Chelsea wanted to go with this, but knew she couldn't say as much.

"I think it's fine, quite beautiful in its own way." She tried to imagine whether she was hitting the right notes here. It really looked to her like, well, just a rock; a bit big, yes, but maybe they didn't have boulders in Ottawa.

Chelsea dipped into her beach bag and brought out her trowel and the hammered-copper urn. Dropping to her knees, she began scooping out sand from beneath her mom's Breadloaf. She worked without looking back. Eyelids raised, it reminded Margaret of grainy movie footage she had seen of soldiers from World War I, attempting to inter bits of a comrade who had taken cover in a shell crater, only to have a second casing fall in and explode beside him. She stepped back and tried to size up the stone. What was so special, she wondered? It was about shoulder high and more than eight feet long, and, yes, it did look rather like a loaf of bread. She moved around it, being careful not to dislodge the cantaloupe-sized rollers at its base; all, she supposed, waiting to upend her.

The Breadloaf's north face, she could see, showed fault lines, deepened by the seepage of winter rains frozen and thawed over a span of centuries. The drag of glaciation had rounded its corners. It did, she began to feel, exemplify the solidity and permanence of ancient granite, its surface dulled but soul undaunted by exposure to a million storms and baked by as many sunlit days. A bed of oddly casket-shaped sand lay at the base of the north face, its beach side bracketed by torso-sized boulders. Perhaps it *was* the most appropriate headstone for Chelsea's mom.

Chelsea finished her excavation. Slowly, reverently, she introduced her mother's urn, pushing wet sand against it, pressing the granulated dampness to smooth it with the palms of her hands. She stood to stare down at the makeshift tomb. Her tears were there, falling into where the urn had disappeared. She didn't try to suppress them. Moving alongside her, Margaret reached for her hand, held it gently, and kept their silence. They remained that way, together in friendship, until Chelsea's tears dried on her cheeks.

Chelsea turned to face the sea. A single plover patrolled the beach, poking holes in the wetness beneath it, seeking lunch. A flock of five newcomers joined in because of the bird's apparent success, quickly to become eleven, all with the same helter-skelter agenda.

The Fontana Resurrection

The women made their way back to the car, before heading to the Coffee Grind for a quiet lunch. Chelsea appeared to Margaret again to have lost herself in thought, her mind perhaps entangled in a net of the morning's events. But it wasn't that. Pushing away the unfinished half of her BLT sandwich, Chelsea sipped at her coffee, set it down, and asked, "Could I impose on you for a favour? I'll understand if you'd prefer not to do it."

"I will if I can," Margaret offered.

"It's large, I think, and it *is* an imposition." Chelsea said, taking another sip of coffee.

"I'm listening," Margaret said, trying to make her tone reflect a probability of acceptance.

"I wouldn't ask this, but I feel now like I have to get home. My husband is alone, except for the company of our little dog. I worry about him, almost always."

"Why is that?"

"He suffers from chronic depression. When he crashes, it's bad. So far, whenever that's happened, I've been there, able to save him from himself, literally. He's had professional help and takes medication for it, but I get nervous after a while whenever we're not together."

She paused, turning the half sandwich on her plate, and picked at a bit of bacon peeking out from under the lettuce. "I wanted to be here longer, but I also don't want to have another catastrophe on my hands."

"I understand," Margaret again offered, "How can I help?"

"I'd like to have a bronze plaque cast and mounted on mom's rock. Do you know someone who can do that?"

Margaret paused. "Well, I know someone who could *mount* it. A man in town does that sort of thing. He'll have the tools or could rent them." She squinted momentarily and then added, "The casting will have to be done at the Lunenburg Foundry, but I can make that happen. They do excellent work. What would you like it to say?"

Chelsea reached into her purse for her notebook, found the page, tore it away, handed it to Margaret, and asked, "Do you think this might be okay?"

Margaret read what she recognized as one of Sara Teasdale's poems:

99

If Death Is Kind

Perhaps if death is kind, and there can be returning,
We will come back to earth some fragrant night,
And take these lanes to find the sea, and bending
Breathe the same honeysuckle, low and white.

We will come down at night to these resounding beaches
And the long gentle thunder of the sea,
Here for a single hour in the wide starlight
We shall be happy, for the dead are free.

"I think it's fine," Margaret said, feeling a swelling in her throat, eyes gathering a moistness she wasn't easily able to control. "I believe it reflects how you feel."

"Yes, it does."

Chelsea groped in her purse for something, found it, and then said, "I'll cut you a cheque to cover this."

"No need," Margaret countered. "I'll send you the invoices later. I'll take care of it, no worries."

Sensing that lunch was done with and that they wouldn't be seeing each other for some time, she added, "When this if over, how about we stay in touch?"

"Absolutely," Chelsea offered, "I'd like that."

They hugged and then each went their own way.

August 12, 2010, 10:16 a.m.
Chelsea settled her account at the motel and drove back to the Moncton airport, her next problem occupying her mind throughout: Stanley. How would he have managed in her absence? Had he been taking his medication? She should have phoned, she knew, but she hated phones. Anyway, she would be home soon. He would be okay.

September 3, 2010, 9:23 a.m.
Margaret made good on her promise. The plaque arrived. She accompanied the fellow who would mount it, scrutinized the stone, pointed

out her choice of location, and watched him mark and drill mounting holes and then screw the plaque into place. He pulled a cloth from his tool kit, burnished the metal until its raised poetry glowed in the sun, the deep brown matted background contrasting with a lighter glint of polished wording. He turned to smile at her, knowing she would be happy with it.

They found their way back across the stream, not saying anything: he a long, lanky man, quick to find humour, seeming to lope rather than to walk and she, a longtime acquaintance, preoccupied by something about which he deemed it best not to inquire.

Margaret found herself glad to have done this for her friend, wondering how she had fared once back home, hoping her husband's dependency hadn't become yet another cross she would have to bear, and hoping also that their friendship would last, that they would meet again.

But she couldn't get past the differences in how they had each viewed the beach. To Chelsea, Margaret knew this was sacred ground: a graveyard, her mom's repose, forever. Margaret, though, had recognized the grit, the seascape's perfection marred. As she looked around her now, she glanced again at her surroundings: at the flagpole, for instance—Chelsea may not have noticed it—its flag tattered, frayed at its snapping end where sun and rain and time had claimed disintegrating bits of fabric, surrendering a losing hold on the warp and woof of Nova Scotia's intended-to-be proud banner. Why had no one changed it, she wondered?

Continuing to choose her footfalls carefully, nearer the artisan's truck she came upon a ring of stones gathered by some earlier and apparently insensitive adventurer—perhaps living a tension between desire and fulfillment—to form a fire pit, ashes abandoned, charred butt of log cold upon a smoked slump of Beefeater flask. It reminded her of Salvador Dali's *The Persistence of Memory*. Malodorous food scraps lingered there, settled amongst crumples of plastic wrap and Styrofoam, feeding opalescent flies, thereafter to host their progeny. Crows, fewer than seven but difficult to reckon due to a masterful aerial ballet *in situ*, landed to exercise a preordained pecking order, sorting their diners from gleaners.

Above, wilier than its competitors, a seagull dropped through them, wings folded as though broken, to snatch preferred bits; others less venturesome, in canopied flight, squalled a cacophonous displeasure.

Quite the scene, she thought; black versus white, like a Boris Spassky and Bobby Fischer chess match, advancing toward the players' objective with all the determination and cunning of a dictator subsuming a democracy, or vice-versa. Stepping again toward the truck, she conceded that this had been—bugs to birds—analogous to humanity's behaviour: the mighty get the most. It had ever been thus, she mused; ever would be.

This, she conjectured, happened on beaches everywhere. But, like Marion's body, such things didn't belong on a beach. Marion's body, though, at least had been tidied up.

CHAPTER 2
The Corporation

Scene 8
Meet Lee...

> *"It's true, I am afraid of dying. I am afraid of the world moving forward without me, of my absence going unnoticed, or worse, being some natural force propelling life on. Is it selfish? Am I such a bad person for dreaming of a world that ends when I do? I don't mean the world ending with respect to me, but every set of eyes closing with mine."*
> *–Jonathan Safran Foer, Everything Is Illuminated*

September 23, 2009, 2:27 p.m.

Tall, slim, and hard of hearing, Lee was a presence that couldn't be denied, wherever she went. In any newly joined leaderless group or setting she had bubbled naturally to the top. She had a buoyant style, which had stood her in good stead whenever she had encountered difficult or slower people at or near the pinnacle of any hierarchical pyramid. She had always been able to see the collective as a potentially new flock and manipulate it to become *her* flock, once she'd broken them free.

Lee revelled in that. She couldn't get enough of life. Insatiably curious, she was always peering around the next corner to see what challenge might await her, or what excitement she could generate.

Such was her mood on September 23, 2009, with the leaves crisp in their curled glory, competing with each other to showcase their most brilliant shades of orange and mottled burgundy.

Turning her head and mind away from the *joie de vivre* that was streaming through her home-office window, she looked again at the doodles that she had pencilled onto a sheet of paper, smudged somewhat, having been brushed over several times by the edge of a closed hand. She reversed her pencil and began tapping its eraser on the small clusters of circled words and misshapen rectangles, filled with thoughts that had ended in exclamation marks, some highlighted by little hearts with arrows through them, pointing toward boxes that contained ideas that she preferred above the others.

It bothered her that she had recently allowed herself to slide toward boredom. She needed something new to do. Not anything she had earlier toyed with, rather something to rake the fading coals of excitement within her—a now-dated excitement she felt age was causing to curl at its edges, deep down, like the leaves on the trees beyond her window.

She looked at the page, not as one who might read the words left to right and top to bottom, but more as a dilettante looking down with a measure of self-satisfaction at what could become, with a bit of touching up, a collectible piece of art. She began to focus on words within the boxes and circles, eliminating some as being capricious or impractical and others as being interesting, but without offering anything particularly new.

Gently easing the page away from the glue binding along the top of her pad, she started anew, disciplining her abstractions into something of a businesslike list, extending an arrow from each surviving item toward an emphatically pencilled cluster of large dollar signs. Cost would be an issue; she was financially comfortable, but not rich.

Whatever this venture was going to become, she would want to arrange her own financing. This was not to devolve into anything that might require either the funding or the agreement of her husband. She loved him dearly, but whatever was bothering her was beginning to manifest itself as a growing desire to prove to herself and to the people in her world that she had the capability to stand alone—this time to stand beside a money tree from which she would always be able to pick, in large denominations.

Her focus returned to the line that said "Clinic for the wealthy elderly". She followed the adjacent arrow to the reality-questioning dollar signs. She supposed this option was likely to involve a lot of money. But that would be part of the challenge, not necessarily a showstopper.

She paused, giving the concept time to flesh itself out. Beginning to feel the adrenaline, she tentatively allowed it to brush aside the other things on her page.

Yes, she told herself, this would be it: a seniors' spa. Not something plebeian, like so many of the newly constructed seniors' barrack blocks. They seemed so much alike, especially after the residents settled in. Hers would be something really exciting, with added space and luxury for each client. These features, still-to-be-imagined, were none that existing facilities had or would be able to afford.

The annoying little cluster of dollar signs crept back into view. Truly this idea was going to require creative financing. She would have to look toward something less conventional than the banking system. But that mustn't be allowed to become more than a hindrance. Looked at in a more positive light, it might morph into a titillating search for a financial partner.

* * * * * * * *

In days that followed, Lee spent the pleasantness of autumn's slanting-sunlit afternoons working through her list of existing Ottawa seniors' residences, ostensibly looking for a happily-ever-after place to settle. Having asked her bathroom mirror to stop lying to her, she admitted she was of an age that would allow this ruse some legitimacy, although the remnants of her vanity precluded her from admitting that she was really *old,* certainly not one of *them.*

The exercise became wearisome. The competing businesses, which so recently had seemed the avant-garde thing for the elderly, were beginning to appear tired, all too much alike, all offering the same amenities. For folks who had decided to make one of these places their final home, it seemed to her that it must have been a bit like shopping for a car: All vendors were bent on pleasing potential leasers, but they all were doing it with more or less the same dab of honey on the ladle. As could be expected, all facilities had nuanced variances, making one or two of them perhaps more desirable in the eyes of shoppers.

Whenever she could, without attracting the attention of any given facility's staff, she had attempted to connect with folks who were living there to see how they really felt about their new lifestyle. Were they truly happy there, she had asked? Had there been any disappointments, and if so, what? She listened carefully to the things they said mattered most to them and, more particularly, to features or services that they would have liked to have had but which weren't part of the package. Interestingly, none of them seemed too concerned about the *cost* of their new digs. Lee found the rent high—approximately the same daily rate charged in most five-star hotels—more, actually, than the daily breakdown of fares charged by some cruise lines. For those who proved at all chatty, she extracted from her purse a small hard-cased notebook with its black, straw-like pen and, in her most friendly manner, asked their permission to keep in touch. She said that she was interested in their views and opinions, and would it be okay for her to be considered a friend? Beyond that, becoming then more selective, she had asked a few if they might be interested in relocating, were there to be a more luxurious, feature-rich facility developed. All who had said yes agreed that it would be fair to expect a higher occupancy rate for something a cut above anything now on the market, in fact they had welcomed that possibility.

"Could you let us know?" they had asked in one manner or another.

"Yes, of course," she had said, adding the words *possible client* beside each promising entry in her notebook.

Taking her inquiries a step closer to the graves of the folks she had been considering, she spent half a day at the White Lilly, Ottawa's most notable and costly-to-maintain palliative care centre. She had introduced herself to the centre's staff as a health-care professional and had asked their permission to introduce herself to their patients. The nurses had been pleased to oblige. They chatted with her briefly, asking about her background and the basis for her interest, to which she replied she was a practicing chiropractor, more recently having taken courses at the Department of Palliative Care, Policy and Rehabilitation, King's College in London, England. She held her breath momentarily, hoping they wouldn't ask her to provide proof. They didn't. She said that she had heard much about the White Lilly's reputation, but hadn't to date had an opportunity to visit the terminally ill who were being cared for there. She wanted to learn firsthand how palliative care was administered at the high end of that specialization, and how the folks who presumably were aware that they would never be leaving the place were receiving it. This type of practical training, she had acknowledged, hadn't been part of her earlier exposure; she asked for their advice on how to better prepare herself to discuss such matters should her own elderly clients choose to bring up the subject.

With tea finished and a tour of the facility behind her—artwork appropriately admired and commented on—her escort happily gave her a printout of the guests and left her to go ahead with her visitations.

That's when she had met Marion Barber.

During that first visit, they had an interesting chat. It had turned out, through various small-gathering Christmas parties, that Lee had come to know and like Marion's daughter Chelsea. Marion had described how, with Chelsea's help, she had made the rounds of and stayed in almost all the better residences available in the city. For her, they had all, in one way or another, been found wanting. At the same time, Mae had confessed to having felt misgivings about the trouble and inconvenience that she had caused her daughter. She had wished that there could be some way she could regain her strength and to again pursue a life independent of her children. Yes, she dearly loved them—both of them—but she knew that her dependence on their help was an anchor that she had preferred to unhook them from.

Earlier, she had said, following the death of her husband, that she had enjoyed being alone and having responsibility for her own affairs. It was just that age had deprived her of something she could no longer buy: independence. And because she had been diagnosed with terminal liver cancer, she could no longer look forward to *any* future.

Lee had counselled her to take courage, to indeed hang on, and that there were medical breakthroughs relating to the ageing process that suggested age itself might be held at bay and even reversed. Research was being conducted at that very moment in Switzerland, she had added—the thought having just come to her—that looked very promising. It was expensive, yes, but, at least experimentally it had held out the promise of a very real fountain of youth—virtually a miracle! In the beginning, because it was so new, it would understandably be beyond the reach of those individuals who weren't financially able to pay. For those who could afford it, it might herald a new beginning.

No, she had answered when Mae asked, the operation couldn't yet be covered by Canada's health plan because it was still unproven to the level demanded by our government's layers of bureaucracy, which they both knew, didn't they, had kept so many promising new medicines and medical procedures out of reach for Canadian patients who really needed them. She said that it was her professional wish that all of that unnecessary caution could be somehow circumvented. She had added that she was staying on top of events in Switzerland. She had believed that their work was at a point where it could soon be shared with other developed countries, at least experimentally, Canada being one of them. She had asked Mae to cling to that possibility—that hope—as a drowning man might to a life preserver. A positive attitude had done miracles for such people before. The Church, she added, had held out all kinds of examples of terminally ill believers who had stepped away from their ailments as the result of their faith, and Mother Church. Our dear Mother of Jesus couldn't be wrong, could she? Lee felt the guilt shudder through her as she extemporized this bit of hypocrisy. But she also felt the edges of a smile creeping up and had to consciously suppress it.

They had agreed to keep in touch, and Lee had promised to return frequently to visit her. She had left Mae with one caveat, however: Don't share what they had discussed with anyone else. When Mae had asked her why, she said that she could be professionally admonished for deemed-unethical medical deportment were it to become known that she was speaking openly about government and medical-profession bureaucracies forming a barrier to the well-being of Canadians in need. Mae agreed, and they had both kept their promises, in Mae's case—forever.

With new hope looming on her horizon, Mae began to rally. Six months later the director of the White Lilly had approached Chelsea to see about relocating her to a less-intensive care unit. The White Lilly, she had explained, was funded primarily by community donations and the daily cost of per-patient care was absurdly high. Donors had been consistently generous, but they had their limits. The usual patient stay was measured in weeks, not months, and the nursing staff was now regarding Mae as able to manage well enough to return to the greater seniors-residence community.

Upon hearing that news, Chelsea had worried her way through the relocation process again and had hatched a plan to recycle her mom, she thought, this time intending to bed her down in the Governor's Walk, a pleasant enough residence, quite to her liking. Mae had never mentioned a word to Chelsea about her late-stage friendship with Lee, and Chelsea had been pleasantly baffled by her apparent recovery. Life, for both of them, might be beginning to take on a new normalcy.

* * * * * * * *

With a spider now at work weaving its gossamer collection of Lee's newly gathered thoughts across dark niches of her mind, she returned to her home office, assembled her pencils, turned over a new leaf on her notepad, and began listing imagined features that the places she'd just seen *didn't* offer.

Her list was ambitious:

An in-house spa; very large, designed to irregularly loop back onto itself with a tall, forest-like fountain as its central attraction. The pool's water would be warm enough that the facility's clients could always see steam floating above it.

A fully equipped chiropractic and physiotherapy facility.

An operating theatre that would give the impression of being the equivalent of that found in a small hospital.

A big-screen movie theatre equipped with surround sound and the latest in 3-D movie projection equipment, including a wet bar, with a built-in self-serve popcorn machine.

A dedicated bridge-teaching room.

Suites offering roominess and high-end luxury appointments. Clients would be invited to preselect new furnishings and discouraged from bringing pieces of their earlier nests along with them. Small bits of bric-a-brac could be acceptable, provided it had been tastefully winnowed down to a few memories of days gone by. The intent would be to have the whole place exude an aura of new beginnings.

A rural, forest setting, quasi-isolated from Ottawa's crowd.

A gated, tastefully landscaped and ornately fenced community for clients and staff, requiring card-key admission to the grounds and buildings by all clients, visitors, vendors, and service-vehicle drivers. These security precautions would be taken in the guise of providing exclusivity and to add snob appeal. Provisioners and service providers would have to be prescreened, without exception.

On a separate section of her page she pencilled in a few additional items, such as things that wouldn't be advertised in her company's brochure. She drew a loosely shaped rectangle around them, then another, slightly offset, and shadowed its border.

A new idea was beginning to morph within her, a still murky thought dark enough to keep her from wanting it to squeeze out of its chrysalis—something she feared might demand that its wings be allowed to dry and take flight—were undisciplined thoughts to linger within that artfully pencilled frame.

She paused and put down her pencil. There, with fingers locked behind her head, she closed her eyes. She became conscious of an involuntary smile pulling at the corners of her lips. Yes, she thought, this was truly evil—but how inescapably fascinating!

She was quite sure nothing like this had been tried before, although she realized there was nowhere she could go to find out. The Internet didn't seem like a safe option; one never knew which authorities might be scouring for any pattern suggesting criminal activity. The police may appear to cynics to spend most of their time in donut shops or issuing traffic tickets, but she knew they were really smarter than that and were doing whatever they could to keep up with the bad guys—and *girls*, she thought, smiling.

Would she ever allow herself to do it? *No*, she thought, knowing all the while "no" was a lie she would soon have to correct.

She looked again into her shadow-margined picture. The smile was still on her face. She read aloud—to no one but herself, which she had taken a moment to confirm—what she had just written:

> *Operating theatre to be located on the floor above the main level, the main level being where all other client-accessible facilities would be constructed. That room would back onto a freight elevator, and the elevator door would remain masked from view except when used.*
>
> *The freight elevator would be operable only by authorized staff: card-key holders whose cards would have an embedded unique key for that function.*
>
> *A special cold-room would be built immediately adjacent to the chef's walk-in refrigeration chamber, the former enhanced as a quick-freeze facility accessible only by authorized card-key holders.*

She looked back to her first page, seeking out her cluster of dollar signs. Finding them, she reminded herself that the kind of venture she wanted to step into here was going to require some creative and unconventional financing. No matter where this facility would be built, it would take a ton of money. She would need to convince someone, perhaps a shady venture capitalist, that she could make the payments—likely very steep payments.

She turned within herself to revisit the places she had recently toured, wincing at the thoughts of the leathery, withered souls she had encountered, shuffling listlessly as they did from one overplayed event or venue to whatever next bit of drudgery might hold out a doubtful glimmer of adventure for them. They had seemed to her to be swathed in an outer layer of pale crêpe, similar to the mythical fabric offering ghosts their translucency. These were folks tired of the world who wanted at last to get beyond it. Their greatest excitement evidently centred on mealtimes. En route to one or another of their three squares a day, they seemed to put added zest into efforts to arrive on time. This usually resulted in a gridlock of walkers, wheelchairs, and crutches, all of which managed to get parked or abandoned in a clutter of geriatric hardware, making adjacent hallways impassable. Only oxygen bottles were likely to make it to where the wraiths seated themselves at their dining room tables.

"Is that all there is for society's end-of-life castaways?" she thought aloud. Could there not be some way of fortifying their final years, perhaps with an offer of revisited youthful excitement? Will money not buy them experiences more fulfilling than what they're getting now? "Self-replenishing excitement," she thought, speaking it into the air around her. It sounded almost plausible—like a slogan—cloaked as it could be with a bit of work in the finest robes of faux legitimacy.

A spasm of uncertainty shivered through her. Acceptance of her final-solution concept for seniors had crept in, virtually unnoticed, like a trickle of sand finding its way through the neck of an hourglass. "*No!*" she declared aloud, trying to double-clutch her brain into reversing her addict's need for whatever she was *on* from carrying her, body and soul, over a cliff. But, even while her mind was struggling to stop it, she began to watch the black stain of evil overcome her attempts at containment.

Minutes passed. Containment? she thought, recovering her composure. Why? Softly, as a reverberation coursing through all the necessary synaptic connections to reach a yes conclusion, the answer began ringing in her head, demanding that evil's door be unlocked. Containment because it's evil, and because it's evil it's exciting, therefore evil must win over doubt. Such a wonderful thought, she mused, compressing what was left of her guilt into a tight, little wad, and like the skin of a discarded orange peel, dropping it into the wastebasket that she kept for discards at the back of her head. Then, surrendering all, she turned the key, and evil was out—her new reality—in her mind spreading onto the page before her, seeming like a tipped bottle of India ink.

She realized she would need to manage the spread of it. All but a handful of people around her—people she would have to find and trust—must see her as innocent.

She flipped back to her first page, looking again for the dollar signs that she had overwritten subconsciously, so many times. Yes, it was all about money; in order to make her bundle, she would need a lot of it, and she would have to be able to—at least initially—dipper it from a near-bottomless well.

Again closing her eyes she chanced a last glimpse into the depths of the abyss she would fall into if her plan failed. The magnitude of her imagined downward spiral pulled at the muscles of her groin, and she momentarily backed away. But even as she did, she realized that this was the excitement she had been seeking. Finally dismissing all uncertainty, she resolved to follow that sensation wherever it might lead her. Was positive momentum not, she rationalized, the genesis of all things worthwhile?

Gathering up the pages of her notepad, she pushed back her chair and walked to the safe her husband had installed for her a couple of years earlier. He had also had one put into his own office, the rationale being that neither of them should run the risk of losing, either to fire or burglary, any of the documents that were key to their family's business or to their individual financial well-being. She put the papers onto the safe's top shelf, closed the door, turned the handle, and twisted its heavy dial. Smiling to herself, she felt a warm rush at having earlier taken time to reset its combination so that only she would know it.

Scene 9
Finding a Place for the Clinic...

"Beneath all untried activity lies complexity, waiting to ingest the intruder."
-David Edey

October 10, 2009, 2:27 p.m.
Lee found herself preoccupied with thoughts of where to locate her new clinic. She could quite readily picture its interior and feel its ambiance, but she wasn't at all sure how to protect the secret of its fundamental purpose. An urban facility, she concluded, either existing or newly constructed, couldn't work. People in the neighbourhood would always be curious about its distinctiveness and could be expected eventually to pry into details related to activities being conducted there. Staffing would also be an issue—a huge one—but she knew she would need to deal with the physical facility first and later work through the security complexities to protect her relationship with her employees.

She decided that the place would have to be somewhere in a rural setting. It could either be built from scratch or, preferably, she could settle into an existing building. She felt if she could find and walk through a few commercially listed places that, once inside, she would know.

She checked the Internet for real estate offerings, outside Ottawa, but within a hundred-mile radius of the city. The area's real estate agents hadn't posted a lot that looked promising. She was able to eliminate several just through their descriptions. Others she scratched off what had amounted to only a short list because they were located within one or another of the area's outlying small towns or villages. That, she sensed, would attract even more curiosity from neighbours than would have been the case in the city.

As her research continued, she began to see that she was looking for a resort facility or, maybe, a small hotel. There weren't many of them. From the online pictures and descriptions, she was able to eliminate all of them—except one. She knew that it must be a wreck, but if memory served her, it might just fill the bill.

The Mont Sainte Marie resort hotel, having brooded over its decades-old emptiness and finally given in to the inevitability of dereliction, was staring sadly at her from her computer screen and was now up for sale. It would likely have been priced right, she thought, although no price was listed. The larger question was, was it recoverable? It was at least worth a look, given the absence of anything else that might hold promise.

Scene 10
Assessing the Mont Sainte Marie Hotel...

"She hoped to be wise and reasonable in time; but alas! Alas! She must confess to herself that she was not wise yet."
~Jane Austen, *Persuasion*

October 12, 2009, 9:34 a.m.
Spirits soaring, camera in hand, she pointed her car north toward the village of Mont Sainte Marie and pressed the speed limit around several dubious curves along Highway 5 at the edge of the Gatineau River.

She had wanted to go there first alone—without any real estate agent—to see whether the place had the good feel she had imagined would be needed to possess her were it to become her new, secretive Gabriel's-Horn location. In any case, the trip wouldn't be a waste; it was a beautiful autumn day, and a walk in the woods would be, if nothing else, a pleasant outcome. Perhaps it would even give her pause to reconsider this quixotic scheme.

She had known the place much earlier, of course. Who in Ottawa hadn't? Although she had never been into any of the hotel's guest rooms, she had been all through the lobby area, its shops, and the lower floor on several occasions during and after dinners that she had enjoyed there with friends. It had been, in its heyday and in its class, unquestionably beautiful. For the Ottawa downhill ski crowd, it was, for a disappointingly short time, the place for the moneyed set to be seen. Built with Switzerland's Oerlikon family money, it had, initially, responded well to an expensive marketing campaign. The location was Alpine-like. Nestled against the steep edge of a nicely forested mountain, it stood tall and proud at not more than walking distance from the Mont Sainte Marie ski lodge and the area's scattering of privately owned chalets.

Curving past the front of the hotel as she drove uphill to its main parking lot, she was a bit taken aback by the extent of the hotel's disrepair. Was this a knockdown, she wondered? Vandals had stoned the ground-floor windows, and there was ample evidence to show that curiosity seekers had had their way with it. There were suggestions that one or two homeless people had taken shelter there; perhaps they were there even now. A construction fence had been erected around the front and two sides of the building. Yellow no-trespassing ribbons reinforced a safety disclaimer that the public wasn't, at least at this time, welcome inside. But none of that deterred her for long. Something about the look of the place made it feel right. On closer examination it looked to be structurally sound.

She had determined earlier that the primary reason the place had gone bankrupt was that it hadn't been built quite large enough; as built, it had insufficient guest rooms. The Oerlikon family had arrived at that sad determination and decided against an expansion.

Another problem they had faced—although diplomacy had precluded the owners making any fuss about it—was staffing. Quality help had been hard to find and even more difficult to train. A long commute from the city meant that local folks eventually had to make up the preponderance of the workforce. They had become difficult to manage, harbouring a parochial inclination to resist being regarded by the hotel's clientele as servants.

The financial loss had been hurtful, both to the Oerlikon family and to the region's economy. Financially, the endeavour had had to be written off; there were no new takers. Gradually, inexorably, the building had grown tired and then had slowly died.

The question now was, could someone—some talented restoration or construction firm—build out and up from possibly sound underpinnings of this ruin? Or was it beyond that? Either way, much of the property's cost would need to be allocated to refurbishing or replacing the building.

From the outset of her walkabout she hadn't relished the notion of destroying the facility's main part. A convention centre behind it could go, but the hotel itself, however haunted it now may look, had a certain cachet about it. The clock tower was a distinctive feature, its hands now frozen in time. The overall angular architecture and the presence of a lot of glass at the backs of all balconies leading to guest-rooms gave it something of a Swiss-mountain elegance. She thought that that could be its saving grace, provided the structure itself was later found to be fundamentally sound.

She knew then that she would next need two things, perhaps three: an engineering opinion on the structural viability of the place and an estimated cost to refurbish it; a real estate agent's price to acquire the property as is; and a determination of the availability of a line of condos that had been built as a rent-by-owner adjunct to the hotel itself. They had been sold and privately owned from the hotel's get-go. All of them, she noticed, had been well maintained over the years. If they could be bought, perhaps separately from the main deal, they would make excellent staff quarters. However, if not—and it would remain a huge question mark—they would represent a security problem because of their close proximity to the main building. She would have to worry a bit later about that. Maybe not all the owners would sell; maybe the price would go up as the first few were sold; maybe she wouldn't be able to put together enough money to buy them all. But, first things first: how much would the main venture cost?

Scene 11
Lee Plans for Clinic Renovation...

October 12, 2009, 11:26 a.m.
The day was young. The sun was strong, and the weather still comfortably warm. She still needed to ferret out a few details.

Working her way around the building was difficult; the security fencing and the yellow tape didn't look like it wanted to be tampered with. After she had picked her way through the trees and rocks to get there, the building's back side seemed to be coming up directly out of steeply sloping bedrock. With every step, footing was tricky, and she had only one hand free, the other was busy keeping her camera from banging against the rocks on her left side and the wall of the building on her right. The kids had obviously been more agile than she was. She finally managed to get to a window. Inside, she could see broken glass wherever and everywhere it had fallen. But, all in all, the interior—at least the part she could see—didn't appear to be too badly depreciated. Looking at the ceiling and walls, she couldn't detect any water damage. The building's ground-level floor appeared to be a poured slab, which also looked to be in relatively good shape.

Moving on, assessing carefully the slope that she was picking her way along, she noticed that all the building's HVAC extensions were there, built out from the back wall and up the slope of the mountain so that they could be accessed from inside through doorways at both the first and second levels. There were no windows anywhere nearby that she could try to peer through. Elevated steel catwalks led out from the doors at both levels from rooms that presumably made up the central core of the building's utilities infrastructure. She managed to get close enough to the catwalks—one of which extended out onto the side of the mountain—to see that they and their protective handrails were still structurally sound. Rust hadn't significantly eaten into them. She was tempted to try to scramble up to the catwalk at its uphill anchor point, but she found the footing too uncertain.

Given that she was now standing in what appeared to be a fairly representative cross section of the mountain's flora, she paused to push the toe of her right shoe beneath the leaf mold and into the sparse topsoil. It was mainly a composted accumulation of detritus from the forest's trees and soft-stemmed ground vegetation. Overall, there wasn't much of it. She had hoped the soil would have been at least moderately deep and, with luck, easily handled with a shovel. It wasn't, on either count. There were to be *parcels* she had counted on being able to inter here; it was apparent now she would have to make other arrangements.

She could see that tree growth on the mountain behind and part way around the hotel was primarily deciduous with a few conifers in the mix. The ones immediately around her appeared to be ironwood. Farther out, others included maple, some oak, and some immature poplar.

Moving cautiously for fear of a fall, with one careful foot placement at a time, she stepped around rocks and tree roots onto the asphalt that paved the building's far side. She moved back to get an overview and take a couple of photos of the loading dock and then came forward into weeds that had grown in front of it for an arm's-length inspection. This looked somewhat more promising. The cement platform itself, when poured, had been steel reinforced to protect it from inadvertent contact with backing trucks. The concrete would need touching up, but was fundamentally a still-intact solid block, designed to accommodate big rigs. Any large vehicle, even a 53-footer if handled by a skilled driver, could be butted up against the ramp and loaded or off-loaded quickly and—of equal importance—done so out of sight of anyone not employed by the hotel.

She had already concluded that the driver would need to be someone under the absolute control of the spa's management team.

Beginning to feel somewhat at home, she stepped back around to the hotel's main entrance. The security screen erected there was actually reinforced construction-site mesh, prefabricated in ten-foot lengths. Each section's end posts were set into the openings of cinder blocks.

Making her way along the fence toward the clock tower, she looked casually for a movable section. Finding one, she looked around, sweeping her gaze over the condominiums that bordered the front of the lodge. Seeing no one, she tugged a bit awkwardly at one end of the fence section that had been left unattached to the building's front wall and squeezed sideways through the opening. She moved quickly to the front doors and—glancing behind her to see no one had observed her little trespass—tried them. Locking hardware for the double doors had at some time been removed or perhaps stolen. Imprints of the locks' faceplates—the faceplates themselves now gone—revealed that the doors, by now a muddy brown, at one time had been painted pink. She hooked a finger into one of the vacant hardware holes and gave the door a gentle pull. It yielded, quite easily. Stepping inside, she could see, to her right, looking down its curved stairwell, that the lower level, which included the kitchen and dining room, was going to need serious work. She decided not to go down there; it was better, she thought, to stay where she was, take some hasty photos and slide out before someone caught her.

Happily unnoticed, but feigning an air of casual detachment in the event she was being watched from a distance, she retraced her steps through the doors and the gap in the fence, nudging it back into place against the wall. Again, being a novice at this sort of deceit, and attempting to appear as if nothing more was at play than displaced curiosity, she wandered across the open patio toward the first row of condominiums. Scanning the blackness of interiors staring back at her through windows along the row of units she now wanted to appraise, her confidence began to grow that indeed she was alone. For a moment she felt a bit silly, or was it, she wondered, just a shiver of giddiness.

She paused to review the photos she had just taken of the hotel's admitting-desk area: The reception lounge, with its stone wall and the fireplace she had remembered, located just beyond the stairwell leading down to the dining room, and, behind the wall, the vista lounge with its spectacular view of the rocky, forested mountain side she had a few minutes ago stepped away from.

The condominiums were impressive. If there was a problem, she thought, it might be that there were too many of them. They architecturally were perfectly integrated with the hotel; although at arm's length, the hotel had been intended to become part of their owners' lifestyle. She felt that they could make excellent away-from-home accommodations for her and all members of her company. Having exclusive use of them could become part of their compensation packages.

Walking along the units, front and back, she found herself attracted to the design and facilitation of their interconnecting wooden stairways and walkways. She stepped toward and onto one of the boardwalks dividing two sections of the condo units, and, suppressing any notion she might be looking too far into the future, picked out one that would become hers.

Maintaining her air of touristy detachment, she retraced her steps onto the hotel's front patio and turned to photograph each separate block of condos. That done, she returned to her car for the drive home.

Scene 12
The Comfort of Le Moulin...

Ever since Adam ate the Apple, man has refrained from no folly.
~Author unknown

October 12, 2009, 2:34 p.m.
Her head was filled with possibilities. It felt like planning for a Christmas friends-and-family get-together: what to buy for whom and how to keep it secret; could she afford all that would be needed; who could do what, collaboratively, to make the undertaking surprising, exciting, and ultimately gratifying; and who to invite and who to leave off the list.

She sped through the village of Lac Sainte Marie, considerably above the speed limit, without noticing how fast she was going or the quaintness of little homes and business fronts that blended in postcard picturesqueness to distract ordinary city dwellers from their Monday-to-Friday dreariness while en route to their lakeside cottages.

By the time she got to the village of Low, several of the possibilities—and problems associated with them—had begun to separate themselves out from a several-day clutter of thoughts and words into separate little bins in her mind. Complexity's initial disarray was beginning to give way to orderliness. Uncertainty was losing out to a growing sense of what could be realized. Confidence is the domain of the self-assured, she thought, smiling her Lee smile.

Almost-unnoticed roadside signs had begun to introduce the town of La Pêche. She still thought of it wistfully as Wakefield, which somehow triggered the notion that she might be hungry. Perhaps not so much *hungry*, she realized, as was her need for a quiet, pleasant venue with a glass of Chardonnay at an isolated table where she could jot down some notes about the hotel: who should staff it, how much it all might cost as an early guess, and where she should begin to look for the funding that would make it all happen.

She slowed the car and turned right off Riverside Drive onto Mill Road, following its twists and turns until she came to Le Moulin's Inn & Spa. She had been there often and had even overnighted in one of its luxurious guest rooms in celebration of a wedding anniversary.

Nosing her car into the inn's near-empty parking lot, she paused before going inside long enough to take in the early autumn rush of colours, glowing as they were from the deciduous density of surrounding forest. She looked left, past the building, seeking again the timeless view of the waterfall's crystalline curtain, ever dividing into fingers of a nature's hand and tumbling over broken and oft-polished Precambrian granite with a force that once powered the mill's turbines. Reluctantly turning away, she slowly inhaled the pleasure of escape that an hour or so at this place would bring her.

Le Moulin, she knew, had had an interesting past. In 1838, a man named William Fairbairn had become intrigued by the power and beauty of the MacLaren Falls, the same rock shelf she had just been admiring. After writing Lieutenant John Colborn, the commander in chief of Upper and Lower Canada, Fairbairn had begun construction of the stone mill for the purpose of milling local grains into flour for farm families of the Gatineau and La Pêche river valleys. He had sold the mill a few years later to James MacLaren, a native of Scotland. MacLaren then had expanded the operations to include a sawmill, woolen mill, and general store. In 1910, a fire had destroyed the buildings. MacLaren rebuilt the following year, expanding the flourmill but discontinuing his woolen mill operations.

The mill's engine room was located in what is now the dining room. The mechanical and electrical turbines that drove heavy steel gears and pulleys required to transport, separate, and grind the grain were below the dining room.

The MacLaren mills operated until 1939, when larger mechanized flourmills made small-scale production uneconomic. From 1939 to 1980, the business operated as a gristmill, producing livestock feed for local area farmers. The Gatineau Historical Society later operated the mill as a heritage museum.

In 2000, two local residents restored the vacant building and its twenty-four acre site. Results of that rebuild had become increasingly familiar to Lee with each passing visit, and were going to be of special interest today.

Original beams inside survived to dominate the present reception area, having previously supported the grain silos above. The grain silos became four particularly prestigious guest rooms, and she had enjoyed staying in one of them. One turbine room had morphed into the new spa, the other into a wine cellar. Overall, Le Moulin by now boasted twenty-seven guest rooms, four executive retreat function rooms, a waterfall, a dining solarium, and a fireplace lounge.

Lee correctly presumed that because not many cars were in the parking lot, the staff inside wasn't busy. Good, she thought, she would ask for a seat in the lounge, preferably by the fireplace, if one were available.

One of the mill's hosts charmingly greeted her. After Lee stated her seating preference, he led her to a space quite familiar. There he stood by, waiting for her to become comfortable before gently inquiring what she might care to have for lunch. Without glancing at a menu she ordered a glass of house Chardonnay and a toasted BLT, the food being less important at that moment than the drink. He nodded obligingly, formally as a butler might, then melted away, shortly to rematerialize behind the bar.

Gazing around the old friend that this room had become, she reminded herself of its subdued opulence. Architecturally, she felt, this was a perfect restoration. She now knew that it was what she wanted to emulate in the second coming of her Mont Sainte Marie Hotel.

But she needed a break from all the intensity, to release her mind from its morning turbulence, having clawed its way through, as it had, everything she had seen of that tattered Mont Sainte Marie ruin. Giving in to that, she permitted a small segment of her cerebrum to remain active—to lock in memory for future reference images of features such as the fireplace immediately to the left of her sofa, to admire its curvaceous, asymmetrical grill and the way it had been inset between two of the building's supporting columns. She might be able to have a skilled craftsman replicate in "her" hotel glories like the ones she was now memorizing. That done to her satisfaction, she allowed herself to lapse into several minutes of mental neutrality, something she decided she would let extend until her lunch arrived. It was a form of meditation her unacknowledged narcissism allowed her to believe she had invented, and into which she would retreat—space and time permitting—whenever the intensity of her thought processes fragmented all new attempts at concentration into a scattering of images and text that defied coalescence. It was a dream state that she paradoxically enjoyed controlling, not believing for a moment that it might reflect, to an outside observer, a glint of insanity.

Not wanting to disturb, her host shook a linen napkin onto her lap and eased a coaster under her drink, lifting the glass with a crisply pressed handkerchief.

Pulling herself away from her reverie that was conscious primarily of the fireplace, she brought herself back to the moment and to her sandwich. Then, with her mind still reassembling itself, she ate it quickly.

Over the top of the sofa opposite her she could see the comfortably spaced pool table behind, looking very much like a well-crafted reproduction from an earlier era. How well done everything was! The support pillars, most of which were set into the beautiful broken-stone masonry that accentuated all exterior walls, were smooth and painted in a muted burnt-earth tone. Some of the casual chairs beneath the stone-slab windowsills were upholstered with the same fabric used to cover the two juxtaposed fireplace sofas, one of which she was sitting on. They were patterned in green and burgundy renderings of weathered-brick French shops, perhaps of a time earlier than that of the mill she now found herself admiring so. "Beautiful, every part of it!" she muttered.

The bar was behind her, stools arithmetically aligned and spaced, but no one, she noted, was polishing glasses. Her host had thought it more discrete to retire to the kitchen until he might again be heralded by this enigmatic presence whose gestures—sometimes inexplicably dramatic—had seemed to him to be coming from some mysterious pocket of her mind.

Refreshed and once again at one with her surroundings, she pursed her lips to sip the wine, turned the glass slowly by its stem, and peered deeply into its promise. Setting it down, she reopened the mental folder she would later title *Hotel Acquisition and Refurbishment—Funding*. Deciding that this might not be the best place for paper and pen, she tasked herself with memorizing the highlights of whatever she might be able to think through during the next thirty minutes.

First, what about cost? She reasoned that her venture would chew its way through several millions of dollars. The questions were and remained: How many millions? And, where to get it?

She decided that her first priority would be to deal with the dollars, but she needed to know how many.

She knew a guy—Sven Martin—who might be able to come close to a bottom-line number with little more than an initial walkthrough; his reputation suggested he was that good. He was a civil engineer that she had met at Stan and Chelsea's last Christmas party. He had a lot of health problems—complications he was born with—which he had overcome with sheer grit throughout and after dozens of surgeries. He lived life for today and crammed as much involvement as he could into each day that followed. The good news, for her, was that he was now CEO of an Ottawa start-up specializing in the development of big box stores, sell-everything pharmacies, and, peripherally, filler new-age mall additions. He was known in Toronto and Ottawa as the go-to guy, having survived, in Toronto, the bludgeoning that chain-store construction funders delighted in handing out. According to the word on the street, his company specialized in fulfilling contracts of her sort, either from scratch or as phoenix-like build outs from the shells of eviscerated has-beens. Like dentists preparing to fit new crowns, Sven's people were known to work with precision to grind away and discard old, decaying material, first confirming, and then saving, a solid base from which to create an edifice to behold. They took pride in each completion, celebrated each victory—just what she needed.

She would phone him and see if he had the interest and time to visit her Mont Sainte Marie ghost and assess whether or not it could be resurrected. It would be interesting to see what price he might place on her visualized subsets, for instance her earlier-imagined centrepiece— the tall fountain—done up as a within-nature waterfall.

Other synapses in her busy mind began to connect, opening parallel streams of thought. There was a possible spinoff from her negotiations with Sven. His wife, Abigail, was a nurse. They didn't have any children, and she only worked part-time. Perhaps she would want to consider a full-time opportunity, were it to pay, say, beyond what any big-city surgeon could expect to make. But, for now, that was a mental note she would have to leave as a to-do item. She would get in touch with her later and propose a nice lunch at Manotick's Three Gondolas restaurant, which was new and—for the village—very upscale.

Bringing herself back to Le Moulin's comfortable couch and fireplace, she moved her head consciously, slightly, as if flicking a lock of hair off her forehead, realizing she must appear to have fallen asleep. She brought herself smartly upright, smoothed her skirt, and catching her waiter's eye, asked for her bill, and paid it.

Before leaving the building she approached the receptionist to request a copy of Le Moulin's brochure. Then, sitting behind the wheel of her car, she reviewed all of its features, looking closely at the photographs to note details of its décor. She knew she'd want to go over these later with Sven.

She had been very taken with Le Moulin's interior stone walls, although realized that replicating them in her new place would be somewhat out of character and undoubtedly hugely expensive. She liked the fireplaces and the restoration of the original plank flooring. The grand piano was a nice touch; hers would be a restored turn-of-the-century Heintzman with a matching bench. She had seen one somewhere, its original wood colours recaptured. It had been lovely. She hadn't cared much for the recently popular and more affordable black-enamel Yamahas nor for other Pacific-Rim competitors' models. And, oh yes, Le Moulin's tray ceilings, with their attractively recessed pot lights, were another must. She would show them to Sven as well.

She started her car, climbed the hill leading out of Wakefield onto Highway 5, and headed home.

Scene 13
Who to Turn to for Funding...

"He who allows his day to pass by without practicing generosity and enjoying life's pleasures is like a blacksmith's bellows --
he breathes but does not live."
~Sanskrit Proverb

October 12, 2009, 5:16 p.m.
The miles were rolling away easily behind her. Her Nissan needed little guidance; she had selected it a couple of years prior for its ease of handling on country roads and now it knew her mind almost as well as she did. Sweeping at speed around patchy asphalt ledges on hillside-to-river curves along Highway 5, almost without seeing them, she let her mind race ahead over distant hurdles she would need to coax a phantasmal black stallion to clear: an imaginary companion she had an Alice-in-wonderland penchant for calling up at such moments. The hazard she most feared he would balk at was a thorny bramble of hedge-apple her mind had titled *Project Funder*. Her black phantom, fearing unavoidable

thorns, wasn't likely to take it in easy stride; maybe she would need a second, perhaps even a third, run at it.

She imagined her funder couldn't be any Bay Street guy. It would have to be some wolf in sheep's clothing: someone presentable, white collar or at least pale blue, whose territory might stray above a shadowy stakeout he had established on the south side of the fuzzy delineator separating lawful from what is not. Someone fronting for the mob, she reasoned, could be a good benefactor. They would have access to the money and would be, if she were lucky, in need of a north-side partner whose wannabe enterprise might launder some of it for them.

The mob, she smiled. It was an amazing subculture that had existed, seemingly forever. A corruption of the Romans, she wondered? Maybe. Who knew? She'd check it out when she got home. Anyway, she reasoned, it was probably made up of more reliable people than could be disentombed from whatever functional parts remained off most Western governments. It had, she knew, an unwritten, unbridgeable code of conduct. Transgressions were dealt with harshly. Deals were made with a passing of envelopes and the nodding of heads to indicate mutual understanding. People could find themselves still alive even while hardening into the foundation of a high-rise tower if they didn't follow the rules. Or at least that's the way she had pictured it. And yet the Dons seemed seldom to be punished, or, in the unlikely event of a conviction, usually were handed token jail time, as if somehow the law couldn't or didn't want to poke a gavel into a hornet's nest. Or maybe it was just a question of which side had, or could afford, the best lawyers.

Who on the dark side did she know? She hadn't spent much time—no time at all, actually—in the back alleys of society and didn't really know where to begin.

Familiar landmarks passed her by, diminishing from her periphery into emptiness. She could see the graying image of some of them reflected in her rearview mirror without knowing why she was even bothering to look. These distractions, though, brought her back to the present and told her she was getting closer to home, nearer where her real life existed.

She knew that the day's explorations, if she were to persist with them, warned her of being within a stone's throw of putting in jeopardy the pleasant life she had had for the past seven decades. Why would she even be thinking about this, she asked herself? It seemed insane, although exhilaratingly insane. A shiver of uncertainty passed through her body as she contemplated risking everything for the sake of little more that a chancy adventure, and that admittedly built around self-titillation. She didn't need the money nor did she fancy spending time in prison were she to make a slip. Her marriage, even now, could be in jeopardy. Carlyle—quiet, lovable Carlyle—recently hadn't been able to make head or tail of where her head might be. And lifelong friends, were she to fall from grace, would have little or nothing to do with her.

But somehow that didn't matter. This was like morphine; maybe she had had a Mephistophelian syringe too many. Her new world was glittering before her like an infinite number of stars in the blackest sky she had ever known. Happiness was a part of it. She was becoming hooked, she knew.

Happiness was such an odd word, she thought. What was it, really? Hadn't she been happy without all this? Pulling down the driver's-side sun visor, she glanced into its vanity mirror. There, darkly reflected, was an image of the upper part of her face. Was that the face of happiness? Is that what it looked like? She didn't know. Alternating glances between the highway and the mirror, she attempted to penetrate beneath the eyes looking back at her. Who was she, really? Did she actually know herself? Had she ever known? Well, let's see, she thought. She had been a gregarious person, a floral presence, really, by choice, within any circle. She accepted that to her detractors her wit at times might have seemed wicked, her tongue perhaps piercing as a thorn. But that had occurred only when she had deemed a retaliatory masterstroke appropriate: a need to map-pin an ephemeral printout of her point of view onto the foreheads of others in the room, painful as that may have seemed to them. What was wrong with that? It was a hallmark, a brand really, that she had claimed as her own. For her, dominance was scintillating; prominence itself wasn't the peak of her ambition. She had always needed to climb higher, to be at the pinnacle, no matter what risk that might entail. And now she was climbing again, but this time without a rope.

This adventure, even the very notion of the adventure, had taken over her being, trumping all options. From first blush her imagination had propelled her into a netherworld. In fact, the doorway back into yesteryears' existence might be now closed to her forever. If this were to become her game, she would have to play to win. She had won a lot of games, she knew, and she felt she could think her way through this one.

The traffic thinned. Home was getting closer.

Braking at the end of her driveway, she reflected on an interesting possibility. Her mind turned toward being in front of her home-office computer. She switched off the Nissan's ignition, killed its lights, picked up her camera while stuffing the Le Moulin brochure into her purse, and then nearly tripped on the top step in her haste to get into the house.

Good, she thought. Carlyle wasn't home. She set down her things on her office desk and, shucking arms free of her jacket, reached to bring the computer's screen to life. Finding her chair by feel behind her, she settled into it, typing two words into Hal's uncomplaining brain. Hal had long been her pet name for Google, ever since Larry Page and Sergey Brin had launched Google's IPO. She wished again she had bought in early.

Her today's appetite, it had seemed to nonjudgmental Hal, was an undefined entry that she had titled *the Mob*. He dutifully presented her with a cornucopian discharge of possible starting points. Scratching at the black rim of her monitor, she teased, "Come on Hal, you know I want you to be more specific than that. No, I don't need to know about motorcycle gangs or assorted collections of ordinary criminals, no matter how popular you might think they are. I want you to tell me about the catholicism of the criminal world's high priests: I want you to tell me about the Mafia and about their order and discipline."

She waited, her lower lip drawn between lightly clenched teeth, biting at the flesh but without incurring tissue injury, like a cat toying its way through the prelude to a fatal bite when displaying a caught mouse to its mistress. "Come on, Hal," she urged. "I need you to focus.

You know Carlyle won't be pleased if he finds me letting you wander around in your too-frequent universe of uncertainty. If you help me now, I won't unplug you."

She tapped at the keyboard again and hit enter. The screen sensed a need for haste while rearranging itself, as new choices cascaded down the glass like a woman shaking her way into a loose-fitting dress, hesitating in flashes of uncertainty, as though Hal were having second thoughts about presenting some of the offerings. She scanned down the tumult for something specific to the organization's early history. "Thank you, Hal," she said, as if speaking to a boy child having just presented all As on a year-end report card.

Settling on a lengthy piece, she paused, closed her eyes for several seconds, and returned then to its start, taking time to absorb the origins of Sicily's most infamous regurgitation of evil onto an unprepared world. It took her a while to absorb the whole treatise, but she was enjoying herself, more relaxed now. Fascinating, she thought, reading aloud to help her capture the essence of it, just as she had done in university when prepping for exams.

> Modern scholars believe that its seeds were planted in the upheaval of Sicily's transition out of feudalism in 1812 and its later annexation by mainland Italy in 1860. Under feudalism, the nobility owned most of the land and enforced law and order through their private armies. After 1812, the feudal barons steadily sold off or rented their lands to private citizens. Primogeniture was abolished, land could no longer be seized to settle debts, and one-fifth of the land was to become private property of the peasants. After Italy annexed Sicily in 1860, it redistributed a large share of public and church land to private citizens. The result was a huge boom in landowners: from 2,000 in 1812 to 20,000 by 1861. The nobles also released their private armies to let the state take over the task of law enforcement. However, the authorities

were incapable of properly enforcing property rights and contracts, largely due to their inexperience with free market capitalism. Lack of manpower was also a problem: there were often less than 350 active policemen for the entire island. Some towns did not have any permanent police force, only visited every few months by some troops to collect malcontents, leaving criminals to operate with impunity from the law in the interim. With more property owners came more disputes that needed settling, contracts that needed enforcing, and properties that needed protecting. Because the authorities were undermanned and unreliable, property owners turned to extralegal arbitrators and protectors. These extralegal protectors would eventually organize themselves into the first Mafia clans.

Banditry was a growing problem at the time. Rising food prices, the loss of public and church lands, and the loss of feudal common rights pushed many desperate peasants to banditry. With no police to call upon, local elites in countryside towns recruited young men into "companies-at-arms" to hunt down thieves and negotiate the return of stolen property, in exchange for a pardon for the thieves and a fee from the victims. These companies-at-arms were often made up of former bandits and criminals, usually the most skilled and violent of them. Whilst this saved communities the trouble of training their own policemen, this may have made the companies-at-arms more inclined to collude with their former brethren rather than destroy them.

Mafia activity was most prevalent in the most prosperous areas of western Sicily, especially Palermo, where the dense concentrations of landowners and merchants offered ample opportunities for protection racketeering and extortion. There, a protector could serve multiple clients, giving him greater independence. The greater number of clients demanding protection also allowed him to charge high prices. The landowners in this region were also frequently absent and could not watch over their properties should the Mafioso withdraw protection, further increasing his bargaining power.

The lucrative citrus orchards around Palermo were a favourite target of extortionists and protection racketeers, as they had a fragile production system that made them quite vulnerable to sabotage. Mafia clans forced landowners to hire their members as custodians by scaring away unaffiliated applicants. Cattle ranchers were also very vulnerable to thieves, and so they too needed Mafioso protection.

In 1864, Niccolò Turrisi Colonna, leader of the Palermo National Guard, wrote of a "sect of thieves" that operated across Sicily. This "sect" was mostly rural, composed of cattle thieves, smugglers, wealthy farmers, and their guards. The sect made "affiliates every day of the brightest young people coming from the rural class, of the guardians of the fields in the Palermitan countryside, and of the large number of smugglers; a sect which gives and receives protection to and from certain men who make a living on traffic and internal commerce. It is a sect with little or no fear of public bodies, because its members believe that they can easily elude this." It had special signals to recognize each other, offered protection services, scorned the law, and had a code of loyalty and non-interaction with the police known as umirta (*humility*). Colonna warned in his report that the

Italian government's brutal and clumsy attempts to crush unlawfulness only made the problem worse by alienating the populace. An 1865 dispatch from the prefect of Palermo to Rome first officially described the phenomenon as a "Mafia".

Mafiosi meddled in politics early on, bullying voters into voting for candidates they favoured. At this period in history, only a small fraction of the Sicilian population could vote, so a single Mafia boss could control a sizeable chunk of the electorate and thus wield considerable political leverage. Mafiosi used their allies in government to avoid prosecution as well as persecute less well-connected rivals. The highly fragmented and shaky Italian political system allowed cliques of Mafia-friendly politicians to exert a lot of influence.

In a series of reports between 1898 and 1900, Ermanno Sangiorgi, the police chief of Palermo, identified 670 Mafiosi belonging to eight Mafia clans that went through alternating phases of cooperation and conflict. The report mentioned initiation rituals and codes of conduct, as well as criminal activities that included counterfeiting, ransom kidnappings, robbery, murder, and witness intimidation. The Mafia also maintained funds to support the families of imprisoned members and pay defense lawyers.

Well, she thought, exploring more references to their initiation rituals and codes of conduct…marvellous!

So, she concluded, it had worked well for them, and was thriving today; bullet-proof, almost, like Kevlar. Unless, of course, the players fucked up.

And, there was one so very close to home, she was almost sure. How interesting!

She pushed back and tried to relax, but on this day the attraction of her grand plan hadn't left her alone for more than a few minutes. Feeling now she had to secure it—the details of it—safely away from Carlyle and the world, she swung closed that portal in her mind, sensing it clang shut like a hatch segregating the torpedo compartment from the command centre of a submarine. She would have to be ever vigilant, at home—everywhere.

Smiling her hedge-apple smile, she realized that she would be captaining a sinking ship if struck from an unexpected quarter, the corpses of her fellow travellers to become companions during her imagined slow descent; bow tilted down, hull grating along rock shelves, bottoming finally into a nature's sarcophagus somewhere within gravity's last abysm; a frond of gray silt blossoming around the disturbance, then settling, leaving only a trace exhalation of bubbles to stream from the broken casing. She would come to know absolute solitude, briefly. Troglodytes, venturing from coral caves into the surrounding gloom of microbially filtered sea bottom light for an inquiring probe would be initially apprehensive, sensing a need for caution, but hunger would centre them on the ship's invitation, sweeping 'round her like beach crabs circling a sandpiper with a broken wing. The spectre who called herself Aloneness would be there to greet her; to breathe toward her from the darkness of death's impenetrably black hood, soothing her softly, patiently, saying "I told you so, Lee!"

It worried her, but only fleetingly. "Everyone dies," she said to no one at all, switching off her computer monitor. "It just makes the game more interesting."

Scene 14
A Different Kind of Lender...

> *"Nothing so soothes our vanity as a display of greater vanity in others; it make us vain, in fact, of our modesty."*
> *-Louis Kronenberger*

October 13, 2009, 10:34 a.m.

She breakfasted late, alone, at the Amadora Cafe in the Village Mews; her head tilted, fingers combing through yesterday's thoughts, a hand unconsciously pushing through the twists of her hair.

The Amadora was in many ways a refuge for her. She appreciated the warmth and ambiance of the place, its ever-changing consignment of artwork and its brickwork fireplace angled into a back-most corner. She always looked for this same table by the fire, happy whenever she found it unoccupied. The Amadora's owner, a tireless, talented, Portuguese philanthropist—a benevolent sweetheart—frequently chatted with her when other customers' needs had been met.

But Lee didn't want that today; today her mind was on quite another restaurant, and for this day she craved aloneness. Keeping her face deliberately toward the gaslit ceramic logs, she absorbed into some inner art gallery their orange and black wickedness, the flames undulating a Mata Harian dance, performed just for her.

Her thoughts floated across town, to another place she also frequented—the Three Gondolas.

Its owner was of a different ilk: flamboyant, vain, and over-the-top showy, bringing to mind a human incarnation of a bird of paradise. Everything he did, every gesture, effervesced a certain Papal richness—a self-assured, loaves-and-fishes, feeding-the-multitudes generosity. All he touched had the Midas Effect, or seemed to.

"Yes," she said, he was that: *Phrygia—the King of Phrygia!* The word had such a delicious texture when rolled round in her mouth, anomalous in sound to a softened, frequently voiced obscenity. Appropriate, she thought, smiling the smile she reserved for unpretending, mirthful moments—her honest smile.

So, this could be her guy. Maybe, just maybe, if she played him right.

It would have to be a multifaceted presentation, necessarily convincing, and by then well rehearsed; a one-shot opportunity to sell her plan, assuming he would agree to meet with her at all.

Were he to buy in, she would need him to up-front the clinic's building acquisition and renovation costs. If indeed he turned out to be a gray-market money dude, it might be best for him to oversee both the location's physical and fiscal security. Assuming he had survived within his milieu this long, he would no doubt be better at it than she would. She would also suggest to him that he and his colleagues install a financial adviser to live on site. The adviser could report to him and her jointly and would assist in persuading clients to move their money out of individual bank accounts and into one or another holding mechanism, thus allowing each to prepay their operation and recovery time at the clinic.

In drafting her pitch, she had rationalized that a client might need to be encouraged to invest in gold bullion in the form of gold wafers, given that gold prices had been on the rise recently and the American dollar was likely to remain in a state of flux for at least the next decade. That could be the clients' hedge against near- and long-term inflation and might well yield them a tidy profit. They would deposit their newly acquired wafers into clinic-supplied safety deposit boxes. Concurrently, they might be advised to liquidate *all* their assets—houses, vehicles, boats, etc.—given that each would want to plan a near-future relocation to a country of choice. Once *in situ*, they would of course need an accepted-anywhere currency. Thus having made their assets readily accessible, they might want to consider giving a proxy to the clinic's lawyer or financial adviser to facilitate channelling smaller amounts of gold-equivalent to them, first converted into a fiat currency. It would all be part of the corporation's package: an extension of the clinic's no-charge legal and financial advice services. If all manner of lifestyle-amenities were to be provided, residents would have no need to monitor their off-site accounts; the clinic would simply offer on-site safety deposit boxes for storage of keepsakes, documents, and gold or currency. Such a facility could be installed to meet commercial bank-vault standards. And, as a bonus, she could pass off her external security arrangements, which were necessarily elaborate—worrisomely so, actually—by telling them that the guards, fencing, and electronic-access system were just part of the need to protect their assets within the clinic's *bank*.

Obviously, that would open a whole new window of opportunity for increasing the clinic's profitability.

But—and this was a big but—it wasn't perfect. The concept had a potential glitch, a problem she would have to further explore, presumably with her funder. It was about how, initially, to get the money safely out of each client's home bank account, be that one or many. Were she to ding each of them half a million dollars for their *operation,* her guess was that any Canadian banker would want to do more due diligence than just raise an eyebrow. So, the question was, how to get her clients to withdraw their money *in person* and hand it over to her and her team? It would take effective, believable marketing to pull it off. Each mark would need to visit—or be chauffeured to—his or her bank to reassure management that such withdrawals were legitimate and were what the client wanted.

This emphasized her need to deal only with wealthy elderlies, ones likely to have had a history of making authoritarian demands of their banking minions to allow large withdrawals. She presumed business people or their widows. Widows would be better, easier, more gullible, if old and lonely enough. She had spent a lot of time earlier thinking about how to price the clinic's service, having more or less settled on a flat half-million dollars, all services included. But was that right? Would potential clients balk at that amount? Not, she guessed if they were rich enough or out-of-touch enough or both. Her target market would have to be further narrowed to family-discarded, en-route-to-dying, upper middle-class or elite-echelon people whose net worth bottom-lined at, as a minimum, two million dollars unencumbered. That would have to become her acceptance threshold, nothing below.

She sipped thoughtfully at a second cup of coffee, continuing to mull over the get-their-money-early question, not wanting it to become a funder-presentation showstopper. She had always had a way of commanding her brain to shift into overdrive when need be, to become mischievously creative, and she willed that capability to self-invoke now. She could almost feel the challenge clicking in. Fresh thoughts emerging from a pupae stage, lining up in some cerebral starting gate, still-wet wings navigating tight turns, scraping but not slowing at intersecting corners of her labyrinthine mind, competing for the prize—a

The Fontana Resurrection

more refined answer, something she believed lurked there, just needing to be fleshed out.

Ah, she paused, tucking her chin toward her throat and blinking her eyes to greet a forming smile, there was one! If, she supposed, her mind plucking the wings off the winning thought, clients were to need a value-for-money comparison, she would give them the China-versus-America organ-transplant model. In China, a kidney transplant operation would run around $70,000, a liver $160,000, and a heart $120,000. Although unattainable to China's poor, the money compared very favourably to fees in the United States, where a kidney transplant can demand $100,000, a liver $250,000, and a heart $860,000. Chinese prices, she would say—providing them with press clippings to back her claim—have made China a major provider of organs and transplantation surgeries to other countries. But would her clients be willing to risk that? From China? She would argue that they would be better safe than sorry: Organs, like a second life, are hard to come by; it's the time-proven economists' law of supply and demand that dictates the price. Often, when Western volunteers—living or the newly dead—weren't available in time for a patient's need, that person would have to resort to a questionable offshore *acquisition,* something still unlawful in Canada. But, not so in China. There, a heart harvested from an executed prisoner—perhaps a Falun Gong transgressor—could be bought, and such transactions were court approved. However, she would argue, even the Chinese weren't offering a second chance at life, not at *any* price—at least not yet, until they can emulate the Swiss breakthrough. So wouldn't hers be a greater value than, say, a heart, the latter being only the price of a decent Mercedes away from a million dollars? Her cost of service was competitive, she would add, and nonnegotiable; folks were already lining up for it, although the clinic's privacy regulations forbade her from disclosing names.

She sensed that the good news was that as soon as she got the money, she would be able to move it offshore and keep it secure until she and the team needed it. She had researched the notion of opening and maintaining at least some of the clinic's bank accounts in Switzerland and such other countries as Belize. She had discovered that the former had recently been taking—at the insistence of the United States—greater due-diligence precautions related to money laundering. The latter, although laissez-faire in its enforcement, looked iffy unless an investor retired there. Even then, it would be difficult to get the money out of the country.

It was a different matter, though, to maintain an offshore safety deposit box. One scenario that looked promising was the Austrian Palace. In fact, she thought it was just about perfect. Carefully hidden money or gold wafers could be jetted from Ottawa to Vienna at irregular intervals, by herself or one of the *doctors* to be deposited without hassle. From that point on it could be accessed without any embarrassing formalities.

But, still the question lingered: how to fleece them of their cash, initially?

Perhaps it would have to become a precondition of admittance. Clients would need to understand that this procedure was not yet an operation sanctioned by the Royal College of Physicians and Surgeons of Canada nor was any part of it funded by Canada's health plan. That's because, her staff would need to say, the procedure, miraculous as it may seem, was deemed experimental in countries outside Switzerland and as such would be forced to endure years of bureaucratic tidying up before becoming mainstream. Although formal certification eventually would happen, it might, by then, be too late to help present-day folks that the clinic was ready to serve. Trained-in-country surgeons were available, here, now. Canada was fortunate to be first in having been invited by Geneva to expand the program. Our doctors were handpicked, much like Dr. Christiaan Neethling Barnard, who—as the clients would be invited to recall—performed the world's first human heart transplant operation, back in 1967. He was South African, educated at the University of Cape Town. That operation lasted nine hours and used a team of thirty people. It was, she would say, miraculous. And, Dr. Barnard later wrote, "For a dying man it is not a difficult decision because he knows he is at the end. If a lion chases you to the bank of a river filled with crocodiles, you will leap into the water, convinced you have a chance to swim to the other side." As you'll recall, she would remind them, many people after that died waiting for the medical miracle to be replicated in other countries.

In short, she thought, *whatever* the fabric of deceit her *doctors,* in their white and green coats, might need to weave would become part of their getting-to-know-your-clients program. What the hell, she mused: priests, bishops, and the Pope can sell Catholics on the merits of tithing to support Mother Church, supposedly to save humanity from damnation; even television evangelists were making tax-free fortunes from the gullible by pitching a variety of good causes, ostensibly to benefit the world's have-nots. Just send money, they would say.

She knew of an example, actually, as near at hand as Toronto.

She had of course brought her laptop to the Amadora with her, wanting to polish the ever-evolving draft of her business plan. Pulling her gaze away from the flame, she broke open the Apple and, stretching her fingers across its keyboard, typed "Okay Hal, tell me what you know about Benny Hinn." Within a nanosecond Hal coughed up an answer, happier this time than before to be seen as unequivocal:

> "Benny" Hinn…is a televangelist, best known for his regular *Miracle Crusades*—revival meeting/ faith healing summits that are usually held in large stadiums in major cities, which are later broadcast worldwide on his television program, *This Is Your Day.*
>
> Hinn was born in Jaffa, in 1952, in the then newly established state of Israel to Palestinian Christian parents. He was raised within the Eastern Orthodox tradition.
>
> Soon after the 1967 Arab-Israeli War, Hinn's family emigrated to Toronto, where he attended but later prematurely left the Georges Vanier Secondary School. In his books, Hinn states that his father was the mayor of Jaffa at the time of his birth, and that as a child, he was socially isolated and was handicapped

by a severe stutter, but was nonetheless a first-class student.

Horseshit, she thought. Good student? She knew Hinn's critics had disputed those claims. She continued reading.

> As a teenager in Toronto, Hinn converted from Greek Orthodoxy to Pentecostalism, eventually joining a singing troupe made up of young evangelicals. Upon moving to the United States, Hinn traveled to Orlando, Florida, where he founded the Orlando Christian Center in 1983. Eventually, Hinn began claiming that God was using him as a conduit for healings, and began holding healing services in his church. These new *Miracle Crusades* were soon held at large stadiums and auditoriums across the United States and the world, the first nationally televised service being held in Flint, Michigan, in 1989. During the early 1990s, Hinn launched a new daily talk show called *This Is Your Day*, which to this day airs clips of supposed miracles from Hinn's Miracle Crusades.
>
> Hinn's ministry began to rapidly grow from there, winning praise as well as criticism from fellow Christian leaders. In 1999, he stepped down as pastor of the Orlando Christian Center, moving his ministry's administrative headquarters to Grapevine, Texas, a suburb of Fort Worth, while hosting *This Is Your Day* from a television studio in Orange County, California, where he now lives with his family.
>
> He is the author of a number of bestselling inspirational Christian books. His thirty-minute TV program *This Is Your Day* is among the world's most-watched Christian programs, seen on various Christian television networks.

> Hinn conducts regular Miracle Crusades—revival meeting/faith healing events held in sports stadiums in major cities throughout the world. Tens of millions attend his Holy Spirit Miracle Crusades each year.
>
> Benny Hinn claims to have spoken to one billion people through his crusades, including memorable crusades with attendance of 7.3 million people (in three services) in India, the largest healing service in recorded history.
>
> Hinn's teachings are Evangelical and Charismatic, accepting the validity of spiritual gifts, and Word of Faith in origin, with a focus on financial prosperity. Benny Hinn Ministries claims to support 60 mission organizations across the world and several orphanages around the world, and claims to house and feed over 100,000 children a year and support 45,000 children daily because of his donors.

Yeah, right, Lee thought, unattended stables are full of this stuff!

> A controversial aspect of Hinn's ministry is his teaching on, and demonstration of, a phenomenon he dubs *The Anointing*—the power purportedly given by God and transmitted through Hinn to carry out supernatural acts. At Hinn's Miracle Crusades, he has allegedly healed attendees of blindness, deafness, cancer, AIDS, and severe physical injuries. However, investigative reports by the *Los Angeles Times,* NBC's *Dateline,* the CBC's *Fifth Estate,* and the Nine Network's *60 Minutes* have called these claims into question.
>
> Hinn has also caused controversy for theological remarks and claims he has made during TV appearances. In 1999, Hinn appeared on the Trinity Broadcasting Network, claiming that God had given

him a vision predicting the resurrection of thousands of dead people after watching the network—laying out a scenario of people placing their dead loved ones' hands on TV screens tuned into the station—and suggesting that TBN would be "an extension of Heaven to Earth."

Hinn is notable for his mistaken prophecies relating to the end times, including the destruction of homosexuals in the United States of America, the death of Fidel Castro in the 1990s, and the end of the world in 1992 and 1999.

In April 2001, HBO aired a documentary entitled *A Question of Miracles* that focused on Hinn and a well-documented fellow Word-of-Faith German minister based in Africa, Reinhard Bonnke. Both Hinn and Bonnke offered full access to their events to the documentary crew, and the documentary team followed seven cases of miracle healings from Hinn's crusade over the next year. The film's director claimed that they did not find any cases where people were actually healed by Hinn. [The film's director] said in a *New York Times* interview that 'If I had seen miracles [from Hinn's ministry], I would have been happy to trumpet it...but in retrospect, I think they do more damage to Christianity than the most committed atheist.'

In November 2004, the CBC Television show *The Fifth Estate* did a special titled "Do You Believe in Miracles" on the apparent transgressions committed by Benny Hinn's ministry. With the aid of hidden cameras and crusade witnesses, the producers of the show demonstrated Benny's apparent misappropriation of funds, his fabrication of the truth, and the way in which his staff chose crusade audience members to come on stage to proclaim their miracle healings. In particular, the investigation highlighted the fact that the most desperate miracle seekers who attend a Hinn crusade—the quadriplegics, the brain-damaged, virtually anyone with a visibly obvious physical condition—are never allowed up on stage; those who attempt to get in the line of possible healings are intercepted and directed to return to their seats. At one Canadian service, hidden cameras showed a mother who was carrying her Muscular Dystrophy-afflicted daughter, Grace, being stopped by two screeners when they attempted to get into the line for a possible blessing from Benny. The screeners asked the mother if Grace had been healed, and when the mother replied in the negative, they were told to return to their seats; the pair got out of line, but Grace, wanting 'Pastor Benny to pray for [her],' asked her mother to support her as she tried to walk as a show of 'her faith in action,' according to the mother. After several unsuccessful attempts at walking, the pair left the arena in tears, both mother and daughter visibly upset at being turned aside and crying as they explained to the undercover reporters that all Grace had wanted was for Benny to pray for her, but the staffers rushed them out of the line when they found out Grace had not been healed. A week later at a service in Toronto, Baptist evangelist Justin Peters, who wrote his Masters in Divinity thesis on Benny Hinn and has attended numerous Hinn crusades since 2000 as part of his research for his thesis and for a seminar he developed about the Word of Faith movement entitled *A Call for Discernment,* also demonstrated to the hidden cameras that 'people who look like me'—Peters has cerebral palsy, walks with arm-crutches, and is obviously and visibly disabled—'are never allowed on stage…it's always somebody who has some disability or disease that cannot be readily seen.' Like Grace and her mother, Peters was quickly intercepted as he came out of the wheelchair section (there is one at every crusade, situated at the back of the audience, far away from the stage, and never filmed for Hinn's TV show) in an attempt to join the line of those waiting to go onstage, and was told to take a seat.

In December 2006, BHM sent out a mailing asking for donations toward a new Gulfstream G4SP jet valued at an estimated US$36 million and costing over US$600,000/year to maintain and operate. The 22-seat craft was purchased in 2007 and christened *Dove One*.

Hinn married Suzanne Harthern on August 4, 1979. The couple have four children together. Harthern filed papers in Orange County (California) Superior Court on February 1, 2010, seeking a divorce, citing irreconcilable differences.

In July 2010, both Hinn and fellow televangelist Paula White denied allegations in the *National Enquirer* claiming that the two were engaged in an affair.

What a sweetheart! Lee said to herself, admiring the success of a fellow traveler. Here the guy is, exposed on the Internet as a scam artist, and still the faithful flock to him. If, she mused, this asshole can suck money out of gullibility's central core, why couldn't she?

Okay, she concluded, enough for now. She'd polish the pitch later, at home. The success of scam artists was all in how they spun their yarns; her people would have to become damn good at it.

Scene 15
The Three Gondolas...

October 15, 2009, 12:36 p.m.
Okay, what about this Three Gondolas place? Lee asked herself, quietly finding a seat in the restaurant's barroom; and more importantly, what about the guy who owns it?

As had happened here during midweek afternoon hours, she found herself being the only customer, not only at her table, but also in the room itself.

The bartender greeted her with an icy smile and picked up a menu before starting toward where she was sitting. She was an attractive Asian—perhaps Chinese, maybe Vietnamese, of indeterminate age, as Asians sometimes seem to Caucasians—who looked young, vibrant, healthy. Not a tall person, but athletic, she had the body of a gymnast or maybe a belted tae kwon do aficionado.

Unusual for a waitress, Lee thought. The lady had fierce, intelligent eyes—analytical eyes. Although polite, she exuded a coolness that her smile couldn't cover. Lee wondered how long she had been doing this type of work. More specifically, she wondered what she might have done before and where?

Putting that aside, she ordered a glass of house white and requested a few more minutes to get to the lunch menu's yet-unturned last page, hopefully there to find something in the way of a more-cultivated exclusivity on offer. Glancing up, she felt somehow that the waitress had been studying her, perhaps had remembered her—unfavourably—from previous visits, a feeling that was suddenly, inexplicably, disconcerting. With self-confidence now in full flight, she wondered whether she had been hasty in ordering just the *house* wine; it may have come across to her apparent, stonily silent analyst as having been a bit plebeian, especially if she were to perk up now and ask for something more in the order of a chef's challenge.

She got over it. Stay calm and carry on, she told herself, remembering the crown-topped slogan she had seen pressed onto some Brit's T-shirt in a London pub.

This historically significant house, she reflected, had been well kept. She knew more than most about it, having looked into the place before returning here this time, including a bit of its history and the sequence of ownership hand-offs before its conversion to a restaurant. She had known Jerome Carmichael—an interesting surname, she'd learned, of Scottish origin, it being a locational name from the parish of Carmichael in Lanarkshire, dating back to the early 13th Century—the building's previous owner before her questionable new friend and presumed benefactor-to-be, Luciano DiPasquale, had wrested it from him.

Gerry, as he'd preferred to be called by friends, had painstakingly reworked the home's interior without sacrificing any of its earlier external charm. He had added an architecturally compatible board-and-batten garage—a very large one—with a full basement beneath, as well as a loft above. He had built an archway between the main house and garage, which lent itself then and now to being a pleasant enclosed span bridging an inviting walkway that ran beneath, the latter leading to the property's rear garden. She had been "invited"—at her own instigation, actually—to visit this house during its previous incarnation, and Gerry had given her a personally conducted tour. He had also given her permission to audio-record his description:

> 1126 John St., formerly 1126 O'Grady Street was built in about 1870 by a guy named Williams, who, around twelve years later—around 1880-1885—opened the first commercial bakery in Manotick. The bake-oven doors still remain downstairs. Horses then had been driven onto the property at the north side of the house, around back, and their drivers would have loaded up with baked goods. I think at some point he operated a pushcart around town, selling baked goods.

Then he moved to Montréal, somewhere around the late 1890s. The house was subsequently occupied by a succession of town doctors. Following that, a family named Hall made this their home in the twenties and thirties.

Then came McColtrum, who was one of the founders of Carleton University. He lived here in the late 1940s until 1955-56. That family made a few changes to the place.

Two or three other owners followed until I picked it up in 1988-89. When I first took the house over I was meeting people that were in their eighties who'd been *repaired* here, and a woman who was born here.

So, the house is Victorian Gothic. The kitchen, as it is now, was an addition. And then the sun porch was added. For years, what had been where the porch is now was just a shed that covered the back of the bake oven. There was a door below that that would let you come into the basement proper. The bakery-era accounts for the three or four chimneys on the house, including the big one going down to the ovens' rock wall, below.

And that had been it—a wrap. Succinct. Nice guy, she'd thought, a bit introspective, but very accommodating in this situation. After all, it had been her idea. She had thanked him for that and hadn't seen much of him since.

She had really liked the house and felt sadness when a guy with a reputation for aggressive entrepreneurship had bought it. The village's old-timers had fought the transition—labelled it a travesty—all the way to the Ontario Municipal Board. The new owner had had his lawyers take it from there, knowing the OMB would rule in his favour. And it had, of course.

But what about its gregarious *current* owner, she wondered? Possibly still on the right side of fifty-five, he had seemingly waved some magic wand over what had earlier been the bakery and later the doctor's house, and had transformed it into a to-die-for dining venue. To do this, she thought, he must have managed to slide down some rainbow's arc and drop arse first into a pot of gold—a big one at that.

There had been an ostentatiousness about him that couldn't quite ooze its way past her bullshit filter. The quintessential narcissist's look-at-me bling, she had observed, was all there: the heavy gold, wherever it might show; the splendorous Swiss-made wristwatch; and a weighty ring with diamonds inset, which she imagined would have triggered, were he still alive, an orgasm right there on Liberace's piano bench. His clothes suggested a new, upscale definition of business casual, all tailored to perfection, all apparently cut from the finest fabrics. There had been the same exacting standard for his shoes. Did he wonder if she had noticed? She hoped not.

Then, there was the car. His car. *One* of his cars. It had been the first time that she had seen it. It was almost too much, that and his flourish whenever he would venture out onto the street to display it. He would wave, with an illusionist's flare, although without the hankie, then fold himself into the open-top black Maserati GranCabrio to bask in the glow of any admiring audience. She had to admit that he had achieved a car-buff's dream, albeit here in sleepy, backwater Manotick.

His home, too, was an effusive excess, a colossus, actually; it was shaded within densely treed acres and set among other McMansions spread along one of Rideau Forest's richest, wending drives.

During meet-and-greet chats with Three Gondolas customers, he had been known to parachute into the conversation a suggestion that he had another place—somewhere in the American Midwest, although she couldn't recall the exact location—where a second Maserati was parked in its garage. He apparently preferred that one over his Manotick showpiece.

Should a thus-engaged customer happen to query the roots of his success, she had noticed that he would drift into obfuscations. She supposed them vagaries to leave the listener believing his financial interests

The Fontana Resurrection

lay in one or another engineering activity in Montréal or the western provinces, somewhere.

The restaurant, he had implied, was a pet project he had wanted to set up as an amusement for his wife. Too often, though, whenever she had been there, there were few others in the place. How, she wondered, could it possibly have been paying for itself?

"Well, close enough," she muttered in what may have been loud enough to be an indiscreet whisper, looking then with a quick twist of her head to see if the bartender/waitress might have heard.

The owner must be *connected*, she concluded. If her hypothesis was right, this guy Luciano DiPasquale might have millions more that he and his buddies could want to wash through an untapped enterprise, presented as a joint venture to masquerade as legitimate. It seemed worth a try, a feeler, anyway, she thought.

She wondered if she was really bold enough to give it a shot, quivering with last-minute trepidation at the possible consequences of being wrong. Well, yes—why not? That's why she was here, wasn't it?

DiPasquale could become her next and perhaps most dangerous conquest, ever, she smiled confidently, broadly, keeping her face turned away from the barkeep.

She had met him at various social activities in the village. He might remember that, if prompted. It was during those soaked-olive cocktails that she had decided to begin frequenting his Three Gondolas establishment. She had made it her favourite, loitering there over afternoon drinks, waiting for a chance to again say hello.

She had noticed him, passingly, while there, often with younger business types who, like himself, favoured colourful, sometimes open-topped roadsters. Some had Québec plates. His, however, was the one they had all salivated over—Corvettes and Porches just weren't in the same league. His was a winner, *the* winner: all beauty and beast, wrapped up in the flawless metal of one of Italy's finest designers. But it was just a very showy thing, she thought now, squirming a bit in her chair as she pictured herself settling into an equivalent chariot's driver's seat. Okay, she said to herself, she could permit herself to envy him that…for now. But her Italian chariot would have to come later, one step at a time. And hers would be a softer colour; feminine, although not pink. It probably didn't come in pink, anyway.

She realized her mind had been drifting. She parked her non-pink Maserati in one of the darker recesses of her mind and returned to the project at hand. She knew she must. Her next move would be the threshold footfall, either she would be allowed to cross over—possibly forever—or she would be turned away. She wasn't sure which call he might make that would be the riskier for her. Once her proposal was pitched, rejection could have consequences more grave than merely having the door slammed in her face.

So, she felt sure by now, legitimizing bad money was the *raison d'être* for the restaurant. This would not be good news for Manotick's heritage defenders, were they to find out. But, it also seemed a door to opportunity—*her* opportunity.

"Maybe," she breathed into a handkerchief while pretending to blow her nose, watching the bartender watching her, "or maybe I'm a dead woman walking."

Earlier, she had thought a great deal about money laundering and what it actually meant. In her home office she had Googled the phrase and printed off some of the references. She had decided to keep them in her office safe for future referrals, particularly if her exploratory discussions with DiPasquale didn't go well. A vindictive side of her suggested she might use this material to piece together an anonymous note to the Mounties, should she not be loaned the money to fund her plan and therefore have to scrub the notion of going ahead with it.

Throughout lunch she mulled that over, remembering one article from the *Globe and Mail* suggesting that laundering had become, for Canada, a widespread problem. Of interest was the RCMP's assertion that in almost every case, lawyers were central. Criminals apparently could acquire solicitor-client privilege for as little as one dollar. Thus protected, they could help move millions of dollars into investments that would hide their illegal origin. The Mounties also said it was twenty times easier to launder money from Canada than the United States, and that Canadian lawyers could be found who would process as much as $200,000 a month through trust accounts in return for a seven-percent commission. Other lawyers used offshore accounts, stock market scams, and foundations to hide illicit cash.

The material she had found went on to say that authorities knew about a lot of money-laundering techniques, and undoubtedly there were countless others they had yet to uncover. The couple that had caught her eye were views of overseas banks and underground or alternative banking. In the former, money launderers were described as often sending money through various offshore accounts in countries that have bank secrecy laws, meaning that for all intents and purposes these countries allow anonymous banking. A complex scheme apparently could involve, the material said, hundreds of fund transfers to and from offshore banks.

The latter example had intrigued her. Some countries in Asia apparently offer well-established legal alternative banking systems that allow for undocumented deposits, withdrawals, and transfers. She had learned that they were trust-based systems, often with ancient roots, which leave no paper trail and operate outside government control. More specifically, if her memory served her right, this included the *hawala* system in Pakistan and India and the *fie chen* system in China. But the clincher was the example that described investing in legitimate business areas. Launderers, the article said, sometimes place dirty money in otherwise legitimate businesses to clean it. They use funds from large businesses like brokerage firms or casinos that deal in so much money that the dirty stuff can easily blend in when meshed with small, cash-intensive businesses like bars, restaurants, carwashes, or cheque-cashing stores. These businesses may be front companies that actually do provide goods and services, but whose real purpose is to clean the launderers' money. This method typically works in one of two ways: in either, the launderer can combine his dirty money with the company's clean revenues. With the first case, the company reports higher revenues from its legitimate business then it is really earning. In the second case, the launderer can simply hide his dirty money in the company's legitimate bank accounts in the hope that authorities won't compare the bank balance to the company's financial statements.

Now that, she thought, sounded like an opportunity waiting to happen, at least for her. And, she felt quite sure that she had been sitting in the midst of one just now, enjoying her lunch.

The article had ended on a note which, for her, represented some astounding numbers: Depending on whatever international agency was updating the figures, criminals were laundering anywhere between $500 billion and $1 trillion worldwide every year.

So, she rationalized, just a few more millions shouldn't greatly impact the global economy, should it? Besides, if everyone was doing it, why shouldn't she?

Now, how to get the backing to make all this happen? Where was Mr. DiPasquale when she needed him? Mr. Glitz, she said to herself, I need you, now.

She was, however, still nervous and uncertain. She hadn't felt this way since her first date. How would it come out? Would he like her? More importantly, would he like her proposal? This would be the iffiest pitch she had ever made; she hoped it wouldn't be her last.

Scene 16
Lee Meets Luciano...

"Avarice, he assured them, was the one passion that grew stronger and sweeter in old age."
~ Willa Cather, *Death Comes for the Archbishop*

October 19, 2009, 10:24 a.m.
In days that followed, during snatched moments when she had assured herself of aloneness in the house, she had prepared draft after draft of her business model—all of them in pencil, all with side notes and arrows and edge-of-lead shadowing to link details that needed rearranging or abbreviating.

She preferred the feel of a lined notepad under her palm. She felt that accumulated editions, having served their purpose, could be more easily and certainly destroyed than if she had committed her efforts to a Microsoft Word file, there perhaps to replicate itself God knows where within the pseudo-safe soft muskeg of her machine's hard drive. Her scribbled sheets could be run through the office's shredder at any time, whereas, with Word, one could never be sure about the ultimate destructibility of anything. Or so she thought. Each evening, or whenever she could hear Carlyle returning to the house from one of his unannounced outings, she would carefully tear the newest-worked pages off her pad, and along with the pad itself, place all the current endeavours into her safe and lock it.

It was, by now, she thought, as good as she could make it. Nothing would be perfect, she knew, and she felt she had poured over every question DiPasquale might ask. She had rehearsed it as one might in preparation for addressing a large audience, trying to memorize as much of it as she could. She then tried putting herself in his shoes, having him, in her mind's-eye attempt to rip her proposal apart. "All the world's a stage," she remembered from Jacques's melancholy monologue in Shakespeare's *As You Like It.*

She knew that it was risky. DiPasquale would understand that *some* risk was unavoidable; risk must have followed him at every turn he had made in his shadowy journey to where he had currently concealed himself. He wouldn't have made his millions playing out his ploys incautiously; he would've known then, and would know by the end of her dissertation, whether to hold 'em or to fold 'em—and maybe to fold her along with them, were she to go in unprepared or lacking confidence.

So, it was time. Steeling herself for possible rejection, she called the restaurant to ask if she might speak with him. She recognized the answering voice as that of her earlier Asian antagonist.

"May I inquire who's calling?" the voice asked.

"Yes, it's a happy customer, and a frequenter of your restaurant. I'd like to say personally to him what a joy it is to have your establishment in our little community," Lee quickly chirped. There, she smirked to herself, stick *that* into your fuzzy little source-of-life's catchment, envying at the same time the girl's linguistic nimbleness. What must have been her first language, she wondered—Vietnamese, Mandarin—*what*?

But, it had connected. With no further masked acrimony she had been able to make an appointment to see him. Today was to be her day.

She drove to the restaurant and found a place to park close to his black jewel. Her unlikely new best friend, the Asian, greeted her with cold displeasure. Behind her, waiting casually, with a smile of anticipated pleasure at the compliment he expected to be receiving, was the prince himself. Having finished pouring them each a glass of *Greco di Tufo*, he picked up them both, nodded unobtrusively to the Asian girl, and escorted Lee to his office, which had been completely remodeled from the space over what had been the garage she had seen in her earlier tour.

She opened her pitch with all the effervescence she could fabricate about how wonderful the restaurant was, and had been, to her and all of those within her circle who lived in or near Manotick. He let her play that out, with gracious impatience, nodding and smiling at appropriate intervals, until she finally ran out of her kludged for-the-occasion vocal excretions. He had always had a nose for horseshit and waited before in the face of disingenuity for the tail of the animal to go down. Then, looking at her in a firm but not unfriendly way, he said, quietly, "Why do I get the feeling that's not why you're here?"

Lee realized with a sudden shiver she had started badly. She scrambled to recover, determined, in spite of her stumble, to become the alpha presence in the room, knowing all the while it was a contest she might lose. "I am a business person, as I know you are, and I have a proposal to put to you."

"Really?" he asked. He picked up his glass and tipped it, watching her carefully over its rim as he allowed his body language to convey to her that he truly approved of *his* choice of the wine. "I understand you usually order our house white."

"Yes, I quite like it. It's not about the money, you know; not for what we're enjoying here," she offered. It bubbled out of her with a shaky confidence befitting Jackie Kennedy describing the president's White House digs to total strangers. But her introduction of that one

The Fontana Resurrection

word—money—just now plucked from within her mind's subconscious lexicon, held out a segue she needed to bridge that river separating a poor start from where she wanted the discussion to go. And, bonus, she thought, congratulating herself, it hadn't been planned!

"Speaking of money," she started, afresh, "I think I'm onto something which could make both of us a great deal of it. But I need a financial backer, a moneyed godfather if you will, and I've chosen *you* to become my funder. Although, dollarwise, I'm in good shape," she lied, "what I have in mind is above my pay grade, somewhat beyond the level where I might have been able to proceed alone."

"Really?" he asked again. "Well, I suppose I can afford to at least be curious. But first, I'll need to resolve another curiosity I have about you. If you can agree to my resolution, we may be able to proceed. If not, I will have lost nothing, and you will have gained a glass of the best white wine The Three Gondolas stocks."

"Can I presume your *resolution*," she asked, sensing a need for caution, "will be some sort of no-contact sport?"

"Not exactly," he said, "but the exercise, if you agree to it, will not involve me."

"Now you've aroused *my* curiosity, although that shouldn't be taken to imply my consent," she offered, feigning confidence. "What do you have in mind?"

"You'll need to endure a visitation from one of my associates. Don't worry because it'll be a female, a person of few words. The encounter should be brief, one way or the other."

"And if I find I don't like that?"

"Then we'll be done here. You'll need to understand, among a myriad of other things, that I'm a man of necessary caution. Success seldom befalls a tuba player whose aspiration is to one day become a symphony orchestra conductor. If, during your audition, you can't project a potential to become first violin, we will shake hands as friends and you can remain a valued customer, but never more than that."

Picking up the phone's handset, he asked, "Which shall it be?"

Bit of a suave, self-assured prick, isn't he, she thought. "Are you always this abrupt?"

"Not really," he responded. "I'm usually a cuddly teddy bear. But playtime isn't to be confused with business, and since business equates to the ebb and flow of the Queen's coin, at least in this country, I find I have to be gentle on the one hand and firm with the other."

"Okay, make your call. I have a feeling I already know who my new girlfriend will be."

He dialed an in-house number, waited for a pickup, and then said, "Qian, could you step into my office for a few minutes, please?" Without waiting for a response, he put the handset back on its base.

In a few moments Lee's Asian nemesis came in and closed the door. Had she been on hold all the time, just behind it? Who knew?

"Qian, would you confirm that it will be okay for me to have a perhaps-lengthy conversation with this lady?" Relishing his moment, DiPasquale oiled his words, oozing the lubricant onto the palm of his tongue like an excess of Brylcreem squeezed onto a scalp to facilitate slicking his hair in preparation for a date. It had resulted in more silkiness than was optimal for the effect he had intended. But it was his way, a very old-fashioned way: the way of his father and of male generations long before that. He didn't much care if any of it was in sync with the times.

Lee wanted to interject a flippant comment that had swept into her mind, but recognized the probably unpleasant, about-to-be frisking mustn't degenerate into a girl-versus-girl smart-ass scene. In the same instant she conceded, only to herself, that she *wasn't* going to be able to dominate the room.

DiPasquale excused himself with a theatrical accentuation of gentlemanliness, pulling the door closed just long enough to hear through it Qian hissing out the words, "Take off your clothes!" Then he graced his way unhurriedly, chuckling as he went, back to the main bar. Time for a second glass of Greco di Tufo.

"*What?*" Lee asked. "Why?"

"Just do it. I need to see what you're wearing. Or not wearing."

"*Not* wearing? Is this a fashion show? What should I not be wearing?"

"A wire."

"Wire? I thought that sort of thing went out with whalebone. I've never needed extra support."

"Don't try to be clever, because you're not. I never judge a book by its cover. I usually just rip the cover off and then read what's under it, if I like the first few pages. You haven't made much of an impression so far, and I have about one page of patience left."

Lee looked at her in nonplussed silence, uncertainty written large all over her face.

"We need to know whether someone has sent you. So, will you take off your clothes, or shall I take them off for you? In the latter case, I can't guarantee you'll come away from the experience not bruised. So, please hand me each of your things as you take them off, including your shoes."

"My, you *are* thorough," Lee offered, not wanting to appear to be the wuss that was morphing within her.

"Are you unharmed, thus far?" Qian asked, honing her sarcasm, wanting Lee to get on with it.

"Yes, unharmed, of course," Lee said, handing over the first of her shoes.

"Then let's keep it that way. I am not your friend. I'll never be coming to your house for dinner, will I? We may or may not become associates; that will depend on Mr. DiPasquale. So, for the moment, keep in mind that you're already skating on thin ice; any hesitation from this point on won't be tolerated without engendering your discomfort. I quite enjoy pain, someone else's pain. Understand that knowing a little, in this situation, can be viewed as possibly knowing too much. And knowing too much means that nothing can be disclosed to anyone without DiPasquale's specific consent. Believe me, crossing that line would lead to consequences you don't want to contemplate." She finished the search, carefully examining each of Lee's garments before offering them back.

Lee unhurriedly dressed, summoning whatever little dignity the situation could be bent toward. She stood in silence, head high, awaiting things to come in whatever, she presumed, would be Act Two.

Qian rapped twice on the door; DiPasquale entered even before the sound escaped, without echo. He looked at Qian, then at Lee, raising an eyebrow in Qian's direction.

"She will leave here only with whatever you choose to tell her," Qian said. "There will be no real-time electronic transmission, nor a recorded one. If, after your conversation, you'd care to allow her to go, that will be fine. If not, let me know. I'll take it from there."

With that, Qian left.

DiPasquale didn't move to sit behind his desk. He instead gestured for Lee to make herself comfortable on his couch, while he settled into one of the two matching armchairs. "So, please tell me what I'm here to hear," he said evenly. "Spare me any fluff—just the bare bones. Call it your *executive summary,* if you'd rather. Any need to go beyond that, you'll be allowed to fill in later. However, I will be the one to indicate where your gaps might call for elaboration. Are we clear?"

Lee crossed her legs and leaned back into the comfort of the couch, albeit uncomfortably. Taking a deep breath, she started into her dissertation, imagining herself to be doing one final run-through in front of her home-office mirror.

Before long she warmed to her story, contenting herself with the small comfort that DiPasquale appeared to be listening, at least thus far, and had the decency—or the interest—not to interject.

Twenty minutes later she finished laying it all out, with more detail than he had wanted. But he had been attentive, she could tell, and he now seemed to be mulling the concept over.

"Did you develop this into a formal business plan?" he asked.

"Yes," she admitted, afraid to be caught in a lie.

"Where is it?" he probed, squinting at her with a concern that his gathering-storm expression telegraphed silently, albeit without the Morse dots and dashes.

"It's at home, in my office safe."

"Are there other notes or related bits and pieces?"

"Yes."

"Where?"

"Also in my safe."

"Was any of this done on a computer?"

"No. I used my laptop only for research."

"Then on what?"

"Just pencil and paper."

"That's all?"

"Yes."

"Have you discussed any of this with your husband? I believe I've met him on one or another occasion, haven't I?"

"No, I haven't; and yes, you have."

"Nothing at all chatted about?"

"Nothing!"

"Might he have seen your notes?"

"No. I have the only combination to my safe."

"That's unusual, don't you think?"

"Not in my case. I'd have about as much to lose as you, were my husband to find out, or even to suspect."

Wisps of assorted possibilities floated through DiPasquale's mind, as he reviewed all the elements with practiced scrutiny, like a physician examining a set of lung X-rays a second time, looking for traces of possible first-missed malignancy.

"Okay. Go home. Bring them to me. And bring me your computer."

"Now?"

"Yes."

"Does that mean we have a deal?"

"It means we can talk. Nothing more. Not yet."

"Okay, I'm leaving."

Qian, having escorted her to a side exit, watched Lee get into her car and pull away. She was also there expectantly upon her return, noting the envelope tucked under one arm and a laptop carried in the other. They didn't speak while walking to DiPasquale's office. Only Lee entered. Qian remained just steps from the door, not eavesdropping, but readily available should she be summoned.

DiPasquale unceremoniously split open Lee's envelope and glanced at a handful of extracted pages—more for authenticity than content—looking next, against a slanting light, at the blank top pages of her notebook, searching for possible pen or pencil-point impressions. He then gathered everything, including the envelope, and dropped it onto the grate in his office fireplace. He experienced a tingle of self-satisfaction at his choice of wood over gas when he had renovated the place, having later found this to be a certain-destruction method, ever better than any known manufactured paper-shredders. Flourishing his Dunhill—there was nothing unostentatious about him, particularly where a luxury item might make an impression—he struck its flint wheel; let the spark have its way with the wick, as might have happened, in an earlier time, from a flint's flash after a musket's hammer-fall onto the weapon's powder pan. DiPasquale's resulting teardrop orange flame hungered for the edges of Lee's musings.

"Come over here," he offered, with unexpected gentleness.

Both watched in silence as the papers curled to feed their burgeoning carbon-tainted yellow oxidation, twisting to blackness where the fire needed to move on, its remnants falling into fragmented crispness of graying ash.

He lifted a poker from its stand and stirred the few residual curls until they disintegrated into powder, as fluff moving within a passing draft to leave its trace on recently cleaned bricks. "Ashes to ashes, dust to dust," he said, not knowing whose funeral to attribute this to, if any. Not yet, anyway.

Seemingly content with what Lee took to be a well-practiced ritual, he placed the poker on its hook and turned his attention to her. "No one is to know of this," he said.

"Of course," she replied, beginning to feel more like a respected combatant in the game, even were it to become a deadly contest, as were the Mayan *ullamaliztli* gatherings—their open-air ball courts serving as places where the veil between living-world and netherworld beliefs thinned to gossamer wisps, leaving the winner to be sacrificed. Each participant knew in advance that her or his death would become the ultimate honour.

"Any e-mails, or Facebook, or Twitter communications to anyone about anything related?" DiPasquale asked.

"No."

"DVD copies?"

"No."

"Absolutely nothing?"

"Absolutely."

"Leave your computer, with its password," he ordered. "Qian will have a look through your hard drive. You realize at this point, don't you, the consequence of not being totally forthcoming? Always? From here on out, secret *means* secret. I—include Qian if you'd like—don't really believe in convenient dodges offered up after the fact to cover mouthed effluences burbled out during moments of overindulgence or overconfidence."

Lee smiled and then offered, "Could you give me your executive summary of that, without the fluff?" Her confidence was beginning to radiate, unfortunately, from mind to mouth, the latter not having been inclined to remain inactive. She had believed herself clever, having remembered his earlier quip.

Too clever for his liking. "Don't get cocky," he shot back, bordering on anger.

"Me?" she said, holding her smile. "I thought it likely you would be more in possession of something like that than might I."

Not to be outdone, now enjoying the challenge, he replied, "Agreed, but mine's not battery operated."

"Mine, on the other hand, doesn't have rigidity issues. Ever," she teased.

"Okay, enough," he forced, unable to think of a rejoinder, a tinge of crimson creeping into his cheeks. "What I'm saying is, 'You don't blab, ever.' Okay? Does that fit within the apparently confined parameters of your vocabulary?" He had wanted it to come off as an insult, but she chose, wisely, not to react to it as such.

"Okay," she said, knowing when to stop.

There followed, for her, what became an uncomfortable silence. "I'm still with you," she offered, all humour gone.

"Our rules," he said, "*my* rules, are Sicilian, and thus final; you might want to think of any journey toward that finality as one where you'd be obliged to pass through a valley—my valley, if you will—of extreme discomfort. And that, of course, would be just before you get to pass through the other one. You understand?"

She demurely pondered his question for a few seconds and then replied "Yes, I do," all the while trying to suppress a shiver cat-squall across her skin. She hoped that it hadn't shown. She had to bite her tongue before getting those few words out, having wanted instead to ask him, "Could you give me that again, please, in Sicilian? It'd be so romantic, so authentic, to hear it done that way." But she decided—and happily for her—that she wasn't ready yet to wander into his *valley*. She mitigated her capitulation, though, with a promise to herself that she wouldn't allow him to treat her as a lesser presence, ever.

"All right," he said, appeased. "What you have here may have potential. We'll go look at the place, and we'll take it from there. Are you available tomorrow?"

"Yes," she acquiesced, exhaling her relief. "What time?" She did, however, savour a subtlety when he said '*we'll* take it from there' and not '*I'll* take it from there.'

"We'll leave at ten o'clock, and I'll rent a car," he said.

"Okay," she smiled, looking again, this time with amusement, at what she took to be his day-to-day sartorial habit. "But I think you had better dress down a bit."

"Don't presume to tell me how to dress. Just be here at ten o'clock. Park in the church parking lot."

"Which church?"

"And don't try to pass off your wit as deer-in-the-headlights naiveté, either. You know the church; the one down the street, near the Mill."

"Shall I say a prayer?"

"If you *do* say a prayer, say it for your plan, or for yourself, or both. You may yet need to. Qian would quite enjoy having a turn with you were you to fuck this up."

Scene 17
Luciano Assesses, Agrees...

"The success of big government, big corporations, and the mob has ever been
dependent on their ability to sustain feigned legitimacy."
-David Edey

October 20, 2009, 1:36 p.m.
When they had found their way out of the Mont Sainte Marie Hotel's ruined interior, DiPasquale turned to look back at the tragedy of its demise and then at Lee, shaking his head, and then muttered a verdict: "The place is a mess. But I like its architecture and the mountain setting. Quite beautiful, actually, once you look past the building's decay. Somehow—why I'm not sure—I'm drawn to the clock tower. You'll have it refurbished, of course. The condos look acceptable to me. Go ahead and buy them and the hotel. This place is geographically nowhere; its relative isolation is just about perfect."

With a breath of relief Lee braced herself for what she knew must come next and then tried her make-or-break question, "And your terms will be...?"

"Admittedly, they're harsh. They'll have to be," DiPasquale offered, measuring his words, shaping them to imply only moderate interest, paying more attention to the neatness of manicured fingernails curved inward toward his left palm. "But then, what choice do you have?"

"I can walk away," Lee said, attempting an aura of confidence she wasn't sure she could sustain.

"No, actually, you can't," he retorted. "You must have realized that yesterday. *In* is for life, however near or far away you may choose to draw that line. Your duration in this world will be entirely up to you."

Okay, Lee thought, this is the tipping point.

She hadn't expected a death threat. She had thought the earlier conversations at the restaurant had just been tough-guy talk. But he apparently meant it. So, no turning back now. Fear was beginning to form a fullness in her stomach, as if she were sensing evisceration. But no, historically, *drawing* was part of a favoured British method for terminating persons guilty of treason. Would this be the brazen-bull treatment he had alluded to? She hadn't realized its implication until she had gone home and checked it out online.

Sure enough, there it had been; the words now indelibly imprinted in her memory: 'The Brazen Bull, sometimes known as the Sicilian Bull, is one of the cruellest methods of torture and execution out there. Designed in ancient Greece, solid brass was cast into the shape of a hollow bull, with a door on the side that opened and latched. To begin the execution, the victim was placed inside of the brass bull and a fire was set underneath. The fire was heated until the metal was literally yellow, causing the victim to roast to death."

How sweet, she thought, still believing he had been merely trying to intimidate her, to subordinate her, to ensure she would stay in line. But maybe he wasn't kidding. He was something of a collector; maybe he had acquired one of these things? He lived in a monstrously big house, perhaps it was somewhere there as a backyard ornament, intended to amuse his friends.

So, nothing to lose. To hell with him, she thought, she would treat him as a partner. And she would become his equal and would begin right now to emulate his manner. He hadn't yet met her wicked-witch-of-the-north avatar. It was time for its introduction. "Spell it out," she breathed toward him, as though through icicles dripping from a winter-frozen eavestrough, eyes squinting her defiance.

"It'll be an expensive makeover," he tossed back, undaunted. "I think I can guesstimate it to the nearest million or so, all of which I can either handle or arrange."

He paused to let that sink in and then added, like nails being driven into her cranium, "From one month after the building's reopening, you will begin setting aside dollars toward repayment of your loan. Interest will be at thirty percent per annum, and you will pay off the principal within three years. The good news is that your first payment will fall due on the last day of your first business year. That should allow you to get comfortably up and running. After your *third* year, you will transfer into an offshore account of my choosing, in perpetuity, fifteen percent of the clinic's annual pretax income.

"You will personally oversee the building's acquisition and refurbishing; the choice of general contractor will be yours to make. My name won't appear anywhere in your business documentation. This will be *your* venture entirely. As you need funds to meet incremental general-contractor's payments, let me know the amounts and I'll have cash delivered to you. It'll be in used notes of varying denominations. You'll need not count it; my bundles are never light. You will first deposit what I give you in various financial institutions, in amounts that won't attract undue attention. I'll provide you with a recommended list. Getting to and from banks will be at your expense; I'll advance you your travel needs as part of the overall loan. From that point on you'll need to manage all start-up expenses, including real-estate acquisitions, your refurb contractor, etc. Always pay by cheque.

"You will handpick your *medical* staff and find a qualified semi driver. Be careful with that. Make all your people understand that any security breach will be a one-time mistake with no exception. I will deal with any indiscretions as need be. You'll merely have to find their replacements.

"My people will handle the clinic's legal needs and oversee all client receivables. Also, I will provide kitchen and dining room staff, as well as cleaners. The same goes for the facility's security specialists; all will report to me. And, yes, they'll keep me informed. Be aware that these won't be your run-of-the-mill shopping-mall guards. Your clients will find our lawyer quite charming and the finance guy impressively knowledgeable, all in a friendly-persuasion sort of way.

"You must, however, tweak your business model—within your head only, nothing on paper—to allow clients the freedom to forego their contract and leave the facility with a smile and all the staffs' good wishes. I don't want unhappy, expectant heirs or relatives sniffing into our bona fides. And don't ingest *any* client who has had a professional medical qualification. Your need for compliance should be obvious.

"Also, you will pay my people a competitive wage and accommodate them, as a perquisite, in your staff condos.

"And, last but not least, you're to name your new phoenix, once it's up from ashes, the Fontana Spa and Clinic. It's actually a personal touch. My mother's maiden name was Fontana, and she used to tease me about it originating from the fountain-of-youth story, which she had always promised me was real. Like Santa Claus is real and God is real, as has been proclaimed happily by parents and the Pope respectively to the young and to their gullible mommies and daddies. Makes everybody feel good, don't you think?

"So, you now must graciously accept, or die along with your idea, whichever outcome you prefer. Naturally, I would rather you choose the former, the latter being an inconvenience I'd just as soon avoid."

Needing to get a grip on her bowel, Lee managed, "All right, I graciously accept." With the ice now gone from her voice, she added, "I may never make you proud—that seems a bar you've set too high—but I can add lots of cash to your stash, wherever you keep it, or them."

"That's what it's all about," he smiled, again checking his fingernails: "The money. A bit of it judiciously distributed in the right places tends to lubricate the gears of a world within a world that remains the domain of those who would risk something of value to enjoy its benefits. I prefer to remain one of them. Others might be content to wallow in their misery; I'll leave it to the Pope to look after them. But *I* will look after me and mine, and, for the next three years, that will include you and yours.

"Don't slip off the path, dear girl," he added. "Bones will be broken if you do, and I'll leave you to imagine who'll do the bending."

Ever the faux Sir Galahad, he opened the passenger-side door for her, and, with a mendacious smile—as would a fox exiting the henhouse after a well enjoyed meal—closed it, gently, allowing her time to ease her skirt in around her ankles.

They drove home in silence, she to say an unspoken good-bye to the world she had that day stepped away from, and to shudder at the prospect of the one she now found herself forced to accept, and he to measure the probability of her staying power while trying to pull this thing off, and how to deal with her disappearance if she couldn't. He did, however, admire her creativity—such visualization, to his knowledge, was a first in the world's broader history of scams. Exploiting people like her could enhance fortunes, most importantly his.

He smiled again at the prospect.

Scene 18
Lee Seeks a Nurse...

> *"It is necessary to meditate early, and often, on the art of dying to succeed later in doing it properly just once."*
> - Umberto Eco, *The Island of the Day Before*

October 20, 2009, 11:16 a.m.
Okay, with the first hurdle cleared, she had the promise of the money. Now she needed a collaborative sidekick, ideally a nurse, someone with a broad knowledge of medicine and in-depth experience sufficient to allow her to pose as a doctor or else to coach an impostor—maybe an actor—to become her doctor. But nothing was bubbling to the top, at least not quickly enough. She scoured her memory with steel-wool determination, upbraiding its uncharacteristic laziness and ordering it to offer up a list of candidates.

Not many came to mind, but she could feel a tingling. She drummed her fingers on the tidy arrangement of her home-office desk. Hmmm, "Nothing in writing," he had said, so there wasn't a need for paper. Yes, master, she thought, I'll keep it all inside my head, even if it hurts.

Seconds turned to minutes. Finally, there was a glimmer—a name, but no list. The name wasn't new, either. She had thought of Abigail before. Abigail Martin. Yes, Abigail, a registered nurse could fit in quite nicely as one of her *doctors*. The big question would be if she would like to become a partner in this venture?

Asking her was risky, but worth a try. She would contact Abigail and offer to take her to The Three Gondolas for a nice lunch—several nice lunches if need be—and ease her gently into the concept. She'd keep her at arm's length from Luciano and Qian though, just in case her feeler were to become an aborted attempt. But she was hopeful.

Having initially met Abigail at the Watson's house, she had later become a member of a Manotick book club to which they both now belonged. She had found, through sidebar conversations during one of their meetings, that they both had a great deal of empathy for—and interest in—euthanasia and assisted suicide. The book under discussion had been titled *Still Alice,* a story about a professional woman who had suffered from a vascular type of Alzheimer's, which Lee knew to be very fast-moving affliction. In the book, as Alice was losing it, she decided that suicide was what she wanted before it became too late for her to be responsible for her own decisions. So she started the process, only to be distracted and then to forget about it until it became too late for this earlier thought process to kick in. Most of the club members felt that God would take Alice when he was ready and it was her time to go. However, both she and Abigail had expressed the view that it would be much easier on the health-care system, on Alice, and on her family, if Alice had been successful with her suicide attempt. And thus they had their first meeting of minds.

They both had their reasons for arriving there. Abigail's were professional; she had seen a lot of dying during her career, much of it having involved end-of-life uncertainties around the medical profession's hesitancy to assist very old people—those who begged to be allowed to die—through their final step. Some doctors acquiesced, when backs were turned, but it was chancy. Canada still deemed this to be an unlawful activity.

Lee had offered as an aside to Abigail that she had just celebrated her twentieth birthday when she lost her mother to a car accident. She had asked herself any number of times since: Is there a God? The unspoken answer that always echoed back to her was no. As a result, she had gone through her adult life absent of any religious belief. She had a personal family experience in want of some relief within that field as she had watched an ageing aunt surrender herself to Alzheimer's. The aunt had died, mindless, in a soiled diaper. Doctors so easily could have allowed her to go with dignity, but their Hippocratic oath or their ever-reinforced obligation to align medical ethics with the country's laws presumably had kept them from it.

Still idling in Lee's memory were notes she had kept on a recent Internet search about euthanasia, all of which she had withheld during her earlier disclosures to Luciano. What he didn't know wouldn't hurt him. But, wryly she thought, it might end up killing *her*.

America still didn't buy it. Doctor Jack Kevorkian had spent eight years of a ten-year prison sentence as his reward for having unsuccessfully tried to press, by example, his nation's government to change the related legislation.

She had preferred the Internet's Swiss-model example: Assisted suicide was legal in Switzerland and had been since the 1940s. A medical doctor even didn't need to perform it. The Swiss Academy of Medical Sciences historically had held that assisted suicide was "not a part of a physician's activity." But in 2003, the Academy performed a U-turn and told doctors they could help the terminally ill die, although only under strict conditions. All assisted suicides would be video taped. After an upcoming death was reported to the police, an officer from the coroner's department and a doctor would attend the death. At that time, family and friends were to be interviewed. It was "a crime if and only if the motive is selfish." If selfish motive couldn't be established, then no crime would have been committed; hence most of these deaths were to become open-and-shut cases.

She had thought it best to check Canada's Criminal Code, finding that the Code's Section 14 read: "No person is entitled to consent to have death inflicted on him, and such consent does not affect the criminal responsibility of any person by whom death may be inflicted on the person by whom consent is given." Further along, she found that Section 241 read: "Everyone who counsels a person to commit suicide or aids and abets a person to commit suicide, whether suicide ensues or not, is guilty of an indictable offense and liable to imprisonment for a term not exceeding 14 years."

Ouch, she had thought, but knew from her own chiropractic practice that rare was the doctor who hadn't, at the request of a patient, the patient's family, or on his or her own accord, decided to discontinue life support. Studies had shown that many doctors had acceded to life-ending drug doses in cases of advanced terminal conditions, which—under Canadian law—continues to fall within the definition of assisted suicide.

On the other side of that coin, she had been encouraged to discover that Canadian citizens had a basic right to refuse medical care and treatment, and that they had a right to decide what medical treatment they may accept or reject, even were that to lead to their death—part of the Canadian Charter of Rights and Freedoms.

So, she had said to herself, worst case: fourteen years in the slammer. If there had been any good news in that to contemplate, it was that she probably didn't have fourteen years left in her to serve. She had rationalized that the Canadian Charter of Rights and Freedoms should take precedence and that she would proceed on that assumption with a clear conscience.

She picked up the phonebook, looked up the number, and dialed it. She was quietly pleased to hear a familiar, happy female voice at the other end.

Scene 19
Abigail's Response...

"It is impossible that anything so natural, so necessary, and so universal as death,
should ever have been designed by Providence as an evil to mankind."
~Jonathan Swift (1667 – 1745)

October 21, 2009, 12:26 p.m.
Abigail was a bit taken aback. She felt flattered to have received the invitation, not yet having had a chance to experience The Three Gondolas. It was a bit pricey, she had heard, a Mamma Teresa knockoff, according to her friends.

She had also felt buoyant about this or any opportunity to get to know Lee better, having sensed from their book-club chats that they had several beliefs and values in common.

The next day they enjoyed a rather lavish lunch—Lee had insisted on ordering for them both, including a carafe of Greco di Tufo—exploring mutual interests and nurturing the beginnings of a new friendship, albeit obscured within the shade of Lee's gleefully presented tree of disingenuity, the foliage of which, throughout the afternoon, shadowed her real intent: Abigail's recruitment.

Toward the end of identically decorated plates of Zuccotto for desert, Lee suggested that they continue their amicable beginning by taking a stroll through the grounds surrounding the Rideau's Long Island Locks. She paid the tab, and they left together for the Locks' parking lot.

With the car locked and left in the lot, stepping cautiously, eyes down over the long-antiquated, time-torqued, and now rotting wooden bridge on their path to the river, Lee picked up the thread of their earlier exchange about euthanasia and assisted suicide. She nudged the conversation toward hazardous ground when she suggested that, in the absence of legal acceptance of euthanasia in Canada, it might be a service to the terminally ill and the very elderly—those who had no further interest in continuing their lives—to somehow help them *out*.

Abigail didn't flinch at this discussion, having taken it as hypothetical.

As they walked on, pausing to push crumpled breath-mint wrappers through the flap of the first of the park's green garbage barrels, Lee began to gather confidence that Abigail's empathy toward all this might align with her own. With a hopeful smile she continued—gingerly at first—down that track, playfully arcing one foot out in front of the other to approximate a straight line as any teenage girl might do when describing to a confidante a previous night's frolic.

She outlined a version of her feelings about a death-for-profit undertaking, offering elderly patients the hope of a fountain-of-youth opportunity to relive their early adulthood. Thus seeming to have tweaked Abigail's curiosity, she began to build on the framework of her business model.

None of this fazed Abigail. Lee's Teflon recruitment style appeared to be succeeding. Abigail agreed to bring her professional expertise to bear in dispatching any of the clinic's elderly who might be willing to pay for a second shot at life.

In turn, this led to Lee's suggestion that Abigail's husband Sven, being a civil engineer, might be interested in having his Ottawa firm bid to refurbish the hotel. Yes, Abigail had agreed, but with the clear understanding that Sven not be brought into the loop vis-à-vis the true nature of their partnership.

Lee stopped them near a tree shading one of the benches overlooking the uppermost of the three locks. They sat down, pausing for a few minutes to take in the detail and mechanisms of this section of Colonel By's oft-refurbished antiquity.

Breaking their reverie, Lee invited Abigail to tell her something of herself.

Okay, Abigail thought, perhaps *something* but not all. Feeling her way cautiously, she eased into occurrences in her life that she had never discussed with anyone, entrusting and embedding them within this tenuous new relationship, just as she had tucked in dying patients, all anxious to meet their maker but disallowed any unnatural haste in the process.

"Well, I went to Ottawa University," she said, "hoping for a medical degree, but I wasn't able to finish it. I did however get my RN, and I've experienced a lot of patients' near-death experience as a result. While attached to the ICU within one of the Ontario hospitals where I worked, I was close to many fragile souls, each like ashes in a crematorium that hadn't yet collapsed into shapeless dust, who were being given medication to keep them alive. Occasionally, one would be given a fatal dose of morphine, always preauthorized by one of the doctors.

"I also spent quite a bit of time at an Alberta hospital. There I worked opposite a person who had agreed we could sign off for each other's charged-out drugs. Drugs sometimes, you know, could go *missing*. Near-death folks were eased out, so to speak. It was possible to do.

"I later worked in Inuvik. The qualifications for doctors there were sometimes iffy; it was difficult to get best-in-show people to work in the far north. I recall one girl who was unconscious, her situation totally hopeless. We put her to sleep.

"I went to Australia for a while and then later to Dallas. So you can see I've been around, I'm no stranger to death, and I'm not entirely innocent about having been party to it."

She paused, letting her mind be distracted long enough to absorb the aesthetics of burnished rust and pitting from timeless exposure to the elements—proudly worn—on one of the lock's nearest winches, admiring its mechanical simplicity and the efficiency of the device's centuries-old design. The bench she was sitting on seemed appropriately weathered, too, its grayed and cracked boards, having yielded to the dictates of decades of rainfall and intense sunshine, were warped now but not broken nor yet ready to break. A gnarled root at the base of Lee's chosen shade tree, having broken through the earth to curl over an edge of one of By's curved foundation stones—in much the same way a U-boat might have surfaced through a froth-capped North Atlantic breaker to greet a Canadian convoy—made footing there hazardous to the unwary, acting as it did as an alternate step down toward the wharf, along which two disparate boats were tied but apparently unoccupied. The park, oddly, seemed devoid of humanity, but for the two of them. Who knew to what place the boats' owners might have dispersed? It didn't matter, though; their softly spoken privacy would not be easily compromised.

Returning to their discussion, she continued "Lee, I'm not at all troubled by what you've told me or what you're proposing. Death comes to us all. If I were later to devolve beyond all desire to continue my life, I would hope someone merciful enough to put an end to me could be found. It would be a blessing.

"If you and I together can do that sort of thing, count me in. I would agree to it on a humanitarian basis; if there's a living to be made from it, I'll accept.

"My private life probably doesn't matter. Maybe, later, we can get into that if you really want to. For now though, how be we leave it here in the park?"

It was Lee's turn, she thought, and asked her for her story.

Scene 20
Lee's Reflections...

"Truth is something which interests only the innocent. That's why we hear so little of it."
~David Edey

October 21, 2009, 2:38 p.m.
Lee had no trouble elaborating; she relished any opportunity to speak of her background to folks who cared—cared enough to listen—and in whom she felt she could trust. Given this situation, Abigail seemed veracious enough. She knew herself to be loquacious and that she would have to truncate many of the details she was, within herself, so very fond of recollecting. Now, beneath this tree, sitting on this bench, she had an audience of just one, but an important one, and she didn't want to lose her. She knew, though, it wasn't always the shiniest lure that caught the fish.

"I was born in Toronto," she began. "I lived in North Toronto in half of a lovely double. Public school was right at the end of our street. I had one older brother, eighteen months my senior.

"My mother was the most delightful, happiest, cheeriest person you could ever want to know.

"My father was a musician, which isn't surprising, I suppose, given that his mother had been a concert pianist. He started to play the piano when he was three; he was a natural. Later he played and taught about twenty-six different instruments, mainly horns.

"He had a heart attack when I was in kindergarten. He recovered and practiced his music every day, whenever he could. He had many different types of jobs along the way. He worked a lot at night and doing weekend gigs. He wasn't a fun person like Mom; he had a wicked temper and drank a bit. Mom mostly sheltered my brother and me from that.

"My parents, when they retired, kept their house in Toronto; they rented it out and lived at their cottage. Father had built it. My family went there every weekend; sometimes we spent whole summers there.

"Friends within our circle were great chiropractic supporters. When I was young, I thought that that might be a neat thing to do. My parents were delighted and strongly encouraged me to carry through with it. So, I entered Toronto's chiropractic college when I was seventeen. I loved the study and the work. I got very involved with student council and drama. I also had a part-time job with a chiropractor, two evenings a week. But, after my second college year, I found I didn't like some of the antimedicine stances held by my professors and wasn't sure I wanted to continue.

"My mom was killed in a car accident. Soon after, I approached Dad and said I wanted to change schools to study mainstream medicine. His response was, 'Sorry!' So I continued where I was. An aunt paid my tuition in my final year. After graduation, I paid her back, which surprised her, I suppose. She said she thought she would never see that money again. She was a nice person, really; she had a flower shop in Toronto. It had been a longtime family business. She eventually died, horribly: Alzheimer's. She left the business and the building to her children.

"My father remarried four years later to someone I had known for a long time. I was living in Ottawa by then, and when Dad called, very excited, to say he had asked this woman to marry him, I was happy for him. I didn't realize at the time that her husband had only been gone for about three months. But I was thrilled for my dad; he'd been depressed and lonely all this time.

"I had to work that day, a Friday, so that night I got in my car and drove straight to Toronto. I didn't arrive at the house until late, probably close to midnight. But Dad, God love him, was up waiting for me, and we had a lovely chat.

"Only then did I ask, 'Dad, I have to know. Did you buy her a ring?' And he said, 'Ah, no, I just gave her one of the rings that I had.' Well, he might as well have hit me with a hammer. I was so hurt, so upset and disgusted I could hardly talk to him.

"The next day, when family members were getting together and I was to meet her, I could hardly look her in the eye. He had given her one of my mother's diamonds as an engagement ring and married her with my mother's wedding ring. She accepted it all, which I thought was in poor taste. I could never understand how she could do such a thing.

"When Dad passed away, which was ten years after he had married this woman, she was very quick to find herself another husband, her third.

"Along about then—there were still some family ties, believe it or not—we were invited for Thanksgiving one weekend. For some reason I think Carlyle was away. Maybe he was painting or something. So when we went to her house, this new fellow's house, Harold I think his name was, I found myself sitting down to my grandfather's cutlery—*my grandfather's cutlery was on the table!* So that was fine, I guess; at least there was nothing I could do about it. But Harold didn't last, poor fellow. He passed away. And then she found herself a fourth husband. She was quite a busy lady."

At that point Abigail began to notice, albeit impatiently, a change in the pitch of Lee's voice, an edgy intensity building in what seemed an emotional tryst with attempts to articulate painful memories. But couldn't she just get on with it? She tried to remember if she had earlier stuffed Kleenex into her purse; it seemed like tears might be on the way. Not that she cared much about the flower-shop aunt's demise or was moved by the Lord-of-the-Rings bit. And she could have gone without knowing about the purloined silverware.

Lee recognized that the levee that walled the streaming of her words was about to give way—it had happened before—and that she quickly would need to sandbag the tops. And, as well, get a better grip on her story. This was business, after all; she hadn't intended it to be all about family.

But she did want Abigail to understand she wasn't heartless. So she went on. No, she told herself, I'm *not* heartless.

"I began to develop an interest in euthanasia. If you've had experience with Alzheimer's, the related memory loss and how insidious a disease it is...." She glanced at Abigail and saw her nodding in agreement. "Yes, I expect you've been there, done that...you'll have seen these people, plopped into institutions, often unwillingly, because they don't know how to avoid it. They end up wearing other people's clothes and lose their false teeth and their hearing aids. They're strapped into chairs with heads drooping down on their chests. That's their existence. For years. Sometimes they need to be handfed, so there's consequential weight loss. It's awful!"

Abigail *could* relate to the disease, definitely.

"Okay, got that, I guess," Abigail said in an inaudible whisper, having turned her head to see if anyone had returned to the boats.

There was an unexpected absence of sound. She brought her mind back; Lee was catching her breath. Here we go again, the words unspoken, trying not to move her lips.

"These people sometimes can't swallow, in which case they have to be fed intravenously, and they become like vegetables. It's not a pleasant thing to watch; it's not a nice death for them. Maybe in the end they might have a fatal heart attack or something, which would be easier. But, in the meantime, their families and caregivers are left holding the bag.

"Okay, enough of that," Lee concluded, sighing. "You're a nurse; you know all that stuff. I'm sorry. I got a bit carried away."

Abigail smiled her best empathetic smile. So what, she thought if her gesture might have seemed disingenuous? Maybe we're getting closer to the part about killing people. Wasn't that what this little visit was to be all about? But no, it seemed, maybe it wasn't, yet. Lee was looking like she wanted to pick up the thread of her history. The killing part would have to wait a bit. Or maybe not. Maybe a gentle interjection was in order here.

"Lee," given there had been a bit of a pause, "Maybe we should talk about your venture, before others come along and get curious about what we're doing here. I know it may look like we're just chatting, but we've been here for a while. If anyone comes back to either of these boats, we'll either have to stop what we're doing or move on to some other quiet spot."

Yes, Lee thought, time to get down to it. I may have been boring her. But Abigail's hoped-for, easy-goes-it recruitment seemed to have gone well, at least so far. She could sense the barb on her hook cutting into a lip's firmness; she had felt a pullback against the lure. Her bait may have been unappetizing, but apparently palatable enough.

She began to map out her intention to rebuild the derelict Mont Sainte Marie Hotel, and why, resurrecting the story from notes she had carried in her head and offering up a second debut of the canvas she had painted earlier—something of a Salvador Dali knock-off—now hanging on a wall somewhere in DiPasquale's mind.

It took a while, but Abigail appeared to have been assimilating the details quite easily. She didn't encounter any discernibly obstructive body language or any of the anticipated pushback.

"I thought," she continued, "we could talk about designing and furnishing an operating theatre for our shop, keeping in mind that it might be difficult to come by whatever medical devices and instrumentation—props, really—that you might feel we'll need in order to effectively fake it without raising suppliers' eyebrows. Later, when you've had a chance to think it through, maybe you could sketch out the room for me as you see it. If you will, include a shopping list that will give me a rough idea of the money we'll need to make it happen. Keep in mind that the whole *operating* scenario—a smallish room, I'm thinking—will need to back onto a freight elevator, so we should put movable screens or whatever in front of its door."

"Why an elevator?" Abigail asked.

"For moving bodies by gurney down to the cold room without our still-warm and breathing clients seeing us. We couldn't have that, could we?

"You'll have a *doctor* there, of course. I have an affable butcher in mind to fill that position. He'll be perfect, if I can just get him. You'll have to tutor him, of course. He'll need to be able to act the part as well as any Oscar-winning movie star. But you'll be the clinic's head nurse, in charge of all things medical—in essence everything we offer, beyond room and board. The doctor will report to you; it just won't have to appear that way to our guests.

"Among my envisaged down-the-road scenarios, I see, in your pre-op work-ups, patients wanting—one at time, of course—to hold your hand, looking to be reassured, waiting nervously for their operation to happen and to be successful. Then, after they've been sedated and wheeled into the operating theatre, the doctor, I presume—stop me here if I'm wrong—will have donned his surgical mask and be inspecting his instruments: scalpels, clamps, whatever. He'll concurrently vocalize, happily, assuredly, the painlessness of his surgical procedure. He'll say that the operation is a piece of cake, really, and expand on the quick recovery period that the patient can expect as soon as the anaesthetic has worn off.

"He will, if our guy turns out to be the type I think he is, exude an aura of self-confidence, that of a busy, patient-friendly surgeon. But more than that, in a secondary but equally important role, he'll become every client's great white hope. To do that—and this is where you'll need to pump him up—he'll have to, early on, become able to morph into that charming actor I've just now attempted to describe. I'm quite sure he has all the makings.

"If we—*we* meaning, collectively, our entire staff—screen the walk-ins carefully, we should be able to tag those deemed gullible enough to become candidates for euthanasia. That lot should be narrowed down to those well-advanced seniors having no notion or recollection of what a real surgery could look like.

"Your happy guy, our doctor, will be available to the clients whenever he's not in surgery, answering their questions and quelling their anxieties. All others on your staff will need to be supportive.

"So, one of your next tasks, I think, should be to identify and schmooze with the people we'll need to hire. Once they're on board, you'll have to train them to a level of, shall we say, confident credibility. We can't have operating-theater staff screwing up, particularly when it comes to some of the anxious questions clients are likely to dream up.

"You also should begin thinking about developing a FAQ list—hypothetical for now, later to become an all-anticipating reference document, evolving as we move into the program. That way, we'll all be reading from the same page regarding clients' apprehensions, so to speak.

"We'll need to steer them all away from any notion of contacting those who have gone through the process, our rationale being that our *graduates* will already have moved on to their new lives, some resettled in faraway places.

"We'll also have to convey the message that they can't expect to be instantaneously whisked back in time to their earlier existence. They'll need recovery time in the clinic, which will require temporary isolation from our other longer-term guests. We'll need to move them, we'll say, onto upper floors following their operation. We can reassure them that, when they wake up, they'll be amongst others making the same transition: in the queue to resettle into their locations of choice. They can be told that their meals will be offered separately, served in the clinic's exclusive—although, in reality, nonexistent—upper-level dining room. Our intention will be to want to work with them to review and close out all remaining documentation they'll need—new identities, passports, bank accounts, all of that—a parallel, we can say, to Canada's witness-protection program. Won't that be exciting for them: a bit of mystery associated with their new lease on life?

"The clinic's chef and other support staff will be in the know. They'll also be in the employ of our funder—I had to agree to that at his insistence—as will the lawyer and our clients' on-site financial adviser. The security team will be his, too. For him, that'll pretty much nail down our accountability. Like Santa Claus, he'll always know if we're being naughty or nice. Unfortunately, if caught naughty, we can expect more than just a lump of coal in our stockings."

So, the funder, Abigail discovered, was a red flag; she was beginning not to like that. Yes, she had always had a mind for intrigue, a penchant for being able to weigh risks, quickly, and to balance them while keeping—evasively, if necessary—on the move, no matter what the action might be. But to do so, she knew it was important to assess all the players and to know as much as she could about them. "Who is this person?" she asked.

Lee paused, then, "I can't tell you."

"Why not? You must have concluded, even before you approached me, that I can be trusted. So tell me. I need to know."

"I can't, Abby. I just can't."

"Is this a life-or-death matter or what?"

"Abigail, *everything* about this venture will be life or death. And if we fuck up, it'll mean our death. Or at least mine."

"So, is this guy connected to the mob or what?"

"Honestly, I don't know. He may just be an *independent*. He's a businessman, terminally so, turns out, and problems facing him quickly become black or white. Noncompliance could be a one-time mistake for either of us. We'll have to live with that."

Abigail was silent for a while, mulling it over. Lee could see that it might be a tipping point for her. "Abby," she said, "I've decided to *accept* the risk. This whole thing, from the get-go, has been an adventure in risk. It's been exciting for me, exhilarating, really. That's why I'm in it. My life before was becoming morbidly predictable, the end of my road in sight. I'm almost as old as some of the people we're planning to snuff, and I just decided one day that I wasn't going to leave this earth quietly. I've *needed* this. I didn't dream it all up just for the money; I have access to enough money. Carlyle has always been a good and generous provider."

Abigail looked at her hard, almost angrily, saying nothing. Lee became a bit anxious. Might she decline, she wondered? "Abigail," she tried, almost pleading, "I need a partner in this, if it's going to work. I've sifted through all the possible candidates I know and, in the end, decided on you, never knowing if you'd be willing, but hoping you might. That's still my hope. Actually, I'm at the point of no return: our funder will kill me if I reveal his name, and he'll kill me if I back out now—he's told me that—simply because I know who he is and the kinds of things he's up to. Please tell me you'll do it. If money is the issue, there's potentially a fortune in it for you. We'll split the clinic's profits, minus the funder's share, fifty-fifty. It'll be millions. Where else could you come by that kind of green?"

Abigail squinted her tiring eyes gradually until they closed. She shifted her jaw to one side, audibly clamping her teeth together, slowly, and then releasing them, as she had always done in anxious moments; the hollow cavern of her mouth echoed a sound like calcareous water dripping from a stalactite. Yes, the money *did* have an appeal. The funder would be a wild card, and she didn't like the not knowing. It stacked the odds against success—*her* success. She had always, in times when it had mattered, insisted on knowing, and eventually besting, all players in any venture she had ever agreed to become part of. But nothing before had been on this scale; nothing had risked death based on a single mistake. Still…millions? She had always had hopes of that. Now, it seemed, were she to be smart enough, and could maybe dodge a bullet, she could have it all—everything she had ever wanted.

Okay, she thought to herself, it'll take me a while, but I'll make it a point to *out* the funder. Not publicly, just for myself.

By knowing the *who* and the *what,* she felt she could cope with any fear tactics he would have used to scare Lee. Maybe the guy, if it *is* a guy, could be beaten, as in a game of Texas Hold 'Em: garner the right cards and he'd be hers.

"I'm in," she said, finally. "All in. Okay now if we work our way through the rest of your stuff."

Lee smiled, blinking away a freed-refugee's tear, reached for Abigail's hand, grasped it, and breathed a relieved, happy "Thank you!"

Composing herself, she continued, trying to pick up wherever she might have left off. "We can't have an army of people up there, but we *will* need enough security staff to keep an eye on incoming and exiting people and their vehicles. We'll do that primarily through closed-circuit TV. Our receptionist can be the anchor person for that activity—continuously in touch with all the funder's guys in black, a petunia in their onion patch—articulate, smartly dressed, politely confident. So, keep an eye out for the right person, okay? We'll have cameras installed at all our key locations: the entrance to our cold room, the exterior truck dock, and others as needed. A bank of TV monitors will be built in beneath the receptionist's workstation counter, out of sight of everyone coming into or leaving the lobby. Along with a high-end card-key system, which I'll have an expert specify prior to installation, she'll be able to tell at any given time who is coming and going, including our pre-cleared clients' visitors, all of whom will be issued access cards.

"When the funder and I did our walk-through of the hotel—my third time into it—he worried about my original business model needing to be modified to allow for a more legitimate seniors' residence, in the sense that it not be just my pet-project killing venue, as I had originally planned. So, we'll have to make the place look and feel like it's quasi-orthodox. Yes, there's some risk, I think, in allowing our clients—some of them, anyway—to come, stay, and later leave. We'll be expected to provide five-star service for them, maybe six if we can achieve it. But we'll charge accordingly; they'll be paying their way, plus. The clinic, on that basis alone, should turn a profit. And that's what the main man is looking for: big bucks."

Abigail *thought* what Lee had said earlier had had a male gong to it—*yes*, confirmed: the funder *is* a man—maybe with a big clapper hanging from too small a bell. Or perhaps the other way 'round. She sensed an unwashed pungency and wrinkled her nose. How off-putting, she thought. Males in that mode usually were. If that's him, he might need fixing, in more ways than one. She could accommodate that and she knew how. A paucity of anaesthetic might be a nice touch, when the time came, and a dull scalpel. It might move the voice up an octave.

"I can see you feel the same way I did about the added risk," Lee managed. "It was imposed, believe me."

Abigail nodded. Yet another flag. What else might be forthcoming, she wondered?

"Our clients' suites will need to be luxurious and single occupancy—no wife-husband situations. Marketing literature and word-of-mouth promotions will need to make this rule perfectly clear. Only widows or widowers need apply. Why? Because any living spouse could become curious or, worse, alarmed, unless he or she happened to be between-the-ears numb. And, I feel that we reasonably couldn't kill both partners, either together or sequentially.

"While we're still on the plan's financial chapter, our funder has insisted on something akin to fractional ownership. Refurbishing, furnishing, and technical setup will cost—this is his best guess—between $12 and $15 million, including acquisition of the outlying condos. You can understand his position, thus the strength of it, given that we need him."

Abigail breathed quietly into the void of Lee's unexpected silence, deciding to remain restrained in speech for the time being. Expecting more to come, she wanted to allow Lee the opportunity to get it all out. She knew she would have her own turn soon and knew that she would have things to say, constructive things about her own potential contribution to the planning of what now seemed a firm offer of partnership in an exciting, if dark, endeavour, and a challenge that had begun to please her. Was it the danger, she wondered? The intellectual challenge? Both, maybe? She didn't know, exactly, but had begun to build confidence that she could master this endeavour and was beginning to want to. Yes, part of it was about the money—things a fortune could buy her, things she had longed for, could never afford, until now, perhaps….

Lee raked together the leaves of her pleasantly breeze-shuffled wits, found her way back into the conversation, and reopened it with a to-the-point question: "Abby, how would you, or the butcher, kill them?"

"No problem," Abigail smiled. That had been coursing through her mind from the moment Lee had hinted at what the game was all about. She knew the options, too, had weighed them, had come up with her preferred solution—with lesser alternatives to offer, if asked—and had been waiting to lay her death-on-demand methodology on the table for some minutes.

To get there, she mused, she had dipped into a well of confidence she knew to be one of her strengths: an academically anchored self-discipline underpinning what had been a relentless, lifelong pursuit of learning.

"Massive air injection," she prescribed. "There would be no traceable residual; an autopsy wouldn't uncover cause. Maybe a track mark, but nothing more and nothing incriminating."

Lee smoked on that for a few seconds, demurred, not wanting to be outdone. She probed her mind for other solutions and revisited a professional past for possibilities. Where *were* they when she needed them, all the known ways? Case studies? Snippets she may have tuned into while brushing shoulders with peers long ago? But nothing came. Uncomfortable with that, she tried to skate around it. "*If* something else," she catechized, "what would be preferable in terms of its pharmaceutical accessibility—on the black market, say, or legitimately—and yet not be traceable? Euthanizing people with drugs used by vets, maybe?"

"There's morphine, of course," Abigail replied. "It's very comfortable. An overdose would do the job. But a good lab tech could find it within forensically captured blood samples, which could become problematic for us. With my method, air would be free. Always. *We* can't live without air," she smirked, "and *they* couldn't live with it. It would improve our bottom line, were that to matter."

"Okay. I'll agree to that. We'll go with your air. Now, talk to me about our clients' final gurney journey—from life to death. What's your preferred sequence?"

"Jesus, Lee," Abigail flipped back, "You're morbid! At first I thought your motive was altruistic, at least somewhat honest, that you wanted to lend a hand to those begging to die anyway."

"It was," Lee smiled, "At least in the beginning. But the whole thing morphed, like a pupa that became the squeaking death's-head hawkmoth, able to mimic the scent of honeybees and capable of moving about in hives without being disturbed and wreaking havoc while there." She'd read *that* somewhere, probably in one or another bookclub study. Or maybe she had seen it in a movie. Yes, it had been a movie. Thinking herself wise, she paused to let it all sink to the bottom, and then said, "But all quite innocent until it crawled out of its hole in the ground. Wouldn't you agree?"

"Okay," Abigail conceded, unimpressed, but faking it. "You must've signed up for a minor in entomology somewhere along the way? Bugs were never my thing. Anyway, I'm impressed. Good analogy."

"Thanks. But no," Lee grinned, "I didn't learn it in school; I memorized it from second and third viewings of the movie *Silence of the Lambs*."

Clever, I guess, Abigail conceded, but just to herself.

She felt a need to reintroduce the wedge of her natural desire for dominance. "Well, usually a surgeon wouldn't be in an operating room until after the patient had been sedated," she said, reaching back to their earlier topic. "A nurse would not, in any real-world scenario, accompany the patient into the OR. She, along with the surgeon, would visit the patient at bedside, prior to or leading up to the pre-op intravenous being administered. A nurse, someone we'll have to find, would give the bedside pre-op medication—Valium or something similar in a hefty dose—and then I'll follow up and administer, via the same IV, a lethal injection of air. In fact, *I* could become your *doctor*. By the way, what's the name of the guy you have in mind for that?"

Lee wasn't really ready to say. What if she couldn't get him? "Well, for now, let's just call him 'Doctor Jekyll'. I don't know, yet, if we can interest him in the project, but I do believe he would make a valuable addition to our team. It's about his charm, you know, his attested-to lightness of being and his reputed good looks, which I believe could tip the scales in our favour in terms of winning over our best-prospect clients for the clinic's *operation*."

"You haven't met this guy, right?" Abigail asked.

"Yes, that's true, but I have it on pretty good authority that he's all I'm making him out to be."

"Whose *pretty good authority,* if I'm not being too pushy?"

"You know him, actually—not Doctor Jekyll of course—the guy who was his best friend through their high school years: Stan Watson."

"*Watson?* You're kidding! Jesus, Lee, he used to be a cop! Is he somehow connected with this?"

"No, he's not, nor will he ever be. I came across Doctor Jekyll, at least his persona, the same time I first learned about you: at one of Stan and Chelsea's Christmas parties. It was all just innocent cocktail conversation, really; everyone was getting to know each other. Quite sinless, wouldn't you agree?"

"Okay. Maybe it was. So, what's Jekyll's story? I may need some convincing. There's a bit of a gap, in my mind, you'll understand, between medicine and cutting meat."

"Now, now; don't become the invidious little creature I may be beginning to sense in you. He'll be a meaningfully contributing member of the team, assuming we can snag him. But *you* will have the final say on everything we do related to medicine—the operating room and beyond and the clients' health-care in general. We won't be killing them all, and the ones who'll be with us longer term are bound to have needs for treatable aches and pains. You'll be there for them. Jek will be an actor; you'll be our real medical presence."

"It sounds to me like you're half in love with this guy," Abigail shot back. "And you haven't even *seen* him! What did Watson regurgitate that elevated him to *surgeon* in your mind?"

"Well, for a couple of years the two of them were the closest of buddies. 'Jek', shall we call him, apparently was able to, early on, shoot a mean game of snooker. Stan couldn't keep up; he usually ended up paying the tab, a quarter, in those days, which is what the village barber, who owned the pool hall, charged. It was the same price as for a haircut. Later, some evenings, they would sniff around the village, looking for girls who *would,* or at least *might,* but apparently they never got lucky. The chase was fun, although it had interfered with their school grades. They had too often avoided their homework and study. I suppose it was a response to the usual teenaged boys' hormonal explosion. They're *all* like that, don't you think?"

"Yeah, probably," Abigail replied, relaxing a bit. "Most young males are little more than walking hard-ons; they can't concentrate long on much else. The two of them doing that doesn't surprise me. Freud had it right, I believe: everything—at least everything *male*—is subconsciously linked to sex."

"So," Lee continued, wanting to steer away from a tangential thesis on psychology, "they did everything else together. They once raided a nest of great horned owls and raised two of the unhappy parents' fluff-covered chicks. They shot blackbirds at the local fairgrounds to feed them. Ted's owl was killed on a highway that ran in front of his parents' home. Stan's got shooed out of town by village elders for stealing some lady's feather-accessorized hat—right off her head, on the town's main street, or so legend has it—during a Saturday night hunt for its dinner, when all the pious victim's country friends were preening their way along the village's two-block-long, storefront sidewalk. Very embarrassing for her, I expect.

"Ted's dad was physically and emotionally abusive. The family was poor, by any standard. His dad had trouble finding steady employment, at least in that town, although he had apparently done okay earlier. So he trapped during the winters and sold the furs for whatever they'd bring. The kids—Jek had four younger sisters—often went without food. They weren't starving, really just hungry, and went to school hungry. One of their teachers sometimes brought them things to eat or took them to a nearby restaurant for a bite.

"Jek's was a tough go. He ran away once and was found, I think, at an uncle's place in Alberta, and was brought home. But by the end of the eleventh grade, he had had enough and left school and lucked into an apprenticeship with a friendly butcher in a neighbouring town. He became really good at it—not just at cutting meat, but also at marketing—charming first-time lady customers into his boss's shop, drawing them away from the competition. And, according to Stan, it wasn't all a put-on. Jek had always been a charismatic, self-effacing person, who was easily met and very easily liked.

"He married a girl from that same town. At some point they moved to B.C., and bought and renovated a home in Summerland. There, his life had had its ups and downs. Perhaps at times he would hit the bottle, perhaps a psychologically damaging imprint from an emotionally and physically abusive father. But he managed to weather a lasting and stable marriage—through good times and bad, as have many of us—and successfully raised a family. In time, he came back to butchering, eventually to blossom into the meat department manager for a large grocery chain in Penticton. Time passed. Decades, as it does for everyone. He was dropped by the grocery store just before becoming pensionable, perhaps so the chain wouldn't suffer the financial drain

The Fontana Resurrection

of it. So, he and his wife relocated to a small town near Cranbrook, Kimberly, actually, if you know it. Far as I know, they're still there.

"He had needed some sort of an income, so he formed a partnership with another guy—also a butcher, as far as I know—offering custom-killing and meat-packaging services to cattle farmers in the region. It was Jek's job to dispatch all cattle selected by his clients. He did this with a .22 magnum, which he carried with him when needed. He shot them in the face. This became routine; he was able to kill without emotion, I suppose, concentrating his mind on getting the job done cleanly. Each animal, once down, was hoisted on a chain—the chain knotted to the bucket of a front-end loader on the farmer's tractor—and eviscerated. Ted's partner's primary responsibility was to do the cutting, wrapping, and freezer preparation of the carcass."

She paused a moment to wonder if she had really got the calibre of his rifle right, or if the animals really were shot in the face. Maybe it had been in some other part of their dumb, cud-chewing, bovine heads.

"I'm guessing," she continued, "that he didn't have, or maybe couldn't afford, a device like the pneumatic skull puncher used by Javier Bardem in the movie *No Country for Old Men*. Did you ever see that?"

Abigail shook her head, no; she didn't change expression and didn't much like movies. Forcing a feigned interest, she wanted this part to be over. Techniques, details, for slaughtering cattle constituted a food-provision necessity she felt she wouldn't be the lesser for by knowing less of it.

"It was a good arrangement; they had lots of business. Both partners were old hands at what they were doing, and the money wasn't just helpful, it was needed.

"Everything looked rosy for them both until, without explanation," she paused, checked to ensure she still had Abigail's attention, smiled, "Jek's partner walked into the bush one day with his own gun and blew his head off.

"Bad scene," she added. Another pause. "That was it. Doctor Jek spiralled into a troubling depression, which he still may be working his way through. That's why I think he might be open to a generous offer—and I'll make it *very* generous—from us. Our budget can handle it, I think, given that our *budget,* if I can call it that, appears to be open-ended—the downside being, like a hangman's noose, it may be waiting for a taker."

Lee was very much enjoying this, the mischievous side of her mind shepherding thoughts from the farthest pastures of her mind, winnowing and culling them into manageable sound bites to be squeezed through deliberately exaggerated pursed lips. It showed in the curled-at-the-corner's smile as she tried to smooth the flow, wanting Abigail to discover that she could be as macabre as need be, all in the interest of preparing for the larger task ahead. What inexplicably escaped her was that her lexical Mephisto Waltz was being received by her sole listener as something akin to staccato spurts of clay-coloured ooze spattering from Yellowstone mud pots.

Lee sat quietly, smile still there, not frozen but permitted to linger, pleased with the tale she had just thawed and unwrapped. Projecting a dominant mental toughness would be something she would continue to work on.

But now, for today, it felt to her like a pause might be called for, a turn in the direction of diminished intensity. It might be her best expedient. Her whole pitch, she had begun to divine, risked unraveling like act three of a badly written play.

Seconds passed. The ensuing silence tumbled into the hiss of weir-heightened Rideau River water, urging its way downstream as the Colonel's heritage locks settled into a latter-day compromise between the prescient officer's engineering attempt to have the when-closed mechanisms remain ever water tight and an acceptance of their century-plus entropic creep toward imperfection.

They let the silence of those moments hang as ethereal in-fill guarding the space surrounding them. They glanced to see if any stranger might have slipped unnoticed into the park—*their* park, they thought, at least for this one afternoon—who might become curious about what could be taken for the dualistic tension of a quarrel…or a conspiracy. But no such intrusion had occurred.

The solemnity remained either of theirs to break, seated as they were on a time-blackened rub of decay which was slowly crumbling the surface of their bench, all just inches away from insect-pocked, edge-curled bark attempting still to protect the trunk of their unconsciously chosen old-growth maple, its lava-emulating root protrusions offering wind-defying strength to the storm-torn limbs above: a tree as old as the giant hand-carved blocks that gave efficacy to the canal system itself. *Their* tree now was now pushing out its shade, ever lengthening a rich shadow of foliage beyond them to envelop most of the uppermost lock's gates and winches.

But, the nature of silence dictates that silence itself ever remain perishable, especially when one or more humans dare pretend patience with it. And so—lit cigarette to balloon—it broke, favouring Abigail.

All's well…*maybe*, she postulated silently, except perhaps her uncertainty about the funder and the financing terms Lee had agreed to. Onerous strictures, they seemed. And what about Lee's grand plan itself? The bigger picture. Might she not have let herself be swept away by the magnitude and promise of it?

Coming back from within her reverie to their bench and looking again at Lee, she muttered something she thought might be safe. "Interesting background, your Doctor Jekyll's," wondering all the while how her dubious new friend had been able to hold all of it in memory. Had she been keeping notes on stuff like this? Had she gone through a similarly exhaustive background perquisition before today's approach? How long had this *clinic* thing been rolling around inside her head? Might there be—and this was scary—an *obsession* here? If so, what risk could that carry?

Abigail tended to juxtapose obsession with addiction whenever thinking of either, apportioning them equal weight vis-à-vis any danger implied. She felt now that this woman had been painting herself stroke by stroke onto a canvass that would need further study—lots of it. Where was the true representation or clues to one that might lead to a clear interpretation of all this? Clues? Really? Maybe there weren't any and wouldn't be any; perhaps it had just drifted along as an unfathomable enigma—an abstraction—like Picasso's *Seated Nude*. Caution clearly was warranted here, although that caution didn't suggest it yet needed to become a showstopper. She would have to watch out for any telltale ripple, appearing as it might as though caused by a periscope cutting through moonlit water. A rogue torpedo wasn't something she fancied, not unless she could possess one of her own. She would need to prepare to counter *any* threat, she concluded, were these uncertain fears to turn toward reality. But she would think more on that later.

"Okay," she offered, pursing her lips into a tight pucker and pushing against her teeth with her tongue, "let's assume you could, *maybe*, get Jekyll, or that you *did* manage to get him. My take is that he wouldn't need to be in the operating theatre, ever. His role would default, at best, to smiling his way through the clinic, room to room, as our main marketing and bedside-manner guy. *And* he would need extensive briefings from me to understand the to-be-faked procedures well enough to confidently answer, or at least skate around, our patients' questions." She paused for effect, then added, "Are you sure you want that?"

"Yes, Lee replied, "I do." She also wanted to end any further debate for now. Jek's recruitment would be at her insistence, if necessary. She was, after all, in charge of this whole affair, wasn't she? It remained her call to make. Why was Abigail being so stubborn? There'd be room for them both. Abigail would just have to accept that.

"Doctor Jekyll will know, for instance," Lee burbled on, "the details about whatever the clinic's cold-room will need to look like, at least on its hallway-facing side, to the occasional passerby, and how it may need to be modified internally to optimize our ease of use. We wouldn't want to be parking gurneys, shall we say, that carry Aunt Martha's corpse, along with several others, in the basement corridors, would we? If, for example, he would prefer shelves to meat hooks, maybe he would build them for us.

"But, more importantly, we'll need his style, his gregarious, optimistic presence, which we'll let permeate our entire clinic. He'll become an adjunct, of course, to your own dominance." She looked for Abigail's reaction and saw none. "He'll offer his own unique, value-added contribution. He's obviously no stranger to death; I'm sure he won't be put off stride when transforming our warm, air-breathing clients into packaged, frozen clunkers, ready for delivery to the sea."

Abigail paused, mulling over risks of the whole Doctor Jekyll issue and decided to put it behind her.

She concluded that she had best change course now and move instead toward a firm attempt at unmasking a doubt she had nurtured all afternoon about the very essence of the Fontana scheme.

"Lee, you seem reasonably confident that our clients' naiveté will be such that they'll buy into the whole hoax that's the foundation of your proposal. What makes you believe they'll be that stupid? If these people have the kind of money you're thinking about having them spend on room and board and an operation that'll let them relive part of their lives, don't you think some of them will be at least doubtful?"

Lee found that a bit harsh. "Yes," she said, keeping her voice steady, confident, annoyed, but still under control. "Actually, I've studied it. Gullibility amongst Canada's seniors increases the closer they come to dying of natural causes. Their brains begin to atrophy—stagnate, if you'd prefer—along with their bodies. It becomes a race to the bottom. Apparently it hinges on a scientific conclusion that *hope* is their common denominator. They want and need to cling to hope, their fingers clutching at the cliff edge they perceive themselves falling over, praying that something, anything, might buy them a bit more time. Compounding that, the more naive among them are inclined to believe that good is more prevalent than evil. Why, after all, would any doctor hurt them, let alone *kill* them? Or even *lie* to them? It's preposterous, they think; that's not what doctors and hospitals and clinics do. They're there to *help* people. And with all the advancements in science and medicine during the last couple of decades, why shouldn't it be possible to live another thirty or forty years? They believe what they want to believe, when they want to believe it. And their money—those that have enough of it—will make the magic of wealth their ticket, their right, in effect, to participate in a program deemed beyond the financial grasp of the ordinary man or woman. They think being rich has its privileges. They've allowed themselves to be lulled into lethargy by their taken-for-granted comforts, have become mentally and physically lazy, like three-toed sloths engaging their brains only when necessary to make their limbs move just the few inches needed to reach and eat a cluster of leaves.

"Here," she said, extracting from her purse a folded page from a recent issue of the *Globe and Mail*. "I brought this for you. If you research *dementia*, as I have, you'll find there's a large body of material like this, suggesting seniors are vulnerable to scams—and continuously falling for them and into them—even when attempts are made to inform them of the risks. Nigeria, for example, has created cartels out of siphoning off money from the West. A scammer there need only have pay-per-hour access to the facilities of an Internet cafe and a creative mind to get started. That's just one example. Then there are the Bible-thumpers and televangelists closer to home who've made fortunes convincing our targeted age-group to give generously to charitable endeavours, for which the proponents purport to act as benevolent conduits, claiming to pass the donors' money on to wretched souls who so desperately need it."

Abigail nodded, agreement being the easier path.

"Ours is just a variation on old-as-time deceptions. I believe the joy here is that we are pioneers in our niche."

Abigail let that soak in while unfolding Lee's newspaper item, although not as spilled water being mopped up with wadded paper towels. Lee had highlighted sections of the text with a yellow marker, apparently to draw attention to the important stuff. But *importance*, Abigail supposed, should be the prerogative of the beholder. What, within the article, might she be being led to *miss*?

"Read that. Aloud, okay?" Lee asked. "It's been a while for me. I'd like to hear it again. It will, I think, make you a believer."

The article was titled *Per-sua-sion*. Beneath it, a quarter-page etching of a human brain stared sightlessly back at her, its convolutions reminding her of wet noodles spilled into a bowl of tomato juice. There, in large serpentine letters, blending with the bends and turns of cerebrum lobes, the illustrator had inked, in a subtle overlay—as camouflage does for a hunter—the word *scam* in capitalized letters. It was clever, certainly an attention-getter. Abigail stared at the word, absorbing its intended message.

The subtitle read *Shadow of a Doubt.*

She started reading, moving her eyes uncertainly over highlighted lines, curious—but passing over—sections that she guessed were to be, or could be, overlooked. In a tone calculated to sound somewhere between interest and obligation, she began:

"The brain's ability to see through misleading advertising claims or even outright fraud is reduced as people age, putting seniors at greater risk of making questionable purchasing decisions."

Her gaze reached for the next highlighted line: "How can you tell that a herbal supplement may not be a miracle pill, or that a Nigerian Prince is actually of dubious nobility? Most people would say it's as simple as using your brain."

She paused until she found the next highlighted text: "But new research suggests that, for some of us, it may not be that easy. The findings have implications for the growing population of seniors, their families and caregivers, and for the advertising industry in general." She looked at Lee, who was smiling her knowing smile and then continued: "A study from the University of Iowa has linked one specific part of the brain with our ability to doubt. When we are given information, we depend on an oval-shaped lobe in the front of our brains to turn on the skepticism. It's called the ventromedial pre-frontal cortex, or the bottom-middle section of the pre-frontal cortex—that part of the brain that is crucial for governing much of our behaviour, including personality traits, social conduct, and decision-making."

Passing over the next stretch of unmarked print, she came again to the becoming-annoying translucent yellow. "Before now, scientists did not know which part of the pre-frontal cortex was responsible for our ability to doubt. The researchers found it by testing subjects' reaction to misleading advertising."

She was beginning to get the hang of reading ahead. Reaching to the start of a new highlighted paragraph, she continued, "Why should those of us without brain damage care about this softball-sized chunk of grey matter? Because it's a part of the brain that naturally deteriorates as we age and is often damaged by a stroke." Then another. "While some people can reach the age of 90 without losing function, at least some damage to this part of the brain is common enough among seniors to raise questions about the ethics of marketing to this segment of the population. And it raises even more red flags about scams targeted at the elderly. 'As you normally age, this is the first thing to go,' said neuroscientist Erik Asp, now a postdoctoral fellow at the University of Chicago and the lead author of the study. 'These are vulnerable populations.'"

And so it went, paragraph after paragraph, but she had adapted to anticipating them, her reading fluid and by now more confident. "That understanding is crucial for caregivers. When an elderly family member falls victim to a scam—or simply makes unwise buying decisions influenced by ads—it can be easy to assume they would have to be stupid to fall for those messages, Mr. Asp said. But very intelligent people can just as easily lose their capacity for doubt if this part of the brain is affected."

Ahead lay a bit more. "That will be a growing concern as Canada's population of seniors grows: people 65 and older are projected to make up nearly 17% of the population by 2016, and will jump to roughly a quarter of Canada's population in the next 25 years, according to Statistics Canada."

Now she could handle it, almost like Peter Mansbridge reading the six-o'clock news. And she did.

> Those seniors are getting wealthier, making them an attractive target: from 1908 to 2005, the median income of married senior couples rose 34%, and seniors living alone saw their median income jump more than 40%.
>
> People in their 60s are the most targeted group in Canada for "mass marketing fraud," including telemarketing scams, identity fraud, and scams linked to West Africa, according to statistics from the Canadian Anti-fraud center. But if the reported cases among people in their 70s and 80s are lower, it may not be because people are less targeted as they age. Seniors' advocacy group CARP also suggests that

among the elderly a large amount of financial abuse goes unreported.

Factors such as social isolation can make the elderly more vulnerable, "This is a targeted group for different reasons—and this is just one more factor to worry about."

Even if it is not a clear scam, people's judgment can be impaired even when it comes to regular advertising, and then can lead to questionable purchasing decisions.

However, it is incredibly difficult to protect seniors through regulation, because there is very little advertising that is targeted toward that group only. Regulators have been able to impose strictures on advertising to children. But a similar initiative would be harder to execute for the elderly and may risk infantilizing or insulting seniors.

"If there's misleading advertising…we're really biased toward believing things. It takes more effort to disbelieve," Mr. Asp said.

Abigail took a minute to postulate Asp's conclusions, looked again at the illustration, looked up at Lee, folded the page, and handed it back. "Okay," she managed, feeling she had best respond positively, "I'll buy that," she lied. "I'm a believer. It's convincing." Or so I'll say for now, she allowed herself.

She was hugely skeptical. Would she bet the farm on this? No, she didn't think so. Asp seemingly didn't have anything to lose, except his reputation; she, on the other hand, might be staking her life on what they were venturing into.

She *knew* that she knew a lot about the brain, but didn't feel it would advance the in-the-moment chemistry of today's chitchat were she to launch into a debate about something Lee apparently held to be a snippet of medical gospel. Abigail was sure that Lee had internalized this stuff because she had *wanted* to believe it.

Anyway, they had said most of what they had needed to say and now knew each other better in the lateness of this otherwise pristine afternoon. Each sensed the essence of where the other stood and realized they would have to step gingerly through this dance to avoid bruising toes. Neither knew yet with any certainty which of them might end up leading, who might bend to whom. In Abigail's case, there was a growing angst that Lee might not easily yield her for-now frontal position. Lee realized she had chosen an unexpectedly strong, wilful personality to become her running mate, and that she would have to remind Abigail from time to time who was on top.

When all was sifted, it had weighed enough—enough for this day—actually a lot. Abigail by then had agreed to bring her professional expertise to bear in dispatching the Fontana Corporation's clients. Lee thought that Abigail apparently knew how to do it, untraceably. "Just pump fifty milliliters of air into an IV," she had said, "If it's to be a central line, all the better," which had met with Lee's uncertain acceptance. It seemed to Lee that Abigail was *enthusiastic* about the killing, as well as about proceeding with their collaborative, equal-partnership approach. She had even agreed to taking responsibility for setting up the clinic's operating theatre and said that she would treat the project as one would hope a motion-picture producer might when planning the finer details of an intricate movie set. Her medical props wouldn't have to work of course; they would just need to look real. Lee was sure that this new best friend would shop around, acquire the hardware and instruments needed, and arrange storage until the hotel's makeover neared completion. Even better: she had agreed—and this was a plus—to involve her husband as the project's general contractor, having exacted a promise that he would never be made aware of what they were up to. Small concession for a large payout, Lee thought.

It was time, at least in Lee's mind, to go home, splash a few ounces of Pinot Grigio into a chilled glass, kick off her shoes, and settle into one of her and Carlyle's river-facing deck chairs. If Carly wasn't home, she would scratch around in her reading pile for a couple of the more-recent women's fashion magazines and place them so their covers could reflect a shiny distraction from the top of her chair-side table, offering at least a partial answer to his unasked question: What had she been up to all day? On her way there—not a long drive—she would concoct a palatable yarn to augment the magazine's window-dressing notion.

They stood and walked back to their cars, saying little, except to themselves. Sugarcoated and disingenuous words about home began coming to her. They would just have to be sorted and better arranged. He liked her words. They would just have to *sound* like the truth. Maybe, she would say, she had been playing a little bridge with friends. Yes, she would develop that thought. Bridge was very time-consuming.

She felt that she had played her cards well today.

Scene 21
Lee Needs a Surgeon...

> *"Life is pleasant. Death is peaceful. It's the transition that's troublesome."*
> –Isaac Asimov

October 21, 2009, 6:18 p.m.
Now to find a surgeon, and after that a semi driver, Lee mused, making her way to the bottom of her second glass of Pinot Grigio. Carlyle hadn't yet come home, which was good.

Details, she thought, this whole venture was beginning to feel like it was plagued with details. Soon she would have to off-load a lot of this stuff onto Abigail. For her own part, she would need to keep a closer eye on the bigger picture. Realistically, she couldn't buy the hotel or the condos until she had all or most of her people lined up, so she would have to get onto that quickly and stay on it. What if someone else bought the damned hotel? No, she told herself, the thing was too much the first-cousin to a knockdown. The only thing saving it was the possibility of a creative multimillionaire willing to resurrect and improve its original architecture. Yes, she would be able to acquire the wreck. She had tapped into her multimillionaire, hadn't she? And she now had Abigail. Next: Doctor Jekyll. "Piece of cake," the wine was telling her, and she said it out loud.

She vaguely knew—as she had glazed over earlier with Abigail, having then gilded the lily just enough to convince her that they shouldn't drop the idea of having a *doctor*—a meatcutter who sounded like he would be a perfect fit, assuming he could be located and cajoled into becoming part of their operation. Her initial lead, as had been the case with Abigail, had come from one or another conversation at one of Stan and Chelsea's parties.

Stan, she had deduced, had a penchant for talking too freely, particularly about what he had alluded to as his humble beginnings. "Just a poor-boy," he had been fond of mumbling, "a failure, really, from a nowhere dot on the map, lost for the most part between gopher colonies on a flat stretch of southwestern Manitoba." In the telling, he had lost his way and had ventured into a tangential tale about another poor boy who had become his boyhood best friend, only later to run away from a brutal father to become a butcher. According to Stan, this fellow had been a real charmer: good-looking, affable, witty, and intelligent.

Poor Stan, she thought. Gullible Stan. Maybe he was lonely, or, worse—to put it less delicately, pityingly—friendless. Good thing he had such an assertive helpmate for a wife, otherwise he would simply disappear through one of the cracks in their floor…possibly never to be missed.

But, beyond his boyhood on the prairies, he never talked much about the two or so decades that had passed between moving east and signing on with Bell-Northern Research. She had wondered about that, since. In the depths of his usually morose countenance might there have been something he had been hiding? Something shameful? Prison, maybe? That possibility could be worth disinterring and dissecting, were she able to lay hands on just the right shovel and scalpel.

But enough of that, she thought, shaking her head to clear away the gentleness of an aura that was intensifying around objects she had been absently looking at for too long. It was an afterglow from the Pinot Grigio, she knew, but she had surrendered herself to its softness, its creep, anyway. Basking in her mischief, she pulled herself up to go to the fridge for another splash.

Unsteadily resettled, thin crystal stem tilting but with nothing yet spilled, she asked of no one but Carly's brown-eyed, black goldendoodle, "How *do* I snare Doctor Jekyll?" She smiled at the questioning turn of the dog's head.

Yes, that would have to be her next outreach, and a worthy challenge it was. Doing so might be tricky, given that her Doctor Jekyll had experienced, at least according to Stan's tale, a lot of bitter-cold winter days in the mountains assisting a trapper buddy. He had been doing that, not for the money, but for the camaraderie. So, she concluded, he'd likely have predatory instincts; he would know what a trap or a thin-wire snare might look like and even smell like to hunted prey, were they not presmoked. So, in her case, she would need to presume that he could filter and recognize her *words* for what they were: a potential trap. She knew that survival in the wild didn't favour the weak, and the strong didn't always reveal their recognition of their prey's vulnerability. It was all part of the chase and, in the end, the kill. In short, if he *was* affably intelligent, which Stan had implied, this Doctor Jekyll fellow might be inclined to beat her at her own game.

All of this—his dispassionate, professional ability to facilitate any animal's death, a lifelong refinement of cutting skills, and an innate friendliness—would make him the ideal candidate for the Fontana clinic's surgeon.

"Okay…lights, camera, action," she whispered to their tail-wagging companion, it having heard his master's footsteps as the opening and closing sound of the front door faded behind the approaching homeowner's advance into the kitchen. "We had better do a credible meet and greet. I'll pour him a couple of fingers of his favourite William Lawson's."

And she did, her greeting smile steady, assured, as she passed it to him. "Come," she said, "let's watch the geese on the river."

Scene 22
The Surgeon Offers a Driver...

October 24, 2009, 8:07 a.m.
Lee flew to Cranbrook, ostensibly to see her daughter Wendy for a couple of weeks. But it wasn't *really* to see Wendy. She had come with, in addition to her bags, a hidden agenda: a "surgeon" agenda.

Wendy had married, had mothered a now three-year-old child, and, after having dropped out of university twice, was taking an online course in an attempt to become a certified organic nutritionist. So, while in Cranbrook helping out with the baby—in order to allow her daughter to spend more time on her studies—Lee began a search for "Surgeon" Arthur E. McMurray, believing he might not be far away. Stan had said he had lived in or around Kimberly; maybe he hadn't moved from there.

Wendy had fallen into a happy routine of sending her mother to her favourite health food store every day, believing the family's nutritional ingestion needed to be organic and the meat as fresh as possible.

Lee thought the store was a convenient place to begin, so every time she embarked on the daily errand she had a little chat with the butcher. After a week, she and the butcher were getting well in-depth about cuts of meat, what was good, what was not so good, and how should it be prepared to best please a fussing daughter.

Then one day, during a segue-yielding pause in their exchange, she had casually interjected the question she had so long been nurturing: Did he know of or perhaps had he had a former colleague named Arthur McMurray?

Well, yes, the butcher had said and had given Lee a pencil-jotted card—tattered, faded but still legible—lifted from his twentieth-century-something Rolodex file, followed by an over-the-counter handoff of the region's phone book. She had anxiously and excitedly confirmed an address, hands shaking, as Arthur's name jumped out at her from a column on the third page of M's.

She had passed a fretful evening and night, trying hard before bedtime to remain up and cheerfully involved with her daughter's family. But her heart hadn't been in it. Sequential successes in her steps along the path toward making her clinic a reality—compounded by a sense of needing to keep it from slipping away like sand through an hourglass because no one was home to rotate it—emboldened her, puffed her up, and made her adopt a caution-to-the-wind approach in meeting this mystical character: the fabled Arthur "Doctor Jekyll" McMurray.

Having rehearsed the coming scene one final time and trying to suppress a growing frustration at driving her daughter's car to and around seemingly defiant streets of Kimberly, all the while trying to locate his house, she had finally arrived, parked, taken a last deep breath, and marched, head held back in a reach for confidence, up to his front door.

And, suddenly, there he was, door held wide in a gesture of greeting, his smile warm as Stanley had implied. She could almost picture the two of them, still as boys, with their owls.

Excitement reigned. Introduction niceties were hastily, smilingly—almost stammeringly—bubbled over with excitement. She was quick to invite him out for a cup of coffee and wanted the invitation posed before he might feel compelled to ask her in for a visit or to meet his wife. That wasn't part of her plan.

He had happily acquiesced, amused and somewhat confused, but flattered by the intensity and apparent determination of this stranger's presence.

He had remained disarmingly casual and charming throughout. She liked him from the get-go and wanted him to become *her* doctor. She was sure of it now.

She paid for their coffee, of course, along with the sticky bun that he relished, licking his fingers to catch last remnants of icing.

On the drive back to his place, she pulled over to a quiet, leafy street's curb, leaving him wondering for a moment, behind the mask of his ever-ready smile, what *this* was to be all about. They had pretty well covered his and her early life story at the restaurant. Before leaving it she had nudged their conversation in the direction of a perceived need, in her view, for the legalization of euthanasia in Canada. She had said that baby boomers were growing old, and not all of them—particularly the terminally ill—wanted to stick around for a dishonourable end. Yes, she said, they could go to countries in Europe to have that service rendered, but couldn't do that—at least not lawfully, not yet—here at home. He asked himself, so now what? That thought lingering, he hadn't been nearly ready for the proposal she was about to make to him.

And she did, couching her pitch in a padded wadding of insincere benevolence. They would be primarily doing their clients a great service, she said, letting them leave this earth with the last thing on their minds being that they had discovered a fountain of youth and were about to experience a rewind of their last thirty years or so. What could be a nicer way to go than that? And if he and she were to make a little money for their trouble, who was morally to find fault with that? So, she had asked, half an hour later, did he want in or not?

In the end, he had favoured it, had bought into the story and the offer that she had made him. Yes, he would be able to deliver on his part of the action, and, yes, it was true: he could use the money. He would have no problem in living away from home and commuting back from time to time, provided she could cover his travel expenses. Well, yes, she had offered, she could and would.

He had brightened when she confided in him that her next task would be to find a semi driver, because, he had informed her, his eldest son was licensed to do just that and probably would be as open to an offer as he had been.

Jay, the son, she was about to find, was a big man: a mountain of a man, really. He was gentle or seemed so. Softly spoken. Attentive. He politely and briefly answered questions in a manner that seemed to invite further questions. He lived in what an easterner might have been inclined to call *the bush*. They had gone to his house to meet him. On their first day, Jay had built them a fire in his well-used fire pit and had offered to barbecue hamburgers, an offer Lee had jumped at, having had a twelve-day run at Wendy's, nibbling little else than lettuce leaves and organic chicken bits. The fire had taken a chill off that late afternoon, and the burgers were delicious.

Art had effused his own view of what an opportunity he felt they were being offered, and he, more than Lee, had convinced the younger man that they should partner as a father-and-son team to take care of Lee's disposal issues.

In the three days that had followed, they had met and again sat on the same lengths of log, asymmetrically nudged into easy reaching distance over the rocks surrounding Jay's fire pit, Lee prodding at char collapsing from split but heavy wood blocks that time and oxygen and the modest dance of flame were reducing to orange embers begging her attention. She had thus imposed a positioning of herself in the developing pecking order as ex officio corporate-meeting host, working out next-step details and the longer timeline that rebuilding the hotel would necessitate.

When, finally, she had said good-bye to father and son, and then to Wendy, and flown home, she had realized that her newest team members would bring to the table—the *slab* she had called it, but just to herself—creativity, daring, and enthusiasm to what all three had come to believe was by now a very feasible endeavour.

Scene 23
The Driver Seeks a Man with a Boat...

"Hope deceives more men than cunning does."
-Author unknown

November 15, 2009, 2:38 p.m.
Before leaving Kimberly, Lee had delegated a mission to Jay: He was to explore one or more stretches of shoreline—of his own choosing—along Canada's East Coast with his objective being to find a fishermen with a suitable boat, who was willing to take up to twelve or fifteen weighted and wrapped bodies at a time out to sea and dump them. Between the boat guy and himself, he was to work out a secure procedure for doing this on a recurring basis. The procedure, however, was

to be understood and *not* documented, anywhere. She gave him *carte blanche* to set up this end of the business: authority to spend whatever it might take to facilitate the recruitment and to establish the fisherman's price for accepting his end of the deal.

He should get onto this project fairly quickly. She would soon want and need the peace of mind of knowing that disposal arrangements were in the bag. He was to give the boatman a clear understanding that drop-offs wouldn't begin for as much as a year; all parties concerned needing to accept that that much time would be required to get the hotel—their clinic—rebuilt, equipped, and furnished. She asked him to track his expenses and to check in with her in Ottawa when he deemed his mission accomplished. She would reimburse him then for everything.

Jay immediately warmed to the challenge. Starting with very little knowledge of the country's East Coast geography, he purchased maps and collected travel brochures to help with planning his venture. He augmented that study with a couple of afternoons in the Kimberly library, burrowing through books and reference materials the staff were helpful in selecting for him.

He found himself drawn to the eastern shore of Nova Scotia as his best starting point. In defense of a gnawing uncertainty, he promised himself that it would be, as a minimum, his beginning. Were that not to work out, the knowledge he would gain from exploring towns and harbours along the shoreline would serve him in good stead. Later, were he to need to revector his search, he would try farther north, perhaps Cape Breton. He deduced that he would be able to learn more from just meeting and chatting with people along the way. He thought that picking out older seamen in pubs and buying them a beer or two should be possible. But just in the more *promising* of places; he must not buy beer on Lee's nickel, at least not just for himself. There wouldn't be time for excesses of that, anyway.

* * * * * * *

At the Halifax airport's row of car-rental counters, he shopped for the oldest model he could find, preferably something low cost, ideally with a few dents and scratches. Definitely, he rationalized, he shouldn't set out on this deception with something too ostentatious. Turned out, finding a yawner took a bit of haggling; he had to settle for a something in between—not a clunker, but near the end of its rentable tenure. It would do; it would need to. He told himself, believing he meant it, that if it rained he would make an off-highway run to splash the car through any muddy stretches he could find and then let the dirt dry on.

His plan, within the annoying uncertainty he had been unable to shake, included poking along the southeast shore. He knew he mustn't lock onto the first location showing potential. He would be able to backtrack to whichever—or all—that might make the cut. He imagined them all, if written down, would amount to just a short list. So, no need to write them down, just to remember them: he wasn't supposed to write stuff down, anyway. Lee had said so. He could only write down his expenses.

* * * * * * * *

He took Highway 102 through to Dartmouth and then turned east onto 107. From there he began his quest. Unsatisfied with the level of detail on the maps he had brought, he had picked up something much better, recommended by the car-rental office: a copy of the *Province of Nova Scotia Map Book,* which, happily for him, divided the province into large-scale, page-by-page sections. He quickly discerned interesting-looking places along 107, and he would look there for a harbour able to tolerate moderate-to-heavy truck traffic, a harbour that opened, essentially unobstructed, to the sea.

He found many of the ports along Highway 207 interesting, but he kept going, knowing he would be able, later, to reconsider them if needed. It was like buying a car. He shouldn't settle for the shiny model gleaming out from the first lot he had visited. He had done that before, and it had been bad news.

He slowed down in Chezzetcook and then again in Musquodoboit Harbour. He also spent a few minutes at Jeddore Oyster Ponds. Keeping any eye on the time, he picked up his pace. He stopped briefly—just long enough to reject—East Ship Harbour, followed by first- and second-look turndowns at both Pleasant Harbour and Popes Harbour. They wouldn't do. He moved on to Sheet Harbour, which had possibilities, but seemed somehow overdeveloped with too much traffic. He was seeking something more out of the way, somewhere discreet, in his own sense of the word (he thought it exuded a trace of his wannabe sophistication). His ideal place needed to be somewhere he could hide his boss's *disposals,* in plain sight, in the dark, because, if he found the right locale, no one would be looking.

Pushing east on Highway 7, he steered his way to Moses River. Un-uuh. Not there. He stopped at Ecum Secum, checked out Spanish Ship Bay, and then paused at Sherbrooke.

Hmmm. *Sherbrooke.* Yes. What a pretty town. He wasn't big on using that particular word— *pretty*—but figured that it applied here. Wanting a rest, he parked along what looked like the town's main drag. A walk would feel good; his legs were numbed, but, more, it might tidy up his now-cluttered mind. He tried to relax as he eased into it; stayed long enough to poke about through the historical fascinations of Sherbrooke Village and then some of the town itself. He liked the place. It didn't suit his mission's basic need, but it held out the possibility it could become a hub for a next-day's search, plus it was a place to buy groceries and other things he soon may need.

He couldn't shut down quite yet for this day, though, tired as he may be. Checking his map, he decided to persist for a bit longer along Highway 211, to follow Indian Harbour Lake down to where the bridge crossed at Indian Harbour. There, he stopped at the bridge for no good reason and lingered, longer than he had intended. Was he just tired or did he like the look of the harbour? By now he wasn't sure. Nice rocky beach, he thought. Then he pressed on to Bickerton West, and did a quick drive past Port Bickerton. Interesting. A possibility, maybe. But time to shut her down, he knew; his head wasn't working any more.

He thought he had seen a bed-and-breakfast back along the way toward Port Hilford, so he went back and, yes, the folks there seemed happy enough to meet him and to have him stay overnight.

He tried to keep his conversations brief while there. They didn't really ask what his business was, and he didn't really say more than was needed.

He decided that the next day he would return to Port Bickerton. It had interested him. He thought it had, anyway, although he wasn't sure now. There had been so many towns in so little time.

* * * * * * *

The morning was fresh and had a clean feeling. Crisp. No fog. He didn't have any more fog in his mind, either. His hostess had agreed to make him an early breakfast. Having slipped an extra ten dollars into the notes he had sorted to pay his board bill, he thanked her for their home's hospitality and comfort, and then left, anxious to resume what he had started the day before.

Shortly after his turn off Highway 7 onto 11, he noted what seemed a relative heaviness of truck traffic: mostly 53-footers, not many short boxes, and some 40- and 25-foot refrigerated rigs. He wasn't sure where the big ones were headed, but thought he would go in that direction to maybe sniff out their destination and, better yet, discover what they were carrying.

He passed through mile upon mile of the boreal forest. It was interesting, but he was used to the forests of British Columbia, so the view wasn't anything new. Breaks in it seemed to come mostly as he approached one or another harbour.

Seeing Port Bickerton, he slowed down, noting the modest collection of houses on its outer fringe. Just beyond appeared to be a trailer depot. All the trailers there, at least on one side of the main building, were 53-footers. He didn't know what they were about, but he assumed the place was related to the trucks he had seen coming this way.

He approached an intersection with a sign saying Bickerton West Fishplant. Turning in the direction of the arrow, he passed churches: St.

Paul's Anglican and a Gospel Light, concluding that this must be a pious community. He wasn't himself, of course, *pious*, but he thought it interesting. These people might even be somewhat honest! Honesty would be okay, as long as they weren't, for the sake of it, overly inquisitive.

On his right was a small post office. Then, he saw a small*ish* store—apparently the only one in the hamlet—a sign proclaiming it to be The Tickle. It promised, inside, that customers would find groceries and ice cream. "What the hell did the name Tickle mean?" he wondered, out loud.

But his interest, by now, was primarily in finding the fish plant. Nearby houses, as he passed them, looked adequate, a few even prosperous, like what he had come to expect a typical east-shore Nova Scotia village to look like.

Yes...*there!* He could see the fish plant on his left—its mottled, mustard-coloured, metal-clad buildings—and he could see where he would need to turn. The place had obviously been, at one time, a substantial operation, probably the community's lifeblood. From where he was, he could see the harbour. To his right was an interesting sign—*Caution, trucks loading*—for a yellow metal-clad building. It looked like a still-functioning, well-maintained, two-story facility, with what appeared to be a refrigeration unit on its upper level.

He had to drive around a truck ramp, keeping the car to the asphalt driveway. Approaching the harbour, he could see out onto the open ocean. Bingo! That's what he had been looking for. Almost straight ahead he could make out a couple of red and white lighthouses on a point, a light flashing in what appeared to be the farthest of the two, although both seemed part of just one facility. He came off the asphalt onto a crushed-stone parking area. All but one of the vehicles parked there were 53-foot trailers. He could see small loading cranes, apparent extensions of equipment sheds: three of them, there to facilitate lifting fish catches onto the dock or perhaps into waiting vehicles.

An assortment of floats was nearby, gathered together in large plastic bins, and cable reels—weeds growing up around and among them—seeming to have been there since Noah grounded his ark. And *very* large, upturned, netted baskets, perhaps used in conjunction with the cranes

The Fontana Resurrection

to hoist seafood catches from incoming boats. But he wasn't sure; all these things were still new to him. Literally dozens of the baskets were stacked one on top of the other, like soup plates turned upside down.

Not a soul was visible on the dock, although one, a watchful one, wasn't yet ready to be noticed.

He was beginning to think this place could be *it:* this harbour. Had he arrived? Could he have been that lucky?

He looked at his watch, found it was already midafternoon. It seemed that whatever was happening here was taking place within the yellow building. The others, except for the crane sheds, were dilapidated.

A fishing boat that he would check out later was tied at the main pier. It didn't look much different from others he had seen; it was typical of what he had presumed to be lobster boats.

The wind in the harbour and sweeping over the pier was high by now and cold. He could tell from the chop of the sea beyond the harbour's islets and natural breakwaters that piloting one of these vessels would require an experienced sailor, a skill set he didn't have.

Turning, he could see the siding on the older buildings in some places had been blown away by winds, exposing what he took to be now-decaying post-and-beam constructs. They still seemed sound enough to keep most everything upright. One of them looked, maybe, to be three stories high and, depending how it had been originally partitioned and built up inside, may have been as high as five. He could see that pigeons and rodents were quite at home. In its own way, it was a colourful place, hauntingly beautiful, even, to a man for whom the term *beautiful* was reserved primarily for flattering women, and the easier they were, the better. He had known more than just a few, amused that they had often preferred a certain softness. No, not of *that*, he smiled: a softness of vocabulary, which had come to him by way of practice during the hunt.

From where he stood, smiling still at his find, he could see a single yellow dory and cormorants, one of them standing on a rock, wings stretched, drying. A plethora of seagulls swept in ballerina-like trajectories, one having greedily laid beak on something no doubt disgusting;

they were ubiquitous and cacophonous creatures, he thought—the sea's garbage collectors.

He walked his incoming route back to the edge of the fish-plant property to find that the original part of the facility truly had become a ruin, beyond recovery. The sight reminded him of ghost buildings he had chanced to explore years ago in California on Monterey's Cannery Row, where fishermen for untold generations had harvested sardines. But the sardines must have moved on, or were fished out, and the buildings had fallen into disarray. These, in front of him, looked very much like Monterey's abandonment, except that some of the ones in California had been turned into upscale restaurants and a network of interconnected boutiques catering mostly to tourists.

Lost in his own fantasies, he became suddenly aware—was it the semi's engine starting?—of a possibly perceived uniqueness in his presence, were he to be observed by a local. Here was a stranger, daydreaming. Here? In this spot? Why? Who could be doing that? All reasonable questions. He didn't need nor want them. Not now, not with this new bit of activity happening around the front of the yellow building.

Refocusing, he concluded he should get out of there and stay overnight nearby. He would come back the following day to find out who belonged to the boat and whether or not it might be possible to engage the captain in friendly chitchat.

He had found himself quite taken with the village's charm: the saltbox homes, many white, one story or one-and-a-half stories, a collection of varying styles. Others were pale blue. Some carried five-pointed stars. He wasn't sure what that was about. He saw, while passing, yet another church, the Bickerton United Baptist Church, and then moved on along the harbour. Several house trailers went by, homes to their owners, looking in their way conservatively attractive.

He moved through a patch of forested area but was aware that—although he couldn't see it—he was still near the edge of the harbour.

At the next intersection, he came on a sign directing nonlocals to Fisherman's Harbour and the Country Harbour Ferry landing. He pulled over and stopped to think about that. Again he checked his watch. It was still early enough to allow him to go to the other side and

The Fontana Resurrection

have a look. Nonetheless, it would be more just a duty trip; he believed the location he had left behind him would do, and do nicely.

But it turned out to be quite a beautiful harbour. Flicking through to the relevant Nova Scotia maps, he decided to take the ferry across and then move on to Isaacs Harbour and perhaps Goldboro. Those communities, the map suggested, opened directly to the sea, although neither appeared to have a sheltered harbour of the type he was seeking.

The ferry turned out to be a uniquely structured craft, at least compared to anything he had seen before, pragmatically militaristic in its design. He explored its curiosities during the crossing; he thought it best, though, not to ask questions of the crew. Yes, after pacing its open deck, he could see that it could accommodate a 53-footer.

Upon landing, he moved along to the nearest intersection and turned toward Isaacs Harbour to take a peek. From where he sat nursing the wheel he could see clearly across the water; at most it would be half a mile. There were few trees on the far side, the usual white and black houses, red and black barns, brandishing white window trim, and a roadway—the *only* roadway into Isaacs Harbour—hugging the shore, within just feet of the sea.

He stopped for a few minutes to take a look at a rather larger-than-life white church on the opposite side of the road. Across from it were a couple of finger docks, pushing out into the water. God's house stood on a redbrick foundation, clad in white clapboard, with a black shingle roof and Gothic windows. The place had a way of catching his eye, had given him pause. The sea winds, over time, had been unkind to it. Perhaps its congregation, if it still had one, wasn't sufficiently large or not wealthy enough to keep up the paintwork. Some windowpanes were broken, although nothing else indicated that the edifice was unused. A graveyard toiled its way up the hill behind it, or perhaps it was down the hill; he didn't check to see who had been planted where, when.

It seemed a pretty enough town, small boats in the harbour—smaller than the one he would need for his purpose. The community, as he came nearer into it, was larger than he had expected.

He turned around when the crumbling two-lane asphalt ended in gravel. On his way back, reflecting again on the finger docks reaching into the harbour and the small boats at anchor there, he realized this site couldn't be good for his purpose. It didn't look like it would facilitate truck traffic coming in, at least not without being very much noticed by the town's inhabitants. Too many houses were right along the road looking over the harbour. There would be too much curiosity. It was too quiet a place to allow much of anything to happen without it becoming the topic of next morning's conversations over coffee. He wondered what they did as a substitute for Tim Horton's.

Maybe it was just the day or maybe it was the aura of desolation hanging over the place. It had bothered him because it looked empty, almost ghostlike. Not a place where he would want to live. He couldn't imagine, apart from its picturesqueness for folks who lived right at the water's edge, a reason for being there. Obviously they all had to use the ferry to get away occasionally, and it was a five-dollar passage each way, unless they could buy, say, a season's pass. So, that would be ten dollars to get out of the village and back. And ten dollars would mean quite a bit more to these folks than it would to anyone in Toronto or Vancouver.

He nosed the car over decaying asphalt toward Goldboro on the other side of the bay. There he came by four parked, possibly dying fishing boats about the size he would need, but wearing the rags of decay about them—of having fished their last season, and, as with aging racehorses, put out to pasture.

Now he could look back across the water and see where he had just come from. He could see the Baptist Church and the pretty yellow boat, a boat that might have worked for him, but it wasn't the right community.

As he moved along the bay's east side, he found himself coming into the next prospect. He could see from where he was out over the ocean. This side, like the other, had houses strung along the edge of the water. It was a rocky harbour with very few trees. Ubiquitous crows perched on power poles angling out of ditches, waiting for any snippet that they might hope to find or steal. Roadkill would be nice. Heads cocked, they watched his wheels. Nothing left crushed behind them. Poe had been right. They drove a cunning beak, any heart would do.

The Fontana Resurrection

Goldboro was obviously a very old community. Homes reflected that, although some appeared more prosperous than others. The town had its own interpretive center, but he wasn't going to take time to look through it. Again, he could tell; this place, like so many others before Port Hilford and Bickerton, wouldn't do. He could see the ocean, yes, but he knew too many curious eyes would be seeing *him* whenever he drove a truck into this part at the edge of the shore.

He pushed on to Drumhead. Not much there really, except the spectacular view of the sea. Some of the harbour islands were visible. Nothing, though, that would make it for him, at least not in terms of what he later would need to do.

He turned into the Drumhead Wharf Road, just to be sure. Yes, there was a pier. He came past the arena where he saw another attractive boat that looked almost brand new. It was of the kind he could use, and the dock looked like it had some potential. The place had perhaps a bigger wharf than the one at Bickerton. No buildings were on the outer edge, and no buildings were close by, except for some houses that, again, showed very little activity. The death knell was its huge exposure to the houses themselves. A truck of any size, even a 25-footer, would be bound to attract attention, especially when making trips, even irregularly, and even if executed by night. It just didn't look like it could be bent into his needed shape.

He drove toward the end of the wharf and noticed that it was barricaded off. It wasn't being used for large boats. There was nothing to offload catches, nothing really but a breakwater and a view of the sea.

The day was wearing on. He knew he had seen enough. His mind kept slipping back to Indian Harbour, to appease some inexplicable magnetism about the beach, and to Bickerton and Bickerton West. He liked that area. Somehow or other it just felt like the right thing, the right setup for him. Of course, no harbour facility or location could be without risk, but minimizing that risk was what his trip was all about.

He now believed that he had to go back to base in Sherbrooke—yes, he would make it his base—and refocus, this time on finding the right captain, his captain, in or around Bickerton.

He turned back and caught the ferry. He had been through enough. His harbour-decision made.

* * * * * * * *

Sherbrooke's Village Inn hadn't been all that hard to find. It was a workable fit for the time he would need to be in town.

He would remain cautiously pleasant with the staff while there, but not so relaxed as to be perceived as willing to enter into any shared memorable moments. *Friendly* was off the table. Best that way to be forgotten.

He enjoyed a light supper and a cold Keith's Ale, celebrating the evening with half his mission accomplished, followed by a reasonably untroubled sleep. The last thing he could remember having dreamt prior to breakfast was how to knock off the other half: finding his fisherman.

Scene 24
Disposal, the Lobsterman...

November 17, 2009, 10:38 a.m.

Jay breakfasted and then drove back to the fish plant at Bickerton.

It was quiet there, with just a single boat and one person working in and around it. He noticed that it was the same boat as the previous day. He wandered over, tourist fashion, to shoot the breeze with the man.

Hands in pockets, his best theatrical smile masking a true countenance, Jay offered, "Hi. Whatcha fishin' for?"

"H'lo," the man replied, in a not unpleasant manner, continuing to go about his business. "Yer not from around here, are yuh?"

"Nope. Just here fer a visit, is all. Tourist, I guess you'd say. From B.C. I'm tryin' to get acquainted with the uth'r end of our country."

"The other end? *Yer* frum th' uther end, wouldn' yu say?" the fisherman offered, a broad smile forming across his handsome, sixty-something face.

"Not 'zakly. I'm a mountain man, have always thought of myself as that. Like it better like that. Always have. I can make my way better when I'm alone."

"Really? You alone now?" the fisherman asked.

"Yuh."

"How did you ever find this place?"

"Oh, just pokin' along the coastline. Gettin' acquainted. No particular destination in mind."

"Where's next, then?"

"Dunno. Maybe just here. I kinda like it here."

"Here? At the fish plant? D'yuh know anybody here?"

"Nope. Don't know no one. I mostly don't *know* folks, anywheres. Bit of a loner, I guess. It has worked best for me. I like to travel though."

"What kinda work you do?"

"Driver. Big rigs, mostly. Work alone. Don't own one. I rent 'em when I can get a load."

The fisherman kept at what he was doing. It looked to Jay like he was tidying up more than getting ready for a day at sea. There was a *possibility* here, he thought. He liked the guy already. The fellow exuded a certain easy sincerity and seemed like a friendly, no bullshit sort. And the boat could work, too. "Are you going out today?"

"No. Just fussin' with the boat. Like to come down to her ever' day, when she's in the water."

"Nice lookin' boat. What's her story?"

"Story? Well, I guess yuh could call it was love at first sight. Had to have her, so here she is. Are yuh sure you wanna hear about it? I'm told I can be kinda wordy, sometimes."

"I've got all day. Not goin' anywheres, except maybe back, after I visit here for a couple or three days. The town looks really interesting."

"Which town?"

"Sherbrooke. I'm at the Village Inn. Maybe I could buy you a beer there, after you tell me about the love of your life here, if you'd like to do that."

The fisherman fairly beamed at the offer. "Well, don't know about the beer, unless you come up to my place for it. There's not much opportunity in Sherbrooke. There's no pub or anything. But anyways, here goes; don't say I didn't warn yuh. Why don't you step aboard?"

Jay did, extending his hand. "Jay McMurray. From a long way from here."

"Glad t' meet yuh. Russell Roude. I live near Port Hilford. Mostly, now, I fish for lobsters. Didn't always, though. Used to fish for fish, *real* fish."

"Maybe we could talk about that over your beer. Now, tell me about your boat. What's she all about?"

"Well, take a seat. Want a Coke? I've got a few in my lunch bag. She's got a fridge with ice. Want some?"

"The can will be fine. Thanks." This was looking better to Jay, by the minute. He popped the lid and took a long sip.

"Well," Russell started, "boats this size could go out overnight or for a week. Cabin in her can accommodate three men. She's got a stove and fridge. I bought her in 2006; my old boat was too small for the gear we had and couldn't handle the traps and gear aboard. Nothing was wrong with it; it was just too small. I shopped for this one for a month and a half, looking all around the shores for the right thing and found her in Publico, close to 200 miles from Bickerton. I sailed her home. She's a 225-horsepower Mitsubishi diesel and a 200-gallon fuel tank, more than enough to get us here. Took her out of the water, hauled her home; I put her back in next season and fished with her. She's thirty-four feet, eleven inches; that's so because Fisheries and Oceans dictate what size boat we can have for whatever size and type of license."

"Nice," Jay said, emptying his can. "Looks to me like you made a fine choice." He stood up, stretched, and took a look around the buildings and at the decaying remnants of something that had stood in or above the water at some earlier period. He could only see the decaying stumps of what must once have been support posts. The sea had reclaimed most of whatever had once been there. "What's going on here?"

Russell followed his gaze and replied, "All in, it's—or was—the Bickerton fish plant. Closed now, except for refrigeration. In its heyday, it employed fifty to sixty folks with cold rooms and cutting rooms, where they would cut and fillet the fish by hand. When finished processing, the fish went out across the road to the freezing plant. They shipped trailers full of fresh fish all the time, as well as trailers full of frozen fish. Eventually they lost the market. They still have the freezer facility; it's that yellow building. It now accommodates shrimps. They come frozen off the boats or ships and are kept frozen until there's a market demand. Then they're loaded onto the trailers and sent off to customers. Twenty-five to thirty years ago twenty or so boats would have been fishing out of this harbour. Now we're the only ones, bringing in mostly lobsters. They get put in tote-boxes—a hundred pounds in every tote-box and then put on trailers and they go down to Cape Breton to a plant that processes them. They cut 'em in two, so many legs on one side and so many legs on the other side, send 'em through a brine and that's an instant freeze, and then they're put in a vacuum pack, then into boxes, and away they go."

They walked around the pier, Jay asking questions and Russell answering them. It seemed an easy time for both of them. They soon found themselves quite at ease with each other.

With the pier well explored, they got in their cars and Jay followed Russell back to his place. Russell's hospitality was gracious, and his home comfortable. They pulled back kitchen chairs, and Russell cracked open a couple of beers. Jay encouraged him to share his life's story. It was a one-way conversation, Russell telling, Jay nodding his head and smiling politely, sipping his beer.

Russell had started fishing with his father and uncles while in he was still in school. "Wages, time of my father and uncles, was maybe a hundred bucks per year. I never was much interested in school; I went to ninth grade. I fished from small boats for some years, but fishing got *cold,* so I left and went back to trades school. I learned about and worked on furnaces and oil burners, and did that for fifteen years so I could make a living for my family. Fishing began to pick up, and I continued that trend. I resumed my interest and was enticed back. I got initial licenses—lots of them—for twenty-five cents. Soon enough they went up to five dollars. Fisheries stopped issuing them, so I had to buy them from someone else. I got one for ten grand. Twenty years later the same license was worth four to five hundred thousand dollars. Some lobstermen are now able to make around one hundred twenty-five, one hundred fifty, and even some two hundred thousand a year from catches.

"As I got older, I handed off responsibility to my oldest son. Now I fish with him. I still own all the licenses, though. Fishing is now better than ever, although fishermen are reluctant to publicly admit that."

Russell got up to get them another beer. He had warmed to the tale and continued it while walking to the fridge and back. He tore the end off a bag of chips and shook them onto a plate for them to share. Then he continued:

"Thirty-five to forty years ago most of the people lobster fished from the twentieth of April to the first of June. But there were also these long liners, and when lobsters were done, they went swordfishing. These boats had a big stand out in front of them, about twenty feet, a big thing you could walk out onto, and, well, they used to harpoon the fish. The boats had a big spar in them, and five men went aloft, and these spars, oh, the top of the spar would be forty to forty-five feet off deck. A mast headsman would go in the top seat on the top of the spar, and then there were two on each side, two more below him. They were lookin' for fish—swordfish—when they would come up to the surface. The sailors called it *finning*. They would stick the top of their tail out and the back fin, about six inches or so, and they could be just barely underwater or they could just be cuttin' the water. You're always lookin', from daylight till dark. You're in the rigging, and you're lookin' for these fish.

"First when they went, they would leave here, maybe June first, and they would steam toward Halifax, and go on refit to get whatever repair they needed for the boat, the engine, the gear, or whatever. They would put their supplies, fuel, spare parts, or whatever they thought they wanted aboard, enough for two weeks, and they would go to George's Bank. That's down off New York. That's where they would meet the fish comin'. These fish—they'd be guided by water temperature, we found out in later years, here anyways—always travel based on water temperature. Some of the older fellows used to use baits so the fish would be at

The Fontana Resurrection

a certain place at a certain time. We found out in later years it wasn't baits at all; it was water temperature. It could be a week early this year or two weeks later this year, all according to water temperature. And so they started to meet these fish in George's Bank, down off New York, and they chased them up, and up, and off the other end of the province and then come down, right off here. Sable Island was the big hunting ground, the fishing ground for fish off here, and I think that's why the fleets around Eastern shore here were big sword fishermen because they were the closest to Sable Island and that's where these fish seem to congregate."

Jay loved it, finding himself lost in the story, in his mind, back there with Russell watching it all happen. He needed to keep it going. "And did they stop because the fish got scarce?" he asked.

"Yup, yeah. They stopped themselves, or the fish just stopped, or whatever."

"The guys that were actually doing the harpooning, was that a sort of specialty function?"

"Oh yeah, that was a specialty function. They called him the striker, and every boat had a striker. If you were a striker, you were pretty well sought after. But you pretty well stayed with the one boat. Of course some fellas were strikers who wasn't really up to par at all, and…the age-old story."

"Well yeah, I guess. God! It wouldn't do for them to miss their shots, would it?"

"No, no. That's the same as hunting or anything else; occasionally they would miss a shot. And occasionally they'd miss a *good* shot. And these fish, when you went up on them, like me understanding where the striker was to strike them, they used to call it, 'he's run around.' In this here, 'running' was that he would get nervous, and he would just take off and he would go down."

"Yeah?"

"And then sometimes, after they did harpoon a fish, the striker would tell you that you had to go in a dory. You had to run a hundred fathoms of line on this dart that you would put in the fish, and the fish went with that, and they had a keg on him, too, so that you could easily

223

find him. And, you picked up that keg and brought it aboard the dory, and you started to haul him back. You had to haul him back by hand. And he was still alive. And, so you started to haul him back, so when you got in the dory, the boat swung to go look for other fish and left you alone. And if you're really careful with him, you might get him, but you'd pull a dart out of him if you came on to him, and you gotta use him with kid gloves. So, you hauled him back and hauled up alongside of the dory, maybe he would be anywhere from four to ten or twelve feet long, the big fish. And, so you had a gaff, and you stuck it in the side of his tail right easy, and you hauled his tail up, and you got a big rope of strap around it, and you got around his tail."

"And he'd let you do that, eh?"

"Oh yeah, but you were just right easy—or you hoped he was played out—and you hauled him and you took a couple of turns around the riser—that's the strip of wood down inside the dory between the top and the bottom of the dory. It took a couple of turns around that, then you reached over and yanked his tail right out of the water, fast as you could, and you took these turns on his rope to hold it. Then all he could do was wiggle his front part; his tail was out of the water, his power was gone, and he was done. And so then if the boat was in sight—sometimes it was in sight and sometimes it wasn't—you put up your oar, and the fellows in the spar, of course, they could see for miles. So, some days you get no fish and some days maybe get ten or fifteen or twenty. Fishing was *fishing*."

"And you've been out in the dory yourself?"

"Oh, yeah. Sometimes it was really a nice experience, and sometimes it was a real scary one. These swordfish sometimes, for some reason, they would chase the rope back. So you got to one side of the dory and you tipped her, and you got that rope back to the stern of the boat, far as you could, so when he came up, he'd be clear of the dory, because he had a sword of bone, and they can come stick it right through a dory."

"Oh, yeah?"

"Oh, yes, they will! Dories have been stuck, and that's when you take off your shirt or your coat, screw it up and stuff it in the hole, and try and stay afloat."

"Oh, my God."

"And so anyway, one fella in Bacchus—he's dead now—but he was hauling a fish back, and the line come slack, and he did everything he was supposed to do, and he crawled up on the seat of the boat he was sitting on and stood up because he was scared to death of getting stuck by the sword. So anyway, he heard, he even *felt* the swordfish when he came through the dory, and he looked around and he couldn't see it, and he couldn't imagine what happened. And he had on a pair of oilcloths, and the swordfish came right up between his boot and the side of his oil pants and right up pretty near to his knee. And that was just how close it was. But that's why he couldn't see the sword."

"Wow!"

"You know, you hear some hair-raising experiences."

"God, Russell!" Jay had almost forgotten his hidden agenda. Russell was an amazing storyteller. Lee's driver couldn't get enough of it.

"But this crew understands that and sort of takes the bitter with the sweet, the big with the big and the small with the small, and so forth, and the sword fishermen, they always made a good summer, you know, like, better than if they had stayed home or went in the woods and worked, or went on construction or something. It usually would end up with more money in their pockets than if they had gone to work at some labour work somewheres. But it was a gamble, you know. Fishing is always a gamble, one day to the next.

That's the way with these lobsters. See, these lobsters are way up, here, so it's just terrific, but we don't have no guarantee that next spring that they'll be there. I would be willing to bet with you now, ninety-nine percent that they will be there, but I couldn't guarantee it. I was lucky when I bought the boat; I paid for it and I owe nothing to nobody. And if there are lobsters there next year, terrific, and if there aren't, well, we're okay.

"My Uncle and his wife didn't have any family or anything, and I sort of was with him all my life. He taught me to hunt and trap and fish and so on, and so I imagine that's why I was in on the swordfishing. Whenever I had a chance, I'd go, and I enjoyed it.

"One year, we went to Glace Bay. A lot of fishermen, when they had smaller boats and they weren't going to Sable Island, would go to Glace Bay swordfishing. The boat Uncle had was just a year or two old. She wasn't that big, not much room. We had a dory and we had some swordfish poles and harpoons, most of the gear we needed. We had a compass, the same as everybody carries, and we had a roadmap. And that was it. And we went to Glace Bay, caught one big fish, and it paid our expenses and paid us wages."

"So, who harpooned him?"

"Uncle did. Yup. I was steering the boat. We had the steerage and the throttle and the shift and everything up at the spar."

"If you take a toss at him and you miss him, you don't get a second chance, eh?"

"Not very often. You're usually heading right toward him, and usually he'll come in under. If you don't run, he'll usually come in under and hit the boat on one side or the other."

"Oh, yeah?"

"Of course the minute he hits the boat, he's gone! And once you fire the bow, then the pole is gone. All you had out there was the one pole. And you got the one shot, and that's it. And, like I say, you never know whether he's going to run, or whether he's gonna come right in underneath or he's gonna be off to one side. So that's the way it goes. It was quite a thing; it was certainly an experience that not many fellas from around my age did experience or ever will experience. And so I was always extra pleased, you know, when I got that chance."

Russell paused for a few moments, his mind sifting through a vastness of cherished memories.

"Now there's this Sable Island—you've heard of Sable Island?"

"Yes," Jay responded, wondering where this might next take him, "I have."

"In those years, you weren't allowed on Sable Island. And you aren't allowed on Sable Island now, either.

"So anyway, we were out there, fishing near the island. One evening, just around sundown, the fish seemed to just go down, and the boats all quit for the day. Our guys turned in, got supper, cleaned up; we dressed our fish, and did whatever else we had to do. I wanted to go ashore. Of course I'd known the skipper and the boat's striker right well; had been tormenting them for days, wanting to set foot on Sable Island.

"We were as close in as we could get in the big boat. The sea was a bit rough, but manageable. I couldn't go alone, so this night I convinced them both to come along. We had two dories over the side; rowed to the beach in one of them. The waves upset us in about two feet of water, so we managed to right her.

"We walked around a ways; I got a bottle of sand—I still have some of it, although a lot turned to salt. And I picked up a bit of the driftwood and so on and so forth.

"It was quite a thing to be able to say, then and now, that I was ashore on Sable Island."

"You can't go ashore now, eh?" Jay sensed that he'd soon have to steer their visit, delightful as it was, more in the direction of his reason for being here.

"No sir, it's completely illegal. It was illegal then, but there was no one to stop you. See, there are ponies there, and I guess they thought if they allowed people there, folks would do this and they would do that and they would upset the balance of nature. If they caught you ashore there now, it wouldn't be pleasant."

"It wouldn't be a good thing, you're saying?"

"No, no, it wouldn't be very pleasant. But anyway that's what the…"

"Who…? Okay, would it be the Coast Guard that would enforce whatever is going on there now?"

"Yeah. The Coast Guard. See, there are lighthouses there, and they were manned. I don't think they're manned now, but there are Coast Guard stations there and there are people there, pretty well all year doing research on seals and doing research on charts and whales and the ecosystems. So when the horses and the shifting sands and the—you know, so it's a job for somebody. They fly out on helicopters and so on, so it's just a zip there and a zip back and so on and so forth. They've got a little pad there and…"

"Okay. And what about this whole area? Is this all policed by the RCMP?"

"Yup."

"Where's the nearest detachment?"

"In Sherbrooke."

"How many people?"

"There's three, I think, but—usually there's three—but maybe two now. There's usually three."

"Okay."

"But they run quite a big area, I'd say maybe a hundred-mile radius."

"So, you know, if a body were found on shore, somebody would be reporting that to the Mounties here?"

"Oh, yeah. Yuh.

"Talking about bodies, I worked with the Coast Guard one summer."

"Yeah?"

"And, uh, I was aboard the *Raleigh*, she was a search and rescue."

"Uh huh?"

"She ran from over at Pictou, over to here, to PEI, Charlottetown, and Summerside, and up to New Brunswick, and we were going as far in as Québec. One night, once a year, the Coast Guard would give us a lobster supper."

"Yeah?"

"So, the night our lobster supper was on, I was out on deck for some reason walking around—we were tied up in port and nothing much was happening ashore—and Lord Jesus, I looked out here comes buddy floatin' by!"

"Oh, yeah?"

"He was lying on his back, his hands sort of folded, and he had some kind of checkered pants on. The knees were completely wore out of them, and he had some kind of—I don't know, they weren't leather—some kind of plastic shoes on, and the toes were wore out of them."

"Yeah?"

"And so, we found out later, that this buddy had come into the tavern, got in a taxi, and went across a big bridge there, a river, going into the harbour, and he told the taxi driver, he said, I got to get out, I got to have a piss. So, the taxi driver stopped for him on account of this

The Fontana Resurrection

big bridge, and buddy went over the side, and up over the rail, and kept on going. And that was in the middle of winter."

"And that was it?"

"Of course, there was a big roaring tide going through there, and they looked for him and they knew what happened to him, and they couldn't find him."

"Yeah?"

"And the body was never found, and, they just said, 'Well, we might pick him up sometime; we might never see him.'"

"Yeah. Ooh."

"So this was buddy, who jumped over the bridge! And on account of his knees, and the toes of his shoes being wore out, he was drifting around under the ice. See, the gas in the stomach had floated him, and he was driftin' around in the tide under the ice, and the knees and the toes of his shoes apparently was the highest things, and they were wore out. So anyway, I went in and told the skipper. I said, 'Sir,' I said, 'There's a body going down by.' 'What?' he says. I says, 'Yeah.' He says, 'Oh, uh, you're joking!' I said, 'No, I wish I was, but I'm not.' So he came out on deck, looked at it, and says, 'Best I'm getting closer.' And so, we had these big wire stretchers, we could put over the side, to pick a buddy up."

"Okay!"

"So I said, 'Lord Jesus!' I had never ate no lobster, but I said, 'If I do eat them, I'm going to lose them, I know that!' So I figured that we had to pick him up. And so, I asked the old man, I said, 'We have to put a launch over and pick him up?' And he said, 'No. Not us!' And I says, 'Why?' I said that I thought we would have to."

"Yeah?"

"'No,' he says, 'Not our jurisdiction, we are for *offshore* as we come into these harbours and tie up, but we are search and rescue. Not our baby. Nope. Let him go.'"

"Oh, yeah?"

"So he says, 'I'll go in and call the Mounties.' So anyway, he went up to the bridge and called the Mounties. 'Now, you know, it's not really our cuppa tea.' 'Well,' he said, 'I'm just passing the word along. He's just going by now, somebody better come and pick him up.'"

"Ha, ha, ha! Nobody wanted the trouble!"

"There was a little harbour patrol there, in the Zodiac, and they had two teenagers aboard, and they patrolled the harbour. And so, anyway, somebody stuck their finger at them, and they says, 'It's up to *you* fellas to pick him up. We got no equipment to pick him up, we got no nothing!' And, so anyway, they got off the hook. So they kept on phoning. And so, there in Charlottetown, there was a city police there—the RCMP was there, but they were out in the outskirts, like you know—and there was the city police right in the city. And so they said, 'We are here in the city; its a *city* police.' So they called the city police and told them, and they said, 'Yeah, I guess it's us.' So they says, 'We have no launch or anything, so however we gonna pick him up?'"

"Haw, haw, haw. They didn't know?"

"So, they went down to the wharf, and they came over to us, and they get one of those big wire structures. They hired a long liner, a boat like that Megan—the Curtis of Megan—and they went over along side of buddy, and they were just, of course, no distance from us, and we were out watching by this time. And so, they lowered this here wire mesh thing underneath buddy and hauled him up and he was in the dip net. And they hauled him aboard, and I figured they'd be right terrible careful with him because I figured he would just be like a bowl of jelly. And why he was still hard, I have no idea. But what do they do? They upset this thing and rolled buddy out on deck! And *pluck!* We could hear him. So anyway, they went into a dock close to us, and they must've called the coroner or the undertaker or somebody, and they come down there with a van, and they had a stretcher, and they rolled him on, onto their stretcher, and we waved good-bye to him! Haw, haw, haaaw!"

"Good luck to you, lads!" Jay offered. "Oh, my God!"

"So, that was my story with the Coast Guard. I'm telling you, you get into some dandies!"

"Oh, that *is* amazing!"

By the time Russell got around to popping the caps off their third bottles they were beginning to feel quite at ease with each other. Russell hadn't invited Jay to go back into his own history, for which Jay had been grateful, and he wasn't inclined to offer it up. He hadn't thought to fabricate a *past* that he might like to have had, and now he wasn't sure about winging it. He was quite sure by now that Russell was a very perceptive guy, and that he would be able to catch a whiff of bullshit as soon as it wafted past him, even if he were then to decide to let it pass as though undetected. So, he concluded, lying was off the table. He would have to ease into it honestly, albeit in easy steps.

"Russell," he tried. "I haven't told you everything about my visit." He twisted his bottle and studied the deer's head on the Keith's label as if seeing it for a first time.

"No?" Russell responded, looking at him sideways, studying him, knowing somewhere within himself that this guy had seemed a bit mysterious, even if sort of likeable.

"No." Jay managed, "I'm here with a purpose. I'd like to share it with you, but I can only do that if it can remain strictly between you and me. Could that work for you?"

"I was sort of wondering when you'd get around to what was real. We don't often get strangers—strangers who appear to be friendly—wandering around the wharf, aimlessly sniffing at decaying remnants of a Jeez'ly ancient dock, and gawking at rusted sheets of corrugated tin hanging off our abandoned buildings. I thought I'd try to see what you were up to."

"It's a bit heavy, and it's on the shady side of the law. If we talk about it, you have to agree that our conversation will go nowhere else. And if that isn't okay, I'll absolutely understand. We'll shake hands, I'll leave, and we'll remember a friendly afternoon spent together over a few beers. No harm done. Okay?"

"Well, I guess you now own most of my curiosity," Russell replied, taking half a minute to think about it. "How *shady* are we talkin'?"

"Russell, have you ever *broken* the law? I don't mean speeding tickets or being caught with open liquor in your car at some barn dance. I mean have you ever been involved in a crime?"

"Maybe. I assume from your hedging that *you* have, but I don't want to press yuh on that."

"Thanks. Do you want me to go on, then? Do we understand each other about the need for absolute confidentiality?"

"Yeah. I think so. Here, have some more chips; I'll break open a fresh bag. Want some cheese?"

"Okay," Jay said, breaking off a length of Russell's delicious-smelling block of cheddar. "Here's the short version. When I've got it all out, you can ask me any questions. I'll answer anything you throw at me."

"I guess then we can have an understanding. Whatever you tell me won't go nowheres else."

Jay took a deep breath; he munched on a chip and nibbled on his cheese. He scraped his chair on the floor as he turned to face Russell front on, wanting to be able to read his reaction. This was a tipping point: either they would go on together or he would have to think about what he might need to do to or with the Russell who by the end of his story would know too much.

He launched into it: about the clinic; what they had been planning and still had to do; why they were doing it; where the funding most probably would be coming from; and what his role was in the overall scheme.

"So, you see Russell, my role is to be their driver. I'm licensed to operate the semis. The company's director sent me to Nova Scotia to find a place to offload their *product*. She and her sponsor seemed to feel, and still do, that the sea is the thing. They've looked at alternatives; there are real reasons why alternate disposal methods would be too risky. Even this one is, but we've tried to think through those risks and to try to find a way to work around them. We think we can do that.

"What's your take on what you've heard so far?" He noticed that Russell had been nodding an apparent understanding. He had shown no body language to suggest he was shocked or offended. So far, so good.

"And I guess you're lookin' to have me become the last link in your chain?"

"Yeah, if you think its feasible. We still have some questions around that, but we can come to them as we go along here, if you think now you'd be interested. As I'm sure you'd expect, we would be prepared to pay a high price to get this done. Call it adding in a *risk premium* if you like. But all of us will be taking some risk, and we're willing to try to manage that. Nobody would go into this all the way if they didn't think this sort of thing could be made to work and to pay handsomely for all involved. You'd be a key part of it. You'd just have to spell out how your end of things should be managed. Do you want to go on?"

"It holds a certain attraction, I guess, like a well-baited hook. Fishermen an' the law have often found themselves at odds, trying to outsmart each other. And it ain't always the law that wins. Nobody knows the sea like us guys who fish her. Nobody. We know her, and we know what she can do for us, and what we can do for her so as not to harm her. The sea's our life. In a way we're married to each other. We *know* each other. If we ignore her moods, or can't see them coming, she harms us, sometimes destroys us. But she is discreet. She keeps our secrets to herself. If there's punishment to be dolled out, she does it. In return, she allows us to make a living from her, and a good living, too. So, yes, go on. I'm okay with what yer sayin' so far. And like the sea, I won't be talkin' to nobody about it."

"Okay, Russ. Can I call you Russ, now that we know each other better?"

"Uh huh. No problem with that, with me."

Then I have some questions for you, though they mightn't come out in any particular order. You've gotta know I don't have them written down anywhere. They're just in my head."

"Okay, figure as if I'm in."

"Russ, if a body were to get away from us—maybe the weights came loose, maybe a belt breaks, somehow or other a *parcel* was just freed up on the bottom—would it be likely to float? And if it did float, where would it be likely to drift? Would there be anything to connect a body found on shore back to our proposed little operation at Port Bickerton?"

"Well, there are the tides and the prevailing winds. The tides would eventually bring them in. But the winds would control them more than anything. And we have a westward flow of a type here, it's always going west. And so, if you went off shore here, say ten miles, fifteen miles, or whatever, a body could land on a point somewheres, but it could go a long ways west, too, before it would come to shore, if it ever did come to shore, and then it could, uh—you know, if the wind were stronger than the tide—it would go whichever way the strongest was, whether it was the wind or whether it was the tide."

"Okay, I'm with you."

"But there's a prevailing westerly tide here, running west—it goes west all the time—and some days it's not very strong, and some days it's quite strong. If there's a strong wind, the wind will take something on the surface more than the other type of ticket, because chances are it's a lot stronger than the tide."

"All right, then. So, if the body got away from whatever weights were holding it down, and it bloated, then it would come to the top and be moved by…whatever?"

"I think a body, after so many days will usually float, won't it? Enough gas forms in there that it'll float. But then don't they say that a body floats for so many days or so many hours and that it'll sink again? I'm not too sure, but I think it goes down again. Now when it goes down, does it stay down, that time? Or…"

"I think generally, once it goes down then, it's gone. But I'm not too sure. It could drift under the surface or along the bottom. I'll have to check that out. When I get home, I'll go online and see what I can find. There's a wealth of information on the Internet, better than any library in the world. Anyway, it's really just an added security precaution. Of course, we don't want a body to get away from us, but we have to think about what our risks would be in the event one does, and whether or not it could be traced back to us. We absolutely can't afford to have that happen, can we?

"The other thing that I wanted to ask you about was, what about the little animals in the sea, like the lobsters and the other little sea urchins, and God knows what else? If a body was in the water, and on the bottom, weighted on the bottom, for a while, would it be likely to get chewed up, much?"

The Fontana Resurrection

"Yeah, yup."

"Fairly quickly?"

"Yeah. It's all according to where they are, but if they're in an area, especially where there are crabs, because crabs seem to be the worst. The worst are the best, however you want to put it on. I know of the body of a fella—he was from Sherbrooke—he drowned down in Country Harbour. And he was under water…I don't think more than 48 hours. I don't think it was there that long, and they found his body, and they asked his brother-in-law to come and identify him. And he was a neighbour of mine, I know him quite well. And he told me, he said, 'I knew it was Billy, I knew it was him.' How he was dressed and his build and his size and everything, but as far as his face, his hands, and so on, and anything that was out in the open, it was just about gone. If I didn't know that Billy drowned there, and they got his body, if I'd a been in Halifax, and someone had asked, 'Did you know this fella?' I would've said, no, I never saw him before. That much was gone. But he wasn't wrapped up in anything; he just fell in the water and drowned.

"Mind you, if a body was wrapped in a blanket, and it would only be a problem then if the wrappings came loose, the rope came loose…. Yeah, if it was wrapped right, the crabs or something might get through it. The sand fleas and little things like that more than likely would eat in through it and eventually destroy it, especially enough that it would never float or anything."

"Yeah, yeah." Jay was focused now on the details. "And so, those critters, in looking for the flesh, would maybe even go through whatever the wrapping was, right?"

"Yeah. Now there are little sand fleas, or some kind of little stuff. We'll, for example, put a bait bag in a lobster trap and maybe have a whole mackerel bag, a mackerel balled up in a ball so to speak, and it'll be in a mesh, oh, a half-inch mesh bag, like. And I've seen them, in twenty-four hours—now this isn't every day and it isn't terrible common—but I've seen them, just the backbone and the head bones, and so on, not one ounce of flesh left. They just got ate completely, and it was some little organisms of some kind. A big fish didn't do it. It were some little sand fleas or lice or I don't know exactly what it was, but you'll get some species of bottom-feeders, some times, so aggressive that you can't keep bait on traps no matter what you put it in. I don't know whether, if you put it in something like, say, a lady's hose, or something like that. They may not go through that and eat it, but anything any bigger than that and they'll go in through it and they just completely clean up. But they don't eat no bones; they must just be suckers of some kind. I've seen just a skeleton, the tailbones and the backbone and the head bones, you know, and the jaws and his skull and so on, and that's all. And then you'll see some that's ate *some* at different times, but there are areas and times that they'll just *clean* everything, just clean as clean can be."

"Okay, I'm gonna see what I can find out about that, and if I can find something easily, it would be good to, you know, just catch a note of that, like what kind of critters we're talking about."

"Well, sand fleas I know about—what we call sand fleas here—they are little things about that long, and look quite a lot like a baby lobster would, and that's what does a lot of this. I'm not saying that does it all. But sometimes we'll haul out a trap, and there'd be a bunch of them still hanging on the brains of the fish or whatever. And a lot of that small stuff, they need a place to start. They need to get into the mouth or into the eyes or.... You know they need a place to start; they can't just land here and keep on going. They need a cut or something, someplace to start.

"Okay," said Jay, "that's good to know. And, what about the effect of storms—storms at sea—on bodies in the water, either submerged or at the top? Does that change where they would drift to?"

"Yeah, it would, but if they were in deep water and weighted down, not likely the action of the sea would have any great effect on them, because when we're fishing, we have to—our traps and our gear—we have to watch it in bad weather. Say we are in twenty feet of water now, and we're given southeast gales, we'll move out to a hundred feet of water. And there, pretty well, the traps are safe. They're okay. But if you had of left them in twenty feet of water, they would've been beat up, and you never would've saw anything again, they would've been gone. So, the deeper the water is, the less sea action or storm action it would have on the body. But then again, if it was afloat, and if it was in anyways soft or starting to decay or anything, in a big sea, it would certainly more than likely pick the body up, you know, and more or less tear it all apart and so on and so forth."

"Okay. And the effect of shoals and sandspits, like Sable Island, and so on…"

"Yeah. The shallower the water you get, the more damage or the more destructive the water is. In shallow water it'll do a lot more damage. That's why this Sable Island—maps that you've seen—is the graveyard of the Atlantic. There are hundreds of boats that went down there."

"And you get used to it?"

"Yeah. Around here we always say that you get salt water in your veins. I've had some, not an awful lot of harrowing experiences, but a fair amount of unnerving times on the water, and I've always gone back. I always swore when it happened that I'd never go back.

"You know, I don't know whether I mentioned it, but there was this one trip, and we came into Bickerton, and I don't know—I maybe didn't explain to you when we were at the wharf—but, you can, by the beacon from the lighthouse, get back in here in a storm. They call our channel the horseshoe; it goes around like a loop. And, normally, with some weather on, you can see a little breaker here and a little breaker there. And that night when we came in, it was maybe five or six in the morning before daylight when we came in, and it was rough. It was blowing and screaming a scorcher, and snowing like you wouldn't believe, and you couldn't see anything. And we get in there, and it wasn't buoyed then, you just went by the light and whatever you thought."

"Um hmm."

"And they were all hollering, 'Where's the horseshoe? Are we up to the horseshoe? Did we get around the horseshoe?' And there was one poor fellow aboard—he's dead now, dead and gone—and that fella he's out on the foredeck, and we were all out looking and, looking for these breakers. And that fellow, how he could do it I don't know, but you'd put your hands up like this to your eyes and try and look out through, and that fella, he could stand there and he could look right into the wind and into that snowstorm and he could see. Yes sir, and he said, 'She's breaking, and she's breakin' up there, and we gotta go out around here.' And the rest of us just couldn't see! And you couldn't stop, you had to keep on going, because if you'd stop, then you'd be gone, you know."

"Yeah, yuh."

"And all those things, but like I say, once you get ashore for a few hours, then you're joking and carrying on, and so on and so forth."

"But there's one thing about a lot of this fishin' that I've done. I don't think that I ever saw hard feelings aboard a boat, and I don't think that I ever saw any harsh words aboard a boat, and everybody was your buddy, and you depended hundred percent on everybody. There was no fella you wouldn't trust, and no fella that was no good or anything. And it was a complete team effort. You know, you're all getting paid exactly equal. You weren't getting ten dollars more than me because you pulled a bit harder than I did. It was a team effort and…" Russell paused, seeming to have lost himself in memories of what must have been, on balance, a good life: a life he obviously still enjoyed.

"It's an interesting assessment, Russ. There aren't many vocations out there where the people who have gone through their careers could honestly say the same things about their experiences, particularly your bit about the camaraderie. They could *say* it, but not mean it. But clearly, you mean it, right?"

"Yeah."

Jay was truly moved by Russell's tales of the sea, not wanting them to end. He contrasted Russell's life experiences with his own and felt a wave of cynicism begin to wash over him. Before he could stop himself, he let a bit of it spill out. "For the most part, in everything else—almost everything else—life's competitive, and the one guy is always looking out for an edge over the other guy, and trying to do a little better and…. So that competition seems to creep into the…the sort of absolute sincerity of relationships, so that relationships can appear to be good, but they are sort of, uh, friendships of convenience, if you see what I mean."

"Well, this is the way, somewhat. What you're saying here is the truth. Because this fishing—like I said—we fish twice or three times now what we used to. And we fish days now that we never thought of fishing before. And we depend on each other to get it done. Because we can."

"And because you have better boats?"

"Yeah, we have better boats, but we equip better boats so that we can do this. But I say it, and I say it in fun, when we haul our gear a day, maybe at ten o'clock, maybe we actually should quit at ten o'clock and go in. But we're still making real good money, and we have sixty days to make it, and if we lose a day, we can't gain it back tomorrow."

Jay didn't want *this* day to end, but he knew he was stuck with a mandate—Lee's mandate—and that he'd better get the business of the day back on the table.

He started back into it gently. "Ah, Russ, just coming back to this stuff, I need to be sure that I get through all of the questions I brought with me."

Russell dragged himself, slowly, reluctantly, back to the present, cast a glance at Jay's empty bottle, and asked, "Would you like another beer? Another chip off the block of that cheese to go with your chips?"

"Umm, maybe I'd best not. Let's get back to why I came here. You still okay with that? We don't have to go there at all if you're not or if you've thought about it and maybe changed your mind. I'd understand. This wouldn't be like fishing, sort of the opposite. You'd be *returning* something to the sea."

"Yeah, I'm okay with all that. I'd like to hear you out."

"Okay..." Jay paused, looked steadily at Russell, trying to read him. He couldn't, but knew having gone this far that he would have to finish the approach. He dreaded to think what an unhoped-for 'No!' would need to entail.

"We think, at the clinic, that we'll need two guys to handle the bodies—the *packaging* at your end. They'll be frozen and put on board a truck, and we'll get them this far. The way it looks, it'll be my dad and me. Probably he'll be the on-site guy and I'll be the clinic's man on the road. But maybe not, that's subject to further discussion with Lee and her team. Whatever we put into play will need to be the best thing, the right thing, for all of us. Wouldn't you agree?"

"Yeah, of course. There's ways it'll work and ways it won't. And ways that it won't is the ways we've gotta steer well away from."

"Once they're here—we talked a bit at the clinic about the handoff—the when and the where and so on. Probably it would be at night, but late at night or early, which? What times might work best for you? And what would the hazards be from friends, acquaintances, and—God forbid—police?"

"Well, even in Bickerton now, there's this long-liner that does a trip maybe once a week, or every ten days, or twice a week. And they go down there and take their trawl—their gear—out of the freezer, out of the shed there, and they put it aboard the boat and leave, maybe at eleven, twelve, one, or two o'clock in the morning. And they go for two or three days. And so if it was arranged for these bodies to come on the night of the seventeenth, say, the trailer was going to be there at eleven thirty, twelve thirty, one thirty, or whatever, well, you go down, you and your buddy, and you take your trawl out of the shed and so on, and you put it aboard the boat. The trailer backs out, and so on and so forth, and you put the stuff aboard. There's just bait to be brought and so on, and you fool around the building enough to sort of cover things up, and so in that way, you certainly could make a trip trawling and make a trip with a load of bodies, all on the one trip. It wouldn't be really obvious what you were doing at all; it would look like you were really trawling, and in the meantime, when you get out there, you'd dump your bodies wherever, whatever position you're going to dump them, and you go to work and set your trawl, and make a trip and come back. It's really legit, and aboveboard, and so on and so forth. You could work that into the equation, right hand-in-hand so to speak, I would think. Y'understand?"

"Yeah, yuh. I gotcha."

"Okay. That's really important. That's great. So assuming there were two guys in the truck, and maybe there aren't two guys, maybe there's just one—one or two guys—if it were you, would you want one of those guys to help you?"

"Uuh, maybe yes, because more than likely, with offloading, it would be the last minute thing. He would back out on the dock, and you would, say, be here at ten-after-eleven or twenty-to-twelve, so he may stop up the road for fifteen minutes or half an hour if he was early. And you have your trawl aboard and you'd be pretty well all ready when he comes, so you could just bail those bodies aboard, untie, and go. Then if anybody happened around, well, there's no seeing and no time to see anything or…"

"Yeah, okay. So now you have an assortment of frail old women and old men—they're going to be lighter than young people would, except some of them might be obese and heavy—so let's say you have, y'know, you have frozen sticks of people—five-and-a-half to six-feet long—and now you've gotta get them off the wharf onto the back deck of your boat, so that there's gotta be two of you?"

"Yeah. Well, you see, you would have a fella with you when you're trawling. There's at least two, maybe three, but you could arrange for there just to be two, so the less the better."

"Okay, so you wouldn't be working alone. Like, if you're doing it, there'd be a trusted person with you."

"Yeah."

"Somebody that was part of it. So, that's kind of cool. So now the eighteen-wheeler is coming right down the wharf, right?"

"Yeah."

"And, fairly quickly, you're getting—okay, maybe the driver's helping to offload and maybe your two guys are on the boat—and you get them down on the boat and you get the hell out of there."

"Yeah. You get them down on board and get untied and you leave. That all happens within two or three minutes. You're waiting for this fella for some extra bait, or you're waiting for him for some reason or other, and he gets there and you're sort of waiting for him, and you're sort of a little ticked off, because he is ten minutes late. You know the story you're telling to your friend or your neighbour or something, and I was waitin' for the son of a gun. He was supposed to be here at eleven o'clock, but it was a quarter after eleven when he got here, and we were running late, and so on and so forth. We just up and threw it aboard and went."

"Yeah?"

"Yeah!"

"Wonderful! Oh, Jesus, this is great! Okay, so now there's you and the other guy. And you're headed out. And, uh, you're gonna set a trawl afterwards?"

"Yeah."

"Okay, so you're gonna do that. So this other guy has got to be knowledgeable enough at least to be useful to you."

"Oh yeah. He's, he's a helper that I have all the time."

"Okay, good."

"And, him being the helper that I work with all year, or in season or whatever, he's perfectly trustworthy and quiet. We can trust him. He's certainly gonna know what I'm doing."

"Yeah."

"And he's *got* to know what I'm doing. And he's got to be trustworthy enough. I can't go here on the street and say, 'I want you to give me a lift tonight for a few hours.' You've got to have someone that you can trust."

"Absolutely! You're in this together, right? If it goes south…"

"Yeah! So, you know, if I get my throat cut, guess what, I'm gonna return the favour…"

"Yeah! And his gets cut first, right?"

"Yeah! Ha! Ha! Ha!"

"Okay. So now, the eighteen-wheeler is on its way back—for the next load. And maybe that doesn't happen right away. Like, maybe the eighteen-wheeler is available, rentable, but it's not coming back and forth all the time…"

"These people that they're, shall we say, *manufacturing* in Ontario or wherever, and they're bringing twenty frozen bodies to me today, they're not coming back for a few weeks, really, by my reckoning. You know, maybe two or three months. They're not killing twenty a week at the clinic, you know; they're killing two or three this week and another in a week-or-two's time. It's not a, really—can't be—a slaughterhouse, can it? It's a slaughterhouse in one sense, but you can't get that many people in and get them through the premises…"

"Yeah. We're going to have a cold-storage facility in the basement of this place. As long as it has remaining capacity, they'll be fine. And, worst case, we can put a few more under the trees in the escarpment, right?"

"Yeah. Yeah, if we really get overrun."

"It's tough digging there though. I've checked that out. The escarpment, there, is a pretty steep slope with a lot of small rocks and not a hell of a lot of topsoil. And we wouldn't want an arm or a leg or anything sticking out, would we?"

"Not really! Ha, ha, ha!"

"Okay. So there's you and your helper, you're in the boat, and you've got the load, and you've got the whole load, maybe as many as twenty, aye? Mind you, they could be two deep, too, couldn't they?"

"Oh, yes. Oh yeah. When those fellas is stiff, you can throw them in; they wouldn't take a lot of room."

"Yeah, yeah. So you're calling the shots, and you're out there and making a determination on how and where you're going to drop 'em. Where do you think that's going to be?"

"Well, I would say, more than likely, if you're going trawling, you could be going fifteen to twenty miles offshore. I would say, you're going there and, uh, there's these humps and hollows, hills and holes, and more than likely you get over a big hole and—especially a big sand hole—and those sand holes are known to be full of crabs, that's where the crabs congregate—so you dump them in these holes. And so the chances of them being devoured is, you know, a hundred percent greater than if you dump them on a hump or something or other. If they go over the side above a hole, they could settle in the silt and the sand and so on, and you know, that's the place for them to go."

"Perfect! And because you know your *patch* out there…uh, what's the term you use, again, for your area?"

"What is what?"

"What term do you use for the area where you fish? Uh, it's not a patch, but it's an area—an area of the ocean, an area of the bottom. What do you call it?"

"I, uh, I really don't know what you mean. If there's a zone that you fish in, like whatever…"

"So, okay, so you know your *zone*. And you know where the holes are."

"Oh, yeah. You have your chart. And you have your water depths and you have your shoals and…. And then you have, like, the computer and everything, and with that computer screen…. By the time she boots up—or whatever you call it, and the screen is full—by that time the engine will have warmed up a bit, and just in time we have everything on and away we go, so we just goes out there and checks that little hole. We looks at our chart and everything's on there, and we just chase our track right through and go out, you know, and then we can go to different charts and, on our computer, and there's an automatic pilot aboard that boat. With the GPS you can punch in the distance, punch in a certain spot, and put her on automatic pilot and she'll come around on the course, and she'll stay on her course and run her time. When she gets to that certain spot, if it's that little pile of gravel, she gets there, she'll go 'ding, ding, ding' three times and that's where you are; you're right there, just like right on the button. That's when you get back there and you start bailing them over."

"Okay, right! Ha, ha, ha! Ah, so, okay, the bodies are being wrapped by other people, and of course the wrapping and everything inside is going to be just like frozen cordwood logs, and you're probably not going to be noticing if they aren't well tied up, aye?"

"Yeah."

"So for the possibility that one might come apart, like if they were just using rocks from the escarpment…"

"No, I don't know where or what to tell you about that, if they were to bring the bodies with any weight on at all. I don't know whether I would make a deal with them where I would have twenty-, thirty-, or fifty-pound weights aboard the boat, or something or other, you know, put them on there, say last week, or were done yesterday or whatever, you know. So these bodies, everyone comes to get them ready, I just tie my own ropes, tie my own knots with the fifty pounds of weight or whatever, tie it onto them, and let them go. And then I know, myself, for my own protection, that it's tied on to my satisfaction. I think maybe that would be a better way. And then there'd be less weight to transport from point A to point B. It would be less weight to load, to unload, and the whole thing would…"

"Are you going to have any trouble getting the weights?"

"No. I shouldn't have. No, no."

"Nobody's going to wonder about that?"

"No. At odd times I can put them aboard, put them aboard at back, and maybe cover them with a tarp. Or have them in the truck for that night when I'm loading, or whatever."

"Okay." Jay thought Russell's approach was the better one; now he would have to change tacks and get to the more ticklish bit: how much to pay him.

"And I'm thinking about your expenses now. Okay? So, I'm from the clinic. How do we pay you?"

"I don't know. You, uh…" Russell paused, took a moment to mull it over, then said, "It's gotta be something that's too good to turn down. It's gotta be something that's going to be a guarantee, you know. I'm not going to come along.… If I meet you on the street corner and talk to you about this and you guarantee me X amount of dollars, I'm going to have to have some proof that it *is* going to be X amount of dollars, and I'm not going to run the chance of doing this and then calling you and you don't exist no longer."

"So," offered Jay, now the negotiator, "We're going to have a bank account opened in a bank in some town or city out here. Of your choice. And, uh, we'll deposit a pre-agreed retainer, with the assurance that, per load, you get so much in addition to that amount."

"Okay," Russell offered, "Again, I'm sure you're familiar with this. How are you going to do this so eventually it can't be traced to you, to me, and this all tied together, and the whole bunch talk, me talk, you talk. You'll have to put some sort of a blockage in the middle there that something can't be traced from you to me, so to speak. You know, if they can trace from you to me, and you're running on home, and these people disappear, and I'm not on the boat making some trips and so on, it's got to be…"

"And, yes," Jay conceded, "You've gotta know from us because we're all going to be criminals, right? You've gotta know from us that you're going to get your money. Like, *assured*. So, we gotta find a way to get it to you, either in a bundle of cash, or…"

"That's about the only way, as little as I know about these things, which is absolutely nothing. That's about the only way that I know that we can run this thing is cash."

"Yeah, okay."

"And it can't be traceable."

"Of course. So maybe, maybe what happens is that the first thing that gets offloaded off the eighteen-wheeler comes out of the cabin at the back, and that's a briefcase, full of cash."

"Okay."

"How much should that be in the briefcase? To make it well worth your while?"

"I don't know. I don't really know. It's, aah…"

"It could be per load; it could be per body…"

"It's not so much the work that's in it, it's the risk that's involved. That's the…"

"Yeah. It's not the work. That's why it's got to be a *lot*. Because the risk is extremely high. It's gotta be a lot. I was thinking about, you know, like, starting at say the cost of a cremation, and at the low end that's somewhere between a thousand and two thousand bucks a body. Umm. But, of course, we can't cremate them. We couldn't. Too many. Heads would turn. They discarded that option earlier, before I came on the scene."

"No, you couldn't, neither there nor here."

"Disposal would be the same risk for us that ultimately you would face, because there'd be too much of the same activity, unless you'd be taking them to different crematoriums all over hell's creation. And then you're going to have difficulty with that, too, because there's a whole lot of paperwork that goes with that."

"Yeah."

"And at the same time, I guess we've gotta look at it from a business perspective and say a price that can't be…can't be out of sight. It can't be probably more than, say, five grand a body. All right?"

"I would say, more than likely, in this case, that it would have to be so much a trip. If I was doing that and I had three bodies or twenty bodies, twenty bodies wouldn't necessarily be any more problem then maybe the three bodies would be."

"Yeah. That sounds like a pretty good way of doing it. Let's work on that approach."

"Okay."

"On your best fishing day, ever, what would you make on that boat?"

"Oh, we've made, I guess, more than five thousand. I guess that's about the biggest day we've had."

"So, okay, would ten grand a trip be…"

"Oh yeah, yeah, I would think so. I do think it would be worth that, for on account of the risk. I think that it would be, ah, fair to all hands. If they had to pay to *legally* dispose of those bodies, it would cost them more than what we got anyway, and, uh…"

"So, well, that's a number we can start with, then?"

"Yeah, because, see, they're gonna have to pay a fair bit of money for just truckin'."

"Yeah. You know what? At the clinic, we're going to have to work that out, too. It's going to look odd, on the books, for a medical clinic to own an eighteen-wheeler."

"Yeah. But again, to my knowledge, around here there's any amount of trucks, that just getting to know the right fella, that they don't need to own the semi. There's any amount of fellas that are willing to bring stuff into the country, and out of the country, for X amount of dollars. And it's being done every day."

"Yeah? Really? Cool!"

Jay let a silence hang between them, pondering whether or not to try his next, last question. Then he did.

"Russell, I have an afterthought. Do you mind if I bring it up?"

"What's that? I don't want no surprises, now…"

"No, Russell; no surprise. It's just a possible extension, an add-on to the clinic's business plan, in case their body output exceeds your capacity to get rid of them."

"Oh? Yuh figure that'd happen?"

"Don't know, Russell. I won't be killing them. I'm just their driver. And, if there's excess, I'm gonna have to dump 'em someplace. Do you know, maybe, of somewhere else I could go look for a backup boat and its captain? It wouldn't have to be as big a boat as yours, just large enough to take a few bodies at a time. Somewhere a good distance from here, so there couldn't ever be any connection drawn between your operation and a secondary one. I won't have time this trip to go and check anything else out, but I thought I would just ask if you might be able to steer me in the right direction. Could you? I'd never, *ever*, link you to a second operator, were we able to find one. He'd never come to know of your existence. Promise."

"Well, I guess I can see your point and theirs at the clinic."

He thought about it for a minute or two. Jay maintained an uneasy silence, respectfully, somewhat unhopefully, but he would listen if Russell had something for him to follow through on.

"There's a place," Russell offered, "that I liked to go to when I was younger, when I sometimes needed to be alone. Just myself. I had some troubles with my first marriage. Wife was cheating, and I needed to get away for a bit."

"Can you share that with me? Would you like to? I've had women troubles myself, several times; things didn't always work out amicably."

"Well, okay, but not about the marriage—my marriage; maybe some other time.

"About where I'd go when I was down though. You didn't hear this from me, understood? Can we agree, for sure, on that?"

"Yes, Russell, of course."

"Okay. There's a little tidal stream just outside Sackville, New Brunswick, in a little community called Wood Point. You head out of Sackville to the West, and Wood Point basically starts where the pavement ends and the dirt road begins, and that little estuary is about a mile and a half, two miles, past the pavement. And it's a little tidal river that empties into the Bay of Fundy. That little fishing spot has been there forever; it's been there as long as I can remember. There's always been one fishing boat, and it's got a floating dock that rises and falls off the mud flat with the tide. It's secluded, and if you were coming along in a fog, you'd never know it was there. It's a beautiful spot, especially on a clear day. And there's no wharf that the guy ties up to. I don't know where he drops his catch, unless he just brings it up and then trucks it somewhere. The fall on the tide is probably anywhere from five to fifteen feet, depending on the season. And that river empties, twice a day, and twice a day that thing is full and all you can see is green grass. It's very secluded. It's so off the beaten path that if you didn't have a reason to go there you wouldn't, because there's nothing there. Wood Point is just a collection of old, ramshackle, low-income housing. As I say, it's not even on the paved road. There's power there, but it's well and septic for everybody else, and it's just the dirt road that goes around the Bay of Fundy, around to Dorchester on the other side. That's basically what it is.

"Now the colour of that water, a reddish brown, never changes, because it's the Bay of Fundy. And there's so much silt in the water, because the tides are so violent, that the water never has a chance to clear, so that it's brown. So I haven't got a clue what he fishes out of there. I don't think there are lobsters in there, because it's a whole sandy bottom. There are no rocks in there.

"He might be able to take a body or two out at a time. And he might need the money. Who doesn't? His boat isn't big; there's a number on it, a registration number, but it never occurred to me to write it down. Never thought I'd need to know until now. I've no idea who the guy is.

"That's about the best I can give you. I expect you've checked out everything there that is along the shore here?" It wasn't so much a question as an accusation.

Jay met his gaze. "Yes, I have."

He hoped his added request wouldn't drop ice cubes onto their burgeoning companionship. He could use Russell as a friend—not *use* him in the sense he'd set out to—but as a true buddy.

He would try to work something out and focus on redeveloping his own character. There would be time on later trips for cementing their friendship. Maybe time itself would make it so. At home he would just have to focus on…what? He knew that he didn't have to ask because the question was self-evasive. It would be *sincerity*, *dependability*, and *reliability*. He knew about these traits' fragility within his true nature; they had been tested before and had failed.

And so the two lads had left it at that. Jay spirited away Russell's phone number and e-mail address, and they agreed to keep in touch.

Jay, before leaving, outlined for Russell the sad condition of the Mont Sainte Marie Hotel that was to become their clinic, and that Lee had made contact with a project manager who would oversee the building's renaissance. The engineer who had appraised it considered it redeemable. That's what Lee had wanted, and it was her project. She apparently had raised the funds to finance the whole deal, and nobody was talking much about where the money was coming from, just that it would be there when needed. So they both—he and Russell—would have to bide their time until the building was refurbished. Jay would let him know when they both could get ready to schedule deliveries.

Without having wanted to, Jay had come to platonically love the guy. What a find; he was a wonderful human being! He knew that Lee was going to be so pleased. He could hardly wait to get home—at least as far as her home or her hometown, Ottawa, to tell her about it. Then he would fly to Cranbrook and his woods retreat to await word from her about when he could start. It should be fun, especially since he would be working closely with his dad.

They shook hands. Jay went back to the motel, pondering his drive back to Halifax to return the rental car and catch a flight to Ottawa, and from there home.

He wondered briefly where he should stay while in Ottawa, so not to pose any risk to Lee's anonymity. She was the boss, after all, and to some extent his benefactor. He had begun to regard himself as her unofficial protector. Not her bodyguard, really, but still, something of a strong man, if ever she might need one. But he would work it out on the plane. There was a nice enough little motel on Prince of Wales

Drive. It had looked like a place where a person like him could fit in unobtrusively. He hoped they would have a vacancy.

Scene 25
Everything Comes Together...

January 18, 2011

Lee knew that she had done well. Her dream had been realized, beyond any hope she had earlier nurtured. In fact, she had recently wondered whether it was all just a dream and that she might one morning unhappily awaken from it to pout her way back onto her earlier path. Not that her earlier path had been at all uninteresting: she had taught bridge at the Bridge Connection and still was enjoying her happy marriage to Carlyle. She presumed he was enjoying it, too. But *this!* This—the clinic thing—was truly an adrenaline rush.

Sven—miracle worker Sven—had been able to deliver the Mont Sainte Marie refurb earlier than even he had hoped. And he had done a fantastic job; everyone who saw the place reassured her of that. Overall, she was quite satisfied—Queen of the May in her own little queendom.

They had spent a sackful of DiPasquale's money, marketing the place, which she hadn't minded at all. It had paid off, a sound investment. Elderly ladies and not a few men had made their way there, some of the early-birds having vied for access to her best-in-house suites, which offered better views and amenities that were a notch up. The high-enders hadn't seemed to care about her roost's five-star price-tag. *And*, they had brought along, or later had transferred, their jewels and money and gold for safe-keeping in the facility's bank. How prescient and generous had been the clinic's all-inclusive service, several clients had effused, upon settling in. And how short a stay many of her earliest arrivals had enjoyed, she mused. Her housekeeping staff had had barely need change the sheets and towels. It perhaps would give those avant guarde one-percenters a heretofore absent understanding of what the unwashed know all too well as "cold comfort."

They had rather taken to DiPasquale's money guy; he had made them feel each was his only client, and he had gone out of his way to make them his friend, as well as their financial manager and investment counsellor.

Speaking of counsellors, DiPasquale's lawyer was also a smoothie. He had been bounced from an Ottawa high-tech firm, essentially for underperformance. They had sent him to California to take whatever additional courses he might need in order to achieve law-practitioner status in that state, an opportunity that he had jumped at. He settled comfortably into posh accommodations and rented a Corvette convertible, all at the company's expense. Nobody there had seemed to notice. What apparently he hadn't done, though, was study. He failed his certification exam and returned to Ottawa, to his previous job, or so he had hoped, with his tail between his legs. Shortly after that, his CEO had fired him, and he found himself embarrassingly jobless. But what he had always been good at was charming the ladies. He locked onto one, a former airline ticket agent, and moved in with her. Her place was decorously appointed; she had previously been matched up by friends with a former professional football player and plastics company owner, and later had been left comfortable when he had committed suicide, so the price for her new guy was right: zero. He had lived off her until those same friends convinced her that she needed to boot him out, and she did. Having then no place to go, although still familiar with the high-life opportunities available along the southern half of California's coastline, he thought he would try to go back there, maybe find somebody who would take him in. Perhaps he might even try for a *job*, God forbid. But, in the meantime, DiPasquale had heard about this guy and had looked him up. "Don Di" had been sufficiently impressed to hire him, in part because he really didn't give a damn about how much or how little this fellow knew about the law. What he had needed was a window-dressing-type lawyer, a smart looking fellow with a vocabulary and demeanour as near as he could find to that of Konrad Schwarz, an entrepreneur whose fortunes he had followed right up until Schwarz's incarceration. Pity, he had thought, that the fellow had had to do time in stir. Really, he should've been able to buy his way out of that. So this new dude had applied to the Mont Sainte Marie Acting School, and there he had performed quite adequately.

The clinic's medical department had gone well too. As an actor, "Doctor" McMurray had been excellent. The clientele followed him around in open areas of the clinic like a litter of puppies following their mother. His white coat was always crisp and spotless, his stethoscope a showpiece always hanging from his neck, and a thermometer's upper end protruding visibly from his coat pocket's plastic pen protector. They would do anything for him and wanted him to do whatever he might be able to do for them. What an easy segue it had offered: identifying suitable candidates for the *operation*. Segregating the co-optees from the general population had been an untroublesome sell. After a few days the folks who were there just to enjoy the clinic's comforts as a high-end seniors' residence offering didn't seem to notice that some of their peers were no longer there.

By their third try, the medical team had smoothed out any ripples in their kill-and-freeze process. Arthur and Jay had set up their freezer with a shelving system that accommodated uncomplaining guests like so many sleeping soldiers in a boot camp's training facility; they didn't really go anywhere until loaded onto Jay's rented eighteen-wheeler. Because the loading was stealthily done, between midnight and two in the morning, none of the in-queue guests had become curious about what was really going on. Jay made his runs, and Russell took everybody out to his favourite patch of ocean. Nobody on the boat ever complained. Meets and hand-offs had seemed to go without a hitch. Russell had turned out to be more than just an efficient lobsterman.

The money and all the gold wafers—where clients could be convinced to buy them—were moved in stashable accumulations to Fontana's safety deposit box in Vienna by Abigail. Lee had designated her as the company's trusted courier. Somehow she had managed always to evade detection, or even suspicion, by either Canada's or Austria's customs-and-excise people. Clever girl, that, Lee thought, given that their earlier pecking-order angst had settled out. Lee was now satisfied that she had won, and had deserved to win, the top-of-the-ladder position.

Their digs weren't bad either. Lee had had her first pick of the condominiums and Abigail second. They were neighbours. Lee had paid, from the clinic's budget, to have both their condos refurbished. Both women had been able to choose colours, furnishings, countertops, drapes, and whatever else they'd fancied, compliments of DiPasquale's largess. He clearly was a mover and shaker, and didn't seem to mind spending to acquire the equivalence of a hotel's five-star rating for his newest amusement. Maybe that was because, at some level, previously it had all been someone else's money.

How could it get any better than this, Lee wandered? She had relaxed comfortably into being the clinic's senior executive, and DiPasquale had increasingly let her grow into that role. She had kept her end of the bargain, in ensuring that he was not publicly associated with the place, and in making sure that whenever they had had to meet that it had been at a location and time of his choosing. She had never been late for one of those meets, and planned never to be. She didn't really regard him as her boss, more as her Godfather. If she'd had to put a corporate title to it, she probably would have chosen "chairman of the board," except of course that the clinic didn't have a board.

Her biggest responsibility now was to keep the ship on an even keel and to ensure that none of her staff would or could make any waves. If she could manage that, it looked to her like she could keep this up indefinitely.

But they were really just early days into their successes, and overconfidence and complacency were slippages Lee wasn't noticing as she did her daily walkabouts. Rightly enough, she spent most of that time socializing with the clinic's paying guests, answering their questions, making them feel important, and offering them assistance in any aspect of their personal lives where they felt she might be able to intervene. She may not have been paying quite enough attention to her staff and hadn't really involved herself in the wrapping-and-packaging aspect of the business.

But how could this go wrong? Lee came to believe that it couldn't. With each designated guest's "farewell", she came to feel that her team was, if anything, getting better and better at it.

She and Abigail were becoming rich. She could see, by each dawn's new light—she was an early riser—a vision, manifesting itself at the upper edge of their mountain-top's still night-blackened conifers, a soon-to-be, spankingly new Maserati. It was an aspiration that lay gently, happily on her mind. There was no rush, of course, she hadn't yet settled on a colour. She just knew it couldn't be black. *His* was black.

So, life was good: Carlyle seemed to have bought into her and the clinic's success, although he'd preferred to stay at their home in Manotick. There, in his studio—enjoying the solitude and his view of the river—his painting and his music had kept him busy. He seemed happy enough, quiet fellow that she revelled in his always having been. "Acceptance" of her tangential adventures was something he'd grown accustomed to.

> Nor had Sven uttered as much as a negative murmur about Abby's upward mobility within her profession. She had seemed happy during their now-infrequent get-togethers; relaxed, even. Her work-load and increased level of responsibility had seemed, to him, not to have fazed her at all. He'd taken to flying back and forth to his parental home in Sackville on weekends, renting a car wherever the plane would safely land him, and spending time in town with whomever was left of his boyhood buddies. He had taken to centering himself within the town's by-now country-wide-famous harness shop, helping out the owner by taking on what had become tantamount to an unpaid apprenticeship as a leather worker and harness maker. The redolence of the place, the quaintness of its antiquities, the joy of learning an ancient craft, and the camaraderie of folks dropping in to the shop for purchases or just to shoot the breeze, had given him a whole new raison d'être. He'd even contemplated moving back to his hometown, perhaps then buying his parents' former home, whenever he might retire.

So, life for him had taken an upward turn: something to look forward to, weekly and longer term. Aloneness didn't bother him much. His first profession and passion—civil engineering—had taught him that life, and work, and relationships, didn't follow a linear path; that a person needed to be ever ready to accept the unexpected, to adjust to conditions and situations that required mental agility and flexibility, always. To not accept *that* was to condemn oneself to a possibly miserable future, something he was determined wouldn't happen to him. He had survived birth, adolescence, early adulthood, and now day-to-day life as person whose health at any moment might take an irreversible downturn. He'd had to live with that, and he had bested it. And he knew, as with planning the erection of a new shopping mall or the rise of a condominium tower, progress often went sideways faster than upwards. Resilience and perseverance were qualities that he'd needed to develop just to exist. And he may need them again. At any time. He wasn't about to give up the strength inherent in his mastery of independent thought—determinations which had got him to where he now found himself. He knew that he'd be able to exercise these qualities anywhere, anytime, forever. Yes, he was a husband, and a good one, but he was first and foremost his own man; always would be.

So, Lee concluded, they were all set: all of them, all of her players, and all of their significant others. What could go wrong?

Who knew?

CHAPTER 3
Demise of a Dream

Scene 26
Jay Gets Caught...

*"To fear death, gentlemen, is no other than to think oneself wise when one is not,
to think one knows what one does not know. No one knows whether death may not be the greatest of all blessings for a man, yet men fear it as if they knew that it is the greatest of evils."*
~Socrates

September 22, 2010
In the early afternoon of this beautifully sunlit day—his father, Benedict, with them for a while visiting from his home in Kelowna, comfortably asleep in one of the lower-level bedrooms—Stanley sat in the living room going through an assortment of books on watercolour painting. It was his newest thing. It had been pleasant to contemplate: something different, something to look forward to.

Reflecting, he knew in truth that he had tried a lot of things in his time, seldom if ever bringing them to fruition. His path through life wouldn't have been hard for anyone to follow; he had left a clutter of unfinished ambitions and incomplete projects halfway around the world. It didn't bother him much, though, not any more, not now. Over the years, stretching back decades, uncertainty and fear of failure had eaten away at his sense of self-worth like a nest of termites consuming externally unseeable channels gnawed throughout the core of an eighteenth-century stable's support timbers: collapse could be imminent without anybody knowing it. It had left him with doubts about his competency, vis–à–vis anything. Whenever he had started something new like this—watercolours being just the most recent—the rush of renewed adventure soon found itself drowning in a pool of uncertainty at being able to do it, or even at being able to be *taught* to do it.

There had been his saxophone foray. He had started out with a student-quality soprano sax, knowing from the outset it was the most difficult within that family of horns to learn to play, or at least to play well. He had taken lessons of course, bought sheet music for all the tunes that he had wanted to learn, and acquired more paraphernalia then he would ever need to maintain and care for his instrument. Then he had decided it might be best to switch to an alto, so he had attached himself to a high-end Yamaha. It was a wonderful thing, but by then his interest had begun to flag. So having convinced himself that buying an even better horn would renew his keenness, he had invested in above any level of competency he could have hoped to achieve. His newest, a Selmer Paris 57, finished in rich bronze plating, was magnificent. He had bought a special stand for it, then a mouthpiece that he was sure would better adapt to his embouchure. He had fussed over the thing, polishing its bronze elegance and wearing cotton gloves so as not to get a fingerprint on it. With a pencil length of sharpened doweling he had coaxed cotton swabs into and around every piece of its valved complexity. Then he had put it back into its case where, as he recalled now, it was still waiting.

Was this what would too soon happen to his newfound enthusiasm for painting? Probably, he thought. It was always like this: a great burst of enthusiasm at the outset, hustle out and buy all stuff necessary to make a grandiose start, grow weary of it somewhere along the way, nest his collected acquisitions into a closet or under a bed, and then wonder once again what in the world he might be good at? The several art books he was paging through—some bought, some borrowed—were wonderfully instructive. They showed so many different styles within the same medium, a whole new appreciation of light and colour, and a justification for the new camera he had bought just a few weeks earlier. He hadn't yet invested in all the materials he knew would become an inevitable next step, but was sure he would do so. He would fix up one of their home's guest bedrooms to become his workshop, although even in his own mind he hadn't pretended to call it a *studio,* knowing he wasn't a tenacious enough student—narcissist though he knew himself to be—to affect that.

His mind, whenever wandering back into this unwanted, please-step-on-my-head garbage, never used the word *failure*. Failure for him wasn't an option. Failure meant surrender, surrender to *truth*, and truth wasn't something he'd ever been able to face easily. Anyway, he had rationalized, truth was a slippery eel for anyone to try to grasp, let alone live by. There was solace in knowing that truth was out there, somewhere, for everyone, but, like the termites in the beam, it took a long time to reveal itself. And what about the universal *anybody* truth? Well, he thought that his favourite example was, who choreographed the JFK killing? Someone had. But who? Somebody still might know. The CIA? Mafia? LBJ and "a cabal of Texas tycoons," as Jackie had alleged? And what about Diana? Who had wanted that? Buckingham Palace? Just a word, perhaps, in the right ear? In a world where, he believed, controllers protected each other, and associates obscured truths of their guilt, unknowable secrets were covered up to keep the underlying cement pour of older ones entombed.

Jimmy Hoffa came to mind.

Putting down his watercolour materials, he went to dig out an old Charles Brandt clip he had recalled filing. Basking in afternoon warmth streaming through the kitchen's patio-door windows, he read it again: 'I heard you paint houses' are the first words Jimmy Hoffa ever spoke to Frank 'the Irishman' Sheeran. To paint a house is to kill a man. The paint is the blood that spatters on the walls and floors. In the course of nearly five years of recorded interviews, long-time Hoffa suspect, Frank Sheeran—nearing the end of his life and seeking redemption in the Catholicism of his Depression Era youth—confessed to Charles Brandt that he handled more than twenty-five hits for the powerful Mafia boss Russell Bufalino and for his friend and Teamsters' mentor Jimmy Hoffa. Sheeran learned to kill in Europe during World War II, where he waded ashore in three amphibious invasions and marched from Sicily to Dachau, compiling an incredible 411 days of active combat in General Patton's *killer division*. After returning home he married, had four daughters, became a truck driver, and met Bufalino by chance at a truck stop in 1955. At age thirty-five, Sheeran's life changed forever. He began doing odd jobs for Bufalino to earn a few bucks, getting deeper into the Mafia way of life. Sheeran soon was killing on orders again. Eventually he would rise to a position of such prominence in the Teamsters and the Bufalino family that in a RICO suit US Attorney Rudy Giuliani would name him as one of only two non-Italians on a list of twenty-six top mob figures. When Bufalino ordered Sheeran to kill his friend and mentor, Hoffa, Sheeran followed the order, knowing that if he ever said no to Bufalino about anything, he would have gone to Australia—been killed himself."

Maybe life was indeed as shouted by Jack Nicholson from the witness stand during filming of *A Few Good Men*: "You couldn't *handle* the truth!"

Yes, maybe so, at least for many folks. But, he was digressing—escaping, again. Swimming against the current of his better nature, he revisited his shortcomings.

It wasn't so much that he couldn't *do* things; it was more a question of his absence of resolve. An only child, he had forever been a dreamer, doted on by an angelic, wartime mother who felt that he had been a miracle—*her* miracle. She had been abdominally injured from a hard fall onto a mudbank during a rope-swing swimming accident, and was later medically proclaimed incapable of pregnancy. He had thus become an accidental inconvenience; she had promised his father that she could never be able to have kids. But, *quelle surprise*, there he had been: fetus Stanley, a bump swelling in her belly, the reason he had to marry her.

No matter, though. Not to young Stanley. At least not for a while. During his early life, *father*—if indeed this man had been his father—had gone to war before they had really come to know each other. For himself, nothing remained beyond a few illusory wisps of a marginally involved male presence. There had been family photos of course, revisited by his mom, particularly when news had come that he had been wounded and evacuated from frontline combat to a hospital in England. But try, as he often had, he couldn't remember more than just an unending pleasantness and the unbridled sense of freedom basking in the sunlight of his mother's love.

Whenever he hadn't finished anything as an infant, she had forgiven him and finished it for him. In the first or second grade, he couldn't quite remember when, he had been required to learn to knit. His first attempt had ended in a mess almost from the get-go: a tangle of burgundy wool, posturing as the start of a scarf that had become hopelessly shapeless within its first five inches—dropped stitches and irregular polygonal openings, making it look more like a web spun by a triple-amputee spider than something any person might wear around his or her neck. She had finished even the scarf for him. The teacher must have known, but she had let it pass.

Gradually he had twigged to the notion that he didn't have to *finish* anything because she would do it all for him. He just had to feign incompetence and look sweetly, sadly, ever lovingly into her eyes. Thus, although together they had been desperately poor—living in a rented, heat-leaking lean-to, built as an afterthought and left to degrade into a mere income-providing ugliness, tacked onto one end of a fairly decent two-story home—he had become a spoiled little turd, floating happily at the centre of the swirl of her attention, until 1946, when his father had returned from Europe. That had been too few months after the end of World War II.

His return had been a shocker; one Stanley was destined never to overcome. By age seven Stanley's life had taken on a rather severe militaristic bent. Parade-square criticisms were spittle-laden and relentless.

Gradually his sense of self-worth had dissipated. In fairness, though, he realized this had been no one's fault but his own; he had allowed himself to disintegrate early in his teen years into a feckless piece of shit who did neither the planet nor the people on it any great favour. On the upside, he had to admit, his dad had taught him to shoot. He had folded his first duck on the wing during the autumn of his ninth year, standing hip deep in cattails along the edge of one of Oak Lake's marshes. They had gone on, during years of his youth, to hunt geese, upland birds, and eventually deer. When times were tough, which were most of the time, they brought home rabbits and pigeons for food. The pelts of muskrats, weasels, and squirrels brought in a few dollars when skinned. A good prairie weasel could fetch as much as four dollars when the villagers saw four dollars as an exorbitant half-day's wage for a labourer. During the course of all that, he had become inured to the nature of death and to the mindlessness of causing it. It was by then to him as it might have been for any farmer chopping the head off a chicken to provide something for dinner: unlikely to affect anyone's appetite.

Okay, he thought, shifting his weight from one cheek to the other on the couch, enough. He had already been over it, in expensive detail, with a shrink. She had helped him a lot. Maybe she had saved him. His doctor had followed on with pills intended to make it all go away. On good days they worked really well. They were working today. Good thing, too.

He set the watercolour books down, went to the kitchen to stir himself a gin and tonic, dropping into the glass's swirl a couple of ice cubes, not bothering with the usual wedge of lemon or squeeze of lime, and then strolled downstairs and outside. There he contemplated earlier events of the day, wondering to himself why his midafternoon venture hadn't bothered him all that much; it hadn't bothered him at all, actually.

What was missing within his psyche, he wondered, looking out at a pair of mallards bobbing for zebra mussels anchored to a nebula of Asian milfoil, the weed working its way toward subsuming the river, swaying now in the current just beneath the surface. Iridescence gleamed from the green heads of the drakes, which weren't as much as twenty feet from where he had settled to contemplate the bigger picture. He and Chelsea had located the outside patio here at the nexus of this curve in the Rideau's Long-Reach stretch; they had selected it for its ever-changing view.

Perhaps he was a sociopath or a psychopath or some intertwining of the two. He didn't want to believe that; he wanted to believe he was just a person bringing justice to a situation that had cried out for it, knowing that without his intervention a tainted clot of humanity who seriously had deserved to die otherwise wouldn't have.

The cubes in his glass continued their flamenco emulation, caught up in a vortex of energy created by his obsessive stirring with one of Chelsea's desert spoons. His choice of glass had been a favourite: one of a very old set; tall, not tapered, frosted by its maker with superimposed red, orange, and green effigies of fresh fruit, making the glass appear wanting to contribute to any holder's contentment. Vivid without being tacky, the images had survived decades of dishwasher cycles. They had added a pleasant tilt for any of his fruit drinks, especially on such warm midsummer's afternoons. Better this glass than, say, a hollowed-out coconut shell. Perhaps, he thought, he might even go inside and pour himself a second, although he didn't want to risk waking his dad; he could do without the old man's company, at least for now. He would wake him for supper, later, after Chelsea had prepared it. No hurry.

Having settled into an Adirondack chair and watching the ducks searching for their late-day snack, he was relaxed. Reality suddenly overtook his unguarded mind as if a view from his brain's rearview mirror. He hadn't wanted the day's earlier memories to return, but, once loosed, the still-fresh neuron stream wasn't to be deterred.

* * * * * * *

This day, this beautiful day, had begun with another interesting call from Corporal Elujah. The RCMP had retried a modus operandi that had worked well for them along sections of Nova Scotia's east coastline when they had earlier attempted to intercept incoming drug shipments. They recruited folks living on heights of land offering a view of docking facilities in and around villages where drug drop-offs had been suspected. Scruffily dressed plain-clothed officers, using older, unmarked vehicles, had sought out and elicited the help of locals—typically seniors known to be discreet—who had agreed to phone in at any time, day or night, any suspicious movement. This recruitment had taken a while, an activity that for obvious reasons they had not been able to rush. For those individuals who had agreed, the RCMP had offered each, as an appreciation of their service, a high-end tripod telescope. Elujah's subdivision headquarters apparently had agreed to foot the bill in lieu of a reward for conviction.

So, tried and true, the approach had worked again. The Sherbrooke detachment had taken a predawn call from a widow who had been more than curious about the offloading of an eighteen-wheeler, first onto the Port Bickerton wharf and from there onto a lobster boat. She said that she had been sleepless, watching the activity from a darkened window at the seaside end of her living room. She had grown to like her telescope and had stashed it in a broom closet during daytime hours to avoid curious eyes of visitors and neighbours. She was pleased that later she hadn't been asked to give it back.

Having crept down to the fish-plant's landside end in a mud-splattered van, engine at a quiet idle, lights out, the RCMP had intercepted both driver and boatman. When searched, neither had been found armed. Outnumbered three to one, neither had offered resistance. The front end of the refrigerated trailer had been packed with beef carcasses that had masked the truck's principal cargo: frozen corpses.

The widow had reported having been able to make out something of the process of their being wrapped and weighted before being stacked onto the open cargo area of a lobster boat. She had said that she knew most of the locals' boats, and she had recognized this one, too.

Both men were arrested and separately interrogated. The lobsterman had stuck to a centuries-old maritime code of the sea: he'd 'fessed up to what had been blatantly obvious; however, he had flatly refused to incriminate anyone else. The other lad, being "from away" and interested in cutting a deal, had offered up what he knew of the Fontana Corporation and its principals in the hope that a court might show leniency when sentencing him. Among those he had named—in addition to his own father—were Lee, ostensibly the clinic's owner, and her partner, the clinic's head nurse. The driver had claimed never to have met other members of the outfit's administrative or support staff, but he had offered that there was a lawyer among them—all watched over 24/7 by an intense, professionally trained security staff. He hadn't known the names of any of the security types, only that they were close-mouthed and businesslike, appearing always to trust no one.

Thus Elujah had asked once again for Stanley's help, or perhaps had just been sharing a confidence, a need, maybe, to share his win—a trust unfortunately misplaced. The clinic's owner, it had turned out, was from Manotick, and chances were he might have known her.

He had paused for a moment when he had heard the name; he had hedged, the corporal having tugged unwittingly at a string wound around the shaft of his brain's gyroscope. This mechanism of mind, in his case more mechanically than synaptically driven, had lifted the wheel into vertical orientation—his sharpest thinking mode—balancing there without wobbles.

Saying that he was "vaguely aware of her, primarily as a person who had lived in the same village," he had lied that they weren't well acquainted.

Elujah then had inquired about the other person: the nurse. He had denied knowing her as well, his of-the-moment credibility enhanced by the corporal's intimation that the nurse had once lived a bit farther away, somewhere in Barrhaven. Elujah had added that she was, according to the driver, now in residence at one of the clinic's townhouses.

Elujah had effused that his people were moving quickly. They had been in touch with the Ottawa City Police and the Sûreté du Québec just hours before about the killings and that arrests were imminent.

The corporal had suggested he not mention any of this, at least not at this time, to Chelsea.

He had agreed, of course. He congratulated the corporal on boxing up this crime; it would be a feather in his cap, perhaps even an added stripe on his sleeve. They had agreed to keep in touch until the case could be handed over to a crown prosecutor.

* * * * * * * *

So, precious Lee—good-natured, gregarious, bridge master Lee—was a serial killer. Interesting. He had actually known something of the clinic's success at Mont Sainte Marie. Everyone had, at least to the extent that it existed and that it catered exclusively to Ottawa's rich elderlies. Its grand opening had been celebrated as the epitome of high-end seniors' care. The elite had been attracted to it like their pet poodles were to overstuffed pillows and platters of pâté. Comfort, after all, wasn't so much where one found it as where one paid to become part of it. And pay they must have; rumour had it that only the top one percent need have sought acceptance. Elitism itself had made the Fontana Clinic the go-to destination for the apex of this province's most pampered sunset resorters.

But he knew beneath all that that Lee couldn't have floated her enterprise without having finessed a financial plinth. She had been financially well set, but she wasn't one of the superrich. She must have had a funder, and it couldn't have been your average, every-day banker. The hotel's renovations would have cost millions and, perhaps oddly in hindsight, no one who'd celebrated the clinic's opening, including himself, had bothered to question just how she had been able to do it.

He had realized, standing there by the kitchen window, that he could waste all day guessing at who might have put the money together for her, assuming it had been her idea from the get-go. He had also known, listening to Elujah, which door he would need to knock on to find out. Yes, that would be the quickest. He would take the accusation to Lee and then offer her an out—one she couldn't refuse, presumably: give up her funder or spend the rest of her life socializing with the idle-no-more crowd in Kingston's women's prison.

Having slid himself into slightly better jeans than he had pushed his legs through when crawling out of bed, he had shaved, puzzled through his game plan, and refined it, all while weighing the impact of his opening question. Recalling a time when that technique—a virtual rifle shot to a deer's heart—had been used against him, he had known his first mouthful of words would have to blaze off his tongue like the flash from the pan of a flintlock. If his verbal aim were off or just inflicted a flesh wound, he would need to be prepared to follow through with the *or* part of his either/or threat.

Done with that, he hadn't been terribly careful in watching the speed limit while driving between his home and hers. Having pushed a tight turn into her driveway he had braked hard, switched off the Echo's ignition, slammed the driver's door behind him, and taken the steps up to her front door two at a time. There, trembling, he had held his thumb against the doorbell until he could see a shadow of movement inside.

Lee had opened the door with a surprised, then warm, smile for him, pushing the outside screen's frame wide ajar to invite him in. Would he care for a cup of coffee, she had asked. But she could see, from an ashen shambles that had taken the place of his face, that he wasn't there for coffee.

He had left her no hesitation in hearing his concern. With anger as much feigned as real, he had spit out that he knew what she had been up to, and knew that she wasn't in this alone. He also knew all about Abigail.

"A wonderful pair, weren't you? Wonderful!" he had blustered. Then he had touched his finger to the trigger of his offer: either she would give up her funder or he would drag her, then and there, to the Manotick office of the Ottawa City Police. Catching his breath while, for effect, wiping the back of a hand across his mouth, he had offered her an out. Were she to tell him who her moneyman was and convince him that she wasn't lying, he would let her go. Why? Because, he had said, modifying his tone, he believed that, at the core of her being, she was a decent soul and that he had known for a long time about her proclivity for wanting Canada to fix its moribund unwillingness to legalize euthanasia as a humanitarian option for people who desperately wanted out. In short, he could understand why she had done this.

A momentary pause lingered between them: he panting, eyes red-rimmed and wet, as though he had been staring into the sun but reluctant to blink and she, contemplative, body erect as a massaged clitoris, mind excavating the narrow space between them looking to disinter words that might help collapse the momentum of his anger, mouth working as if on a nip of snuff and in need of a spittoon, eyes focused on her opponent's reddened rims, determined not to be first to break contact.

He had shifted, accused Lee of killing his mother-in-law, although Chelsea didn't know it yet. She would inevitably find out. This had been his *piece de resistance*—what he had practiced in his mirror while shaving. Chelsea's vengeance might be more than just unpleasant, he had said, less forgiving than his. Had she ever seen Chelsea in a maddened rage, kitchen knife in hand, uncaring where along any antagonist's torso it might end up getting shoved? He lied that he had and it hadn't been a pretty sight. He had survived, however, testicles intact.

Their standoff had held: a silence, their breaths laboured, hers weighing a possible best next move. Then he had sniffed her resolve wilting, her bowels loosening. She had telegraphed a wound, but was trying a last, transparent offensive.

"Stanley," she had coughed, "this is utter nonsense. You must've suffered a fall or lived through a bad dream. You've taken leave of your senses. I'm going to have to insist you go, now. Get off my property, or I'll have Carlyle arrange to sue you both—if that's the kind of thing your wife's vocalizing—for defamation."

"And who will be your witness, Lee?" he had retorted. "There's no one here but you and me, and you know you're just hissing through your teeth. And by the way, you might want to change your undies. Tell me who is behind the clinic, and I'll let you go. You can invoke Plan B. I'm sure you have one. And, if you'd like, you can take Abigail with you. There's still time, *maybe*, but not much. I know for a fact that the police are prepping, as we speak, to come here and arrest you. And if they do, you and Abigail are cooked. But go, if you want and find a life somewhere else. Experience tells me that in a scam as elaborate as the one you've cooked up, there's a back door to slip through. And, believe me, the shit has hit the fan, like leakage 'round a proctologist's probe into an unwilling patient. So your clock is ticking. Which way do you want it go: I take you to the police now or you make a run for it?"

He remembered, smiling, how Lee's face had contorted, her upper lip quivering. For a few seconds she had seemed not to know which way to turn. But she had bought his bluff and accepted that someone must've been in touch with him, someone in the know. She had felt boxed in and knew she didn't want to rot in a cage.

"How much time do you think I have?" she had asked.

"Maybe an hour, maybe as much as three," he said. "I'm only guessing here. But I do know that within this day, unless you go now, you'll be in handcuffs and wearing prison pajamas from tonight through to your eternity."

"Okay," she had replied, regurgitating her confession like a gush of muddied water busting from the mouth a sewer pipe after a hard rain. "My guy is DiPasquale, owner of the Three Gondolas. He's connected to the mob. I've been laundering money for him and his associates. That's the truth, my truth. Now, if you'll excuse me, I have a couple of rather pressing things to attend to."

With that she had pulled closed the screen door and turned away to disappear into an awaiting gloom of her darkened hallway.

He had been left standing there, pleasantly fazed, trying to fit this offering as a piece into the day's larger puzzle. A picture had begun to emerge. It still had gaps and holes, of course, but enough sections were pieced together to let him see much of it.

DiPasquale. Well, Mister Pretender DiPasquale, Manotick's latter-day Giacomo Casanova. Interesting. Suddenly it had made a lot of sense.

He asked himself what to do next.

And, with that, he had known what to do. Err? Perhaps, but err on the side of justice—or, his interpretation of it.

He had come home and rummaged through Chelsea's fruit cellar, separating out various bits and pieces from his long-untouched archery gear, focusing on the crossbow and its bolts. Then he had shopped around various hooks protruding from the bare two-by-fours making up the framework of the little room's walls, looking for something—anything really—that might be long enough, straight enough, and rigid enough for his need. In haste, and in the absence of a better option, he had grabbed a cross-country ski pole. He had thought that it would have to do. He didn't have time for measurements; his guesstimate would have to be close enough. He had peeled off a garbage bag—on a second, thumb-licking try, the slippery son of a bitch that it had been—from the black stack inside its box and then, using a hunting knife unsheathed from the belt of his hunting pants, had punched half a dozen holes through it, however awkwardly. Nervousness, uncertainty, the rust of age; all had begun to get the better of him. So, okay, he would stop now and take a couple of deep breaths. But he would do this all the same, for Marion. Yes, she had told him any number of times that he would be going to hell; maybe this would be his time. But she *was* Chelsea's mom and that needed to be redressed.

The anxiety had passed. By then composed, squinting, he had switched on the crossbow's sight battery to see if it had gone dead, although it didn't matter, because he had a spare if needed. *Yes,* there had been the three vertical red dots, indicating ranges in increments of ten meters. Finding the crossbow's cocking mechanism, he had dropped it into the outfit's carrying case, along with all three bolts, although knowing he would probably need only one. On his way out he had lifted the leather hoop of the ski pole off its nail and tucked it under his arm.

"What's best?" he had muttered to no one on his way upstairs, except maybe to Cleopatra, his little dog. "The van or the Echo?" Cleo had managed to intertwine herself in an anxious dance around his feet and pant legs—ever the trip hazard, he had thought, annoyed—wanting always to be with him, hoping this might be her walk time. He had brushed her away.

No need to have pondered which car, he remembered thinking. It was a no-brainer; he would take the van. As soon as he was inside the garage, he had tossed his gear onto the Caravan's back seat and backed it out, fingering the automatic door closer as he cleared the opening.

He had navigated back-way streets to bypass the village core, feigning elderly uncertainty about where he might've been wanting to go. In the course of doing so, he made a couple of slow passes along Dickenson Street to reacquaint himself with the Three Gondolas—more particularly, its entrances.

Yes. No surprise there, he had thought, eyeing DiPasquale's Maserati, gleaming black and beautiful in the afternoon sun with its top down. No need to have feared rain because no rain was forecasted.

He had sized up the walk his target would have to take when leaving the restaurant to the car and then drove to the riverside's dead end on O'Grady Street to bring the van around to face the O'Grady-Dickenson intersection. He had stopped on the street's north side, backed incrementally to a point where he had judged he could open the driver's side window and remain unnoticed when sitting behind, on the vehicle's mid-bench seat, obscured by the vehicle's smoked glass side and back windows.

Leaving and locking the car, he had strolled into the bar, mustering all the confidence he had left, intent on confirming his target was inside. Okay, the *car* was there, but if he was to wait him out, he would need to know that his guy was *in the house*—an affectation his Mister D was known to advertise—and not out for a walk to grace one of Main Street's shops with his presence.

If he weren't there, he would have to try again, but no later than that evening, before sunset. Dusk wouldn't be an option. His scope didn't like a paucity of natural light nor would a fresh attempt be possible tomorrow; Lee might by then have given him a heads-up, and, the next day, the police would be all over this place—he could have fled to somewhere in Europe.

He confirmed that the man had been in the bar, leaning against back-wall cabinetry, tilting a glass of red, pussy lips as if well-practiced at doing so, swirling his few ounces of Merlot as might have a connoisseur, elegantly dressed as ever, ensuring his body language conveyed to staffers his every expectation. Happily enough, several people were seated at the bar, enjoying a late lunch or maybe just munchies, not one of whom he had recognized or had recognized him. DiPasquale hadn't so much as lifted his head, intent on the wine's quality. Maybe. Or maybe he hadn't. Maybe it had just appeared that way. The nature of the game could've shifted with deadly blowback if the position of observer had shifted, undiscerned, in favour of the observed. What might a person, a stranger, DiPasquale could have been asking himself, be doing walking through his restaurant—not sitting down, not ordering anything from the bar, not ducking into the can for a leak—if he hadn't been *looking* for somebody? But who? And why? Always there were these Damoclean questions: Would the terrier get to shake the rat, or would the rat turn and bite the terrier and then chase him down and finish the challenge, helped by fresh rats shaken from the gamer's sack? Certainty of outcome was never sure.

Returning to the van, he had unlocked it and climbed onto the middle bench. He had unzipped the crossbow's case, brought out the bow and its cocking mechanism, cocked it, and inserted his first bolt into the launching track. Then he had placed the ski pole, sharp end on the van's dash, handle and strap pinched into the gap between one of the bench seat's down-pressed headrests. He had settled in comfortably, had regained his composure, and was satisfied with his relative obscurity. His sight's middle red dot centered on the top of the Maserati's steering wheel. He had found it offered a perfect focal point within the circle of the scope's sight picture. He just hoped DiPasquale wouldn't sink too far into the driver's seat the moment he eased himself into the car. He had guessed the distance between the Maserati's windshield and the crossbow's end to be about fifteen meters. At that distance the bolt's trajectory would remain flat; it'd be essentially a rifle shot, but without the noise.

His wait had seemed endless, and he had been growing a bit anxious. The afternoon sun had begun to sneak across the sky with the inexorability of sand dropping through an hourglass. But the sun's angle, he had calculated, would remain okay; it wouldn't have gotten in his eyes when the time came. And there would been no wind.

More time had passed. But it had still been bright, warm, and pleasant enough as patrons began to leave. Nobody had seemed to notice the van nor could anyone, he had thought, have picked him out. Within his nest he had forced himself to be confident and had disallowed complacency, his essential tremor-stricken left arm having settled into the job at hand, the ski pole its prop, on top of which he had been able to anchor the crossbow's forearm almost tirelessly. He had waited in blinds before, dozens of them. Now was time again to call on the needed patience, stillness; it was time to keep a clear mind and a steady right hand.

And then his man had appeared. No one had come out with him. Typically DiPasquale had stopped just outside the front entrance, stretched, glanced with a characteristic sense of ownership of all he had surveyed, extracted a soft cloth from his shirt pocket and shook it to polish the lenses of his sunglasses, put them back on, and sauntered to the side of his car.

From the van, each footfall had been studied. He had stopped at the driver's door to take a last look around, possibly in the hope that someone would see him getting into his black beauty and envy him driving away in it. Pity, though, nobody had been watching. Except one. DiPasquale hadn't so much as glanced at the van.

With left-hand fingers and thumb locked around the intersection of the ski pole and the crossbow's forearm, the hunter had decided to hold—having been tempted to take the shot while his target was questing about for admirers—until the guy had settled behind the wheel.

The scope's middle dot found its margin-of-error comfort zone between the back of DiPasquale's head and his right ear. The crossbow had a characteristically stiff trigger pull, heavier than any rifle he had known. He had earlier reminded himself not to *pull* the trigger, rather to squeeze all fingers as one, gripping the stock's thumb-holed handle ever more firmly, willing his right forefinger to become just an extension of the hand's overall contraction. If he did that with enough discipline, he knew, the bow's release would come as a surprise.

And it had. He had been unable to track the bolt's soft launch toward the car, but had caught its disintegration as it had shattered against the restaurant's brickwork, leaving within its trajectory a slowly blooming rosette bleeding down into the hair of his man's carefully barbered neck.

Knowing there would be issues with fingerprints if found on any of the bolts, he had wiped all three of them clean. The one he had fired, having passed as though unobstructed through DiPasquale's head, would have been smeared clean by blood and brains. There was a high probability one or more part of the bolt would have torn off inside the cranium; there would be no identifiable trace of origin, he had hoped, either on whatever was left of the shaft or any piece of fletching embedded in the wound.

Okay, so he had managed that. Wearing his cotton gloves, he had wiped down the crossbow's stock and moved the gloves thoroughly over the complex mechanism of the machine's compound bow. He had then done the same with the handles on the bow's cocking pulley and, still with gloves on, had put the crossbow, the two remaining bolts, and the cocking device into his black plastic bag and tied it.

Sliding open the passenger's side rear door, he had moved into the driver's seat, driven unhurriedly past the Mill, crossed over the two Bridge Street arches, went east to River Road, waited for the light, and turned north to drive to Parks Canada's Long Island Locks.

The park was quiet. Again he had been lucky. Having encountered no one, no other vehicle, he had risked a walk to the weir controlling the river's main-channel water level. Moving to the barrier's downstream side, he had checked to see which of the gates was active, glanced 'round the park's far-shore periphery to satisfy himself he was still alone, and then dropped the garbage bag over and down into a roaring turbulence of yellow-green froth, rushing away, soon to dissipate into a patchwork of weaker undulations at the downstream end of Nichols Island, merging there with the passivity of leakage from the three ships' locks.

He had returned hastily to the van, driven home, found and burned in the downstairs fireplace all receipts and documentation related to his years-ago purchase of the crossbow, and then had settled into the serenity of his living room's couch, there to rekindle in his mind something akin to domestic tranquility. He would have to be living that, or convincingly faking it, by the time Chelsea got home.

* * * * * * *

Oddly, he thought, the transition hadn't taken long. The watercolour books had helped, of course. He had been surprised, in hindsight, how easy it had all seemed. This had been, after all, a first for him—not a first kill, certainly, but the first kill of a fellow human.

He wondered if this is what it might be like for a contract killer. No, he had concluded, there would be a skill gap between an amateur and a professional. He had just been lucky, at least, so far.

In the half hour or so that had followed, he had managed to rationalize that this particular human being hadn't deserved to live; that if he hadn't done what he had done, then there would have been a likelihood that the guy's lawyers would've gotten him off, either entirely or with a token incarceration, allowing him to be back on the street within a few years. Chelsea wouldn't have wanted that, he knew. But then Chelsea would never know, would she? He would make sure of that. There would be no talking in his sleep or slippage in the midst of a gin-slurred moment during some evening's happy hour.

Did it all matter? Maybe not. Vigilante justice, he knew, was unlawful. *Now* it was. A person couldn't—at least any longer—hang a man off the back of a horse or shoot someone that he didn't really care for, no matter how richly that dude might have deserved it. But was such justice *immoral?* He had managed to rationalize that what he had done was okay, which concurrently had conjured up the realization that this must have been similar to whatever had gone through Lee's mind while preparing herself to take the lives of dozens of elderly Ottawa citizens.

And what about Abigail? How would she be making out along about now? If he had to bet on the survival of either of the two, his nickel would have been on Abigail. Had this been the Titanic, he reckoned, she would have been early into a lifeboat, prying swimmers' fingers off its ratlines.

Anyway, it was over now…at least this part. He could relax and let things settle back to normal. This would be big news in the village by tomorrow; he would just have to act as surprised as everybody about what had happened. He knew he could do that; he had faked such things before, just nothing this big. He had done something tantamount to acting for a living once—pretending not to be things he was, and just as often feigning things he wasn't. But he had never been proud of that; it had been why he had switched horses in midcareer, only to pick a loser for the second half of his life's work journey.

Well, what the hell, he thought, sipping at the edge of the melting ice cubes in his drink, he could still afford groceries, and the house was paid for.

*   *   *   *   *   *   *   *

Something caught his eye, and he looked up. Chelsea was coming across the lawn to greet him, glass of white in hand and a ready smile on a face he had loved for as long as he could remember. She settled into the Adirondack beside him. Together they watched the ducks continue their quest for mussels. She'd had a good day, apparently.

Life was good, if you just let it be, he thought, smiling. As was death, apparently.

CHAPTER 4
An Odyssey's Fulfillment

Scene 27
Angeline's Visit...

> *"You've thrown down the gauntlet. You've brought my wrath down upon your house. Now, to prove that I exist I must kill you. As the child outlives the father, so must the character bury the author. If you are, in fact, my continuing author, then killing you will end my existence as well. Small loss. Such a life, as your puppet, is not worth living. But... If I destroy you and your dreck script, and I still exist... then my existence will be glorious, for I will become my own master."*
> *~ Chuck Palahniuk, Damned*

September 25, 2010, 9:47 a.m.
Having gotten up later than usual, he found Chelsea had breakfasted early and left in the Echo for an early tee-off.

 He hadn't slept well; the adrenaline rush he had experienced from yesterday's activity had leaked away into the night's abyss, leaving him emptied. Standing there now on the deck, looking down over grass cut just a couple of days earlier and at the placidity of the river's eternal flow—calming as that usually had been—he gnawed on a bone unburied: whether he might have left a tell-tale detail at yesterday's Three Gondolas retaliation.

What about the crossbow's fired bolt, he asked himself? Would Ottawa's forensics sniffers be able to trace whatever might have been left of it? Yes, they would no doubt identify its manufacturer, but could they then track its factory-to-customer delivery? Parker was a big company, which, he thought, was in his favour: American, with possibly thousands of client outlets, big and small, all across the continent and even in Europe.

He had bought his archery gear from a small, home-based hunting enthusiast's shop near Perth —a game warden, actually, and the store had been in the guy's basement. He had sold the business a few years ago. Might he have kept the shop's records? He may have been required to, as a Revenue Canada stipulation. And he would have a memory of the transaction. After all, how many of these crossbow kits might he have sold? Probably not many; his had been a Safari Classic, *very* high end. But—and maybe this was a good *but*— the bolts hadn't been a separate purchase; they had come with the package, and he had never gone back for more.

It was worrisome, though. When the police had a mind to, they could be tenacious as hounds at a fox hunt. And a records-search could determine an estimated geographical area of purchase with a deliberately elastic order/delivery timeframe.

Thus lost in a mental labyrinth that the event's analysis had visited upon him, he didn't hear the patio door ever so gently open and close behind him. He didn't turn around, actually, until he became conscious of his granddaughter's dovelike greeting floating across the short space between them.

"Hi, Grandpa." It was just above a coo.

"Angeline! Whatever are you doing here?" Her presence always seemed to him ethereal. She wouldn't be there one moment and the next she was. Tall for her age and svelte, she seemed to drift from place to place rather than walk, or shuffle, as, he thought, most new-age young people did, almost as if gravity had graced her with a lesser drag than weighs down humanity's other seven billion.

"Oh, I just woke up with the thought that I might be able to be with you today."

"That's nice, thank you." He had meant it, he knew—and hoped she did as well; it wasn't just a platitude. "How did you get here?"

"Mom dropped me off. I told her I was coming to practice."

He concluded—wrongly, it turned out—that she intended to practice the piano, given that Chelsea had been teaching her. However, he thought that this morning an imperfect sonata might not be such a good venture. Wanting to ease her in the direction of an outcome less likely to become volatile, nonetheless wanting to encourage her to stay and visit, he tried, "Well, you're great-grandfather is here from Kelowna. Your playing might annoy him. I think you know what he's like: a bit impatient around young people. Always has been. Blows hot and cold. You never know what mood he's liable to wake up in." As soon as he heard himself say it, he knew it had been weak. He hadn't offered her anything in the way of a desirable alternative. Actually, he hadn't been able to think of one, not in time, anyway.

"I know," she said. "But I came here to be with you, not him."

"Well, young lady," he tried to make *young* not sound like a condescension, "I may not be the best of company today. I've been a bit absorbed."

She smiled her prescient, mystical smile. It had always reminded him of an hour he had spent standing at the back of a crowd, trying, as had millions before him, to puzzle out the meaning of the Mona Lisa's smile as she looked out from her veiled presence, hanging there on a wall in the Louvre. Had Leonardo perhaps reached forward to paint that same enigmatic expression—patient layer upon patiently varnished layer, four years in the doing—as well onto Angeline's countenance? The arts community, he remembered in a moment of self-indulgent distraction, had given that technique a name: *Sfumato* they had called it, emulated by subsequent masters, although never with quite the same dimensionality as had been achieved by the world's most important painter on the world's most important painting. And there standing before him, he found himself looking at it all over again.

She sensed that his mind was drifting, as it was inclined to; she knew it to be her onus to bring him back. "It's okay, Grandpa. I'd just like to sort of hang out with you. I won't get in your way; just be somewhere in the house or in the yard. I won't go down to the lower level; I know my being there might be bothersome to Great-Grandpa."

"Then how will you practice?"

Angeline caught his drift and calculated a best response, perhaps too rapidly. "Oh, another time; maybe when Grandma's here. It's better then. She helps me a lot, and I like the way she gently brings my *ability* along; I know it needs work. It doesn't seem like school at all; she makes it fun, always." Again, he thought, there was the agelessness of that little smile. "If it's okay, I'll just browse through Grandma's library; maybe I can find a new book. I'm more in the mood for reading anyway, although I'll stay close by, out of your way."

It was Saturday, so why not? It was nice to have her here. "Okay, girl, fill your boots, and your mind!" He liked the way she tried to hide a little grimace whenever he used the first part of that expression.

Turning then in place, like the *tamasha* sway of a cobra, undulating trancelike from its basket under the spell of its charmer, she eased her way back through the door and disappeared behind a reflection of sun on glass.

Stanley lowered his head for a minute and closed his eyes, pressing against the deck's railing while he let his mind find its way back to his mother-in-law's disappearance. Before he got there, though, he wondered briefly how Angeline had known that Chelsea wasn't home. But he didn't dwell on it; there were other things to think about, like survival.

* * * * * * *

Benedict, or *Ben* as he'd preferred to be called, his now-ancient father, emerged from the patio doors below the deck, audibly sucking on his ill-fitting upper plate, easing it forward with his tongue so that the two front teeth, affixed with wires and having gaps on either side, emerged between his lips and remained there while he worked at dislodging a real or imagined food particle from its roof. Apparently satisfied, he hooked the underside with his tongue and pulled the protrusion back into place, neither of his hands having had to leave whatever task he may then have been wanting them to perform.

Interesting, he thought: the old man carried a golf club in his left hand. Focusing on it, he could see it was the putter he had given him three years earlier, a gift of no particular occasion. It had been handcrafted by a woodcarver living in the same building as the old lad, who, as a sideline, had customized and sold putters as trophy items. He had cast its foot from bronze and turned its wooden shaft on a lathe, then had personalized it with text he had chosen: simply *Ben Watson*. But when the putter had been delivered, for whatever reason, the craftsman had added, midway down the shaft, the word *Stanley*. He never gave any explanation; Stanley had simply accepted the finished piece and given it to his dad. Apparently he had liked it; he had brought it to Manotick with him, packed away somewhere within his assortment of cardboard boxes and tattered suitcases. Stanley looked at the old man's other hand to see if he had brought out a couple of balls to tap around the lawn, but could see none. The grass between the patio bricks and the river was neither short enough nor the ground even enough to be anything like a golf green, but the man may not have cared. And, he didn't care that this person—the person who had raised him—didn't care.

"The person who had raised him," he thought, mouthing the words. How different from his dad he had become, and how often he had wondered—and tried to determine—whether or not this person was his biological father. It may not have been so; it must've been a close call. Whenever Stanley had attempted the math around his own birth, the date of his father and mother's marriage, and the best date he could pin down for when they had met each other, he always came up with a doubt that he nurtured, still. Why? Because he didn't want it to be true; he didn't want this man to be his dad. This guy he was about to confront was in so many ways the antithesis of everything he had valued, and he held out an undying hope that some other male had managed to get to his mom, Elizabeth, first—so much so that he wished he knew—knew for sure.

The guy that his mother apparently had loved and wanted to marry was Charles Billington, who had inherited from his own father a small but tidy smoke shop and magazine stand. But a profoundly Irish James T. McLeash, her dad, had forbidden the union, believing that Charles was too old and socially beneath his eldest girl. So when her next catch came along and Elizabeth had announced that she was pregnant, Jimmy, as he'd preferred to be called, must have felt he had little choice but to accept her new bedfellow as an unwanted son-in-law.

It was a choice everyone in the family would come to regret.

Looking down on his father now, the long-moribund anger again welling up within him, Stanley decided it was time to bring his uncertainty to the fore, eyeball to eyeball. Busying his mind with how he might introduce the subject without driving the man into one of his infamous rages, concurrently making his way down the stairway to the home's lower level, he worked and reworked in his mind the words he would air.

At the bottom of the stairs, he paused, uncertain but determined. Crossing a distance of parquet that covered the rec room's floor, he could see that Ben had settled into one of the two plastic lawn chairs on the patio, a few feet beyond the screen door. The old man was half in the shade of the deck above him and seemed to be pondering some detail of the putter as he rolled its shaft between left thumb and forefinger.

Taking a deep breath to assuage his uncertainty, Stanley slid open the patio door without realizing that he had not—anywhere during his passage through the house—noticed where Angeline may have settled herself. So concentrated was he on what he was about to say, that he had for the moment forgotten about her.

He had, in effect, brought Ben home from Kelowna, to be away from the intensity of his third wife's dislike for him. His predilection to dominate those around him through verbal bullying and physical abuse may have exacerbated her mental frailty. She had told Stanley, explicitly, that she wanted her husband dead and hoped that his failing health soon would deliver him from her.

He and Chelsea had made several trips to Kelowna in ever-deteriorating attempts to resolve their differences, but the underlying problem persisted, and by now it was presumed irreconcilable.

Images of the beatings that Benedict had visited upon Elizabeth were indelibly etched in some recess of his mind. The re-emergent anger that accompanied them strengthened his resolve.

He pulled forward the empty chair beside his father, watching him fondle the putter. The old lad seemed quite pleased with it, as he had at the time the gift was presented. He gazed at it for some moments, and then at his son. "This is nice," he said, quietly, as he sometimes did when restrained within the good side of his Jekyll-and-Hyde personality.

"Dad, I have a couple questions for you."

"Oh? And what might those be?" Ben asked.

"It's something I've pondered for a very long time, Dad, but couldn't bring myself to ask you."

Ben stiffened, visibly. A frown of anticipation pulled at the corner of his lips, and the Windsor-blue of his eyes paled, as often happened when conversations chased him into a dark alley that led to the fight-or-flight barrier he feared would force him to turn around. He verbally didn't reply. His right eyebrow raised in a high arch whereas the left one squinted down over a half-closed eye. It was his way of communicating that he already didn't like what he expected was coming. Body language and visual cues had always been something he'd invoked as part of his way of controlling whoever might be displeasing him, a sort of early-warning sign.

Stanley blurted, with fear in his belly, but knowing it was now or never: "Are you my real father?"

He had been right; his dad didn't like the question. Ben turned in his chair to face him directly, moving the head of his putter down to the patio bricks and grasping its handle between his knees. He stared intensely at his son and then asked, "And what's your next question?" There was malice in the message, and the blue in his eyes continued to fade. Stanley had hoped the confrontation would go better than it was, but he was determined still to prevail.

"Why did you so often beat my mother?" he tried, without faltering.

A malicious Hyde transformation found its way through the brume of Benedict's split personality and instantly escalated the confrontation into a scene Stanley hadn't anticipated. Jumping to his feet with an agility that must've been his while a soldier confronting the German enemy during his contribution to a Canadian Army attempt to drive opposition troops into the River Seine, he raised the putter over his head and, bending his knees to put greater energy into his swing, began to bring its bronze business-end down toward Stanley's forehead. Stanley hadn't expected anything like this reaction and wasn't prepared for it. He pushed back in his chair defensively, the hangdog resignation of his childhood having again overtaken him. He looked up at the glowering face of his momentarily insane *father* preparing to divest himself of what may have been a lifetime accumulation of guilt. For Stanley, the world seemed to gel in time, the next few seconds playing in his mind like slow-motion frames from a silent movie.

Then, with a stunned initial reaction, Ben's face relaxed completely. Rather than helping him put force into the putter's arc, his knees buckled beneath his weight and he collapsed face first onto the aghast frame of his son, who had more or less frozen in place.

Trying to collect his wits, Stanley struggled with the weight of the corpse on top of him, pushing it forward and sideways, toppling their now-shared chair, one hand on the bricks, trying to regain his footing and stand to see what in hell had happened.

Dazed, he tried to take it all in. Benedict lay ruined, on his side, almost as if he had fallen from the deck above. Stanley bent over him, looking first at his face, which seemed to be—for the first time in his recollection—totally at peace. Then he looked for a cause, his eyes coming to rest on the feathered shaft of an arrow protruding from Ben's back. As he watched, a red stain looking like the petal fallen from a post-Christmas poinsettia seeped downward from where the broadhead had incised a hole in the dead man's shirt. Although Stanley could not have known it then, an autopsy later would show that the arrow had shattered a vertebra, its tip having passed though the body to embed itself in the sternum's manubrium. The shock of it, given his advanced years and weakened heart, had killed him instantly.

Becoming aware of his gratitude for having been thus spared, Stanley shifted his attention to locating whoever may have been his avenging angel. It took only a moment to find her: Angeline was standing in front of the open door to his garden shed, there having edged herself into the boughs of a tall fir, its sprays of needles obscuring her presence from any boat or kayak that may then have been easing, unheard, a south-to-north passage along the river. Good prep and positioning, he found himself thinking. He glanced over the water to make certain they were alone and then looked back at Angeline. She stood motionless; even at that distance he could see her head held erect, smiling that quixotic smile that so mysteriously masked the prodigious maturity that had been characteristic of her throughout her transition from child to girl and, prematurely, from girl to woman. Hanging from her right hand, string angling toward the ground, was Jeremy's compound bow.

She ambled across the grass to the edge of the patio and then to where he stood. She said nothing, just stood there, smiling her Mona Lisa smile.

Regaining himself, he asked "Where—where *really*—did you come from, and why are you here?"

Through the confident shape of her smile, in a quiet, composed voice, she said, "I knew you'd be needing me today, and I came to help."

"Thank you for that," was all he could manage.

Her smile said, without speaking, without equivocation: You're welcome. And the smile stood there, waiting for whatever was to come next, knowing it was his turn to take the lead and somewhat self-assured that, this time, she wouldn't have to cajole him through it.

"How did you know?"

"She asked me to come."

"Who?"

"You know."

"No, I'm not sure I do."

"Yes, in your heart you do."

"Elizabeth?"

"Of course," said the smile, looking almost heavenly in its composed serenity.

"Yes. Yes," he offered reflectively, her calmness infusing itself into his psyche. "I've often sensed her presence in the river—the sometimes stillness of it—just at sunset, when a crimson sky will reflect itself, air and water divided in the mind's eye only by a blackened line of trees mirror imaged at the water's edge."

But he knew that a here-and-now decision had to be made, and, by now clear-headed, he made it. Elizabeth would have to settle back into the stillness of whatever benign force had lifted her ethereally to oversee this, unseen but there, as mist sometimes weds itself to morning air with the coming of the sun.

Taking off his shirt, he bunched it into his left hand and, wrapping a dangling sleeve around his right, dragged the fabric up and down the arrow's shaft several times. Then he reached for the bow and took it gently from her, painstakingly wiping it, only then to grip it, bare handed, throughout its length, using his palms and all his fingers. Setting the bow down on the bricks, he reached out to the shaft in Ben's back and imprinted his destiny onto that.

Mopping up complete to his satisfaction, he turned to face her and urged, "You'll have to go now. Find your way home—cautiously but not furtively—okay? I'll deal with this."

Without a word, she turned and drifted toward the stone steps leading to their upper driveway.

He would not see her again, he knew, until she would be able to visit him in prison.

He faced the river, paused there, trying to stare into its heart, its soul. His eyes squinted, blurred, went teary. He became, for a moment, again a child. Thus transfixed, he finally managed, "Elizabeth, look after her, as you looked after me while I was a boy. She'll need you again… and she will listen."

Then, walking proudly, with straightened back and a new resolve, he stepped through the patio door.

Picking up the bar phone, he called 911. He then went outside to sit down beside his father, there to wait. The sound of sirens took only a few minutes.

Finally he felt like the man he had always wanted to become.

He knew now that his deliverance was part of Angeline's mission; that it had little to do with life or death, at least not as humanity had chosen, erroneously, to interpret those things.

And he knew that Angeline would be okay.

CHAPTER 5
Exodus

Scene 28
Abigail Flees, Goes for Money...

October 31, 2010, 5:42 p.m.
Abigail, the surviving partner in the Fontana scheme, had settled comfortably into the daily laissez-faire that the allure of St. Bart's held for her. No one had seemed unduly curious about her presence in the small unit on Rue du Bord de Mer that she had leased months earlier and left unoccupied until now. Presumably she had been imagined rich, and wealth coming into the island, via cruise ship or private yacht or through surviving the tricky landing—as she had—at the island's Gustav III Airport, was welcomed with nodding politeness from officialdom and gleaners alike, their acceptance extending to not querying any newcomer about where their money had originated.

About the origins of her money, she had presumed she was in good company. Historically, she had recently learned, discretion and judgment favouring the island's economy had been the norm. Back in the day, the port of Gustavia had served as a centre for provisioning and commercial trading. During the colonial wars that raged in the Caribbean at the end of the eighteenth century, the Swedes had made it possible for a boat captain to sell his plundered treasure and at the same time replenish his ship.

Good, she had thought, perhaps not much had changed. For her, the inquiries she had made from home suggested St. Bart's might offer a safe haven until she could find somewhere more permanent—another island, perhaps, maybe larger, or one of the countries of South America. She knew she mustn't go back home, knew she would have to resettle somewhere having no extradition treaty with Canada. But for now, St. Bart's offered at least a few weeks of rest, with time to think.

On arrival she had rented a car, determined to explore the island from every vantage point. It had been, for her, like the first few days of a honeymoon or an ocean cruise; she hadn't been able to get enough of it. The wonderfully colourful shops that lined Gustavia's streets—each intersection holding a promise of more to be discovered—had played to her need to find uniqueness in the little things that she had purchased for her temporary nest. She had strolled among glittering jewellery stores and designer boutiques and had admired the restored facades of handsome wooden and stone buildings that remained from the Swedish era. Later she had walked the Gustavia Lighthouse grounds on the crest of its hill north of town. There had been the island's three forts, built by the Swedes for defense purposes. One, Fort Oscar, on the far side of La Pointe, had offered a wonderful view out to sea, although she had noticed, with some trepidation, that the ruins had been replaced by a modern military building to house the local gendarmerie. The town of Saint Jean also had had its attractions. Crime does pay, she had concluded, having learned that corsairs once protected the enclave from the middle of the bay with a battery of canons—*their* town, presumably. Even better, the settlement had offered her the second largest shopping area on the island.

On the harbour side opposite Rue du Bord de Mer, the street which had become her favourite haunt, there were more restaurants and businesses, as well as the fascinating Wall House, a renovated survivor of the

Swedish era—the island's library as well as its principal museum—where she had spent leisurely hours soaking up details of the island's history.

But all that had grown old to her. More recently, she had preferred settling in for people-watching on the terraces of waterfront cafés, where she would daily allow herself to be fascinated by the harbour's line-up of anchored sea-going toys.

* * * * * * * *

She had taken to sleeping late, having come to enjoy a near-noon cocktail. She would carry it to a small grassy patch she had found on Rue Samuel Fahlberg to amuse herself with the comings and goings of the princes of industry and their women, preening as they did whenever disembarking their moored yachts. That, she thought, on a particularly glorious Tuesday morning, sun bright enough in an azure sky to make her squint behind sunglasses, was an idyllic lifestyle—conjuring up halcyon imaginings of a life partially at sea. But she wasn't part of that set, at least not yet.

It had worried her that St. Bart's was, as a French protectorate, part of the European Union. The island's inhabitants were French citizens with EU status, holding EU passports. The euro was their currency. France was responsible for the island's defense, and as such had stationed a small police and security force here. Even the notion of small law-enforcement bothered her: extraditing her to Canada, she knew, wouldn't take an army to achieve, were she to be found out. Then there would have been the unavoidable rabbit track that she had left behind in coming. Probably the RCMP even now was attempting to sniff her out. Her earlier attempts to acquire a forged passport had been abandoned; perhaps, she thought now, she should have persisted. But getting away from the clinic long enough to accomplish that would have been problematic, unless she had risked attempting it during one of her runs to Vienna. But she didn't have the language nor did she have the contacts, and naive inquiries would have been a flag to the authorities, particularly in Austria.

But clouds darkening her mood began to drift away, chased by the sunshine and the coolness of her drink. An interesting notion had begun dripping into the well of her discontent. Absently poking her straw through what remained of the ice cubes, pausing to swirl bits of fruit around the bottom of her glass, she allowed ethereal fragments of this new thought to gradually coalesce.

Yes, she conjectured, there could be a next step, a notch up, to move into the one-percenters' league and be accepted by them as a peer. She would need to find an exceedingly rich mark, perhaps one sheltering a closeted vulnerability, exposed just enough to let her lamprey his assets. She was coming to believe she could yet morph from middle-class caterpillar to big-league butterfly and enter the world of the untouchably wealthy. Doing so would necessitate an elegantly opaque scheme, impenetrable enough to either draw in, or compel through blackmail, an entrepreneurial criminal like herself, but one who had been more successful. Such a score could mean a sister ship to one of the luxury boats she had been eyeing—yachts the length of football fields, gleaming hulls implying greater comforts within than the newest cruise liners.

How, she asked herself, might she approach this? How had Lee, her now-charred partner, managed from the outset of her doomed scheme to become so quickly successful, apparently with so little effort and such little planning? The lesson learned from Lee's adventure was that it had been too complex, like a busker starting out by spinning a plate on a stick; it had required increasingly frenetic attention as each new plate was added. The end was predictable. That's why she had evolved her own scheme within a scheme—to escape and take everything with her.

Wasn't it clever, she reflected, that she, the ever-faithful second-tier associate, had ended up with Lee's entire share of their offshore stash? With pouting lips a picture of disingenuous regret, she recalled that everyone on Lee's flight—the late-night plane that she had raced to catch, with Ottawa's city police and the RCMP closing in behind her—had died when the Halcyon Air Embraer ERJ 145 tumbled from the sky into a tree-lined, uneven field just miles beyond sparsely inhabited countryside trailing into emptiness beyond Ottawa's urban sprawl. How unfortunate for Lee that she had taken with her the gold-plated bronze Buddha that Abigail had given her just a couple of months into their partnership.

Relaxing into a welcomed reverie, she settled her back into the shallow-cut grass beneath, allowing the joy of reliving a much-prized coup to overtake her. Eyes closed, sorting through clearing wisps of memory, her mind touched down at the afternoon she had shopped for the Buddha. She hadn't known it was to *be* a Buddha; she had actually set out to buy any sort of decorative hollow metal container. But there it was, her buddy the Buddha—a miniature of the Tian Tan Buddha on Lantau Island in Hong Kong. She had started with the necessary bargaining prattle, following through without acrimony to an agreement on price. And now there she was, exiting one of Westboro's finest antique shops with the bronze prize under her arm. About the size of a large grapefruit, it had apparently languished there, long unloved, its patina dimming over time under a quilt batting of dust, seemingly awaiting her arrival. The Asian gentleman who she had presumed owned the shop seemed happier than she with the transaction.

At first opportunity she had driven it to a Montréal jeweller and had it gilded. That done, she had then pussyfooted her way along a convoluted path into Montréal's criminal nether land, seeking the services of a competent bomb technician. Eventually, painfully, she had made contact: first with a cautious, edgy bartender, who had introduced her to a shadowy deal broker. A final handoff had left her in the company of a full-patch Hells Angels' up-and-comer who had been designated the organization's primary point of contact. What she had wanted, he had told her in a flat monotone, would cost her ten thousand dollars, take it or leave it. She had taken it, that amount having been earlier hinted at by the bartender. The Patch had called himself *Bill,* ponderously counting her money as if he had just learned how. Satisfied, he had wadded it into a back pocket, fumbling to button the flap. Jesus, those had been really pretty, brand-new hundred-dollar bills. Now they were like a crushed toilet-paper roll.

"Bill?" She ventured, "how very original!" He drove a look that she interpreted as "Don't fuck with me, lady, or I'll break that smile, and your jawbone along with it." She allowed her smirk to fade, no time to be a smartass.

She surmised that the deal was done. Leeringly he added a side benefit, one for himself: a roll in the sack at the close of business. He hadn't put it quite that way; his analogy for her preferred turn of phrase for that particular activity being, in her opinion, unnecessarily blunt—a crudity she had chosen to soften in her mind while recovering from the unpalatability, literally, of his suggestion. But this, she considered, nodding toward him with an acquiescent smile, might work well for them both. She suffered through several more minutes of awkwardness, attempting to establish terms and limitations. Apparently he didn't like compromising, and he insisted on the full-meal deal. Sensing he had been a while without, she offered coyly to make it quite worth his while, that she knew what went where and how to get it there. He had taken her capitulation to be disingenuous, but the implied outcome was where he had wanted to get. If necessary, he would *take* her there. Grasping both cheeks, forcing her to look him full in the face, he sealed the arrangement with a sincerely meant threat. If, after the fact, she screwed up, she would spend eternity holding hands with Jimmy Hoffa in hell. Again she nodded, lowering her head slightly, feigning submission—a younger sister giving way to an incestuous older brother. We will see, she thought, raising her eyes to meet his, with all the happy anticipation she could fabricate. The show must go on, winner take all, as always.

Prerequisites finally out of the way, he drove her to The Sands of Time, an upscale St. Xavier Street eatery. She had never been there before, and didn't quite know where they were. It looked to be first class. Although not many patrons were inside, no expenses on the decor were spared. The staff seemed to know Bill, nodding at him. He weaved her through a labyrinth of stainless-steel kitchen essentials into a back-hallway utility closet and closed the door behind them. Nobody had seemed to notice. Chefs continued cooking, and waitresses went to and from the kitchen, serving; it apparently was business as usual. Amid buckets still wet with mops dangling their musty cording over rims, he hooded her, harshly. She hadn't seen it coming, thought he must've used a potato sack. The fabric was course, probably burlap; she sneezed at her next inhalation. It chaffed her neck where he had begun to tighten it, so she thought there must be a drawstring. He slapped her hands away when she had tried to find the noose, wanting to loosen it. Inside the bag she sensed a dusty, filtered light, emanating as though through the warp and woof of a caned chair seat held up to a window. Instantly she felt off balance. He didn't try to steady her. A door opened, one that had been retrofitted inconspicuously into the closet's back wall. He nudged her through it. She heard the click of a light switch. Toeing her way across a flat space under her feet, she sensed it had a front edge.

She asked him if there were steps.

"Yes," he said, then silence.

"Many?" she asked.

"Nine." Again silence. Nothing more from him.

What she couldn't see was a crude cement staircase descending toward a landing that ended at another door. She felt for a nonexistent railing, stumbled, nearly fell on the steps, touched walls that had the granularity of patchwork cement. He made no attempt to help her. "Bastard," she muttered to herself, "I could've broken an arm, or worse, dropped the Buddha. Inconsiderate prick!"

A key turned in a lock—he must have been in front of her—the screeching sound of a steel door infrequently opened, hinges complaining at the disturbance. He pushed her through, closed the hatch, and locked it. Turning her slightly by the shoulders, he reached up, shook her hood, in part to make sure it was tight, in part to shake out a little more dust, and tugged its forward corner in the direction toward where he wanted her to move. She closed her eyes to avoid the stinging particulate that was beginning to make her breathing difficult. Focusing her mind on what must lay ahead, she vowed she would sort him out later. He was a muscular lump of shit, she thought, the pile topped with a Shar-Pei face. She recalled having noted several tattoos, one of the Harley-Davidson logo stitched into his neck. She had paid attention to that—below his left earlobe, about midway between the curve of his jawbone and shirt collar. He had caught her glance. She had complimented him on it; he had brightened. Young, she had thought then, young to be a full-patch Angels' guy. Probably he would be brutal if pushed. She would have to be sweet with him, and precise.

With her rocking from one foot onto another, arms extended like a kid playing blind man's bluff, they reached the bomb maker's studio—a musty excavation of concrete-lined misery cached behind a boiler-plate door pocked with rows of hammer-mushroomed rivets. Bill untied and lifted her hood. The drawstring caught under her nose, tilting her head back as the sack swept her hair into a disarray of broken straw. She coughed up burlap filament that she had inhaled within this little cavern that passed for fresh air. Looking back through the portal just as he was closing it, she concluded they must be somewhere within an unfathomable web of Montréal's utility tunnels. Passage walls were flanked on either side with cable trays supporting telephone and hydro conduit. Pipes of varying diameters, joined and elbowed at irregular distances, dripped condensation into small pools on the floor. She had no engineer's sense of their various purposes, as she knew Sven would have, were he here. To her it was just a subterranean rabbit warren, and it would feel damn good to get out of it.

The tech guy had been impatiently awaiting them. He had preassembled her order according to dimensions that she had provided to the Angels. All that remained was to install this newest contrivance within the cavity of whatever vessel she would be bringing him. He knew its approximate size and that it was bronze, nothing more. He hoped she had her measurements right. The opening's diameter would be critical.

He was good at conceiving these things on short notice, he knew, and was proud of it. It had become his *raison d'etre*. As a younger man he had learned the precautions needed to stay alive while handling highly volatile substances. He had been a militia guy and had even achieved military-expert status at disarming landmines and other nasty bits of enemy ordnance. There he had learned what went into making them, and where later he would be able to source chemical and electronic components, untraceably. He still had all his fingers and wanted to keep it that way. His dick would need that. Loneliness was a major presence in his life. Sex workers had been disinclined to accommodate him. He wasn't a pretty sight, he knew; mirrors weren't something that he favoured. Whenever he did look, he would wince at an encroaching sallowness, his disconcerting pallor. There had been a premature desiccation, overall, no denying it. He had been tall but had developed a stoop to accommodate his studio's low ceiling. Perhaps, he had thought, his disagreeable countenance had been the outcome of a long-term coexistence with apprehension that had oozed from his pores whenever contemplating that one wrong move: the mistake that would end it all.

A key tumbling open a heavy lock and the portal's scraping swing on its rusty hinges let him know that his client and escort had arrived. So, he thought, seeing Bill with her—asshole Bill, errand-boy Bill—the sometimes Angels' wet-work cleaner who would do whatever unpleasant chore the organization might need taken care of at any given time. Apparently he was good at stuff like that. Maybe somebody one day would *clean* him. He had never known Bill's real name and hadn't wanted to. He didn't want to now.

Bill stayed, crumpled hood in hand, loitering close to the steel door that he had clanged shut and then locked behind them. He was visibly nervous, seemed to want to get back into the tunnel, but stayed. Perhaps he had been ordered to hang in. Just a goon, obeying, the tech thought. But, an errand boy with larger ambitions, willing to do anything that would help him rise within the organization. He wasn't a dude to trifle with.

Abigail's eyes—burning, accustomed uneasily to the small, underlit, windowless prison—swept it with a nurse's eye, passing over oily dust bunnies on the floor—what an irregular concrete pour it had been, she noticed—populated randomly with twists of discarded coloured wire, apparently offcuts from this or another project. She glanced at the tech's wastebasket, found it had frequently been dented, possibly kicked in frustration, overflowing now with torn plastic packaging and rejected components maybe tossed away in favour of more technically advanced or safer options. She suspected that he was an expeditious worker, possibly impatient. Not good qualities given his profession. Electrical and mechanical parts lay everywhere—apart from on his bench—much of it in a marginally manageable disarray on shelves, stacked in boxes on the floor, dangling from pigeonholes shadowed inside a cupboard that, due to an unintended slope of the shop's floor, leaned against one end of the workbench—all the necessities of his trade within easy reach.

His bench presented quite a different topography: orderly arrayed tools, finely tipped needle-nose pliers, various sizes of wire cutters and insulation trimmers, two electrometers with alligator clips hanging over the bench's front edge, callipers, a digital vernier scale, and other very small instruments she didn't recognize but assumed had been designed for use by watchmakers. Off to one side lay a neat row of double-ended picks, pieces perhaps lifted from a dentist's office or bought from a medical supply house. At eye level above the circle of white light brightening the focused area of his bench craned a tall, elbowed magnifying glass. And there, shadowed in greyness where the light transitioned to the room's relative darkness, lay his cell phone.

Moving with slightly dramatized awkwardness toward the tech, sidling crabwise as if to avoid encroaching on his personal space in front of the bench, she leaned against it, near the phone. Smiling, submissively maintaining eye contact, she handed him the flex-nylon travel case containing her Buddha. He held her gaze without expression, assessed her, felt no words need be exchanged. Unzipping the travel bag he lifted out the effigy and focused his magnifying glass to scrutinize its head, then turned the casting over to gauge the opening in its base. Setting the callipers aside, vernier scale in hand, he measured the wall thickness. Apparently satisfied, he set it on its base and again studied the icon's nose and ears.

Throughout the IED's insertion, she had leaned partially over the tech's shoulder to watch, glancing back at Bill to see what might be preoccupying him. He seemed to be salivating over one of several decades-old centerfolds, apparently pulled from archived issues of *Playboy* and stuck to the cave's wall, perhaps with chewing gum. Interesting pose, she thought; the girl in the picture bent fully over, knees locked, buttocks facing the camera, a trim of fluff the only disorderliness masking what he must have been searching for. Her body was horseshoed around toward the happy photographer to put what he must have considered her second-best face forward. Good! Abigail concluded, cautiously reaching over the bench with a cupped hand to sweep the tech's phone into her jacket pocket.

Drawing open a drawer beneath the bench top, the tech lifted out a Dremel drill, changed out the tool's bit for one of a smaller size, plugged it into a vacant slot along his bench's extension-bar, and bored holes through small indentations cast into the Buddha's nose and ears. His objective, Abigail surmised, was to allow outside air to flow into and out from the casting's interior, obviating a need to have any flow through the base's opening. With a round file he de-burred the edges of the bit's four pathways, then burnished them with a few moments' spin of a Dremel-fitted buffer. Hands moving surely and elegantly as a ballerina interpreting Swan Lake, he inserted the one-off K-4 package loosely into the Buddha's cavity, connected its wires to an altitude-sensitive ignition mechanism, and packed loosely woven steel wool around the device.

Repressing questions she had dared not ask, Abigail watched him begin to close the aperture, inserting first a length of flat steel bar, 1/32" narrower and 1.5" wider than the opening, noosed at approximately its midpoint with a pencil length of nylon fishing line. Pulling the bar tightly against the bronze casing inside the hole, he asked her, "Hold this line, okay?" She moved around him obediently, pinched the filament between thumb and forefinger, and drew it taught toward her.

"That's good," he said, reaching for and uncapping a small plastic squeeze-bottle of i5 Instant Metal Bond. "Hold it there." He ran a seam of the adhesive around the edge of the hole, bonding the steel bar instantly to the Buddha's casing. He quickly snipped the fishing line's noose and said, "Okay, pull it out." She did, moving again out of his way. Turning the Buddha upside down, he squeezed a generous layer of the glue over the exposed area of the bar, adding more to the circle where the two metals joined.

"This stuff's expensive," he said, "but it's worth it. All part of the service!" Then, reaching a hand into one of his cupboard's pigeonholes, he dragged a finger through dust on its base, gently puffed a film over the fast-firming patch, and watched it solidify and discolour to a graying shade of taupe. The seal looked instantly old to Abigail. That's what he had wanted.

"Why the steel bar?" she asked.

"Because when this thing blows, you'll want all its energy pushing out against the entire inner surface of the casing, not just blowing through the base hole like a cannon going off with no ball in its barrel."

Handing off the now-deadly ornament, again nestled into its bag, he assured her it would withstand gentle knocks and bumps. "You'll be able to handle your little piece of shelf shit with relative impunity. Just don't climb a mountain with it."

She thanked him, smiled again, and said good-bye. Over at the door, Bill looked back at the tech and nodded. They stepped out onto the tunnel floor, Bill obviously relieved. Shaking out the hood, he tied it again around her neck.

When they arrived back at the hatchway entrance leading up to the utility closet, Bill stopped her. He unlocked and opened it, put a hand to each of her shoulders, and steered her through. Behind her she could hear again the scratching complaint of the door closing, then a key turning in the lock.

"Can I get out of this now?" she asked, setting her travel bag down and tugging at a corner of the hood. He untied the drawstring, loosened the sack, and lifted it off. She shook her head with theatrical exaggeration to make a point, testing the extent of her coif's disorder gently with fingertips. "My hair feels like a strawstack. Mind if I get my comb out and straighten up a bit? I don't want the people up there to see me like this, including your patrons. They'll wonder what in hell we've been up to."

"The staff already knows what we were doing."

"Oh, really? Still, I would feel better if I could appear outside at least half presentable. Give me a minute to regain my composure, okay? I don't do this every day. And, I *am* the customer in this situation, you know." She felt she was pressing him a bit here, but it was time. Instinct was apprising her she would have to soon try for a shift in their relative positions of dominance. No more Miss Meek-and-Mild.

The landing at the foot of the cement steps was small, not much more than room for the two of them to stand comfortably. "Go ahead," he said, "Get it done. We've got somewhere to go."

"Where?" she asked with feigned innocence, sensing that his runaway libido might be working in her favour.

"Our agreement, remember? There's a place I use not far from here."

"Oh. Yeah. While I was in the bag, I guess I momentarily forgot. So this should be the pleasant part, right?"

"For me, anyway."

"And for me," she offered coyly, demurring with the hope he would relax a bit. "Could we maybe catch a drink first? My throat feels like a porcupine's backed down it." She set the Buddha's case on the bottom step, her purse beside it, and then crouched down to shuffle through the assortment of femininity's ubiquitous necessities inside. She came out with a compact and held it up in her left hand with a soft rotational wave, like the Queen acknowledging a crowd. She popped it open and, ostentatiously rubbing her lips together, glanced in the mirror's circle of reflected dissatisfaction to ask of no one in particular, "Okay, where's my lipstick?" With her other hand scrabbling inside her purse she muttered, "Comb!" Instead, in a side pocket she found what her fingers really wanted to embrace, opened it with practiced dexterity, stood suddenly up to him and plunged the blade of a straight razor through readily capitulating flesh, bursting open like a popped grape from the authoritatively torqued entry at the centre of his Harley-Davidson tattoo. Twisting the blade to approximate a horizontal plane, she swept it under his jaw in a sibilating disseverance, casting arterial blood onto the door beyond to form a red-ochre simulation of the Niki arc. Her movement was ballet-like, the sweep of an Ultimate player's arm tossing a Frisbee to a scoring teammate.

Grabbing his throat with fingers convulsing into the weakness of an enervating fist, Bill stumbled back against rough concrete, reaching out uncertainly as he did with his free hand to grasp some part of her. She parried with her left forearm, leaned back into a fencer's brace, and then swiped at the offending appendage with a second sweep of her

Grandpa's instrument. It caught his palm, lifting flesh to let the blade scrape against a whiteness of bared metacarpals.

"So, big boy, you want a feel?" she asked vengefully. "Go for it!"

The precautionary second cut wouldn't have mattered. Bill's knees were already buckling, his good hand still at his throat, trying but failing to staunch pulsing blood now forming rivulets in the creases of his shirtfront, pooling in his lap as his back abraded in its slow descent to the floor. He began making suffocating, sucking sounds; he was choking, his severed trachea becoming clogged. His legs pushed outward, a shoe nearly striking her. Dancing to avoid it, she stepped over him onto the stair holding her bag and purse.

He was fading fast, his body uttering spasms like a child in the throes of an epileptic fit. Soon he began to quieten, became still.

"Okay, Romeo," she said by way of a good-bye, "there's your night on the town. Sorry about the tattoo."

Avoiding the curl of blood spreading outward on the floor, beginning to take the shape of an artist's pallet, she stepped into a clear space and bent down to go through his pockets. His keys in hand, bypassing his wallet, she turned the weight of his sorry corpse sufficiently to one side to expose the back pocket that held her cash. Unbuttoning its flap, she extracted the wad and shook it out loosely into her purse.

Standing over him, she did a quick survey; she bent to wipe the blade on a trouser leg, one side then the other. She had laid hold of her grandfather's razor with her mother's consent when they had cleaned out his apartment following his restful demise. She had kept his strop as well and had honed the steel lovingly, in memory of him, believing it might someday be of use.

Before picking up the bag and her purse, she extracted a pair of soft wool gloves from one of the travel bag's side pockets and stretched them on. Remembering the bomb maker's phone, she reached gingerly into her jacket pocket and extracted it, gripping only its edges, wanting whatever pints were on it to remain unmarred. She stood and looked down on her diorama as she surmised a coroner might. Stooping over Bill's undamaged hand, fondling Kleenex tissues to keep her gloves clean, she manipulated his fingers to emulate a pointing signpost. Then, a few inches out from it, she splashed the phone into a firming kidney-shaped thickness of blood.

Again she stood, rechecked her work, the nurse within her demanding Hippocratic professionalism, ticking off all details against possible errors or omissions.

"Good enough," she said. "I'm outta here!"

Before emerging into the hallway she locked the utility-room's inner and outer doors, checked the corridor to see if there might be an alley exit from the restaurant. "Yes!" she muttered, looking back to see if anyone might be watching her leave. "Nobody. Perfect!"

Silently welcoming freedom, turning her head both ways, she headed down the alley's shadowed, brick-lined corridor in the direction of passing cars. It took her minutes to locate Bill's car, and she lost more time driving around trying to get oriented. Finding her bearings, she drove to Montréal's Central Station, parked, and wiped clean any surface she thought she might have touched earlier while a passenger. She locked it, walked to the station, hailed a cab, and had the driver take her to the Walmart lot where she had left her own vehicle. In three hours, she guessed, she would be safely back in Ottawa.

And she was.

Parking, then closing her car door in the lot overlooking Hog's Back Falls, she walked into a misty spray that made its underlying Precambrian rocks slippery. Pausing to savour the moment, she tossed Bill's key ring in a high arc to watch it descend and disappear into the roar of the Rideau's cascading turmoil of frothy water.

* * * * * * * *

From the outset, Abigail had known that if Lee were planning to flee without her whenever their little golden-goose enterprise would be decapitated—which surely it must—she would be inclined to scoop up the Buddha and pack it into her checked luggage. After all, she had have known, because Abigail had made sure she did, that it had been gilded with two millimeters of their scammed yellow metal.

Abigail had dubbed this her either-or plan: Lee either would fly away with it or the Buddha would be found by airport security during a routine pre-flight baggage scan. She would be arrested and detained while her lawyer chased his tail trying for a possible but unlikely bail arrangement. That in turn would give her the opportunity to beat Lee to the Vienna safety-deposit box and disappear with all that was in it. But, whatever baggage scan might have taken place, if any, it had missed Lee's glittering treasure and, when the aircraft ascended to near cruising altitude, the explosion had torn a massive rent in its underbelly, ripping around the fuselage with the suddenness of a barn roof lifting off in a hurricane. The tear had subsided just inches above the row of starboard passengers' windows. Against that late-hour darkness it had flashed momentarily inside with a whistling, plaintive slipstream shriek, like a snared rabbit's scream, thrashing its way to stillness, having tried in vain to escape the wire loop it had innocently hopped into.

The wound suffered by the plane's body, as pieced together later by a forensic reconstruction team, had the stale, archived appearance of an inverted lightning bolt, asymmetrically ragged and blackened along its edges. All cabin pressure must have been sucked away instantly through this passenger-compartment rupture, leaving screaming occupants groping in the dark for masks that would have showered down on them like prizes tumbling from a struck piñata.

The blast had disabled the plane's tail control surfaces. The starboard engine had died, its portside twin, sighing, defeated, soon wound down to nothing. The pilots struggled to bring their craft into some semblance of a controlled glide, believing, hoping, they might yet coax it away from the tumble it seemed determined to maintain.

But it hadn't worked out that way. On contact, the second explosion, this time fuel-fed—roiling within itself—had insinuated its ascending torchlight vapour into the night's enveloping blackness. In a smaller way it was reminiscent of the Bismarck's shell strike on the Hood's munitions magazine that had obliterated the pride of England's navy, in an *augenblick*. The traumatized passengers hadn't lived past impact to witness any of this.

All was being imagined, however, by Ottawa's on-duty air traffic controllers, huddled together in their tower, listening with hanging heads and grim resignation to their receiver's ever-lengthening sound of silence, the spectre of a grim-reaper's skeletal hand having pointed out to them a flat line of emptiness moving away from the heroically even and steady dialogue that, although now only recorded, had been a living, necessary stoicism: the unfalteringly exchange between the aircraft's captain and first officer as they had struggled to keep the plane from going in heavy.

Each controller could picture the scene: an angry, upwardly billowing column of red heat, blossoming as it ascended, pluming into darkening variegated orange, gracefully swirling outward in charcoal-fringed, puffing curves to exhaust itself and become one with the night.

To the tower staff, eyes closed, footage still playing in their heads, it had seemed reminiscent of fires set by the Iraqi army while retreating from Kuwait's oilfields.

* * * * * * *

Pity that, Abigail thought, sitting up, mind sweeping forward through the mists of her reverie, anxious to resume her Internet search.

Gazing out over the masts of boats in the harbour, she sucked noisily on her cocktail straw, frowning as she poked at the spent, bottomed-out fruit bits; ice cubes now reduced to rattling, misshapen pearls.

She felt that her colourful double-rum Tuesday's special, as had the one before it, helped her considerably in coaxing Google to locate fissures in the armour of the überrichs' defenses against people like her. Yes, she had chased down some ratholes, but she remained undiscouraged. She would continue that, looking for any breach through which her mind might crawl to latch onto resources the elite surely must be hiding from her.

Swirling her glass, she lifted her head, narrowed her eyes unhappily at its pulpy, exhausted residue, and watched the day's homecoming flotilla of private ships—beautiful things that they were—rippling toward their private moorings.

One day, she had determined, one of those ships would be hers, as would a crew to sail it. She would need enough money to buy a handsome captain as part of the package.

"It can be done; I've come this far," she muttered, with total self-assurance, snapping shut her laptop and setting off unsteadily in the direction of the bar, like a tightrope walker without a balance bar, to get another tequila sunrise.

Scene 29
Stanley in Prison...

> *"All changes, even the most longed for, have their melancholy;*
> *for what we leave behind us is a part of ourselves;*
> *we must die to one life before we can enter another."*
> *~Anatole France*

January 18, 2011

When the court sentenced Stanley to life imprisonment for the murder of his father, he had quickly found that day-to-day penitentiary routine was not all that bad. The internment process had gone well enough; he had remained polite and attentive to the directions of Kingston Penitentiary's authorities throughout. The fact that he now had a lot of time to himself was perhaps, for him, the antithesis of punishment. Actually, he had been able to acquire almost everything he could want, missing little except his family.

Chelsea had come when she could, and she had understood and empathized with his *crime* from the outset. But it was a considerable drive from Ottawa, and she had a life of her own that he had encouraged her to live. Whenever she was able to, though, she had brought news of their children and the grandkids. This first Christmas, alone, so to speak, had been comfortless, but he had gotten through it. Chelsea had been expected by the family, naturally enough, to be with them in Ottawa, realizing that he couldn't be.

The Fontana Resurrection

He had fallen into a rather happy ritual of hunkering down, for all the time available to him, in the prison's library. It had become a solitude—his, he felt—alone there in the midst of strangers, appreciating each day that he wouldn't be expected to make contact with anyone. The history of nations had always been an interest, as had global geographies and the political demarcations that all national boundaries suggested, their ropelike outlines being containment indicators of peoples and their differences or of wars won and lost. Then of course there were all the books and reference materials related to languages he had spent so much time earlier in life learning, as well as an opportunity to learn others. Early on, in the library or in his cell, he had been able to look back on stories written about the prison itself; it had been his way of getting to know the place.

Life as one of society's outcasts, tucked away in this institution, had changed considerably since it had opened in 1835. Back then inmates had lived under a strict code of silence. Although required to work together all day, they weren't permitted to communicate with each other. If they needed, they could make hand gestures to get the attention of the guards. They also weren't allowed to interrupt the so-called harmony of the prison. Offenders were routinely given six lashes for laughing or fed bread and water if heard vocalizing anything. Prison food had been purchased primarily from the dregs of Kingston's local markets. Given that there were no proper in-house food-storage facilities, meals, as prepared by inmates, were often soggy and flavourless.

But it had improved. Prison wardens since 1935 had come and gone; some okay, some not so much. Then, seemingly as an act of divine intervention, a *saint* had been visited upon the place. Born in Ireland, John Creighton, a printer and later owner of a bookbindery and stationery store, was elected the city's mayor in 1863 and returned by acclamation in 1864 and 1865. In 1866, he became police magistrate, and in October 1870 he was induced to accept the position of warden by Sir John A. Macdonald and Sir Alexander Campbell. As a single parent responsible for five children, Creighton found himself troubled by the prospect of raising his family in the penitentiary's proffered in-compound apartment. So, Sir John—by then Prime Minister as well as Minister of Justice—approved the construction of a wardens' home outside the prison's gate. Built entirely by convict labour under the supervision of staff trade instructors, the house took nearly three years to complete. Designed in the Italianate Vernacular style by penitentiary architect Henry H. Horsey, it was mortared together using a combination of local Kingston limestone, quarried on the penitentiary reserve, and given added Ohio sandstone accents. Later dubbed Cedarhedge, the house remained the official residence of sequential wardens' families until 1933, when it was converted to administration offices for the prison. At its peak the property boasted apple orchards, greenhouses, a grape vinery, and a conservatory. Inmate gardeners tended to the extensive terraced grounds each day.

Considered by many to be the first true humanitarian to hold the position, Warden Creighton improved the prison's lighting, heating, and ventilation as well as provided better shoes, uniforms, bedding, and a more varied diet to the inmates. Exercise periods were increased and extended to all prisoners. He began a lending library and night classes, and improved school equipment. He introduced prison entertainment by and for inmates on holidays and visited the inmates in their cells, in the workshops, on the farm, and in the quarries. In fact, he even ate his meals in the inmates' dining hall. In 1873, when 119 inmates boarded the steamer Watertown at the penitentiary wharf for their transfer to the new St. Vincent de Paul Penitentiary in Laval, Québec, many of them made it known that they did not want to leave his humane custody.

Interesting stuff that year of 1873: With its exodus of prisoners, Stanley mused—a sort of March East, to Laval, albeit over water—a newly minted North West Mounted Police had begun to coordinate its famous March West that same year. Macdonald had seen the need, given all the reports about American whiskey traders causing trouble in the region. The last straw for Macdonald had been the Cypress Hills Massacre.

The policing initiative was to be organized along the lines of a cavalry regiment in the British Army, structured partly on the Royal Irish Constabulary model. Its troopers would wear red uniforms. The initial group was assembled at Fort Dufferin, Manitoba. They departed

Dufferin on July 8, 1874 with their destination being Fort Whoop Up, the notorious whiskey trading post located at the junction of the Belly and Oldman rivers. Having arrived, finding Fort Whoop Up abandoned, the troop continued a few miles west to establish its headquarters on an island on the Oldman. They named it Fort MacLeod. Part of that story was that, in 1873, Lt. Col. Acheson Gosford Irvine retired from the military and was appointed assistant commissioner of the Force, to become its commissioner by 1880. He commanded the NWMP during the North West Rebellion, more commonly known as the Riel Rebellion of 1885. That, too, was interesting in that he resigned from the NWMP in March 1886 to become an Indian agent on the Blood Reserve, followed by an appointment to warden of Manitoba's Stony Mountain Penitentiary in 1892. In April 1913, at age seventy-five, he was appointed warden of Kingston Penitentiary, right where Stanley found himself now. He thought that Commissioner Irvine wouldn't have been very proud of him had they been serving at the pen, on different sides of the bars, at the same time.

Well, Sir John, it seemed had been a busy guy. It was a poignant recollection for Stanley; he had been a resident of the fort's replica in the town of the same name—Fort MacLeod—as a young constable, proud then of his red coat, his high boots, the shiny spurs, and flat-brimmed Stetson. The fort's log bastion remake had been quite comfortable, its modern amenities hidden away, unseen by the public, and just a short walk to the town's detachment offices.

Coming back to the moment, Stanley reflected on his discovery that these earlier prisoners had been builders. Besides the warden's house they had done other good work—*outstanding* work. The prison's population must have included talented, or at least trainable, masons and carpenters.

The most noteworthy example he had come across was *The Church of the Good Thief*, designed in Romanesque Revival style by architect Joseph Connolly and constructed of random-coursed rusticated limestone ashlar. Built between 1892 to 1894, the church was enhanced with rich masonry detail; its square bell tower rising above the main body of the building, visible from a considerable distance; its mixture of historic styles and the tower's single turret giving it an asymmetrical appearance; a slate-clad gable roof decorated in a polychromatic pattern, the roof's ridge topped with wrought-iron detailing. At the peak of the church's facades, front and back, stone crosses had been added. And here was the kicker: Convicts had quarried the stone and carried it to the church site and were paid twenty-five cents a day for their efforts. In recognition of its links to the prison, the church was named in honour of St. Dismas, the Catholic patron saint of prisoners. Dismas, also known as the Good Thief, was one of the two thieves crucified beside Jesus.

* * * * * * *

How gentle a people we've become, he thought, by now almost civilized, at least in this country. Prison, here, wasn't quite the hellhole its original staffers may have preferred it to be. He hadn't known, for example, that he, like all other Kingston Pen prisoners, would get paid—not a lot, but something—for work they might be willing to do. Niceties were available. From the get-go, he had been allowed cable television and a stereo system. He and his colleagues were able to enjoy socials with their families and even conjugal visits. What could be wrong with that? Unlike the old days, friendly contact with inmates was encouraged; although *friendly contact* might be a stretch for him—there were nasty people here, some not very interested in civil interaction.

On the other hand, he had to admit that he hadn't felt threatened. He had told no one, of course, nor would he, that he had once been a police officer. The bars of his cell, thus far, had protected him from the world, more so than the other way around. He would be required to remain locked in his cell much of the time, unless in the library or involved in one or another productive activity, but even there, protected either by his bars or the library's staff, he could read and think and reflect. He had worked at maintaining a respectful demeanour with both the inmates and the prison staff, although at mealtimes he had tried to eat alone. With showering, old age had been his friend. He hadn't needed to keep his back to the wall. He thought of all this as his managed solitude. Thus far it had worked well for him.

He had also been happy to learn that he would be allowed to advance his education. Yes, he would have to pay for university courses, but at a reduced rate. And, should he need help dealing with any returning shadows of the depression he had for so long battled, counselling was available. No wonder keeping him here cost his fellow Canadians $113,000 per year. But, to their advantage, he knew he could at best expect a dozen more years of being anywhere. The grim reaper would catch up with him by then, in prison or wherever.

* * * * * * * *

He had had few friends and fewer hobbies in his life. He had been keeping an eye out for a benign chess partner, but hadn't found one yet. The prison had a good library; its staff encouraged inmates to use it. Why wouldn't they? He had been spending all the time he could there. So, between the library and his cell, there had been a lot of days and weeks to think back over his life, to take a hard look at where he had gone wrong, and the fewer times where he had maybe done something right. Just surviving, he had concluded, more than anything he had learned in schools or from the myriad courses he had taken, left him with a distillation of what he had come to suppose was wisdom. But that didn't mean *good* wisdom: at the core of his soul, if indeed *wisdom* was the withered raisin remaining of his life's gathered grape, festered a dark cynicism about humanity's inability to correct injustices that shackled much of the world's population to the daily struggle of gathering enough to eat and finding shelter from the elements. Part of that had been a consequence of the larger world's not having tried adequately to stem Third World population growth, thus leaving the exponential curve of humanity's numbers looking like an inverted shelf hanger as viewed from its side. Ninety-eight percent of those starving, he knew, lived in developing countries, their most common cause of starvation being the economy. Poor people sometimes couldn't buy enough foodstuffs. By comparison, his life in prison was a life of luxury. And it would continue to be.

He knew his in-the-moment thoughts shouldn't be allowed to stray into those shadowy corners any longer, but he hadn't been able to shut down his mind in time. There it was, he believed, the root of the problem: a prevailing Western view that the world turns—and *must* turn—opportunistically, allowing individuals, those who could, to develop—often then to lose—any of the declining job or entrepreneurial openings. That had worked well for the strong, particularly in this century, but not for the weak. It has left much of the world divided into rich and poor, with the gap between them ever widening. The West's middle class had been eviscerated, but remained complacent enough to do nothing about it.

Admittedly, he hadn't had many viable solutions to propose. Whenever he had tried, nobody had listened—or almost nobody. Maybe that was because his solutions were too idealistic. So now, he supposed, he was waiting for some magical knot of pathfinders to succeed where he had not been able to find his way out of the starting gate. He had always been an observer, perhaps like a sports announcer doing his best to work up a crowd with pregame prattle. He had come to think that that's where most ex-middle classers now found themselves. The warm sand they had been keeping their heads in was simply more comfortable than whatever might be awaiting them should they risk pulling their toupees above it.

The what-to-do thing had crept into his thoughts insidiously for about the past decade. He had become fascinated by the fundamental limits of humanity's consumption in a world of uncontrolled population growth. Western civilization's leaders seemed to him to be totally disinterested in allowing themselves to be made scientifically aware that there might be a problem. And the people following them were as bad: like blackbirds in a cornfield—whenever one rises into the air, the entire flock lifts up with it, drifting above the cornstalks until another chooses to settle, at which time all follow. And eat.

He remembered having read Hugh MacLennan's *Barometer Rising* and later having watched the documentary *City or Ruins-The Halifax Explosion*. It had played on TV a few times, then found its way into the shadows of too-seldom visited library shelves. He recalled the scene where a mesmerized public had gathered on the city's docks to watch the Mont Blanc—having just collided with the Imo in Bedford Basin—begin its historic fire at sea. They had stood there fascinated, perhaps somewhat titillated, conscious that what they were witnessing must spell danger for someone, definitely for the sailors aboard her. And, if indeed that was what they were thinking, it was the last thing that went through their minds. Halifax, in a split second, was afire: thirty-five tons of benzol, ten tons of gun cotton, 2,300 tons of picric acid, and 400,000 pounds of TNT having ignited while encased in the steel hull of a small ship would do that.

Maybe, he thought, most everyone thinks what is coming next to the world may be only a small bump in the road, something to be amused by, but nothing humanity need have an anxiety attack over. A prevailing notion in North America has been that some quasi-magical intervention will make it all right before humanity gets into too much trouble. And, admittedly, maybe this magnificently complacent nebula will turn out to be right. Who knows?

At the bottom of his crucible he could see that humanity was little more than an evolved disparate family of apes, little better—if any—than the rest of the primates. If humanity's cousins had the power of speech, he thought, society would have to accept them as *human;* and if society didn't have the power of speech, it would merely be a little higher, still, in the branches of our tree, but there nonetheless. Of course, except for a minority of folks—primarily the scientific community—he felt that people had preferred to think of themselves not as being that at all. For adherents to any of the world's organized religions, humans have had a special place in the world and a divine destiny, provided they deport themselves appropriately in this life. Degrees of belief in the various doctrines vary, he knew, with some holding firmly to the notion that what their God had to say in the beginning and was recorded by his disciples is absolute. Armies had killed in defense of that belief; many still do.

He felt that so many things were wrong with the human condition that he hardly knew where to begin quantifying them. He believed that humanity had started out badly because it's in the nature of primates to be combative. From the moment one of them picked up a tree limb and figured out how to use it as a club, the stronger and cleverer among them had killed the weaker, for various reasons, not the least of which having been for personal advantage. Over time, humanity had gotten very good at that, on all fronts. Winning in combat yields power to the victor and leaves the vanquished, at best, in a position of implied or real subjugation.

So began the origins of power, and the realization that power is the most assured route to acquiring wealth and domination. Humanity had begun to test the limits of that with Hiroshima and Nagasaki, and it hadn't stopped since. He had felt that this endless struggle had created a highly stratified and divided global society, with those having the power taking for themselves most of whatever they perceived to be of value, with the rest of the people left to divide up whatever might be left. And that quickly led to a world populated by the rich and the poor, layered within a human pyramid that leaves the poorest at the base and the rest somewhere in between. Throughout history there has been a to-and-fro struggle between the classes, with the poor sometimes dominating… but only for a while. Power itself seemed to him inevitably to bubble to the top in human form, not infrequently from within the ranks of the poor who initially were struggling against it. With that, historically, a new dynamic tension has taken hold, keeping everyone more or less in his or her place.

Collectively, humanity had moved on. Wars have been started, won and lost. Power hierarchies, after each, settled out according to their own specific gravities.

It was interesting to him that the stratification of societies in the world had always been elitist-led, in that people within a given strata were and are ever upward looking. People had tended not to want to identify with those at the next layer beneath them, and, opportunity permitting, had tried for an open fissure through which to crawl where there might be the hope of acceptance at the next level up.

Humanity has come to accept that as being the way things are. The societal mechanisms for ensuring a relative stability of the status quo can vary from country to country, but they are all tentacles of cliques who exercise state control—the people and organizations at the top of that country's pyramid.

Oddly enough, that has led to an inured state of being for the common folk. They know they are unlikely to ever break out of it, and they have decided to support the status quo in order to make the best of things for themselves and their families. Rocking the boat is not the accepted thing to do. Control mechanisms contain or punish those who push the envelope too far. Children are taught to follow society's accepted norms of behaviour, and the church—wherever religion is a factor—reinforces that precept. Power, in its several guises and manifestations, remains at the pinnacle of the pyramid.

Humanity has wobbled along in this fashion, getting it wrong, mostly, for dozens of millennia. Humanity has toiled in its tree, albeit in the lower branches. Indeed, humanity may never get below or beyond that. Within the past century, it has ventured into patterns of behaviour that unless modified soon could lead to a cataclysmic outcome for everyone.

What changes could humanity make and that might put it on a better track? What could people try that hasn't been tried before? The issues, for the most part, are easy enough to identify. Trying new solutions would be difficult on two levels: first, because almost everything that could be tried *has* been tried; and, second, getting any sort of consensus on actually doing something and then following through with it isn't something that humans can easily be persuaded to become their cause.

* * * * * * * *

Anyway, whatever. All of that had been a field he had plowed and harrowed before, to no avail. He was here, in Kingston, in a penitentiary, to stay, probably. He knew he would have to make the best of it. Odd, though, he had calculated: he was in for a murder he hadn't committed, and hadn't been found out—at least not yet—for one that he had. That latter, he had decided, was a sleeping dog best left not prodded. From what he had learned in the library:

> *Most of Canada's federal offenders serve only part of their sentences in prison. Part of their time is served in the community. The first steps toward (attitudinal) change are taken in the prison setting. But if the change is to last, it must continue in the community, where almost all offenders eventually return. Conditional release occurs only after a thorough assessment of the safety risks that offenders may pose to society. Offenders who appear unlikely to commit crimes or break certain rules may go on conditional release, as an incentive to make positive changes in their lives. In addition, the law requires the release of offenders who have served two thirds of their sentence, but only if they are not considered dangerous. Both types of offenders must abide by specific conditions when they are back in the community, and (must be) carefully supervised. If offenders violate the rules, they may be sent back to prison.*

How sweet, he thought. Who knew: maybe they would let him out one day for being Mister Nice Guy, in which case he would find Abigail, wherever she was. After he first shopped for a crossbow, new or used.

While thinking through all of this, he had composed a short poem, written on a napkin. He folded it now and put it in his pocket for another day. Maybe another year. Maybe when he wrote a book or something.

On Being…

**I am not what I have done,
nor what I do.
I am what I think,
and so are you.**

The Fontana Resurrection

Your inner self, and mine
are infinitely more complex
than the universe we share
with others.

How late it is
we come to know that.
Too late, perhaps
to make a difference.

But we must try,
for if we fail,
cloaked greed and cunning
still will smile…and still prevail.

AUTHOR'S ACKNOWLEDGEMENTS

This book would not have been possible without the tireless help, persuasion, and patience offered by some very special people.

Patricia Spratt gently prodded me into expanding the *Fontana* story into something beyond what had been shelved as a dusty, long-forgotten short story about a troubling dream that I had. Her ideas led me to other folks who could and did offer their expertise: Lynn and Steve Smith, who toiled patiently to provide invaluable medical and engineering input, and who found a way to have me meet Joe Furlong, who in my opinion is the most charming and fascinating storyteller on Nova Scotia's east shore; Marcia Anderson, who guided me to a better understanding of the flora and fauna of that province and who assisted with Sherbrooke anecdotes and insights that made me feel like I wanted to belong to that community; and to Ted Murray, a lifelong friend who brought his career-long knowledge to bear when helping me get my mind around the nuances of what goes on in the cold rooms of meat markets.

My heartfelt thanks goes out to them all.

ABOUT THE AUTHOR

David Edey had stints with the Royal Canadian Mounted Police as an intelligence officer and at Nortel, retiring right before the company ceased operations. Although much of *The Fontana Resurrection* is drawn directly from real-life experiences, it is a work of fiction. Based on a dream that he had about his mother-in-law, he first wrote it as a short story. After encouragement from family and friends, he extended the story into a full-length piece of fiction, highlighting the story of exploited seniors who are more susceptible to scams.

When writing the full version, he traveled to Nova Scotia and British Columbia to research the settings and characters for authenticity.

In addition, he co-authored and edited the book, *Prairie Crocus: The Clays—Their Family, Friends, and Their Place in Canada's History* with Shirley Black. He and his wife, Linda, live in Manotick, Ontario.

CPSIA information can be obtained at www.ICGtesting.com
Printed in the USA
LVOW11s0223220915

455169LV00001B/214/P